Critical Praise for

FENICUS FLINT &
THE DRAGONS OF BERATHOR

MILES AWAY
TIME CRISIS SAGA: BOOK ONE

C.W.J. HENDERSON

FIRST KNIGHT PRESS
CASTLETON • NEW YORK

Printed in the United States of America

First Printing, 2016

ISBN: 978-0-692-56932-0

First Knight Press
50 Campbell Avenue
Castleton, New York, 12033

www.firstknightpress.com

www.cwjhenderson.com

ACKNOWLEDGMENTS

I would like to thank all my beta readers for their help in making sure that this manuscript is the very best it could be: Andrea, Tim, Chrissy, Becky, Don, Colleen, Fran, Theresa, Gianna, Julie, Rebecca, and Megan. I would also like to thank Faye and the rest of the research department at the Globe Theatre in London for setting me on the path to some great source materials about Southwark in the early stages of writing. And last, but certainly not least, I would like to thank Nikki Lombino for her inspired cover art; your concept and design brought everything together in the end.

DEDICATION

To my twin sons, Alex and Tristan—no matter how many stories I write or novels I sell, you will always be my greatest creation.

To John—your strength and courage in your battle against cancer helped me face my own diagnosis head on and beat it. You will never be forgotten by your family, friends, or students. I wish I had the chance to know you better.

To Julius—father, grandfather, great grandfather, and a member of Americas greatest generation. Though a quiet man, your love and dedication to this family was undeniable. Your passing left a massive hole in our hearts. You will be forever missed.

CHAPTER ONE

Miles Draven watched the clock, willing each minute to tick by so that his agony might pass. While Mr. Hannigan's world history lessons dripped the kind of boredom that made him want to slit his wrists, the stinging jab of a needle-sharp pencil at the back of his neck is what stirred Miles' need to flee.

Miles spun around in his desk and scowled at Jack Warren. The super-jock stared back with a wry, knowing grin perched on his etched face. With his sinewy, muscled forearms and massive hands, Jack grabbed the sides of the desk, leaned forward, and whispered, "Turn around, asshole."

"Is there a problem?" Mr. Hannigan barked from the front of the room.

The whole class went silent and stopped to gawk at Miles and Jack. Miles had a sinking feeling, the kind he always felt in these situations. He wasn't going to win, no matter what he said or did. Jack was the prodigal son, or something like that, and everyone looked the other way when he broke the rules. Miles, on the other hand, had a notoriously bad reputation. He spent the better part of his days in in-school suspension or the principal's office. This little tussle had all the earmarks of turning against him.

"Miles?" Hannigan called him out specifically this time. He spoke in a slow and deliberate manner. "Is there a problem?"

Jack fell back in his seat, blasé about the whole situation. He ran his fingers through his obnoxious blond hair. Each strand fell back into place like strangers coming together at the start of a flash mob. Every aspect of him irked Miles to the core.

Miles turned back around to face Mr. Hannigan at the front of the room. He clenched his fists so tight that each knuckle popped aloud. "No," Miles shot back, defeated. "There's no problem."

Beeeeeep!

A firm hand slammed Miles across the right side of his head. The force of impact nearly knocked him out of his desk. His skull throbbed and a ringing sound deafened his right ear. The whole classroom spun and tilted around him like some sort of nauseating amusement park ride. Seething with anger, Miles stumbled to his feet only to find Jack out of reach, mingling with his crew out the rear door of the classroom. He held the side of his head and fought to focus his wavering eyesight. His feet faltered beneath him, his legs rubbery. Maybe he was better off not confronting Jack at that moment, he decided.

Miles steadied himself against the desk, gathered up his books, and clumsily slid them into his backpack. A congested throng of students pressed close together in conversation and moved from the room at a sloth-like pace. Head down, Miles slipped past them and into the hallway. Merging with the flow of bodies, he decided to take the scenic route around the media center on his way to gym. The shortcut would lead him past Ms. Mitchell's classroom where Jack had study hall next, and Miles wanted to avoid any further confrontations. If he could make it to the gym unscathed, he'd get a break from Jack for a while.

Having made it around the media center without incident, Miles took a right turn at the main lobby and headed down the pallid, windowless guidance wing. A few offices broke the monotony: the office of the athletic director, the faculty lounge, and of course, the guidance suite. A quick sharp left at the end and Miles would be in the clear.

As he reached the final hallway intersection, Miles slowed in his gait and stopped. His head seemed clearer now, his footing more firm. He snuck a glance around the corner and down the hallway to the right to see if Jack was outside Ms. Mitchell's room with Kyle White and Dennis Green, his henchmen. A sigh of relief escaped him as they were nowhere to be seen. Without looking to his left, Miles turned to head toward the gym and ran into a large, muscled body. He knew that smell—*Drakkar*. It enveloped Jack like a cloud. To Miles it reeked of cat litter, but it somehow made the girls melt in all the right places.

Don't look up, Miles told himself. Not only was Jack far stronger, but he also stood about a foot taller than him. If they locked eyes, then a confrontation would ensue. Desperate to get away, Miles brushed past Jack and kept walking as if his nemesis wasn't there.

Jack, however, seized the moment to tenderize his favorite chew toy. He clamped a powerful hand around Miles' neck from behind and shoved him brutally into the brick wall that lined the corridor outside the gym. His face scraped across the rough stone. His body thudded against the wall. Miles began to crumple from an ache that radiated down his side, but he steadied himself with his hands and continued walking on unsteady feet. A swipe of his palm across his cheek made him suck in breath through clenched teeth. Searing pain shot through his face. Looking at his palm he found a fresh smear of blood. He began to feel a bit dizzy. Then the taunts began.

"Hey, faggot," Jack shouted at him, "bet you can't wait to get in the locker room so you've got something to jerkoff to later!"

Oh, that's original. Miles just shook his head and kept on walking, ignoring the taunts. He tried not to bite at the bait laid out before him. Giving a response would only give Jack what he wanted. Besides, Miles heard the same old bullshit day-after-day, making him numb to its effects.

Then Dennis chimed in. "Yeah, homo, gonna get hard watching the guys change?"

Miles had nearly made it all the way to the locker room and to relative safety. He passed by the trophy cases and watched Jack and Dennis' reflections in the glass. Their long strides closed the distance between them. Along the hallway, students stopped to watch; the girls snickered nervously, the guys waited for action.

"Bet your parents abandoned you because they knew you were a fuckin' queer," Jack laughed as he jabbed with an exceptionally sharp barb. "Probably sold you for a bowl of soup."

That one hit the mark! Miles had no family, no real family that is. He had a foster family, the Lyles, but his own parents had abandoned him at a hospital just hours after they brought him into this world. Once the other kids got hold of that bit of news, especially the cruel ones who felt great joy at making others feel like shit, the relentless taunts began. It was the one thing he couldn't ignore. He stood at the brink of snapping. All he needed was a little nudge.

"Faggot!" Jack barked and shoved Miles in the back, sending him lurching forward.

All the jokes, all the heartless taunts filled his mind and clouded his thinking. A deep, primal rage surged through him from his brain down through his body. The pain, the discomfort he carried vanished in a breath, and his blood surged with adrenaline.

Whipping about to his rear, Miles swung his textbook-laden backpack off his shoulder and hurled it like a basketball chest-pass straight at Jack, who never saw it coming. His anger poured forth with a thunderous war cry. The bag struck Jack in the chest, knocking the wind out of him. He teetered backwards on unsteady legs.

Though Miles' foster parents never paid for him to take martial arts lessons, he spent many lonely hours in his room watching old Van Damme and Bruce Lee movies, mimicking the moves he saw on screen until they became instinct. Miles rushed at Jack and planted a violent front kick where his school bag landed. The strike knocked his nemesis off of his feet and flat onto his back against the hard tile floor. Jack's head hit with a crack. He winced with a pained expression and grabbed for the injured area, leaving the rest of his body unprotected.

Miles surrendered to the beast that lurked within and let go of all control. He brought up his leg and stomped on Jack's stomach. The crushing blow doubled him up. And when Miles' foot hit the floor astride his enemy, he pivoted on the balls of his feet and drove his fist downward with a perfectly aimed left cross to Jack's eye that hit with a loud crunch. Without breaking stride, Miles continued to land a flurry of punches to his chest and face. Then Miles felt someone grab a fistful of his shirt and drag him backwards off of Jack.

"Get the fuck off him!" an unidentified voice growled in effort.

Miles stumbled over Jack and then found his footing. With a quick spin, he rounded on Dennis and swung his foot straight up into his balls. The force of the kick made his target crumple to the floor like a paper doll in a moaning, achy heap.

Miles stood, chest heaving, scanning his surroundings for other deserving targets to unleash his fury upon. His heart, which thumped like a piston beneath his ribcage, began to slow. The rush of adrenaline that fueled his onslaught receded. All that remained were subtle tremors that tickled their way along his body and a sudden clarity of thought. He felt as though he had awakened from some kind of dream. A makeshift audience of still bodies stood in a misshapen circle around him. They all wore contorted grimaces of shock, gawking at the carnage he had wrought. Miles looked down at his fists, splashed in blood. Beyond them laid his handiwork; Dennis lay on his side, moaning like a dying heifer, his hands cradling his battered balls. And next to him lay Jack, a bloodied, motionless mess. Miles' message was evident—he was done taking their shit. He moved from the defeated figure beneath him. The deliciously gratifying sense of victory that he always believed would accompany his revenge, of having vanquished his foe, did not surface. Instead, a frightened helplessness filled his thoughts. *What did I do?*

Though Miles hated them all, the release of his hurt spilled forth as tears. He screamed, "Fuck you!" and made a mad dash down the hallway, knocking students out of the way that blocked his path. The teachers on the scene let him go for the moment and focused their attention on the injured bullies.

CHAPTER TWO

Miles' knuckles were raw and torn. He picked off the loose tags of skin and hissed when the salt of his fingers burned at the exposed flesh beneath. With his thumb and index finger, he rolled up the strips of skin and flicked them across Principal Dempsey's office while he waited for her to interrogate him. He bounced the rolled-up wads off of her furniture and even landed one well-aimed shot into her coffee mug that read, "World's Greatest Principal."

A muted voice outside the office brought his clandestine aerial assault to an end. Trying to look innocent, Miles browsed over the familiar surroundings. The inside of her office was a testament to her lifetime of hard work and dedicated brownnosing. Miles had spent so much time in there over the years that he had memorized the unchanging landscape like it was his own room. Elegant frames filled with a myriad of objects covered the walls: staged photo-ops of her glad-handing politicians, degrees from the College of William & Mary and the University of Virginia, and an array of assorted educational certificates and awards. Absent from the whole scene, however, were any pictures of friends or family. She had no husband or children that anyone knew of, and she became quite flustered whenever anyone referred to her as Mrs. instead of Ms. Miles loved to push that button, especially when passing her in the hallway.

The click of a door latch sounded behind Miles. Through the door walked Ms. Dempsey with a very determined, calculated gait. A low rumble of thunder traveled through the floor with each movement of her thick, curvaceous body. Her hips were a good three feet across, stacked upon short, cellulite dimpled legs and a rear end that matched her hips in width and surpassed them in volume. The top half of her wasn't much different—thick upper arms and breasts atop a disproportionate waist. Combined, they gave her the appearance of two enormous arrowheads being stacked, point down, on top of each other. She resembled the patch arrows on a Cub Scout uniform, only jiggly. Her chubby, red-cheeked face sat atop an equally stout neck. She had a soft, grandmotherly look without the deep wrinkles and cracks of old age. Wisps of gray streaked her dark brown hair, which was styled in a short bob that framed her face.

Ms. Dempsey's outfit swished as she crossed the office floor to her desk. She wore her typical administrator attire—a black skirt and business jacket over a white blouse, sheer pantyhose, and black flats. Taking hold of the armrests of her chair, she wedged her hips between them and settled in. Then she tossed down a referral on her desk. Her eyes scanned over the details scribbled upon it. She pursed her lips in a disgusted frown, flared her nostrils, and looked up to glare at Miles. Her hands sat clasped together on her desk.

Miles attempted to return her cold glare, but she would have none of it.

Ms. Dempsey leaned forward aggressively in her chair. "You're about this close," she pinched her fingers nearly together, "to getting an expulsion hearing before the superintendent and the board of education."

Miles slumped back in his chair, trying to act tough and disinterested. He folded his arms and huffed his standard response, "Whatever."

Ms. Dempsey didn't act impressed by his show of bravado. She countered by leaning back and yawning. She stared at him for a moment through narrowed eyelids, studying him. Then she shifted forward in her seat and asked, "So you want to tell me why you attacked Jack or should we just sit here and stare at each other all day?"

"What do you want me to tell you?" he questioned sharply. "Jack's an asshole and I finally got sick of his shit." He thought back on the foul epithets Jack threw at him in the hallway. They reverberated painfully in his mind. It wasn't bad enough that Miles had no real family of his own, but cruel kids like Jack thought it was fair fodder for amusement. Over the years, he came to understand why kids snapped and went into schools with guns and hit lists, ready to make their tormentors pay for their transgressions. Miles wasn't that crazy, however, nor did he have a grandfather in the militia with a small arsenal from which to select his tools of destruction. And now that Miles finally fought back against the most popular kid in school, he was going to have to pay for it.

"Watch your language," Ms. Dempsey corrected him, pointing a chubby finger his way. She shook her head, glanced down at the referral, and scanned it over. She shrugged her shoulders and looked back at Miles. "Well I don't know what Jack did to you, but the referral says the attack was completely unprovoked."

Miles gasped. "Unprovoked?"

"Yes. And apparently you beat him so bad that his mother had to take him to the emergency room with," she paused and picked up a report from the school nurse. When she was finished reading, she continued, "With broken ribs and suspected internal injuries."

Miles, uninterested in Jack's problems, continued his own investigation. "Who said it was unprovoked?"

"Umm," Ms. Dempsey groaned as she looked down at the referral again, "Mr. Hannigan. He said you jumped Jack without cause or provocation and, even after he was in a prone position, you continued to hit and kick him." She tossed the referral aside like a card dealer at a Texas Hold'em table. It was one of her many signature gestures he had become familiar with over the years. It was her way of acting aloof when she was really pissed. Miles, however, could not disguise his anger.

"What?" he protested. His voice raised several octaves out of sheer disbelief at what he just heard. "So Hannigan didn't bother to mention what Jack does to me every day?"

"No, he didn't."

Miles sensed that the "good'ol boy network" was at play. Hannigan was protecting Jack. That much was certain. Like the dirtbag needed any help. Miles clenched his jaw, grinding his teeth with displeasure. "Then he left out quite a bit."

"Really?" she asked with an unmistakable air of doubt. "Like what?"

"Oh, let me see," Miles said sarcastically, as though he needed to really think of reasons. The list seemed endless. "He stabs me in the neck with pencils, slaps me around, calls me a fag, loser, dirtbag, slams me into walls. Oh, and his new one today was telling me that my real parents were so poor they sold me for a bowl of soup. That's just the highlight reel of course."

Ms. Dempsey wore a doubtful smirk beneath narrowed, probing eyes. "That doesn't sound like the Jack I know." He could feel her looking through him, trying to find an angle of attack. Her features relaxed again, and she said confidently, "So why should I believe you? If that was really happening in his class, Mr. Hannigan wouldn't overlook it."

He locked eyes with her and snapped back, "Yes he would!" Miles felt his composure slipping away. "Think about it. Hannigan's the varsity football coach and Jack's his star running back. The last thing he's going to do is write him up in-season, especially with the playoffs coming up. Instead, he goes out of his way to nail me on everything I do wrong and lets his little golden-boy get away with murder."

Her next line of questioning completely ignored the connection that Miles attempted to make. "How many referrals have you gotten so far this year, Miles? Fifteen? Twenty?"

Miles shrugged his shoulders. "I don't know. What's your point?" He knew where this interrogation was headed; he was a troublemaker, there was no mistaking it. It was the only way he got attention from anyone. His grades sucked, he had few real friends, and his foster family was beyond lame. So he caused mischief. So what! It was the only fun he had in this world. But his mischief making had earned him a bitter reputation that now stood in the way of finding any justice. One of the fastest ways to tear down a witness or accuser was to bring their character into question. It was a perfect strategy and Miles knew it.

Ms. Dempsey unbuttoned her jacket and sat back in her chair. "My point is that you do nothing but cause trouble around here. I don't know how you can expect me to take you at your word." She picked up her coffee mug and took a sizeable swig.

Miles cracked a wry smile. He breathed out a muted laugh through his nostrils at the whole situation, let alone his discarded flesh the

9

principal no doubt just ingested. "I don't know. I guess I don't expect anything. But Hannigan isn't telling the whole story."

Ms. Dempsey leaned forward and clasped both hands together. She smiled at Miles. "So you say."

Miles looked down at the floor, despondent, shaking his head. He huffed out an exasperated breath.

"Look, without a report from Hannigan, there's nothing I can do."

"Bullshit!" he spat back at her.

"Watch it, Miles," she pointed threateningly at him again. Her voice dropped several octaves. "You've got a short leash on this one."

"Just talk to Hannigan," Miles whined, his arms wide in an expression of exasperation. "Look into it for yourself if you don't trust me."

"Even if you're right, which I doubt, it doesn't excuse what you did to Jack. There are other ways to deal with bullying. Besides, I don't think you have anything to worry about after the beating you put on him."

"Oh yeah," Miles scoffed, "I've got it made. Now all I have to do is worry about all his roided-out friends coming after me."

Ms. Dempsey clapped both hands down on her desk. "Hey, all I can do is look into it. I'll talk to Hannigan and see if he can corroborate any of your story."

"Oh," he replied sarcastically, "I'm sure you'll look into it. Just like when he pulled the fire alarm last spring or when he was caught throwing a beer bash over Christmas break. The whole school knew he was guilty, but he managed to slither out of it with a slap on the wrist."

Dempsey gasped audibly. "What are you insinuating?"

"Who's insinuating?" Miles leaned in and pointed at her menacingly. "You let him off easy."

"Easy? He was suspended for two weeks from school and athletics once we put it all together."

Miles rolled his eyes. "You mean when you conveniently decided to punish him during the break between basketball and baseball. God forbid something gets in the way of him getting a scholarship or our school being splashed across the sports page." Miles could see he was getting the better of her. He knew he had gone too far this time and was ready to finish what he started. If he was going down, he was going down swinging. He slurred the words at her with intent, with an accusation of impropriety. "He plays you like a fool."

"I've had about enough of you today."

But Miles wasn't finished. Determined to say his peace, he cast the final stone. "His parents have money, power, and influence. Everyone knows it. Everyone knows you're his bitch."

Ms. Dempsey launched from her chair, her hips popping through its arms. Her face turned bright red. Seething with fury, she shrieked, "That's it, Miles! Get out of my office. Go sit yourself out by Mrs. Clancy's desk and wait for your mother."

"She's not my mother!" he shot back with equal intensity.

"I don't care. You can tell it all to the superintendent. Your fate's in his hands now."

"Fine," Miles retorted. He stood up and slammed the chair backward with a violent thrust of his hand, knocking it into the wall with a thud. "Fat ass," he muttered under his breath.

Dempsey glowered at Miles as he opened the door and threw it shut behind him.

CHAPTER THREE

Miles watched through the glass partition as his foster mother, Carol Lyle, strode angrily and with purpose through the outer double doors, into the high school lobby, and toward the main office. Her teal nursing scrubs hung upon her gaunt body like burlap sacks on a scarecrow's frame. The brunt of her brunette hair hung in a ponytail out the back of a surgical cap. It snapped back and forth from the briskness of her movements. Miles looked to her feet. She still wore her shoe covers. He knew he was in for it now; they pulled her out of surgery to get him.

With a violent yank, Carol opened the door to the office. The aluminum blinds clanged against the wire-reinforced safety glass. Her eyes locked on Miles, and she stalked toward him. A foot from him she stopped, glared, and shook her head with displeasure. The smell of cigarette smoke wafted from her clothes.

"Mrs. Lyle," the principal's secretary, Mrs. Clancy, broke the silence.

Carol quickly composed herself and turned to face her.

"Ms. Dempsey is expecting you."

His foster mother glared back at him. "We'll talk in the car," she grumbled low. The veins in her neck bulged. Miles knew she was really holding back. She whipped around, walked down a short corridor, and stepped into Ms. Dempsey's office.

He waited a good half hour before Carol finally emerged. While she looked pissed before, she now seemed despondent, unsure of what to do. The wrinkles around her eyes appeared more distinct, pronounced. In her hand he saw the pink carbon copy of his referral. Calmly, Carol drew near Miles and resignedly said, "Let's go."

Miles stood up, grabbed his bag, and followed her out the door to the van. She didn't utter a word the whole way. The rumble of the Dodge Caravan coming to life seemed to be the only sound that hit his ears. He could swear even the birds stopped chirping. It was an unnatural silence. The moment the van left the school grounds, Carol lowered the driver's side window and lit up a cigarette. She took long, concentrated drags. With a half inch of ash dangling from the glowing tip, his foster mother finally broke the silence.

"I'm trying, Miles. I'm really trying to understand you." Carol shook her head. "Why would you do that to someone?"

Miles kept his emotions hidden away. He stared out the window, not making eye contact with her. "He deserved it," he uttered flatly.

"Deserved it? Miles, you sent him to the hospital. Who deserves that?"

"You wouldn't understand."

"Try me."

Miles lost himself in the blur of green pastures and sweeping hillsides passing by. He couldn't admit to her why he beat Jack to a pulp. The thought of exposing a weakness to her, of telling her that other kids abuse him would let the sturdy wall surrounding his emotions crumble. Besides, what could she do? Talk to the principal? Talk to Jack's parents? That would only make things worse. They'd feign ignorance, and then Miles would be made out to be a bigger liar than they all already thought he was. The volatile persona and the dangerously short temper he put on display today, he decided, would serve him far more than opening up to his foster mother. She'd be pissed for a few days, just like his foster father would be once he found out, but their anger would subside. The added ridicule and bullying he'd suffer as a result of whining about being picked on far outweighed any benefits he might reap.

"You can ignore me all you want, Miles, but your father won't stand for it."

He glared at her out the corner of his eyes. "He's not my father." Miles plugged his earbuds into his ears and pressed play on his mp3 player, shutting her out.

Carol took a long, hard drag of her cigarette and exasperatingly puffed out the smoke.

As the short drive home passed, Miles couldn't help but try to make sense of what he felt back in the hallway outside the locker room. Jack deserved what happened. For as much as he terrorized and ridiculed Miles, he wasn't the only victim. Like a quintessential bully, Jack fed on the weak, the smaller, and the insecure. No one dared stand in his way for fear of what Jack or his parents might do. Rest assured, sooner or later he was bound to mess with the wrong person and be put in his place. Maybe, Miles thought, Jack was lucky it happened now when he was still a kid rather than as an adult. Kids can only do so much damage. Adults are another story. Jack probably never counted on someone smaller than him fighting back. But through all his rage and anger at Jack and even his foster parents, Miles' true hatred, the root of his anger stemmed from his real parents. Why did they give him up? If they hadn't, maybe his life would have turned out far better. Maybe he might even have been happy.

Before he could entertain that thought any further, Miles saw the Lyle's raised ranch roll into view. With an aggressive turn and a squealing of the brakes, the van came to a stop. Miles reached for the door handle and popped the door ajar. The firm grasp of Carol's hand on his arm kept him from jumping out. With a frustrated yank he pulled his earbuds out of his ears.

"What?" he snapped at her.

"I have to get back to the hospital," Carol replied with a calmer, measured tone. "We'll talk about this tonight."

"Sure," he replied apathetically. He pulled himself free of her grasp, hopped out of the van onto the damp asphalt, and slammed the door shut.

Within moments the van was out of sight and Miles was alone in the house. He descended into the darkened basement and to the small walled-off space he called his bedroom. The flimsy door opened and a flood of light washed over him from the lone window that revealed the outside world. Posters of Bruce Lee, Cam Newton, and bikini bimbos covered his meager bit of wall space. In the corner opposite his bed sat a worn-out, dial-tune television and a collection of retro video games he haggled from neighbors at garage sales. His foster brother had a nice HDTV upstairs in the living room and all the newest gaming systems. It was okay though, these were his. After all, things could be worse; he could live in a closet under the stairs.

Miles threw his backpack across the room where it landed on his duct-taped bean bag chair. Then he moved over to the edge of his bed, knelt down, and pulled a tattered cigar box from under the frame. Turning and sitting with his back against the bed, Miles lifted the top off the box and laid it on his lap. Inside rested an eclectic combination of items that he had collected in his travels. Miles had lived with so many families and in so many homes over the years, he kept a memoriam of sorts from each. Most of the items meant little or nothing to him in the grand scheme of things. A few, however, held special meaning: a tattered John Franco baseball card, a few seashells from the Outer Banks, and a ticket to Busch Gardens. In his seventeen years, these three moments stood out because they were the only truly happy times in his life. He spent the better part of his life feeling unwanted and alone. Family after family passed on him after a few years of care, not ready to "adopt" him. By the time he was ten, he stopped letting himself get too vested in his foster families or hope that someone might offer him a permanent home. He kept his distance and wouldn't let anyone in.

But it wasn't those happy memories from the past that Miles sought at that moment. His heart ached, not because he had to listen to the taunts of a bully or because he brutally repaid that bully in kind (deserving or not), but because the people who could have prevented him from ever having to listen to such heartless insults had cast him out into the cold world, naked and vulnerable for vultures to pick over. He dug through the contents of the cigar box for their photograph. Sliding it out from under the weight of the other trinkets, the photo came into view. It was from one of those instant cameras, a *Polaroid* he was told, with its white paper border surrounding the developed picture. It was taken at the hospital the day he was born. Small creases and discoloration marked the picture, but he could still see his parents clearly despite the wear and tear. He held it at arm's length and studied the two strangers he saw.

Miles' father looked no more than twenty, maybe twenty-two, with closely cropped brown hair, a distinct, pointy nose, and a small scar over his right eye. He had the look of a rugged man, the kind that worked with his hands, and that work made him tough. Yet the smile on his face showed sincere love for both his wife and the small son she held wrapped in her arms. His mother, on the other hand, had shoulder-length, curly red hair, high cheekbones, and an equally beaming smile. She had a chubby, childlike face, probably from carrying him for nine months. Examining the picture for the thousandth time, he couldn't understand how they could just abandon him if they seemed so incredibly happy. Though she smiled, tears streaked down her face. Did she know that she would never see her son again? Is that why she was crying? How could they do it? Not knowing made the hurt inside Miles all the more unbearable. In the quiet safety of his room, he let all his pain out in a crescendo of agony. He clenched his right hand into a fist and swung it brutally against the side of his bed, pounding it over and over again. The mattress bounced and lurched from the power of the blows.

"Son of a bitch!" Miles bellowed as his hand struck the edge of the metal bedframe. He rose from the floor onto his knees, clutching his throbbing hand. The photo fell from his grasp, and the box of trinkets spilled across the rug. "Why did you do this to me?" he screamed, pressing out every molecule of air in his lungs. He began to hyperventilate from the sobs that racked his body and the thunderous pumping of his blood. Like an angry hammer, Miles brought both fists down hard upon the thinly carpeted floor. This time he felt no pain. His sense of self and connection to reality left him in his rage. He recklessly flung the spilled belongings from his box to the walls, putting as much power and malice into his movements as he could.

With both hands he snatched up the last two pieces, two crystal spheres with letters etched upon them, and squeezed them in both hands as he howled. Miles closed his eyes and focused his thoughts on his parents; he summoned all of his anger, all of his loneliness, and all of his pain in an attempt to crush their memory. Miles squeezed the seemingly fragile orbs as he wished he could strangle his parents and to turn them into nothing. Yet he heard no cracking, felt no sting of glassy shards rending his palms. Instead he felt something, something he couldn't explain; a tingling of sorts akin to sticking his tongue to a 9-volt battery. It raced up his wrists and held them tight like a squid squeezing his forearms to bursting. He fought the sensation, gritting his teeth, hoping that what he sensed were splinters of glass deepening into his nerves and flesh so his physical pain might equal his mental anguish. But Miles couldn't endure it any longer. His hands opened from the unbearable discomfort and the spheres fell with a clunk.

Opening his eyes, Miles immediately perused his arms. He looked them over, front and back, and felt utterly befuddled. Though he wasn't certain whether his eyes were playing tricks on him or not, he thought he saw minute blue threads of energy pulsing along his forearms before fading into oblivion.

His breathing slowed, and the storm within him subsided. What his parents did to him had taken a back seat to this mystery. Miles rubbed at the ache that began to nibble once more at his now bruised right hand. He ruminated over the event.

"What the Hell," Miles mumbled. He scratched at his head and shrugged. Miles didn't realize just how much of a mess he had made until he surveyed the carnage around him. With a burst of energy, he gathered up all his valuables, placed them back in the cigar box, and thrust it under the bed. Then he threw himself down on the mattress and stared at the ceiling, no longer consumed by demons of the past. A new demon had taken its place.

CHAPTER FOUR

June 5th, 1613

A gentle, drumming knock interrupted Gaius Lloth's evening nourishment. The demon's gaze shifted from the pale-gray, boiled haggis that lay dissected on the porcelain plate to the man who stood silently beside it. With a nod of the head, Gaius sent the man across the room to an oak door that separated the manor's dining room from the foyer. Jerking the doorknob, he opened it to a chorus of groans from ungreased hinges. Through the door walked a tall, slender man with salt and pepper hair and aged features. He wore brown britches, a white shirt, leggings, and brown startups covered in mud. His feet scuffed along the floor at an intolerably languid pace as he approached. The height of his gaze never rose above floor level. He stopped a few feet short of where Gaius dined.

"What is it now, Brutus?" Gaius wiped at its ginger beard with a handkerchief, brushing away the bits of food that lingered there. The demon wondered how any humans could find such fare delectable, but it had no choice. Though it didn't need to eat, the meat sack Gaius inhabited needed nourishment and satiation. One downside of possession was being subject to the host's natural inclinations for food. Though it supplanted their consciousness and essentially their soul, wisps of what made them who they were still lingered. They were essential to assuming their identity, but next time the fiend vowed to select a human host with better hankerings.

"M'lord," Brutus croaked with a grave voice, "a traveler seeks an audience with you."

Gaius slowly closed its eyes and took a deep breath. The demon's consciousness extended out from its human form with ethereal fingertips. The fiend's essence swirled like an invisible fog down the leg of the chair, poured across the knotty floorboards, slid beneath the chamber door, and expanded out into the foyer where the supposed traveler awaited. The man wasn't much to speak of at first blush. But once the demon's essence closed in around him, it knew for certain that this man was whom he claimed to be. Though he appeared to be a mere twenty or so years old, his body told a different story. Like a mind, a physical form has memories, a record of all the experiences that have come its way. This shell had seen some ninety odd years. But above all else, he carried a chronoperpetua, the mysterious device that opened portals for his kind to travel to other times and realities. Its presence verified his identity as one of their Order. Gaius recoiled back into the host body with a jerk and opened its eyes.

"Bring him to me."

The manservant nodded deep and fast, his movements indicative of his eagerness to leave Gaius' presence. He passed through the door without looking back. Seconds later, a young man stepped through the doorway and into the room. From head to toe, this man reeked of confidence. While he wore clothing tailored of the finest cloth, his attire did not portend opulence or even the slightest hint that he appeared in James' court—quite typical of a chronoshifter. They always seemed to possess ample financial means, but their pathetic ilk avoided power and influence, preferring to lurk in the shadows and avoid making marks on history as it unfolded. While they chose such a life, Gaius had no choice but to hide. The demon knew from previous encounters with other shifters that if it made too grand an effort to seize power and means that it would quickly find itself on the run again.

The chronoshifter cast back the hood of his cloak with one deft movement, letting the light of the room fall on his features. His relatively short black hair lay pressed forward and together at the apex of his scalp in a manicured coif. The etched cheekbones, pointed nose, and strong chin gave him a smoldering look. Then he adjusted the fall of his cloak lapel to reveal the pommel of a gladius he carried at his hip.

Gaius narrowed its human eyes at the traveler and then stood abruptly. The chair it sat in groaned painfully as it shot out from under the demon. The young man who stood there reacted in an instant, dropping his weight into a defensive fighting stance while his hands grasped for his sword and its scabbard.

The demon laughed haughtily. "Oh, you are a nervous fellow, aren't you?"

The traveler shook his head and sneered at Gaius. "And you're too trusting, demon."

"Quite the contrary, sir. You're not here to kill me because you can't. Yes, you've come into my home, armed for combat, but only to defend yourself if necessary. Unless of course you're an imbecil, for you know that if you kill this vessel," Gaius spread its arms in a welcoming gesture, "I'll walk out of here in your skin. Just think of the damage I could do if I took over one of your kind, freed from the shackles of time."

"Enough," the traveler barked, jerking his hand away from his gladius and letting his cloak fall back upon his frame. "You're right, I'm not here to fight. I'm here to talk."

"So then tell me your name, traveler, and by all means, talk." Gaius used a breath of its limited power, reached out with spectral hands, and drew out a chair for its guest to sit upon. The demon gestured with its physical form for the young man to take a seat.

"Traveler," he uttered coldly as he settled himself down upon the oak chair with an uncomfortable grimace. "That's the name you get for now."

"Fair enough." Gaius brought its own chair back to the table, sat down, and willed a goblet and a bottle of liquor to cross the table toward the chronoshifter.

"No, thank you," the traveler refused.

"Have it your way. It's a perfectly good bottle of ale." Gaius took a mouthful from a nearby goblet. "So, talk."

The man appeared pained by the thoughts that swam in his mind. The demon wished to plunder his mind of all thoughts and cut to the chase, but it was a power the fiend had yet to reconstitute since being summoned all those centuries ago. So it waited and watched. Gaius suspected why the man had come to see him under such conditions, but it needed to hear this traveler say the words himself.

"I'm here to make a deal."

"A deal? Of what sort? I'm a simple creature. I find contracts and agreements don't suit my purposes. I generally just take what I want. But I'll hear your offer."

The man closed his eyes, exhaled deeply, and groaned, "I'm tired. Tired of fighting. Tired of watching those I love grow old and die while the rest of us try to find a way to stop you. It's all useless."

Gaius cocked a curious eyebrow at him. "Useless you say? I think your Order has done a fair job of keeping me in check all these years. You must have seen something, something to make you question your piety." It leaned toward him, a hunger brewing within to hear the traveler pour forth his deepest pain and secrets. The demon fed on hurtful emotions and agony, more so than any morsel of mortal sustenance it could ingest physically. And when such succulent fare was freely divulged, its taste brought pure ecstasy. Gaius sensed the human vessel it inhabited struggling to maintain shape and contour against its hideous form, eager to break free and devour its victim. Bringing itself under control, the demon drew a sleeve across the gaping human mouth to wipe away a tendril of spittle seeping from within.

"What did you see?" it rasped eerily.

The traveler seemed taken aback by the feral persona that peered from behind the demon's mask of flesh. He replied, "No matter what we do in the end, you win. Every action we take, every time we think we've stopped you, the end result doesn't change. And when you're immortal as long as we are, you forget what happens when time catches up to you. I had to watch someone very close to me grow old and die. I've had enough of being on the losing side."

Gaius leaned back in its chair. The demon narrowed its eyes, taking measure of the man before it. Everything about the traveler—his stench, his demeanor, his resigned calm—spoke to the demon's instincts. There was no attempt to deceive. It made the negative energy pool generated by the man all the more delicious. Gaius simmered in the sauce, quietly gleeful; this time it was careful to not show its intent. Coolly, calmly, Gaius inquired, "So what's your bargain?"

The traveler's eyes locked on some knot or other detail in the woodwork of the table, though they didn't seem to be looking at anything in particular. His fingers drummed uncomfortably. He looked like a man struggling with the words he wanted to say. For several seconds he sat silent before he spoke. "There are others, like me, who want out of the Order."

"How many?"

"Enough to swell your ranks," the man answered quickly, snidely. He glowered at the demon and spoke with deliberate emphasis. "Enough to put an end to the Order. And they'll agree to join you in exchange for something only you can grant."

The demon cocked its brows with intrigue. "And just what is that?"

"Immortality."

Gaius guffawed, "You've already got that, traveler," and took a swig of ale.

"No, not truly immortal. Our lives can still be taken. We're still mortal, flesh and blood, unlike you. In the meantime, we lose track of time and the passage of years, and before we know it, time catches up to us. And then we start to age, while the rest of our loved ones have to watch us grow more fragile and helpless until we die. We want immortality that doesn't come with a caveat. If you want our help, it's the price you must pay. A small sacrifice of your power."

A tiny brass bell lay on the table next to Gaius' hand. The demon shook it, letting out a high pitched cacophony. A door behind it, much like the one that the traveler entered by, creaked open and another servant came in from the kitchen. He lifted the half-eaten plate of food from the table and quickly ducked away. The door clanked shut behind the servant. Gaius rose from its seat, walked the length of the table, and stopped across from where the traveler sat. The demon leaned over the table, hands supporting its weight, and responded, "But you do know that's a power I can't grant in my current state."

"We're well aware of that." The traveler reached into his waistcoat and removed a crisp piece of parchment. He unfolded it and slid it across the table to Gaius. "We can get you the object of power you need, if you will give us what we ask."

Gaius lifted the parchment and examined it under the flickering candlelight. It was a drawing of a sword, an ancient sword, Celtic in design. Below the sketch, a cypher comprised of numbers, letters, and symbols lay written in black ink; none of it made sense to the demon. "What is this?"

"A promise," the man snickered. "That's the object you need. The encryption below it is its location. But without my help, you'll never find it."

"Making me jump through hoops will only delay your prize. Tell me its location and I'll give you what you want tonight."

"I could, but it would also leave me no bargaining chip. And frankly, if I told you how to break the cypher, you'd have no use for me. I'd prefer to walk out of here alive when our business is completed."

Gaius, recognizing the sound strategy of its unlikely visitor, nodded respectfully. "Very good."

The traveler rose from his seat and pulled a pair of black riding gloves from his cloak. He swung the pair with his right hand into his left palm with a clap. "To be honest, the encryption has yet to be solved. I'm not sure where the object is yet. But I'll have it soon." The man locked eyes with Gaius as he tugged the gloves over his fingers.

"So why should I trust you?" the demon inquired reservedly. "Other than a boastful claim that you can help me find one of the artifacts, tell me why I shouldn't have you torn limb from limb right now?"

The traveler crossed his arms and leered at the demon. "Because we can also help you blend in and hide from the Order. You'll be able to move about freely and reconstitute all your power without their interference. It's truly a win-win situation for everyone."

"An interesting bargain." Gaius nodded, thinking over the proposal. "I'll agree to your terms, but you must do something for me first. We demons aren't the trusting sort. You don't appear dishonest, but the flesh I'm trapped in prevents me from properly reading you. I require proof that you're what you say."

"What kind of proof?" he asked, his body posture and attitude were aloof, confident.

Gaius smiled menacingly. "The children. I want them eradicated."

The smugness that hung on the man's shoulders crumbled away. He looked visibly shaken, perhaps unprepared to accept such a term of agreement. His voice cracked, "Why?"

"The prophesy. If there's even the slightest possibility one of those progeny are the foretold deliverer, I want them wiped out."

"But there's no proof that any of them are the deliverer. No twins have been born of our Order yet."

The demon shook its head, clicking its tongue against the roof of its mouth in protest. "You're beginning to sound like a man whose bluff has been called."

"No," the traveler gestured with a pointed finger at Gaius, "not at all. It's just that what you ask is no easy task, Gaius. There are hundreds of thousands of permutations of each of them living throughout time, and only one true, living version of each."

"I know you have ways of finding them. Bring me their heads, and I'll promise you what you seek. Betray me and watching your loved ones grow old will be the least of your worries."

"Alright." He nodded with worried eyes. "It'll take some time."

Gaius laughed warmly. *How ironic.* "What else have we got?"

CHAPTER FIVE

"Why can't you stay out of trouble?" Karl Lyle barked across the dinner table, his mouth full of meatloaf and mashed potatoes.

Miles stared back at his foster father, arms crossed, trying to put on an indifferent front despite wanting to shout back with equal vehemence.

"Sometimes I wonder why we didn't get rid of you sooner."

"Karl," Carol pleaded, "take it easy." She laid a calming hand on his arm, but her gesture didn't work. He pulled his muscled, greasy forearm out of her grasp.

"Kid doesn't have a fuckin' brain in his head!" Karl shoved his chair back, stood up, and lumbered across the hardwood floor to get another beer from the fridge. He took a long, hard swig as he stood over his chair. After letting loose a foul belch, he dropped back into his seat and began shoveling food into his face again.

Frustrated, Miles finally broke his silence. He uttered under his breath, "He had it coming."

Karl narrowed his eyes at Miles and leaned closer. He held the fork and knife in his hands in an oddly threatening manner. "What did you say?"

"Dad," his foster brother Simon drew his attention, his mouth equally full. "Jack's a total douchebag. He probably deserved it." Simon, a senior, spent his school days at the vocational center working in the auto shop instead of taking classes. He was a lot like his father, at least physically: tall, muscular, and a total grease monkey. The big difference was he had a calm demeanor. Some of his friends were a lot like Miles, so he figured that he understood him and didn't give him grief for that reason. It was probably the same reason why Simon spoke up once again on his behalf.

Karl shot Simon an angry stare and jabbed his food-covered fork in his direction. "I don't recall asking for your God damn input."

Simon shrugged and went back to cutting his meatloaf. "Fine."

He turned his ire back to Miles. "And I don't give a shit if that kid was beating your ass to a pulp, you don't do what you did today. That kid's father is the God damn district attorney. If he decides to press charges against you, you're on your own, pal." Karl waved a dismissive hand in his direction. "We've had to bail your dumb ass out over and over again and now you go and pull some shit like this? It's bad enough we're going to have to foot the bill if they expel you. Maybe Jack should have busted in that stupid skull of yours. Teach you to keep your mouth shut and toe the line."

"Your father's just frustrated because this puts us in a real bind," Carol explained, nervously puffing on a cigarette. Her eyes shifted uncomfortably between Miles and Karl. "If you get expelled at that hearing next week, you'll have to go to private school or be home tutored, and we just don't have the money to pay for it."

"Actually," Karl added, "what I'm saying is you're a God damn idiot."

Miles, finally having had enough abuse, shot up from his chair and violently shoved it back under the table. He stalked away and muttered the word "asshole" under his breath.

Karl jumped up from his seat, fists clenched, apparently ready to perform the beating he said Miles deserved. Carol grabbed him by his flexed bicep and dragged him back down to his seat.

"I swear to God, Carol."

Bounding down the stairs from the dining room, Miles finally escaped to the solace of his room. He couldn't believe how heated Karl had gotten. He'd seen him worked up in the past over his shenanigans, but Miles knew to look out when his foster father drank. Though he never laid a hand on him before, when Karl's rage spilled over without the censor of sobriety, it scared Miles. He couldn't push from his thoughts the memories of his foster father backing him into a corner, standing over him red faced, veins pumping through his thick neck, and bellowing at a body penetrating decibel that made him want to wretch. One uncontrolled swat from his bearlike hands and Miles knew he'd be waking up in a hospital if he ever woke up at all.

Through the ceiling, Miles heard his foster parents bickering loudly. Most of it was unintelligible, but he caught wind of his name enough to know what it was all about. He didn't want to hear it anymore. Leaning down, he picked up the controller to his NES, threw the power switch, and plopped down on the edge of his bed to play *Final Fantasy*. His mp3 player and earbuds sat next to him, so he plugged them into his ears and powered it up. After hitting the *next* button a few times, Miles settled on some *Alice In Chains* and drowned out the world.

"I'll go over in the morning and talk to Mr. Warren," Carol cajoled her husband while carrying a stack of dirty dishes to the sink. They clattered when they fell from her hands. "Maybe I can convince him to go easy on Miles. Tell him we just can't afford a lawyer to defend him."

Karl stood, half drunk, in the archway between the dining room and the kitchen. Another can of beer dangled from his fingertips. He fell against the archway, letting it support his slumping frame. "Oh yeah," he slurred, "I'm sure that'll work."

Carol turned away from the dishes and put her hands down on the edge of the butcher block island. She lifted a smoldering cigarette from the pea-green ash tray that lay there. The tip glowed and crackled as she sucked in a lungful. The smoke left her body in two concentrated tendrils through her nostrils. "Do you have a better idea?"

Karl staggered toward his wife. The can of beer collided with the side of the island, fell from his hand, and spilled all over the hardwood. He swore under his breath, smacking his hands against his jeans to wipe away the beer.

"Damn it, Karl!" Carol growled. She whipped off a few handfuls of paper towel from the roll and held them out toward him.

"I'm not cleaning this shit up." He stepped over the mess to head toward the fridge. "Need another beer."

Ding! Dong! The doorbell rang in airy tones throughout the house. Both Carol, who knelt down to mop up the spilt beer, and Karl, cracking the tab on another can, paused to glance in the direction of the front door.

"Were you expecting anyone?" Carol looked to the display on the microwave. 7PM.

"Nope," Karl barked, slamming his beer down on the countertop. Froth crested through the spout and down the sides of the can. "Probably more fuckin' Jehovah's Witnesses!" He blundered out of the kitchen.

"Karl," Carol scrambled to her feet, tossed the soaked towels in the trash, and followed behind him. "Are you sure you should be answering the door? It might be the police looking for Miles."

The two of them passed through the living room where Simon sat in the recliner watching the news. He made no effort to get up, let alone recognize their presence.

"Good, maybe they'll cart his ass off to jail. Let him rot there overnight. Maybe that'll get through to him." Karl stopped, locked eyes on Simon, and hollered, "Get off your lazy ass and go clean up the kitchen."

Simon threw the recline lever forward, which made a loud clank as the footrest collapsed back into the frame. He complained with an audible sigh that immediately garnered a death stare.

"Don't give me any of your shit, boy." He leered angrily at Simon. "Move it!"

Ding! Dong!

"Can you please calm down!" Carol begged. "I don't need to bail you out of jail too."

A few steps later, Karl stumbled down the first half of the staircase to the landing and the front door. A hard fist knocked on the door.

"Keep your damn pants on!" Karl snapped aloud at the insistent visitor and drew near the door.

Carol stood behind him, peering over his shoulder, arms crossed. His fingertips reached for the cover of the peephole. He flipped it up and pressed his face against the door. A sharp snap of glass and wood rattled the airwaves. Blood, splinters of bone, and chunks of brain splashed across Carol and the far wall. Karl's limp body fell back from the door and tumbled down the steps to the lower floor. Carol's shrill screams of terror ripped through the house. With a bang, the door blew open in a cloud of dust and splintered wood. She fell away, scrambling up the stairs in panic. Two men, clad in black from head to toe, crashed through the doorway and moved in on her. The crisp bang of gunfire silenced her cries of terror.

A distant, muted sound penetrated Miles' shell of isolation. It sounded distinct, alarmingly different from those that he usually heard through the din of his music. He shook his head. *Those idiots are still fighting upstairs?* He could feel slight tremors rattle down through the house and into his bedframe from the wall. Miles ripped his earbuds out and listened. He heard heavy footfalls from above and male voices arguing. *Damn, they're really going at it.*

Then something weighty and large hit the floor above. One of the male voices shouted in protest. Something was wrong. Miles got up and cracked open his door to eavesdrop. Then he heard it again; no longer distant or muted, the unmistakable report of gunfire rocked the house with amazing power. He flinched instinctively away from the sound; the cadence of his heart tripped into overdrive. It felt as though a vice-like hand had a stranglehold on his nerves. Miles found it hard to move out of fear, but the flood of adrenaline pouring through his bloodstream beckoned him to move.

With shaking hands, Miles pulled his bedroom door ajar and peered out into the rest of the basement. He immediately caught sight of Karl. Twisted and contorted, his lifeless body lay at the foot of the stairs in a glistening puddle of blood. A grisly entry wound took the place of his right eye. Hand over mouth, Miles stepped out from behind the doorway to get a closer look. Panic consumed him.

"What the fuck?" he gasped.

Before he could move any closer to Karl, Miles heard the clatter of foot falls carefully descending from the first floor on the wooden staircase. *Oh, God! They're coming!* He backpedaled toward his bedroom door, catching a glimpse of black canvas military boots rounding the corner of the landing to head down to the basement.

Miles ducked back inside and pushed the door shut, twisting the feeble locking mechanism. Then he made a mad grab for his box of memories from beneath the bed and shoved the box inside his backpack.

The small window at the back of the house that brought sunlight into his room now served as his only escape route. Desperate, Miles lunged for the latch. Just as his fingers wrapped around it, he heard the sound of the doorknob being twisted in vain. Miles felt like he was stuck in mud—one of those nightmares where you can't move. He slid the window open with a hard shove, threw his bag outside, and climbed up into the frame. Tumbling head first, Miles hit the dewy lawn with a thud. He rose to his feet with as much urgency as he could, grabbed his backpack, and ran. Behind him, the crunch of boot heels kicking open his door filtered out into the night air.

A frantic instinct drove Miles' legs into action. He rounded the backyard with reckless abandon and raced across the front lawn to the sidewalk. His feet hit the concrete with a splash.

"It's Draven!" he heard a harsh male voice utter. "Don't let him get away!"

Miles glimpsed over his shoulder as he darted away from the house. Two shadowy figures fell upon the sidewalk to his rear and pursued him doggedly. He saw the faint metallic glint of the handguns they carried reflecting the street lights. All he could do was run, run as hard and fast as his legs would carry him and hope they held out. Their footsteps, however, were closing.

A loud bang rang out from behind. Miles flinched to his right, narrowly avoiding a bullet meant for his head. It hit the side view mirror of a truck and sent shards of glass flying everywhere. An intersection only a hundred feet away or so gave him hope; if he could get there, he might be able to slip into the nearby woods and hide.

But before he could take another step, a topless jeep screeched to a halt atop the intersection. A figure cast in the glow of street lights rose from the driver's seat and brandished a handgun at Miles.

"Shit!" he swore to himself. Miles skidded to a halt and made an effort to duck between two cars when a hail of bullets erupted from the gunman in the jeep and those pursuing him from behind. He covered up and ducked down, waiting for the rending tear of hot metal to rip through him.

The gunfire ceased. Miles wondered for a fleeting moment if he was already dead. However, the beating of his pulse that boomed in his ears told him otherwise. *What happened?*

"Miles!" a voice shouted out to him from the direction of the jeep.

Still crouched and shaking, Miles lowered his hands and arms away from his face to cautiously look upon the mystery gunman. He still stood tall, his firearm aimed in Miles' direction but not exactly on Miles. He subtly flicked its steaming muzzle about in the cool night air, seeking other targets to take down.

Miles stole a quick glance to his rear and found no one on his tail. No one alive at least. Two fallen men laid in slowly expanding pools of their own blood beneath a flickering streetlight. Dissipating wisps of steam rose from their entry wounds. They wore black fatigues, black boots, and carried the kind of firearms he'd only seen in military video games. He could have quickly turned away and ran, but Miles made the mistake of looking into the eyes of the man who lay dead only feet from him. It was the only part of him that showed through the black cowl that covered his head. A cold, lifeless stare marked the eyes and sent chills down Miles' spine. He'd never looked into the eyes of a dead man before. It made his insides knot and churn. Rising to his feet, Miles turned away and covered his mouth with the back of his hand. He swallowed down the wretched taste that burned in his throat.

"Miles!" the man shouted even more insistently this time. "Get in the car!" The faint cry of police sirens grew in the distance.

Miles turned in the direction of the high-pitched wails and then back to the man in the jeep.

"We need to go!"

He had spent enough time in trouble at school and with the police to know that he wanted nothing to do with this situation. But Miles couldn't sponge away the gruesome image from his mind of his foster father lying dead in the foyer. *He may have been a dick*, Miles thought, *but he didn't deserve that. And what about Carol and Simon?* Part of him wanted to run back and see, but the rest of him lacked the courage and conviction to do so. The man in the jeep had saved his life. He wanted answers and perhaps his mysterious savior could provide them.

With hesitant, shuffling steps, Miles backed away from the corpse, turned on the balls of his feet, and ran to the jeep. As he approached, the man tucked his firearm away into a shoulder holster and dropped into the driver's seat, revving the engine. Miles popped open the door and threw his backpack into the passenger's side floor. The man who sat in the driver's seat didn't look much older than him. But something about him seemed oddly familiar. *Who the Hell is this guy?*

"What about the Lyles?" Miles pleaded as he scrambled up into the springy passenger side seat and slammed the door shut. "We've got to go back for them!"

"I'm sorry," he responded curtly, throwing the jeep into gear, and cast Miles a cursory glance. "It's too late for them." With an aggressive step on the gas, the man sent the tires into motion, squealing as they fought to grip the asphalt. They took hold and the jeep pulled away just as flashing lights began illuminating the neighborhood streets from afar.

CHAPTER SIX

Miles sat with his arms wrapped tight around his backpack. He stared blankly at the road ahead of him, rocking in his seat, the last few minutes replaying time and again inside his head.

The jeep had a musty smell to it, like the top was left off in the rain too many times. He felt the cold of the vinyl seat through his clothes. If it was a dream, he wanted to wake up, urgently.

"Are you alright?" the driver demanded.

Miles continued to rock, unaffected. The words did not register in his mind.

"Miles!" the driver barked sharply. The boy's head snapped to his left. "Are you hurt?"

"Huh?" he asked languidly as he slowly came back to reality. In the driver's seat, a man not much older than himself came into view through the clearing cobwebs. He wore very nondescript clothing: a brown and white collared t-shirt, faded jeans, no socks, and beat up sneakers. His hair seemed quite tousled, dirty blond in color, and a little too long on the sides and back—definitely a comb and gel number. He seemed in pretty good physical shape, though; the kind where Miles didn't want to screw with him too much or he might get flattened. Around his mouth sprouted the hint of a goatee. With a stranglehold on the wheel, the driver steered haphazardly through the streets. He shifted gears violently, braking and accelerating with wild abandon while ignoring stoplights and signs all together.

The driver took his eyes off the road for a moment to look Miles up and down. His voice was much calmer. He deliberately enunciated each word. "Are you okay?"

Miles grew suddenly angry at the absurdity of the question. "Okay?

33

A bunch of men just murdered my foster-family and tried to kill me. No, I'm not okay. What the Hell's going on?"

"Were you hit?" The driver asked while perusing the rear and side view mirrors.

Miles scanned the roadway behind them too. There didn't seem to be anyone else on the road. Miles then patted himself up and down, searching for any signs of blood or injuries. His hands wouldn't stop shaking. With the adrenaline pumping through his veins, he figured he could have been shot through the chest and wouldn't know it. To the best of his knowledge, he was okay. "Outside of being seriously freaked out, I'm still in one piece. Now will you please tell me what's happening?"

Though his eyes still appeared to be scanning the road behind them for other cars, the driver eased up on the gas and began to drive like a normal human being. He breathed out a huge sigh. "I wish I knew, kiddo. Thankfully I got to you before they did."

"They who? Who'd want to kill me?"

The driver shook his head and grimaced. "You weren't ready for this," he said under his breath. "Not now."

Miles hit his limit of impatience and blustered, "Either you tell me who you are and what's going on or let me out of the God damn car!"

The jeep slowed as it rolled up to an amber streetlight amidst a quiet intersection. The driver stared at the road for a few moments and then contorted himself around to face Miles. He scratched his head. "No matter how many times I practiced saying this, it never gets easier."

Miles grabbed the latch on the jeep door to get out when the driver threw his arm across the boy's chest to stop him.

"Wait a minute!" he begged. "Miles, I know you're not going to believe me, but you've got to." The driver paused and breathed deeply, as though trying to steady himself. "I'm your father."

"Bullshit!" Miles snapped back. "You're what, twenty? My father would be probably forty by now. Who are you? Really?"

"Like I said," he chuckled, "you're not going to believe me."

Miles cocked an eyebrow at him. "Are you seriously trying to tell me that you're my father?" *Okay,* he decided, *I'll make this nut-bag try to prove it. At least I'll get a good laugh out of it.*

"Yes," he responded with unwavering confidence.

"Then what's your name?" Miles fired back.

"Matthias Draven. And I'm actually 193-years-old."

Whoa! Miles' thoughts raced to try to grapple with the lunacy. *This is getting good.* The man's determination to stick to his story was impressive.

When the stoplight finally turned from red to green, Matthias stepped on the accelerator and they were off again.

Miles' tone turned sarcastic. "When was the last time you had a CAT scan?"

"I'm not insane. I was born in 1752 in Worcester, Massachusetts."

"Well, one thing's for sure, Dad," Miles rudely stressed the word *Dad* with air quotes, "you sure as Hell can't count. If you were born in 1752 that would make you," he paused to do the math in his head before saying, "258 years old. Nice try though."

"So if I'm so full of it, then explain the picture."

Miles recoiled a bit in his seat and narrowed his eyes at Matthias. "What picture?"

"The one you carry with you all the time." He glanced with intent at Miles, his eyes boring through him. "The Polaroid your mother and I left you the night you were born."

Suddenly, the parts of this odd exchange that had entertained Miles had started to send uncomfortable chills down his spine. "How do you know about that?"

"Because I've been watching you your whole life, Miles."

"Watching me? What are you some kind of stalker or something?"

"No. I was waiting for you to grow up, for you to be ready to accept the responsibility that comes with being who we are."

Miles shook his head vehemently. "This is nuts! What responsibility? What are you talking about?"

"Calm down!" he yelled back. "Do us both a favor and take out the picture."

"Why?"

"If you can honestly say that I'm not the man in the picture then I'll pull over and let you out."

"And if I can't?"

"Then you've got to trust me."

"Fine," Miles grumbled and threw up his arms in surrender. Turning his backpack around, he yanked the zipper open on the main compartment and pulled out the cigar box. From inside it he withdrew the photograph and squinted at it in the dark. Matthias reached over and flipped down the visor in front of Miles, activating the vanity mirror light.

"Thanks," Miles groaned. He held the picture under the light. There he examined the face of his father. Then he turned and compared it to Matthias. His stomach lurched and knotted up. The two were a perfect match, right down to the small scar above the right eye; there was no mistaking it. But how was it possible? Miles couldn't wrap his brain around it. "How can this be? If you're my father, and you're, what did you say, 193, then why haven't you aged?" He was starting to hyperventilate.

Matthias stepped on the accelerator, zooming through a yellow stoplight. "I know how hard it is to believe, to make sense of it all, but there's still more to tell you."

"Oh, my God!" Miles laughed. "I don't think I can handle anymore."

"Miles, the reason I haven't aged is because I'm a chronoshifter."

It sounded like gobbledygook. Miles narrowed his eyes at Matthias. "Huh?"

Mathias repeated it slowly "A chro-no-shifter, or what you'd call a time traveler."

Miles fell back hard against his seat, holding his forehead in both hands, shaking left and right. "No, no, no! It's impossible! There's no such thing. This is all some kind of screwed up nightmare."

The jeep slowed down and passed by a large wooden sign that read "Memorial Park." Matthias steered the jeep into a large, vacant parking lot. The brakes whined as it slowed to a stop. He shifted it into neutral and pulled on the parking break. Raindrops began to fall, pelting the leaves of the maples that edged the lot. Overhead, one of the few streetlights left illuminated flickered out. With a twist of the keys,

Matthias shut off the jeep. He stared out into the night. "Miles. I wish I could make this easier on you, but it's the way things have to be. What you're feeling is the same thing I felt when my father told me."

Miles looked around and realized where they were. "What are we doing here?"

His father opened the door and hopped out. Miles followed his movement around the outside of the vehicle. The rear gate swung open. Matthias reached in, pulled out a canvas duffle bag, and exclaimed, "Let's go! We're tethering."

"Tethering?" he inquired, dumbfounded by the odd usage of the term. He didn't see any rope. Miles opened the door and groaned while he climbed out of his seat. "So what, you left your time machine sitting out in the middle of the park? In the rain? I don't see any DeLoreans."

Matthias stood back from the Jeep and surveyed the area. He shrugged and inquired, "What's a DeLorean?"

"Doc Brown, Marty?" he appealed, waiting for some sign of recognition. All he got was a blank, unknowing stare. "Never mind," Miles droned, his shoulders slumped.

Matthias moved aggressively toward Miles and took hold of him by his upper arm, tugging him onto the grass and through the tree line. Beyond the maples, the field was pitch-black. Miles couldn't see two feet in front of him.

"Hey! Slow down!" As he said it, his right foot struck an obstruction jutting up from the ground. He tumbled out of Matthias' grasp and sprawled across a muddied patch of coarse dirt. "Oww!" he cried. Peering through the darkness, he found his foot got caught on a white baseball base. Rolling onto his back he grabbed at his ankle. It stung a bit, but it wasn't broken. He watched Matthias extend a hand out to him to help him up. Accepting the assistance, Miles rose to his feet and hobbled for a moment on his tender ankle. "Thanks a lot. Would you mind taking it easy? I can't see a damn thing out here."

"Sorry," Matthias apologized. "We've got to hurry. I don't know if we've been followed."

"There hasn't been anyone behind us the whole ride." Miles surveyed the park in all directions. Nothing.

"It isn't cars I'm worried about."

"Then what is it?"

"Clearly," Matthias stressed, guiding Miles toward one of the covered dugouts, "I've already told you too much tonight. When we get to safety, then we'll talk some more."

Under the cover of a dugout, Matthias dropped the duffle bag and opened it up.

"I know I haven't seen you in seventeen years, but is it necessary to have a game of catch right now?"

Matthias laughed. "At least you've got your mother's sense of humor."

Miles smiled back. His mother. As crazy as the whole thing seemed, the possibility that if he wasn't in some kind of dream that he could soon meet his mother made him very happy yet nervous inside. But he wondered when the bottom was going to fall out. When was this guy going to reveal himself as some kind of pederast or child killer who lures his victims in with his stories?

"Take off your pants and shirt," Matthias ordered him.

Oh shit! Get the Hell out of Dodge! his inner voice screamed at him.

Matthias threw a pair of grey canvas trousers and an off-white cotton shirt to him. "Put these on."

Oops! Never mind.

As uncomfortable as it was, Miles did as he was asked. First he removed his shirt and tried on the one his father gave him. It was a bit baggy but otherwise okay. Then he removed his sneakers and pants and tried on the trousers. The waist was quite loose, so he tucked in the shirt and pulled the attached suspenders up over his shoulders.

"Does this look okay?" he asked his father.

Matthias looked him up and down, nodding. "Sort of. We'll get you some tailored clothes that fit better when we get home."

"Home?" Miles questioned, his voice rising with eagerness. "Where's home?"

"Not so much a question of where but when." A confused expression marked Miles' face. "You'll understand in a minute. Here," his father said, placing a pair of tall leather boots besides his feet. "Put these on."

Miles sat on the dugout bench with his father as they both pulled on pairs of matching boots. His father then stood up, gathered up all their shed clothes, along with Miles' backpack, and stuffed them in the duffle.

"Time to go," Matthias ordered. He motioned with his head for his son to follow.

When Miles stood up, he noticed that the pants rode up into his junk a bit, the shirt was kind of scratchy, and the soles of the boots didn't have the give of sneakers. Still, he didn't mind them all that much. If those skaters in school could live with painted-on-jeans, he could learn to live with these. He shrugged his shoulders and followed close behind his father who now led the way across the ball field with a bouncing beam from the flashlight.

Directly in the middle of the field, with a cloudy sky overhead, Matthias stopped and pulled from his bag two sets of tangled straps or belts, Miles couldn't tell in the dark. Affixed to each were metallic pieces that clinked and clanked as they dangled in the air. Matthias tossed one set to Miles who caught it awkwardly, like trying to catch an octopus. "Put this on," he said.

Holding it up in the air, Miles examined it and attempted to untangle the straps. They were made of tanned leather and quite sturdy. "This is kind of kinky," he muttered under his breath.

Matthias, who was straightening out his own mess of leather, looked up at Miles. "What?"

"Nothing," Miles snickered. "Are we going climbing or something?"

"No," Matthias countered with no hint of amusement. With a few deft moves, he arranged two straps over his shoulders, two more around his waist, and one strap up between his legs and slipped their metal tongues into a central, five-point buckle. "It's a tether harness for tandem jumping."

"Kind of like skydiving?" Miles asked.

"Kind of." Matthias tugged at the end of each strap and pulled the slack through the tongue adjuster, tightening them snugly against his body. He moved closer to Miles to help him get into the harness. With each strap fastened, Matthias pulled from around his back a thick, braided length of rope that hung from his rigging like a tail. A belaying clip was attached to the end. He attached it to a ring on the chest of Miles' harness and jerked hard at it. "That should hold."

"Why do we have to wear these?" Miles squirmed around uncomfortably. He felt the strap between his legs cutting into his crotch. *Some body parts just aren't supposed to be compressed this much*, he thought for certain. But try as he might, Miles couldn't adjust the straps to make it fit any better. He hoped there wouldn't be any violent yanks upward against the straps or he may come out of this little adventure a soprano.

"It's just a safety precaution. But if for some reason you lose your grip on me, we don't want you floating around the vortex forever."

"What the Hell is the vortex?" his voice rose a few octaves higher. He wondered if he was losing circulation in his crotch.

"You'll see," Matthias answered. His eyebrows rose devilishly and a small laugh escaped him.

Miles watched Matthias pull a round, shiny object from his pocket.

"Come here. I want you to see this."

With a few tentative steps, Miles drew near his father. From where he stood, the item looked like a large pocket watch, but he couldn't be sure in the dark. Whatever it was, it appeared to be made of some sort of polished metal.

"Nice pocket watch. You know, you really should pick up a wristwatch," Miles commented, searching the grounds for any sign of a time machine. "They're a lot more convenient and easy to carry around."

Matthias chuckled. "This is no pocket watch." He pressed a small, recessed button on the side of the object, just below a series of holes that appeared to be made for fingers to slip through. When the side flipped open on its hinge, a brilliant, crystal blue light burst forth from its inner workings. It illuminated his face and chest as though he held a small star in his hands.

"Son of a bitch," Miles croaked and leaned in for a closer look. He shielded his face against the blinding intensity while he waited for his eyes to adjust to the illumination. Instead of seeing the expected clock face with three rotating arms to keep track of hours, minutes, and seconds, Miles saw something completely unexpected. From within the core of the device, a circular panel of glasslike material flipped up and stood on end. The panel itself couldn't have been much thicker than a quarter; it gave the impression of being incredibly fragile. Within that wafer-thin glass swirled a sparkling blue mist that produced the luminous glow. On the face of the panel sat five inset circular panes, each marked with a different number in black calligraphy, with openings filling the gaps between them. And at the base of the panel rested a larger, circular hole that had a ridged ring surrounding it.

Miles read aloud the numbers upon the panel. "1863, 5, 17, 14, 57. What do they mean?"

"May 17, 1863. 2:57PM."

"That's the time machine?"

Matthias shook his head. "I never said there was a time machine." He grabbed the ridged ring with his thumb and index finger and twisted it. It emitted several loud clicks, and then a high pitched whir filled the air. His father slipped his fingers into the device and uttered, "This is a *chronoperpetua.*" Pressing the cover shut, they both fell into darkness.

Blinking away his sudden night blindness, Miles asked, "Do you have a glossary with all these terms in it? What's a—"

"Later."

Miles could faintly see Matthias again. He slung the duffel bag over his shoulder and across his chest. With a pull against the strap, the whole thing tightened around his body.

"Promise me you'll do whatever I tell you to, no matter how scared you might get."

"Why?"

"Don't argue with me!" his father commanded. "Promise."

"Okay, okay, I promise."

"Wrap your arms around me from behind and hold on tight." Matthias turned so his back was to him. Miles shook his head; he never wanted to get this close to another man. Letting out a big sigh, he did what was asked of him.

Standing about the same height as Matthias, Miles looked over his shoulder at what he was doing. He held the chronoperpetua in his right hand, extended away from his body like he was aiming at some invisible point before him. Matthias clenched his jaw and seemed to lower himself by bending slightly at the knees. Miles followed his lead. Then a sudden tension overcame his father's body. With his left hand, Matthias grabbed hold of his right forearm, bracing it.

"Ready?" he asked Miles.

"Yes!"

Matthias snapped his thumb down on a small button on the side of the device. Lithe strands of blue light reached out from the back of the chronoperpetua, snaked up his wrist, and crisscrossed around it like a squid attacking its prey. The moment the tentacles latched on, a howling beam of brilliant blue light burst forth into the darkness from the other end of the device; it swirled and pulsated, setting everything around them aglow and causing the air to hiss. But it did not go on without end. About twenty feet from where they stood, it sliced through the very fabric of reality and peeled it back to reveal an expansive tunnel of pure energy that extended beyond the limits of Miles' sight.

Miles gasped aloud, awestruck by the display. *I can't believe this is happening! He isn't crazy!*

An odd cacophony of sounds emitted from within the conduit, kind of like overlapping radio broadcasts without static. They drowned out the hiss made by the beam. Miles sensed invisible waves of force pulsing through him with the same frequency as the light pulsated. Though they didn't hurt him, they made his insides quiver awkwardly. His knees weakened beneath him, but he held on tight to Matthias for support.

"Hold on!" Matthias yelled over the din as a wave blazed toward him along the beam of light. "Here it comes!"

When the ripple hit, Miles felt a surreal sensation coming over him, unlike anything he ever felt before, except maybe in his dreams. The closest he could come to understanding it was that every cell of his body was being stretched to unbelievable lengths. He struggled to keep his eyes open and hold on to his father as he was told. Then the mouth of the tunnel came racing at the two of them and devoured them whole. With a flash, the beam of light, the vortex, and the two of them were gone.

CHAPTER SEVEN

The first is always the worst. It's a mantra that Miles would carry with him for the rest of his life. He just wished his father had warned him ahead of time.

For the brief moment he traveled through the void, as his father called it, Miles felt his body turning inside out. Images and sounds swirled around him at a deafening volume, yet he felt them more than heard them with every cell of his body. The ebb and flow of time rippled through him as pulsating tendrils of energy reached out and penetrated his flesh. The result was a dizzying sensation that caused his consciousness to begin slipping away. Finally, a blinding, brilliant light swallowed Miles and Matthias.

When it receded, he felt unbearable pain. The sounds of the world echoed mutely in his ears. The Earth, now concrete and material again beneath his body, exuded warmth he never knew before the cold vacuum of the void. Though he wasn't quite sure who he was or where he was, a subtle sensation of the world spinning overtook his sense of balance. His eyes snapped open and the effect increased tenfold. Everything spun so rapidly that he couldn't make sense of where or when he was nor the clearer sounds now registering in his mind. A nauseating pang assaulted his innards. Convulsing violently, a plume of vomit erupted across the ground.

Loud booms sounded nearby. A tremor shook the ground followed by a pelting rain of dirt and debris. Through the din, what seemed like thousands of angry voices could be heard.

A loud, stern voice called out urgently to him. "Get up!"

Miles tried to do as the voice demanded, but he couldn't move. All he could do was groan as a pair of rough hands took fistfuls of his clothes and began dragging him across the ground. The dry, gritty soil tore at his skin.

"Oh shit!" the voice yelled.

Miles felt the weight of this other person collapse on top of him. Then the sound of a more powerful boom hit his ears. Again, the ground shook, but this time the stinging spray of flaming debris stung his skin. The hands grabbed his shoulders and pulled Miles to an upright posture.

"Miles!" the voice bellowed.

Opening his eyes, Miles realized the spinning sensation had lessened. He also recognized the dirt-streaked face before him. His short-circuited memory came back. It was his father, his real father. Somehow this bizarre dream hadn't ended. Matthias' face looked terribly worrisome to Miles, more so than when he rescued him about an hour before.

"We've got to get the Hell out of here!" Matthias shouted over the overwhelming swell of noise.

In his periphery, Miles saw the source of his father's concern and the explosions; they had arrived in the middle of a battlefield. Cannon fire whistled as it cut through the air overhead. Muskets snapped off shot after crackling shot. To his left, an army clad in dark blue uniforms marched toward them in neat, horizontal lines like waves in water. Each of them wore a slouching, blue cap adorned with a brass bugle. Some of the soldiers wore bloodied bandages over their wounds, many of which looked too serious to keep fighting. They also seemed to be of all ages, even boys that looked his age or younger. On the other hand, many looked way too old, well past their prime.

Whipping his head to the right, Miles saw a similar force moving their way. This group, however, seemed a bit more ragtag. Their uniforms were a drab gray. The boys and men who wore them appeared a bit malnourished and not as cleanly kept, yet they had a battle hardened look that made them just as menacing as their opponents.

Oh my God! Miles gasped at the thought. *The Civil War! I'm standing right in the middle of the freakin' Civil War!* A sudden mix of panic, excitement, and fear overcame him.

A loud shout came from a sabre-carrying Union soldier on horseback at the front of the foremost unit. Miles knew he had to be a general or a lieutenant from watching *Glory* in social studies. The firing lines halted.

"Reload!" he barked over the mass of soldiers.

Miles watched as the men, in response to their commanding officer's order, turned their muskets muzzle up with the butt resting against the ground. Then each man reached into a black, leather pouch on his belt and drew forth a white paper cartridge. With their teeth they ripped the package open, stuffed it into the muzzle, and with firm thrusts of the ramrod, packed it down into the musket. Lastly they attached a small, flint cap to the lock and pulled it back into the fully cocked position.

"Ready!"

The men in the front line dropped to one knee while those directly behind them took a step forward, tight at their backs. The butts of their rifles rose to their shoulders as they looked into the eyes of their fellow countrymen whose blood they were about to spill.

Glancing over his shoulder, Miles watched as the Confederates prepared to return fire. They clamored to prepare their muskets before the Union forces could, but it seemed unlikely they would catch up. Looking back, his gaze met Matthias'. A silent decision was made, and the two scrambled to their feet, racing for the woodland edge. While the woods were only a few hundred feet away, Miles felt a lump rise in his throat, fearful that they wouldn't make it. His feet felt like he was moving through quicksand, unable to find purchase as he ran. Matthias, on the other hand, seemed to move on steadier, more confident feet. But his speed was kept in check by the length of rope that still connected the two tether harnesses together. The line drew taut, snapping Miles forward a step or two while pulling Matthias back.

"Aim!" came shouts from both armies' field commanders on such a short delay that the voices sounded like an echo. Every soldier immediately pulled his musket tight against his shoulder and lined up his sights at the intended target.

An involuntary howl escaped Miles. He ran as hard as he could, pushing his body until his legs burned with effort. The whole landscape and looming tree line bounced in his field of view.

"Fire!" The crackling roll of hundreds of musket balls blasting across the battlefield erupted all around.

With a desperate, heaving thrust, Miles launched himself through the air. Behind him, stray fire shredded the foliage that lined the forest. He crashed through the brush and onto his side, slamming into several hard roots that jutted up from the soil. He finally came to rest against his father who lay in a heap. Miles' whole side hurt. He felt like an apple that was dropped too many times and was all broken up and mushy inside.

Matthias rolled to his side and sat up, groaning loudly. "Sorry about that."

Miles gritted his teeth and held his ribs. "So you didn't plan on landing us in the middle of a battle? That's good to know." He twisted his torso at his hips to try to stretch out his ribs. Inside he felt all kinds of uncomfortable popping and stopped when the pain caused him to become light headed.

Wincing noticeably, Matthias struggled to stand. When he got to his feet, he stood bent over at the waist, hands on his knees, and then slowly inched his way up until he stood straight. His hand moved to the iron ring attached to the buckle of his tether harness. With a quick twist, the straps fell from his body into a jangling pile on the ground. "Unfortunately," Matthias added as he bent over backward to stretch, "chronoshifting isn't an exact science."

Miles didn't bother to get up just yet. He unhooked the connecting tether between the two harnesses and then disconnected the tongues from the buckle. He languidly peeled it off. Deep indents in his skin lingered from the force of being dragged through the void.

"Now what do we do?" Miles asked as he heard bayonets and sabers clashing in the distance. Explosions of gunpowder and the painful cries of fallen soldiers echoed just a short distance away.

Matthias packed the tether harnesses back into his bag and threw it over his shoulder. He looked over his son toward the clatter of combat. "We're not safe here. The battle might spill over into the woods."

From his pocket, Matthias pulled out what looked like another chronoperpetua. Overcome by curiosity to see the strange device again, Miles ignored the discomfort in his limbs and got up. But when he drew near his father he discovered that it was nothing more than a simple compass. Its copper casing was worn and dented, and the glass that covered the magnetic needle had scratches and blemishes all over it. He watched the pointer bob and rotate until it finally settled. Matthias looked back across the battlefield with a sour grimace.

Miles didn't like the look one bit. "Don't tell me," he groaned. "We're on the wrong side?"

"Yup," Matthias affirmed. He shrugged his shoulders rather nonchalantly. "Looks like we've got to go around."

"Are you kidding me?"

"If we stick to the woods we should be okay. There's enough cover to deflect most of their stray shots. We are going to have to steal a few horses too."

Miles thumped the palm of his hand against his forehead in utter dissatisfaction and then dragged it downward, slurring his features into a ghastly look. "Oh, this just gets better and better."

"Stop your whining," Matthias ordered with a harsh tone. "Keep low and follow me closely."

After a quick visual scan of their surroundings, Matthias pushed through some low lying shrubs and moved deeper into the forest. Miles tried to do as his father asked, but his boots, which were neither broken in nor as easy on the feet as his *Vans*, were terribly uncomfortable. From what he could tell, large calluses had started to form on his instep and the outer part of his foot by the pinky toe. Each step caused the leather to bend and flex, rubbing harshly against his skin. If that wasn't bad enough, thorns hooked at his skin from the underbrush. He was hot, sweaty, and covered in tiny red cuts along his arms and legs. Yet through all of this, Matthias seemed to move with a boundless energy, not at all put off by the physical labor. Miles didn't think himself to be out of shape or fat, in fact he always pictured himself as being quite thin and muscular, but he just couldn't catch his breath. Maybe it was some kind of lingering effect of going through the void. Either way, he had already had his fill of 1863.

About thirty minutes later, his father brought their march to an end. Sweat now soaked Miles' shirt, and his trousers itched at his skin, especially in certain unmentionable areas that were starting to chafe. Their journey took them all the way around to the other end of the field. The two of them knelt down behind a sizeable oak. All along the edge of the woodland were several smaller trees, and tied to some of them, a line of well-fed horses. They chomped away on a heaping pile of straw, seemingly undisturbed by the constant crackle of musket fire. True war horses. A little farther into the field stood the command tents of the Union army. Through the flapping entryways, generals and other commissioned officers could be seen milling about in darkened shadow. Soldiers came and went, no doubt delivering news from the battlefield. No eyes seemed to glance their way.

Miles felt a quick tug on the back of his shirt. He looked at his father who had a singular finger pressed against his lips. *Father!* He couldn't help but scoff at the idea, even with the situation at hand, that this man who appeared no older than twenty-two could be his father. Giving him any serious measure of respect was going to be a struggle. He looked like the kind of person who he'd try to act badass around, to show off to. But Matthias had proven himself so far to be what he said, so he owed him a small gesture of respect. Besides, Miles knew he was totally out of his element. Nothing felt right here. Nothing felt comfortable anymore. This wasn't the time or the place to be obstinate, so he obediently nodded to his father who then gestured for him to stay put.

With the cunning and stealth of a jungle cat stalking its prey, Matthias slunk along the tree line toward two brown mares that had eaten their way into the underbrush. They did not seem aware of his movement behind the low-lying shrubs. Amidst the snapping off of musket fire in the background and the tinges of battle, he didn't seem to make a sound. Matthias moved slowly, deliberately, until he reached the horses. They nickered quietly at his presence but were otherwise unperturbed. From his bag he removed two hunks of carrot and offered them to the mares while smoothing the fur from below their eyes to their muzzles. They gobbled up their precious snack with relish. As they munched, Matthias unwrapped their reins from the trees and with gentle tugs on the leather straps he urged them deeper into the woodlands. Their massive bodies disappeared into the trees and no one was the wiser.

Matthias waved at Miles to follow him. Staying low, he slunk along behind the horses until they were all well out of sight of the encampment. Having reached a small clearing along the side of a road, they stopped.

"Do you know how to ride?" Matthias asked while checking the fit of the saddle and the bridle. "I'm guessing that horsemanship isn't a commonly taught skill in 2016."

Miles shook his head and looked over the animal from head to tail. He'd never seen one up close before. They were much larger than he previously thought. Its physical power and beauty took him by surprise. "No, I've never even been near a horse before."

Matthias quickly showed Miles how to fit his foot into the stirrup and use the saddle horn to pull himself up onto the horse. It took a few tries before he generated enough lift to swing his leg over its back and settle onto the worn leather of the saddle. Then he unwrapped the reins from around the horn, and after a few simple instructions, Miles had his mare trotting along beside his father's. It took some time to get used to the feel of it. Horses didn't have much to offer in the way of comfort. The constant bouncing of his rear end against its thick, hard back brought about some aches and pains that would surely linger for a few days. Steering wasn't too troublesome, though his horse didn't always seem to respond to gentle suggestions. Every once in a while he had to give the reins a good yank to bring her to a halt or to make a sharper turn. But every time he had to dig his boot heel into the mare's ribs to urge her to move faster, he felt a pang of guilt. He understood it was how the whole thing worked, but it probably didn't feel too good for the horse.

Their ride took them through the Virginia countryside, past stately homes, and countless farms. It was a landscape Miles felt truly alien in. Nothing looked as it did in his time. The roads were all cut straight out of the earth, made of dirt and stone with deep gouges where wagon wheels wore away the ground. The concrete and asphalt highways of the early twenty-first century were still a distant dream to these people as was the internal combustion engine of Henry Ford. It all made for a terribly inconsistent ride. Those people in the horse-drawn carriages they passed by on the road winced as they rode over each bump, bouncing out of their seats. Meager springs set beneath the benches of the carriages that were meant to soften the ride did little to actually allay the abuse of their butts.

For the most part, the homes were much like the ones he knew in his own time. The only noticeable differences were the lack of vinyl siding and the old, wavy panes of glass in the windows. They looked like the glass was slowly melting. Dogs and children still played in yards, and grass still grew tall and green. Just add a basketball hoop or two in a driveway and an in-ground swimming pool in the back yard and Miles would feel more at home.

The biggest difference he noticed aside from the way people dressed came in their temperament, in how they carried themselves and dealt with others. Those whom they passed on the road always went out of their way to tip their hat in Matthias and Miles' direction, to wave to them, or even to say, "Good afternoon." His father didn't claim to know any of them. Yet, he responded in kind to their gestures like it was second nature. They were all just strangers passing by each other on a late spring afternoon, showing each other "proper Christian manners" as Matthias told him. It all made him feel very uncomfortable, especially since the only time he ever heard anyone talk about being a Christian was right before they were about to say something rather unbecoming of a Christian. Miles guffawed at the idea. He viewed religion to be a dark plague of hatred and intolerance, and he rarely kept his views to himself. However, he remembered that this was a very Puritanical society and his opinions would need to be kept in check. Either way, he understood manners, and it was clear to him that these people had them in spades. He wasn't used to that. Being shown respect and, quite honestly, showing respect to others was not something that happened too often in his world.

Daylight soon began to wane. Wispy clouds snaked along the sky and bathed in fluorescent hues of pink and purple. A light breeze blew in from the south, rustling the leaves of the trees and making the long grass lurch at its urging. It was a beautiful afternoon.

The roadside along which they traveled opened up into fields of lush, green grassland surrounded by sections of roughly hewn split rail fencing. A faint hint of cedar filled the air as the wind shifted in their direction. Miles breathed it in deep. He loved that smell.

Eventually, a road covered in crushed stone cut a swath in the grassland to their left. Matthias brought his mare to a halt and Miles followed suit. His eyes drifted upward to where a curved sign, forged of wrought iron, read "DRAVEN STABLES." Miles looked to his father for confirmation.

Matthias smiled warmly and said, "Welcome home, Miles."

Miles shook his head. "I can't believe this is happening."

His father chuckled. "I know. It's a lot to take in in one day. But believe it, son, you're finally home."

Miles leaned down against the neck of the mare and lay his head against hers, closing his eyes. *Please don't let this be a dream.* The horse nickered at the soothing gesture.

"C'mon," Matthias encouraged his son. "Your mother's waiting." With a whip of the reins and a jab of his heels, he urged his mare into motion, galloping up the stone path.

A lightness of spirit ran through Miles. He felt his whole body tingling and his pulse quickened. His mother was only a few hundred feet away, waiting at the farmhouse. With a hearty yelp, Miles cracked the reins and set his horse in pursuit of his father. The scope of the ranch opened up to him as he rode. His high school didn't even have this much land for athletic fields and parking lots. Taking it in it almost seemed like too much space, like he might get lost or not know what to do with himself in such a place.

The two-story farmhouse grew larger with each clop of his steed's frantic hooves. A large wrap-around porch accented the first floor. The railing, along with the shutters and the molding around the roof and windows, provided a dark green accent against the rest of the white siding. It lacked the luster of twenty-first century homes, yet something about it felt homey, familiar even, like a dream Miles had night after night but could never remember once he woke up.

What Miles saw next was no dream or distant memory. Their horses seemed to slow to their own gentle gait within thirty or so feet of the house and then halted several hoof-falls later. Out of his periphery, Miles saw his father dismount and draw near, but his gaze locked unwaveringly upon his mother. Still young and vibrant like his father, Elizabeth Draven rose from a creaky rocking chair to look upon him. She did not wear the classic Victorian Era clothes he expected from Civil War movies and television documentaries. Instead, she wore comfortable looking tan breeches tucked into calf-high riding boots, and a white blouse with the sleeves rolled up. Her long, curly red hair lay bunched together over her left shoulder. Around her neck she wore a glittering gold necklace with a small trinket of some kind dangling at its nadir. The look on her face was much like the one in his precious picture: high, blushing cheekbones; big, brown, earthen eyes; thin lips; and a proud snub nose, much like his. The corners of her mouth rose in a joyful grin, making her eyes narrow and her cheeks glisten in the waning, golden sunlight.

The tingling that Miles felt earlier turned into a stomach churning nervousness. *My mother. By God, my actual mother!* His limbs vibrated like he had the jitters from a hangover. He lowered himself down from the saddle, not letting his eyes leave her as she descended the front steps. Miles nearly fell when his unsteady feet met the loose stone of the driveway, but he managed to steady himself against the horse before he took a few unsteady steps in her direction. His mother's careful pace quickened as did his. Miles always wondered if his mother would recognize him if they ever met. *Would she know I'm her son? Would she love me at all or care about me?* For as long as he could recall, these thoughts plagued him and made him loathe his parents, believing that if they could let go of him so easily as a baby that there was no love, no care at all for him. But as mother and son closed the final few feet between them, Miles saw that her face was wet with tears and her open, welcoming arms were those of a caring, loving mother he had only dreamt of. And the power of their embrace, the warmth of her hand cradling the back of his head and holding it against her own as she sobbed joyfully, made some of the pain and anger in his heart melt away for the moment. But there was still ample hurt and questions that needed answering.

Elizabeth pulled back from his arms and gently touched his cheeks with her hands. She sniffled and gushed, "Oh, my beautiful, beautiful boy. Let me look at you."

Miles watched her eyes examine every aspect of his face. Her gaze crawled across his features like a painter studying a landscape before making their first brushstroke. For a few seconds, he didn't understand the scrutiny. Then he remembered that this was likely the first time since they abandoned him that she had seen his face. Though he was her son, Miles was as foreign to her as anyone she would cross paths with on any street or in a crowded market square. The realization brought his anger back to the surface, the frustration of those lonely nights in his room where he cried himself to sleep wondering why they left him behind.

Miles took her hands in his and pulled them down from his face. His eyes met hers, but he did not return the same tender expression; his face wore the lines and contours of frustration, of years of pain about to be released. He let her hands fall from his trembling grasp. Their tender moment came to an abrupt end.

His voice left him in a low, agonized tone. "How could you abandon me? Didn't I matter to you? Was I that easy to throw away?" Miles struggled to not lash out, to not alienate the people he always longed for in his life. He felt his lip quivering and tears collecting in the corners of his eyelids.

Elizabeth bit her lower lip and frowned sorrowfully. Her solemn gaze fell upon Matthias who in turn drew closer to them in response.

"Miles," his mother whispered and tried to lay a comforting hand on his shoulder.

Miles, however, flinched back away from her touch, shaking his head. His voice rose sharply, "I want answers, damn it!"

"And answers you'll get," Matthias interrupted. "But this is a conversation best kept behind closed doors." He motioned with his arms for everyone to move up the front steps and into the house. "Let's calm down and go inside."

Miles wasn't ready to listen to his father. The pot had boiled over, and years of misguided resentment had finally found their long overdue, intended targets. Tears streamed down his cheeks and into his mouth. The salt on his tongue, a taste he had come to detest, made his rage surge to such levels that his head swam with dizziness. "Why? Why?" his voice crackled. "Why the Hell did you leave me there? Do you have any idea what you've done to me, the life I've had?"

"Honey," Elizabeth begged, "please calm down. It was done to protect you, to keep you out of harm's way." She stepped closer and attempted to put a comforting arm around him, but Miles reeled away from her touch so vehemently that he lost his footing and stumbled again, falling to one knee.

The lightheaded sensation intensified. His world began to spin. When he tried to stand again, Miles saw his parents reaching out to help him up. He motioned their hands away with a wave of his arm, trying to act strong. "I'm not going to calm down," his voice stammered. Miles slowly rose to full height again. The sensation of teetering was difficult to fight off. "Out of harm's way?" he scoffed, aghast at the presumption. "Being bullied and beat up, no family, feeling unwanted and unloved all my life? Oh yeah, you protected me. More like threw me to the wolves."

Miles lurched forward and grabbed hold of his head.

"Are you okay?" Elizabeth gushed with concern as she dashed to Miles' side along with Matthias. They ducked under his arms and supported him with their shoulders.

He struggled against their assistance, but they did not relent. Then a sudden wave of popping, flashing lights went off in his sight, and Miles felt the world closing in around him. All strength left his body. His knees buckled beneath him and he collapsed into his parents. A pool of overwhelming darkness swallowed him up.

CHAPTER EIGHT

A familiar aroma roused Miles from a deep, restful sleep—bacon. The smell of crisp, greasy bacon swirled about in his nostrils and teased his mouth to watering. Through closed eyelids, he could see the glow of sunlight washing over him. Something seemed wrong—his room was usually dimly lit, but today it seemed bathed with light. Then he remembered. His father, the void, time travel...it did happen. It wasn't some hyper-realistic dream he had the night before. It was real. The sunlight was real, and its warmth radiated through the bedding he lay huddled beneath. Groaning, Miles rolled away from the light without opening his eyes. He didn't want to see where he was. The last twenty-four hours had taken a toll on his mind, and as long as his eyes stayed shut, he could deny what he knew to be true; the bed beneath him wasn't his own. With a grunt, he pulled the sheet and heavy blanket covering him up over his head.

Unable to resist any longer, Miles let his eyelids open. A little sunlight passed through the linens into his protective cocoon. He blinked his eyes a few times to wipe away the foggy gloom that clouded his view. Immediately, he saw that someone had undressed him down to his boxers, likely the same person that put him in bed. At least they had the common decency to not strip him down to nothing.

Beneath him, the mattress lacked the springy nature of his cheap one back home, and he found himself longing for it. This one felt like a huge, flattened pillow. His whole body felt stiff from sleeping on it. His shoulders ached, his lower back felt like it was twisted and knotted, and he couldn't feel his right arm. Then it began; a horrid tickle crawled along his numb limb before it quickly grew into a dull ache. He had slept on it. Miles dragged it out from beneath him and held it tight as the blood flow returned.

The gentle clack of knuckles rattled against a nearby door. It sounded thick and heavy, unlike the hollow doors in the Lyle's house. When he didn't answer, a newly familiar voice called out to him.

"Miles," his mother's voice penetrated the door, "are you up?"

He felt his heart flutter at the sound of her voice. It seemed odd that for the few words she spoke to him the day before, he knew the sound well, almost as if it still lingered in some primal, ancient corner of his mind from after his birth, and he found it naturally soothing. However, the years of abandonment quickly swept away the comfort of her voice. Anger and confusion took its place. He found motivation in his want to interrogate them and wring from them the answers that made his first seventeen years of life a living Hell. But this was his *real* family. Miles knew he couldn't treat them like he treated the other people in his life. To get his answers and not piss away the one thing he always wanted more than anything, he had to temper his anger, manage it. Part of him wondered if he could. His mother knocked again. This time he answered.

"Yeah," his response curt and gruff, "I'm up."

He heard his mother twist the door knob and push the door open without so much as a creak. The swish of a skirt and feet padding around the bed preceded the sound of drapes being thrown open and the light intensity of the room growing two-fold. Even through the sheets the brightness was too much for him. Miles threw his left arm up to over his eyes and let the numb one fall to the bed. The tingling was too much. Tossing aside the bedding, he sat up with his back to the windows and shook his arm to get the blood flowing better.

His mother, dressed like one of the Ingalls girls from *Little House on the Prairie*, came into view. He just couldn't wrap his mind around the fact that *this* was his mother—this young, vibrant woman of no more than twenty years. She had not a wrinkle or gray hair of note. Her long, curly red hair fell over her shoulders and framed a figure that had no signs of age or wear. *This is going to take some getting used to*, he concluded. She held a neatly folded pile of clothes in her hands much like the ones he wore the day before, only the pants were tan instead of gray.

"Put these on," Elizabeth spoke in a soft, careful tone. She laid them down on the bed beside Miles and smiled. "I'll wait outside for you."

Once the door closed behind her, Miles rose from the bed and began dressing himself. He took stock of his new bedroom for the first time. Massive windows with white molding stretched from only a foot or so off the floor to about a foot from the ceiling. Miles could literally jump through the windows with minimal effort. Each wavy pane of glass revealed the sprawling grassland of his parents' land and the forest beyond.

The rest of the room possessed a few distinguishing features. Knotty planks of sanded lumber stretched across the floor with a few areas covered by small throw rugs. White wainscoting covered the lower few feet of the interior walls. He had seen it before in friend's houses but wasn't aware that it had been in use for so long. Exposed red brick and mortar stretched from floor to ceiling along the center of the far wall, and a small, pot belly wood-stove stood beside. A length of curved, tin exhaust pipe fed smoke and soot into the main chimney from the diminutive firebox. A few feet to its right sat a cherry rocking chair. The damn thing looked so hard and uncomfortable. Pulling the suspenders of his breeches up over his shoulders, Miles looked down at his bed—a very nice sleigh bed that matched the color of the rocker. He rolled his bottom lip and nodded. *Not bad for a living museum.* Before he could join his mother, a nagging sense of lacking made him uncomfortable. Miles grabbed at his left wrist and realized the problem—no watch. He scanned the area around the headboard and found it lying on a small nightstand. Strapping it to his wrist, he felt whole again.

Ready to face his family, Miles opened the bedroom door. Elizabeth leaned against the wall nearest the doorway, waiting. She smiled at him and nodded. "Not bad. You almost look comfortable in those."

Miles squirmed about under the clothes and grimaced. "Yeah, almost," he grumbled and pulled at the snug collar. "They don't wear as well as they look. Too used to my old clothes."

His mother pushed off the wall with her shoulders and drew near. She made small adjustments to his clothes—tugging the tail of his shirt out of his breeches a bit and unbuttoning the collar of his shirt. "We're not in church, Miles. You don't need this buttoned."

"Church?" Miles inquired painfully. In a mocking southern drawl he begged, "Please tell me were not 'God fearing' Christians."

His mother narrowed her eyes at him and pursed her lips as if to ruin his whole time travelling experience. She said in a measured, deliberate manner, "It's part of the life we lead. You don't have to believe it, but if we want to blend in and not stand out, you've got to suck it up. Think of church as a social gathering." She shrugged and waved her hand as if to dismiss the whole affair. "A place to meet people and see friends." Elizabeth paused again and looked him over. "Better?"

Miles wriggled his shoulders and hips about in an odd way, trying to find comfort in his new duds. "Good enough."

"Good. Your father's waiting downstairs."

Miles followed his mother down the length of the upstairs hallway. He ran his hand along the glassy smooth railing as he passed by two open bedrooms, a few doors that remained closed, and then back around to descend the stairwell. The look and feel of the rest of the house flowed along seamlessly from room to room.

At the base of the stairs, a massive foyer unfolded before him. It was the hub of the lower floor. Apart from the front door, two larger rooms connected to this area. Elizabeth took hold of the newel post as she reached the last stair and swung herself into a tight right turn and then a few feet later turned again through an archway that led beneath the stairwell. Miles kept close by. Thinking back on his trek downstairs, he wondered how hard it must have been to carry him upstairs into bed. He wasn't a little kid.

Passing through the archway beneath the stairs, Miles entered the spacious country kitchen. Though the basic décor of the rest of the house flowed seamlessly into this room, it felt far more lived in, comfortable. The walls weren't stark white like the rest of the house; these seemed more ivory in tone, kind of like the look of French vanilla ice cream. On the opposite end of the room from where he stood, a large stone and masonry fireplace mastered the far wall. It was enormous. A notched crane arm held a large, cast iron pot over unlit timbers. It stretched from one side of the fireplace to the other. Miles also noticed two small iron doors on opposing sides of the outer brickwork, but he wasn't sure what they were used for. To the left of the stone hearth, a dizzying number of cabinets lined the upper and lower portions of the wall. The lower cabinets supported an authentic marble countertop that shimmered in the warm sunlight that spilled through a curtained window. To the right of the fireplace, he saw what appeared to be a massive cast iron stove. It looked nothing like a modern stove top, but he could tell by its design that the two were related in some way. Like the fireplace in his room, a tin pipe branched off from the back of the stove and connected to the chimney.

Stepping further within the kitchen, Miles made note of a few additional pieces of ancient looking equipment. To his immediate right stood a wooden cabinet starkly dissimilar from the woodwork upon the outer wall. The top of it came to his waist and there was no marble top to it. Instead, it had a hollow top that a copper bowl sat within, just beneath the spout of a cistern. As far as Miles could tell, it had to be some form of an early sink before the advent of indoor plumbing. Turning about to his left, Miles found a dough box standing beside a large wooden table whose surface appeared to be unvarnished. His eyes finally fell upon his father who sat at the table, reading from a tattered old book and sipping from a steaming mug. His mother moved across the room and drew a nearby chair out from the table, motioning for Miles to come sit beside him.

Matthias broke from his reading to peek at what had stirred Elizabeth. His gaze then locked on Miles. A contented smile broke the rigid lines of his stern face. "Miles," his father announced with joy, flipping his book closed. "You're awake." His high voice and rapid gesticulations gave away his excitement. "Come. Sit and eat. You must be starved."

Miles scratched at his scalp, still not sure how he felt about all of this. He still felt quite overwhelmed by the events of the last twenty-four hours, but if any of this was to make any sense, he had to go along with it. Plodding across the room with reluctance, he plopped down on the creaky wooden chair.

Matthias leaned back in his chair and solicited with eagerness, "How did you sleep?"

Miles shifted in his seat. He didn't share Matthias' cheerful disposition. "Fine," he answered curtly.

Elizabeth placed a heaping plate of breakfast in front of Miles: flapjacks, ham steak, two poached eggs, biscuits and gravy, and a tall glass of milk. He glanced at the plate, feeling a sharp pang of nausea move through his guts. Then he turned a disgusted grimace her way. "What's this?"

"Breakfast," she answered. He could tell she was disheartened by her smirk and the way her small hands sat upon her hips. Miles wondered if she was going to whip out his middle name already. "Didn't they feed you in that Godforsaken time?"

"Sure. It's just a bit much. Eating early always made me feel kinda sick."

"I'm sorry. I didn't know what you'd want so I made everything I could think of."

Elizabeth reached for the plate to take it away. Out of the corner of his eye, Miles took notice of the pile of dirty pans lying on the stove. She had put a lot of effort into making him happy, and his insides now added guilt to the nausea. He quickly grabbed the plate and pulled it out of her reach.

"No, it's okay. Thank you." *Thank you?* It wasn't a phrase he had used much in his life, nor had he often cause for using it. But he meant it. Come to think of it, no one had ever made him a breakfast anything like this. Maybe his foster parents threw a bowl of cereal, a piece of fruit, or a *Pop Tart* his way, but nothing quite like this. Even if she only prepared it for him because people ate this way in this era, he couldn't ignore the fact that his mother made it for him, and he owed her a bit of courtesy.

With the edge of his fork, Miles chopped off a hunk of syrupy pancake and lifted it to his lips. He sniffed at it with suspicion. It smelled fine. The syrup seemed a bit thin, but he doubted they had *Mrs. Butterworth's* way back when. Despite the knots in his stomach, Miles took the tiniest nibble. He couldn't control the flaring of his eyelids in surprise. Miles nodded and exclaimed, "It's good!"

Elizabeth smiled and patted him on the shoulder. "Thank you. Just don't push it. I'm glad you're trying it, but don't make yourself sick for my sake."

Miles hacked another larger portion off with his fork, leaned over the plate, and shoveled it in, wolfing it down with only a few chews. "I'm fine," he countered, waving his fork. Small bits of pancake sprayed from his lips as he spoke.

Matthias brushed some of the crumbs into his hand from off the table. "Well, eat up. We'll discuss table manners another time."

Suddenly self-conscious, Miles considered his posture and how he was eating. He shot his mother an expression he hoped she would understand. He felt relief when she exaggeratingly straightened her posture—a suggestion for him to emulate. Miles immediately sat up straight. He continued on with his meal for a short while in silence, devouring the pancakes, a bite or two of the biscuits, half the ham, and a refill of milk. Filled to overstuffing, he pushed the plate away and let out a sigh. Elizabeth quickly took up the plate and scraped the leavings into a tin pail that sat in the cabinet beneath the water pump. She lifted the bucket and took it out through the back door. Through the window, Miles watched her take it some distance behind the house and dump it before she came back inside.

"I guess you don't have garbage trucks in the 1800s," Miles mused as he turned back around in his seat to face his father.

"No. Anything the horses or the pets won't eat we have to burn. If it doesn't burn, we have to bury it. It's no wonder the world is in so much environmental danger in your time."

"You know about that?"

"Of course. We're historians, Miles. That's what we do."

"I thought we were time travelers."

"Chronoshifters," Matthias corrected.

"Whatever you call it. Just warning you," Miles pursed his lips, thinking of the best way to phrase his academic pursuits, "history isn't one of my better subjects."

Matthias chuckled, "Let's be honest, Miles, you really don't have *any* better subjects."

Miles was taken aback. "How would you know?" He felt violated. Since this whole odyssey began, he surmised that they had to have been checking in on him from time to time, but just how much did they know? As much as they were his real parents and had some right to know how he fared, the thought that some shadowy figures have been lurking about him his whole life, keeping track of his every movement and mistake, made him uneasy. The cauldron of anger began bubbling over again. His voice rose in intensity, on the verge of yelling. "Are you telling me that you knew what kind of life I was living and just sat back and let it happen?"

Matthias wrung his hands together in apparent nervous discomfort. "Yes, in a manner of speaking."

"What?" He couldn't believe what he was hearing. "How could you do that to me? I'm your son, God damn it!" Miles ran a hand through his hair and looked away from the two of them. "I think I was better off believing you'd just abandoned me."

"Miles," Elizabeth spoke with gentleness, hands clasped under her bottom lip as if in prayer. "Please believe me. If I could have done anything to stop your suffering, I would have. But we had to let you grow up. If we had interfered in your life, you wouldn't be as strong as you are today."

He did believe her, but he also didn't care at that moment. He had come all this way, found his family, and had a chance to set things straight. To do that, he had to say his peace. The truth was going to hurt. "Strong? You call this," Miles guffawed, gesturing toward himself with his hands, "strong? I'm a fucking mess." He jabbed an accusatory finger in the direction of both of his parents. "And it's your fault."

His insides knotted up. He was getting out all his pain and anger, even some of it newfound, but it taxed his mind. The fainting sensation that came over him the day before started again. With the world beginning to spin around him, Miles grabbed for the table top with both of his hands for stability. Then he found his center again. Across the room and behind his mother, he took notice of an odd artifact that his foster mother had in his time—a small, antique coffee churn. The dull surface of the wrought iron device made him feel somewhat at home and calmed his spirit.

Miles exhaled a slow breath and looked to Matthias, who returned a saddened stare. Then he turned away from his son and shared a frown with Elizabeth. They reached for each other's hand and let their fingers intertwine.

"You're right." Elizabeth sighed. "It's our fault. You have every right to be angry. But I beg of you to try to understand why we did it. We're constantly on the move, travelling from one time to another, constantly hunting. It would be nearly impossible to raise a child or keep it safe. "

She reached across the table to take Miles' hand. He wanted to pull back, to keep her from making that connection, but the look of sadness in her eyes and the ache he felt inside wouldn't let him.

"You may not see it or feel it, but by letting you live your life it *has* made you stronger."

"But," Miles attempted to interrupt her, but his father cut him off.

"Listen to me, Miles. We've all had it rough. My parents, your grandparents, left me to fend for myself in New York City in the 1700s. I barely survived my childhood. After they kicked me out of the orphanage, I had to fend for myself on the streets, doing anything and everything I could to find a way to survive to see the next day." Matthias glanced away from his son. He pinched the bridge of his nose with his fingertips. His hand trembled. "I killed another boy when I was your age because he wouldn't share a stale loaf of bread. The scar over my eye is from his knife. He was my best friend, Miles, and I took his life so that I could survive." His eyes locked back on Miles and thumped his fist on the table. "Do you understand what I'm saying?"

Miles had no idea what to say. He couldn't return his father's penetrating gaze. All he could do was nod.

"That boy you beat half to death," Matthias continued, "a weaker man wouldn't have fought back. He was twice your size, but you weren't afraid. You showed restraint, taking as much as could be expected of anyone. But when it was called for, when he pushed you too far, you let the wrath inside take over."

The concept started burrowing through his protective wall of anger.

All the pain, all the hurt he lived with for the past seventeen years, it served a purpose. As much as he hated his parents for what they did, they were right, it did make him stronger. Miles didn't have any fear when he turned on Jack, he just made up his mind to go after him and didn't even let a thought about what might happen to him enter his mind.

"I think I understand, but don't expect me to be okay with it for a while. Just give me some space to get used to all of this."

Both Matthias and Elizabeth nodded.

"I hated my parents for many years," Matthias added, "but over time that hatred faded. I came to terms with it. In their later years, before it was too late, I told them that I not only forgave them, but I loved them dearly. It's a journey we must all take."

There was a lasting period of silence as Miles made peace with the situation. In the calm, the bigger questions that plagued his mind crept to the forefront. "Speaking of journeys, you never told me why we're time-tra, I mean chronoshifters. And why did those assassins come after me? What did I do?"

Elizabeth threw Matthias a doubtful look and shrug before she stood, fetched herself and Matthias cups of tea, and returned to the table. Matthias pursed his lips, not quickly forthcoming with details. He leaned his elbows on the table and tapped his fingertips together. Then he laid his arms out before him, and rubbed the wooden top. He leaned forward and spoke.

"I guess I'll answer the easy question first. They tried to kill you, from what we can surmise, because you're one of us."

"But I wasn't a chronoshifter then. That doesn't make any sense."

"Yeah, but one day you would be. One day we'd come and get you and bring you into the fold. Someone was trying to stop that from happening. Someone's trying to wipe out the next generation."

"Who?" Miles pleaded. "More of our kind?"

"They did the dirty work," Elizabeth answered flatly as she sipped her steaming tea. "At least I think so."

"There's no proof of that, Liz," Matthias countered, seeming to not let her theory gain too much traction with Miles. "The only thing we know is that Gaius was behind the slayings."

"Who the Hell is Gaius?" Miles questioned.

"Yes," Elizabeth admitted with a hint of reluctance. She continued on as though she didn't even hear her son. "But someone stole the anchors and used them to track down the children. He can't do that. Only a shifter can."

"Hold on!" Miles snapped at them both, his voice booming. They fell silent. "Can you please just tell me what's going on here?"

Both of his parents apologized for forgetting him amidst their disagreement. They then exchanged curious glances, appearing to silently decide who would do the talking. Elizabeth raised her eyebrows at Matthias, and he replied with a simple shrug. Without warning, Elizabeth began to explain the sworn duty that all members of the Draven family and their forbearers had been charged with; keep Gaius Lloth, an unspeakable evil from the foulest reaches of Hell, from reconstituting its power and plunging mankind into an eternity of darkness. Over a thousand years ago, it is believed that an unknown sorcerer or imbecile of lesser talent and intelligence summoned the unclean spirit to the mortal realm to serve some dark purpose. Then it is believed that the summoner either neglected to build strong enough wards to control the beast, or they unleashed it purposefully upon the Earth.

Armed with the powerful artifacts collected in order to summon it to this world, Gaius Lloth took possession of a skilled tribal chieftain and wreaked havoc across the globe, laying to waste to countless nations. No one could stand toe-to-toe with the demon in combat or outwit it tactically. It could see the future and knew every move its enemies would make. But then twelve brave warriors, some who had already suffered losses at the hands of Lloth and others who had yet to, experienced what could only be called visions. They understood that they did not make war against a man but a timeless evil that could not easily be destroyed. Together they rallied the last of the brave men and women who still had fight in them for one final battle. Reeling, the last hope for mankind stood fragile and exposed like a baby sparrow fallen from its nest. But instead of defeat, one woman landed the luckiest of blows against the demon. The cleaving wound split its host's body from neck to navel. It fell limp to the ground. Gaius' forces, in utter shock at their master's collapse, could no longer hold their lines and floundered. Those who survived the battle believed, like many, that the evil that nearly tore our world to pieces died on the pitch that day. But evil like that never dies.

Months later, a wizard, not long for this world, visited each of those twelve warriors in their homes. He warned them that the evil they defeated still had a firm hold on this world, though greatly weakened by its loss on the battlefield. He pleaded with them to remain vigilant and pursue the demon until they breathed their last breath. To assist them in their efforts, he presented each of them with two curious objects.

The first object was a journal. It possessed intricate scribblings in each warrior's native tongue, but what was written therein made little sense at first blush. Those words, when processed through a complex cypher, however, would reveal the secret hiding place of one of the artifacts of power used to summon Gaius to Earth. Once found, they were to protect that object from the demon, who now resided in an unknown skin, by keeping it on the move and away from those who might wish to make use of it. If Gaius were to regain the objects, the demon's strength and power would be reconstituted so that it could once again wage war against mankind.

The second object was a mysterious device unlike any the warriors had ever encountered. Circular in shape, crafted from copper, and small enough to rest in their hand, the chronoperpetua would be the key to staying one step ahead of the demon. The demon can't survive on Earth without living within the body of a mortal, so its true form is always concealed and nearly impossible to find. But it also means that the demon is bound to present time, the point in the time-space continuum where history is being written.

The future, though generally moving along a predetermined course, can be dramatically altered in the present. Every moment of present time creates its own tangential future. The events change slightly from strand to strand, but major historical events generally go unchanged. But Gaius is not a part of the mortal realm. Its influences and actions, especially if they fall outside of the destiny of the human it inhabits, will greatly alter the outcome of history. So by using the device to chronoshift, the wizard gave the warriors a way to track Gaius Lloth's movement; look for massive ripples in history that surround the locations of the artifacts, and they'll find Gaius.

"For over a thousand years, our kin have tracked Gaius to the ends of the Earth and fought to keep it from regaining full strength," Elizabeth wrapped up the tale. She reached for her son's hands. "Now it's your turn."

Miles felt the overwhelming weight of truth bear down on him. If this wasn't a dream, if this wasn't all some fantastic hallucination, all the troubles that he left back in the twenty-first century felt oddly trivial. A fate unlike any he had ever dreamt for himself had been revealed, a fate that had not only provided him the answers he had so desperately sought his entire life, but now begged of more questions.

"So when is present time?" Miles asked, trying to make sense of all he was told. The words felt utterly foreign as they left his mouth. "Are we there?"

"No," Matthias corrected Miles. He leaned back awkwardly in his chair, squeezed his hand into this trousers pocket, and withdrew his chronoperpetua. Matthias opened the device, and perused its inner workings. "Back about two centuries. June 6, 1613."

"So if Gaius is back there, why are we here?"

"For safety," Elizabeth explained. "The same reason we left you in the later twentieth century. We live in one of a myriad of time tangents. It makes it impossible for Gaius to find us. It's even a challenge for most chronoshifters. At least that's what we thought."

"What changed?"

"We were betrayed," she answered.

"How?"

"As your mother said before, some of us believe a few of our kind went rogue, joined Gaius. Helped him hunt down the next generation."

"You mean kids like me?" Miles inquired.

"Yes," Elizabeth answered. Redness ringed her eyes. She held a hand to her mouth as she turned aside. "We were the lucky ones." The sobs she attempted to strangle down still bubbled forth, though muted.

"What do you mean lucky? How many of us are left?"

Matthias cracked his neck with a twist of his head. He smiled an uncomfortable smile at Miles, the kind that spoke to how grateful his father was that his son survived and how guilty he felt that all other families lost their children. No words were needed.

Miles felt his insides sink. *I'm the sole survivor.* They were the lucky ones indeed. "How many were there?"

"We're not sure," Matthias replied as he stood and moved behind Elizabeth. He leaned down and wrapped his arms around her for comfort. "We're not close to all the clans, but from what we know, there were six."

Miles closed his eyes and fell headlong into memories of his narrow escape from the hired guns who chased him down the sidewalk in the dark of night and the sensation of gunshots ripping through the air within inches of him. Five others like him died at the hands of these men. *What a horrible way to die.* His mind went deeper down the rabbit hole.

"How did they find us?" Miles asked, thirsty for more information. "I mean, I get that this Gaius bastard can't time travel so you know he didn't pull the trigger. But why do you think another chronoshifter did it? Couldn't Gaius have just written letters to his future self or assassins in the future to hunt us down?"

Elizabeth broke from their embrace for a moment and wiped the tears from her eyes. "That's a good idea, Miles, but it isn't that simple. There's no one future. Any letters he sent or attempts to communicate would have only travelled forward in that time tangent. You, the true you, was alive and well in a wholly different reality. If they did kill the Miles from that reality, the real you would have survived."

A realization hit Miles that shattered his whole outlook on reality. "Wait!" he grunted as he shot up from his chair to pace back and forth, rubbing at the back of his head with both hands. Trying to order his thoughts so they came out making sense seemed a tall order to Miles. Then he stopped, put one hand over his mouth and the other on his hip, and stared at his parents. His hand slid down off his mouth to his chin.

"So if I understand what you're saying, then my foster parents aren't dead?"

"No, your foster parents of that future reality are dead," she explained. "But nothing in that or any future has actually happened yet. They're all just shadows of probability. When present time catches up to 2016, only then will those events be set in stone."

The thoughts swam in Miles' head, making him question his whole life, everything he ever learned, and every experience he ever had. Did they really happen? Was his whole life just a dream of what could have been? That sensation of light headedness came back. Miles stumbled forward, catching his weight with his hands against the table. He squinted to fight off the dizziness. Matthias made an effort to scramble around the table, but Miles shot him a cross glare and held out a halting hand, determined to shake it off without help. Matthias did as was asked, giving a classic "hands-off" gesture. His father did not return to his seat or Elizabeth's side. Instead he stood still, keeping vigil over Miles' condition without violating his personal space.

Miles exhaled deeply, sensing the worst of it was over. "That sucked. I'm sorry, this is all a little overwhelming."

"We understand, son," Elizabeth consoled him. "Take your time."

He nodded. "I'm okay. You were telling me how they found us?"

"Oh, yeah. So they had to find you another way," Matthias added. "The only way to find you is with one of these."

Matthias reached into his other pocket and withdrew a familiar looking object; a crystal sphere with the initials "MiD" etched into its surface. He held it out to Miles.

"Hey," Miles gasped, grabbing it from his father's hand. He examined it closely, tossing it up and down a few times. "I've seen these before. I've got two of them in my backpack."

"That's right. We call them anchors. They allow the chronoperpetua to hook onto a living thing's genetic signature. Every organic object has one, and each one is specific to each time tangent. It's the only way to find other chronoshifters as they wander the different threads. They're what helped us get back to you each time. We left two of them for you the night you were born. Another couple had left a cigar box behind, so we put those and the picture in it with a note that they were your inheritance."

Lurking in the back of his mind were the memories of what happened with the two anchors the day his father came to get him. Now that he understood their purpose, the oddity he witnessed took on an even more bizarre and mysterious meaning. He kept it a secret for the time being. "So how do they work?"

Matthias popped open the core of his chronoperpetua and placed one of the anchors he held within it. "Place an anchor in the core, close it, and activate the energy pulse." When he snapped the device shut, the whole thing whirred to life and a soft, blue glow emanated from its seams. "Nice, neat, simple. It will automatically take you to wherever that person is, regardless of which time tangent they're in. It's what kept all of the children safe."

"But only family members or close friends carried those anchors," Elizabeth added, standing from her chair to place her empty cup in the dry sink.

The guilty party seemed so obvious. "So someone close to us was responsible?"

Matthias pursed his lips and leaned back against the cabinetry, arms crossed. "Not that we can tell. You see, a few days ago, a rash of robberies plagued the countryside. Our ranch was broken into, but we didn't think anything of it. Some cash was stolen, a few odds and ends, nothing important. But then we found out that some other members of our Order experienced similar robberies all throughout time. That's when we figured it out."

"What?"

Matthias continued, "They weren't simple thieves. The trivial items they took were meant to divert attention from what they were really after."

Miles regarded his father with a questioning glare.

"It's easier if we show you," Elizabeth answered this time. "Come on." She waved at Miles to follow her toward a door at the side of the kitchen. Matthias followed closely behind. The door creaked open to reveal a narrow flight of stairs that disappeared into a damp basement.

Elizabeth paused for a moment to take an unlit gas lamp from off of a hook before continuing. Small windows evenly spaced along the top of the walls provided enough illumination to avoid bumping into things, but not much else. Odd shadows played about the space in the crossing streams of light as Elizabeth led them across the floor to a far wall. When they stopped, Miles noticed an iron hatch built into the brick with the word *COAL* emblazoned on its face. He surveyed the rest of his surroundings but saw nothing else of worth. Miles shrugged at his mother.

"Excuse me," Matthias grunted as he put a hand on Miles' chest and urged him to step back. Then he bent over and worked his fingers into the gaps in a rusty looking drainage grate in the uneven concrete floor. The massive grate swung up and over on a concealed hinge. With the grate removed, Miles attempted to peer down into the exposed passage beneath, but it was too dark. The crackle of a match and the smell of sulfur preceded a swell of warm light that emanated from his mother's lamp. She held it out toward Miles. Pensively, he took told of the thin wire handle that it hung from and passed it over the opening. To his surprise, the passage went down several feet, was wide enough for a person to fit into, and had a visible landing at the bottom.

"What's down there?"

"Everything that matters," Elizabeth replied.

Matthias crouched down, put his hands on both sides of the opening, and lowered himself. Having reached the landing below, the top of his head was even with the basement floor. He reached up through the opening. "Hand me the lamp, will you?"

Miles leaned down to hand his father the lamp. He watched his father bend low and heard the sound of feet tramping on damp steps. The passage below became visible as the lamp light washed over it.

"Come on down, Miles," Matthias' voice echoed up through the hole. "There are footholds in the wall."

Miles turned to his mother who returned his glance with a nod of approval. Crouching down, he followed his father's movements. The concrete floor was cold and clammy to the touch, almost slimy. Blindly, he groped the wall for somewhere to put his feet as he dangled half in, half out of the hole. Finally, he found a cutout that he could squeeze the toes of his boots into. Two steps down and he had solid footing on a slab of stone. He noticed Elizabeth hovering over the opening above. "Are you coming down?"

"Not in this dress," she quipped. "I'll see you when you come back up."

He returned his attention to the passage that lay before him. A wall of dirt blocked his view. Squatting down, Miles saw Matthias standing about fifteen feet away, at full height, holding the hurricane lamp aloft. The walls of the tunnel did not appear to be stone but soft earth. Roughly hewn, thick beams of wood ran in parallel along the outer corners of the passage ceiling, supported at intervals by equally stout vertical beams. Two more slabs of stone below the landing acted as steps. Miles made his way down and found the ground to be solid beneath him. Additional flat pieces of stone covered the passage floor and gave him firm footing.

"Have you ever seen anything like this?" Matthias boasted. His voice echoed.

"No. Never." Miles could honestly say he never had. In many ways, he wished the pleasure had been indefinitely postponed. The tunnel gave him the willies. The cold, clammy nature of the whole place, the claustrophobic feeling of the narrow passage, and the fear that the damp soil might give way at any moment made his insides quake with discomfort. But he put on a strong front, not wanting to appear afraid. He walked with firm, deliberate steps toward his father, but kept his attention focused on the flickering flame in the lantern's chimney so that he didn't obsess over his surroundings. Matthias rounded on his heels and continued down the passageway. It ran what seemed like a good fifty feet or so before they came to a rickety wooden door. Splintery ridges ran up and down its length, daring anyone to run their hand across it.

Matthias reached out with his right hand and placed his fingers beneath a curved, rusty piece of metal that protruded from the wood. Lifting it up, the door lurched open a few inches and came to rest. "If you thought that tunnel was something, this will make your head spin.

Stay here for a second."

Miles did what he was told. His father disappeared inside the pitch black chamber. The wait felt interminable, but in reality it lasted only seconds. Then a flash of light flooded the interior chamber and spilled out into the outer passage, stealing his power of sight. He averted his eyes from the blinding radiance and threw his arm up over his face in protest. Miles tried to peer into the light, but a blue splotch dominated his eyesight. Squinting and blinking, the obstruction gave way and his eyes adjusted. The information his eyes sent to his brain, however, didn't make sense. While he saw no electricity being used in the ranch and was pretty damn sure it wasn't used in homes during the Civil War, this underground chamber somehow had power. Brilliant, shimmering sparks of iridescence hung at equally spaced intervals along the length of the ceiling. Every light Miles knew of had a discernible bulb or glass encasement, but no matter how much he concentrated on looking at the source of the light, all he saw was pure radiance. Even more bizarre, there appeared to be no wiring or fixture; the lights truly appeared to hang of their own will.

Jaw agape in wonder, Miles stepped through the doorway. "Holy shit!" he gasped, quite dumbfounded by it all. His eyes roved from one end of the chamber to the other. This room had nothing in common with the outer tunnel. Countless red bricks and mortar made up the outer walls. Lumber of a finer quality than the outer door made up the vast ceiling and floor. There was no mud, no dripping water, nor fear of collapse here. It didn't take long for Miles to forget the chamber lay beneath a significant chunk of dirt and rock.

Rows of bookshelves at the far end of the chamber held hundreds of dusty and not so dusty tomes. Every one of them looked to be copies of the same textbooks. Then something moved amongst the stacks, something very small, bright, and fast. Miles craned his neck as the fluttering movement took off and threaded in and out of the rows. Then more of them came into view, sprites and pixies dancing amidst a forest of books.

"Nanobots," Matthias' voice burst into his ears. The suddenness of his voice made Miles' heart jump in his chest. He turned with a start to his father who stood nearby with a Cheshire Cat grin on his face. He walked toward Miles and added, "They manage and repair all our texts. Help us keep track of all the tangents we visit."

"I've never seen anything like them before," Miles countered, trying to track their movement. "Where did you find them?"

"A few decades after your time, some groundbreaking advances are made in nanoscale science and cold fusion. They usher in a technological renaissance that changes human history," Matthias explained as one of the nanobots landed on his palm. It looked no bigger than a poppy seed but radiated a sapphire glow. "These were a few of the initial inspirations of the time."

"So they're from the future?" Miles asked as he squatted down and leaned closer to inspect the marvelous piece of machinery.

"Yes, just like you."

"But what if they escape? What if someone from this time finds them?"

Matthias shook his head. "That's unlikely. They're incapable of moving more than fifteen meters from that beacon." His father pointed to a small blue dome affixed to the ceiling. "If someone carries them beyond that point or the beacon loses power, the cold-fusion reactor that powers them will implode safely."

"Incredible," Miles responded, awestruck.

The nanobot zoomed from his father's hand toward the outer wall. Miles tracked its movement as it flew by a series of wooden racks that lined the perimeter of the room. Each one held a diverse array of handheld weapons and firearms. Unlike the tiny robots that roved the chamber, all the weapons came from his time or before. For a brief moment he hoped he might get to lay his hands on a phaser or ray gun like those in *Star Trek*, but nothing stood out as being so advanced.

His gaze moved to the center of the chamber. A large white mat monopolized the landscape. It sat about a foot off the floor on some sort of wooden platform. The whole thing had to be at least twenty feet wide. Miles stepped up onto it and felt the floor give a bit under his weight. He pushed down against it with his legs and the whole platform pushed back like a weak trampoline. Miles grunted thoughtfully and kept bouncing as his eyes inspected the rest of the mat. Faded red streaks and spots that resembled dried blood stains marred the center stretch of fabric. And a few feet past those markings, a gray, hexagonal pad drew his attention. It appeared to be a few inches thick and about three feet wide.

"What's that?" Miles inquired, pointing to the object.

"That's the simulator," his father answered. "You'll get acquainted with that later. Some things like tethering can't be simulated. But others things like martial arts and weapons training can be."

"Martial arts?" Miles questioned excitedly. He couldn't hold back his smile.

"Yes," Matthias laughed while crossing the mat to stand beside the simulator. "I had a feeling you'd like that. Its AI processor will assess your physical traits and then pull from its database to tailor a martial arts style specifically for you."

"I can't wait to try it."

"One thing at a time, Miles. You have to learn to crawl before you can walk."

Miles understood his father's cliché. His family had been doing this for hundreds of years, and there was probably a process to it all. Nevertheless, he itched to begin.

The cloud of awe that had taken hold of his mind began to dissipate. Miles started noticing some of the more trivial characteristics of the chamber. Two nondescript wooden tables sat on the nearside of the white mat and a wash basin with a hand pump similar to the one in the kitchen stood in the adjacent corner. One thing he noticed made his pulse quicken several times over and a small wave of panic swept over him; several bundles of wired dynamite sat nestled into the ceiling amidst what appeared to be acoustic insulation. "What's with the explosives?"

"That's our contingency plan. If something goes wrong or we need to leave in a hurry, there's a pipe that leads up to the garden. It helps feed us oxygen when we're down here, but it also contains the fuse leads. Drop a cinder down the pipe and BOOM! All the evidence is gone."

That's a scary thought. Miles then remembered they had come down here for something specific. "What was it you wanted to show me down here, besides all this?"

Matthias snapped his fingers and pointed at his son. "Thank you. I almost forgot." He then made his way to one of the two nearby tables where a small, metal lockbox rested. Miles followed, moving around to the side opposite his father. Three small, revolving tumblers operated the locking mechanism. Miles watched as his father manipulated them until an audible *click* emanated from the box. Matthias lifted the lid and spun the box around so that his son could see within.

The inside of the box had a red velvet base. "Anchors?" Miles questioned.

"Yup. We keep a pair for each of us down here, in case of emergency. We thought they were safe."

Miles examined the anchors. Two with *MD* etched into them, two with *ED*, two with *AD*, and one with *MiD*. He knew three of the initial sets. But the *AD* set he did not understand. "AD?" Miles asked as he glanced from the box to his father.

"That's your brother, Alistair Draven."

Miles felt his heart flutter. He never knew he had a brother. "Umm—when—"

"Tonight," his father cut him off before he could finish. "You'll meet him tonight. He's out on recon."

Trying to calm his nerves, Miles looked back to the box and cocked his head sideways in confusion. "Why is there only one for me?"

"That's what they were after, Miles. The reason we know it was a shifter who went after you and all the other children is because the extra anchor was stolen. They only serve one purpose, and only to a very specific group of people. I guess by stealing the normal items, they hoped we wouldn't figure out that your anchors were stolen until it was too late and you were..." Matthias didn't finish saying what was on his mind. He just starred at Miles with that pained smile again.

Miles had finally gotten some answers: he knew who he was, he understood why his parents abandoned him when he was a baby, and he knew that one of his own kind was responsible for the attempt on his life and the death of his foster family. Now he wanted to know how he fit into it all. How did he become a chronoshifter?

"So," he asked his father with confidence, "when do we start?"

Matthias nodded and cuffed Miles on the shoulder, "Now."

CHAPTER NINE

Miles stood with his father by the table closest to the door. Matthias spoke aloud as if talking to the room itself, "Execute command; retrieve Raleigh Colony incident volumes."

A disembodied, female voice answered back, "Command accepted. Executing." The voice sounded ethereal but wholly human. In fact, Miles found it kind of sexy. It had a distinctively European accent.

Amongst the book shelves, a whirr of activity commenced; a host of nanobots swarmed down the middle aisle. Miles heard the distinct friction of what sounded like sheets of corduroy being drawn quickly against each other. A few seconds later, two texts floated across the room toward Miles and Matthias and settled down upon the tabletop with a gentle thump. The flea sized servants that delivered them raced off toward the bookshelves in a flash.

Both father and son settled themselves into adjoining chairs. Matthias pulled close one of the texts. Hundreds of pages sat nestled between a coarse, brown fabric cover. The gold foil letters embossed on the front spelled out *American History: 1492-1955*. Not only was it a history book, it was an old history book to Miles. He let out a bothersome grunt.

"Don't worry, Miles," Matthias chuckled, "you won't need to read all of these."

"But I will have to read?"

"Eventually. But right now I want to show you what we do with all of these history texts." Matthias quickly passed his hand across the landscape of the chamber like a game show assistant revealing the potential prizes.

The excitement of being a chronoshifter, of chasing demons lost a great deal of its excitement at that moment. Miles felt more like the person who picked the wrong door on *Let's Make A Deal* than the lucky winner. He leaned forward, laying his forehead in his hand. His whole body slumped.

"C'mon, kiddo." Matthias threw an arm around his son, shaking him good humoredly. "This is the easy part. The physical preparation will really bust your balls."

Miles shrugged his shoulders. "Oh. Wonderful." He picked his head up and did his best to feign interest.

"This will be quick. Trust me. Be glad you weren't around a few hundred years ago. We used to spend almost all of our time reading new copies of each text and comparing them to the old ones to look for the slightest change. Now the nano do it for us. They can process a five hundred page book in minutes." Matthias reached for a small strip of blue satin that hung from the head of the book and lifted it up. The spine cracked as he separated the weighty bulk of pages and let the front cover flop over onto the table. An old, musty smell radiated from the crisp pages. "Here, Miles, read these two paragraphs." He pointed to the last two paragraphs on a page shortened by a large painting of early colonists being taught by natives how to harvest tobacco.

Miles read the two short paragraphs. They detailed the history of one of the early American settlements on the island of Roanoke. A man named John White brought his family and 114 souls with him on the journey, at the behest of the British crown, to build a permanent colony there. It mentioned how the colony prospered with the help of the nearby Croatoan tribe when John returned to England for three years. Having finished reading, he shot his father a "so what" glance.

"Seems pretty innocent, right?"

"Sure," Miles answered with nonchalance, shrugging his shoulders.

"Watch this." Matthias pulled the other historical tome close. The book was identical except for a black "X" drawn across the upper right portion of the cover. Matthias once again grabbed the blue satin bookmark that hung from the head of the volume and flipped it open. Though the preceding page appeared the same, the page that once detailed the story of John White's colony was starkly dissimilar from the other text. This one possessed a painting of a similar landscape, but only a few cannons and an awkwardly bent fence post remained where a thriving colonial town once stood in the other book's painting. There were no buildings, no crops growing in the background, and no hearty colonists. Miles cast his eyes across the table to the other text to make sure his eyes weren't playing tricks on him. They were not. Bringing his gaze back to the book before him, the bold section header on the page told Miles all he needed to know. "**LOST COLONY OF ROANOKE.**"

Miles squinted and shrugged his shoulders. "I don't get it. How could two of the same book have totally different versions of the same event?"

"I told you, we look for ripples in history, places where major events have been altered. The actions of a simple man should go relatively unchanged from tangent to tangent. There will be differences, but usually not anything great enough to rewrite the course of history. Gaius wasn't meant to be part of human history. When it takes possession of a human vessel, it dramatically alters their destiny by its actions. That can result in massive changes in history if the demon intercedes in the wrong events."

"But how do you know that something didn't change with—" Miles paused, scrolling the page to find the name of the colony's leader, "John White? Maybe something in that tangent made him turn left when he should have turned right."

"That's a great theory, Miles, but this is a major historical event that changed. And it wasn't changed in some random, unwritten part of the future. It happened in the present."

Miles just stared back at him, not quite understanding the significance of what his father said.

Matthias gave a frustrated sigh. "History, unchangeable history, can only be written in the present. The same time that Gaius can't escape."

"Okay," Miles acknowledged his father's point, "but how is that alone proof it's this demon."

"It isn't. There's more," his father continued. "Ambrose Viccars, his wife Elizabeth, and their son were passengers on John White's ship, the Lion, in 1587. They too were chronoshifters."

A sudden synapse of understanding fired inside of his brain. "Oh." Miles glanced back at the distorted copy of the textbook. "And they disappeared?"

"Yes," Matthias answered with excitement. "Along with the Talaria."

Miles had heard the name before, but he couldn't remember where he heard it. "What's the Talaria?"

"Hermes' winged sandals."

"Oh, my God!" The rare times his literature and history teachers covered ancient mythology, Miles loved it. Whether Greek, Roman, Norse, or Celtic, he loved the stories of the old Gods and some of the ridiculous things they did. The realization that even part of those ancient tales was true blew his mind. "I remember them. Weren't they made of gold?"

"Yes, in one myth. The artifacts appear all throughout history, but as different objects in each culture. The energy that they're made from changes shape depending on who is handling them. It's all a matter of perception. But each one grants a very specific power to those who possess it; the Talaria grants the power of teleportation by thought."

"Really? So if I had it I could just teleport to Australia by thinking it?"

"Yeah, but you might not want to travel there in the present day. It's all wild, untamed land. Civilized man isn't expected to arrive there until the late 1600's. Unless, of course, you want to spend time with the aboriginal tribes."

"Well, I didn't mean going there in the present. I meant taking the artifact back to my time and using it there."

Matthias adjusted his posture and shook his head. "That wouldn't work. The artifacts are a lot like Gaius. They exist only in the present. If you try to take them to the future or the past, they get stuck at the opening of the vortex. It has something to do with the power they wield. Believe me, it's been tried countless times. If we could hide them in a time apart from that demon, we would."

Miles rethought his plan. "Well, what if we found that artifact in this time and tried to use it? What then?"

"It would be no better than a shadow, kind of like everything in the past. They're powerless anywhere but the present. And because the artifacts were used to summon Gaius, it's drawn to them like vultures to carrion. They're kind of like missing puzzle pieces. Once they're all assembled, the demon will be unstoppable."

"How many are there?"

"There are eight in total. Now that Gaius has the Talaria, only seven remain hidden, including ours."

"Hmm..." Miles took a moment to skim over the page in the altered history text. Nowhere did it say what fate befell the members of the lost colony. The only clue as to what transpired there was a single word carved into a tree where the colony once stood—*Croatoan.* "But why are you convinced Gaius got ahold of it. There's nothing in this book that hints at a demon being responsible. Just the name of a nearby tribe and island."

"Look, Ambrose was my friend. He kept going on about how he thought Gaius and his operatives had discovered where they had hidden the Talaria. So he packed it up in a locked chest along with his wife and son and got on that ship. They weren't alone."

Matthias pulled the altered history text in front of him and fanned the pages, looking for something. He stopped, flipped back a few pages, and pulled out a folded up piece of white, unlined paper. When his father unfolded it, Miles could see that it was a photocopy of a handwritten ship manifest for the Lion. Matthias pointed to the bottom of the page. Three of the last four names on the passenger list were members of the Viccars family. Scribbled beside each name was the date they were added to the passenger list. "They were added to the manifest a day before it left for Virginia."

"What about this woman?" Miles pointed to the final name on the list. "Gail Shulot. She was added the same day as the Viccars."

"She wasn't supposed to be there either."

Matthias picked up the other text book and dropped it down on top of the altered copy, going through the same motions before pulling out a similar sheet of paper. He unfolded this one and placed it side-by-side with the other photocopy. "See," he stressed and pointed to the bottom of the new page which had none of the final four names on it, "none of them should have been on this manifest. Your brother and I visited several other tangents established before 1587. Their names didn't appear on any of them. And really look at that woman's name."

Miles looked intently at the name on the document, feeling quite stupid that he couldn't see what his father expected. Then it suddenly clicked. His mind rearranged the letters in her name. "Holy shit! It's an anagram. Gaius Lloth!"

"Yup," Matthias replied. "Demons are powerful and dangerous. But one thing we've learned over the centuries is that they're also vain."

"That's fucked up."

"Wow!" Matthias' eyes went wide and glared with irritation at Miles. "We really need to work on how you talk."

"The way I talk?" Miles asked, taken aback.

"The vulgarity," Mathias refined his point. "Only criminals, rabble talk like that. If you walk around talking that way in this time it'll reflect poorly on you and us, and could bring unwanted attention your way. We try to blend in, stay out of history's way, pretend like we're from this time."

Miles felt his pulse quicken. Anger rose inside him once again. "Are you serious?" he barked at his father. "After all that you just told me, you're going lecture me about the way I talk?" he asked aghast. "How can you warn me about that when you're changing history just by being here, by living in this house and having all this technology? And your friends, the Viccars, how great of a job did they do of staying out of history's way?"

Matthias huffed in an exasperated manner. "It isn't as black and white as you're trying to make it, son."

"Then explain it to me, *Dad*," Miles snapped back, sarcastically stressing his title.

His father looked pissed. His lips were drawn into a tight pucker of contemplation and aggravation as he brooded in silence. Miles felt the whole table tremor under Matthias' drumming fingertips. He wondered if steam might plume from his father's ears as he sat across from him, in apparent contemplation of his response. He finally broke his temporary silence.

"What happened to my friend and his family is exactly why we have to be careful. Ambrose thought bringing the Talaria to America would get it out of the demon's reach. I kept suggesting he move it back to Cairo since he so often told me about how much he missed his home. But he just wouldn't listen. He became obsessed by the idea and forgot his sworn duty. That carelessness resulted in the loss of one hundred and seventeen innocent lives, gave Gaius Lloth a portion of his power back, and dramatically altered history from every recorded tangent we had ever researched. If he had listened to me," Matthias repeatedly jammed his fingertip into the altered text book's pages, "none of this would have happened.

"I know harping on your use of language seems hypocritical given what I've told you and what you've seen, but what happened to Roanoke is exactly why I'm concerned. You never know how big of an impact the smallest action can have on future events."

"Like the Butterfly Effect," Miles offered, trying to understand his father.

"Impressive," Matthias acknowledged. "You're familiar with Chaos Theory?"

Miles shook his head. "No. It was in a movie. But I get the idea."

"Oh," his father grunted, sounding let down. Then he gave a dismissive wave of his hand. "Doesn't matter how you learned about it, you're right. And I know how this all looks; all the technology and even our involvement in this time seems like we're altering history, and to some extent we are. But I assure you, we take great pains to make sure our impact is limited. All these safeguards," he gestured in the direction of the explosives and the nanobots among the stacks, "are here to make sure nothing goes wrong. It's why we regularly tether to this and other futures to check on our historical footprint. All we've ever found were records of land ownership and business records. Not once have we left a mark in any historical text. And if we did, we'd make sure to go back and alter our course."

Miles didn't feel so irked now. His father did a decent job of explaining away his misgivings. If all the failsafe measures worked as well as Matthias proclaimed, then without direct interference in major historical events they really did stay out of history's way. Miles still didn't see how dropping f-bombs here or there around real 1863ers could really alter history, but he recognized that his understanding came from an array of fictionalized accounts of time travel. His father's knowledge came from actual chronoshifting. Much to his chagrin, Miles needed to heed his warnings. Something, however, still didn't make sense to him.

"I don't understand why you'd need to worry about our impact on other tangents. I thought you said that history is only written in the present, like what happened to Ambrose. Don't our actions impact only the future here?"

Matthias scratched at his scalp. "Not exactly. Normally, only events in the present can change the future. However, we learned the hard way that we're essentially part of the present. Even though we live out of sync from it, our actions transcend all tangents."

"I don't understand." Miles felt like an idiot. It all sounded like gobbledygook.

"How do I explain this?" Matthias deliberated aloud. He sat quite still for a moment and then sprang out of his seat. "Got it!" With a few jogging steps, his father disappeared down one of the bookcase rows and came back with another book and a sheathed dagger. Sitting down, he opened the cover and started fanning the pages. "You see how all these pages are blank?"

Miles nodded. It was a clean journal. Looked like a couple hundred pages thick.

"Imagine each page is the unwritten future of another tangent. The one we live in is just one of these pages, and every page is blank because the present hasn't yet caught up to them to write history. Do you understand so far?"

"Sure." It was a simple enough concept.

Matthias closed the book and lifted up the dagger, removing its scabbard. "Now imagine this dagger is one of us interfering in a major historical event."

Without warning, his father raised the dagger and brought the tip of it down with great strength at the book. Miles flinched away. The whole table shook and wobbled on its legs from the force of impact. His father had buried the knife so deeply that he had to wiggle the blade back and forth to pry it loose. Laying the knife aside, Matthias lifted the cover to reveal a deep gash that penetrated every page. He fanned them again.

"The actions of a chronoshifter are just like this knife. We aren't sure why, but what we do influences every other tangent, regardless of whether we're in the present or the future. Everything we do is reflected infinitely throughout the space-time continuum."

A spark of an idea came to Miles. "It's kind of like standing between two mirrors. The reflection goes on and on into infinity."

"Yes. Great analogy."

"Thanks. What about the past, though?" Miles speculated. "What happens if we go there? Is there some kind of paradoxical ripple that happens?"

"No. Nothing like that. Like I said before, the past is just shadows. You can't actually affect anything there. It's like watching one of your television shows, except it's happening around you. You can touch things, smell things, experience the past in every way, but everything's impervious to you."

"Does anyone know why we affect all the other tangents? It just doesn't make sense. We're here, not there."

"No one knows for sure, but some of us have a theory. Our ancestors, the first chonoshifters, lived in the present day. After a few generations, they realized that their actions in opposition to Gaius had too profound of an impact on the outcome of history. That's when they decided to start living in the future, to try to minimize the damage. But after a while, they noticed they were still causing ripples in the texts they studied. They figured they could do what they wanted in the future because it had yet to be written. They were wrong. We believe that even though you and I were born outside of the present and have no physical relation to it, we're still a product of the present. Our ancestors are our link. Nothing else in this future is real except for us. It kind of makes sense in an odd way, like an author who writes the ending of a story before they ever start writing the beginning. It's the main reason we have to be so careful, Miles. If our actions affected just this tangent, then it wouldn't be such a big deal. What we've done here and in other times wouldn't have any bearing on the present. Unfortunately, we're too important."

"I think I understand now," Miles answered after letting his father's words set in. The specifics of the theory were still a bit murky in his mind, but he felt certain he'd straighten it all out in time. "Have you found it hard to live that carefully, avoiding all contact with history?"

Matthias shrugged. "I try not to worry about every single action. I know enough about this time period to avoid the moments that truly shape the fabric of time. That's the best we can do in our situation."

Miles nodded. It didn't sound too difficult. It seemed to be the one advantage to studying history.

His father continued, "They did notice one positive side effect of chronoshifting though."

The thought that life wasn't a total pain in the ass in 1863 nearly made him fall over in his chair. "Oh?"

"You've probably noticed that we don't seem to age."

"Yeah. I figured something was up with that. Are we immortal?"

"Sort of. At first, we all age. Whatever year you're born, that time period becomes *your* time. Where the aging process comes to a halt all depends on when you first tether to another time. In your case, you stopped aging at the age of seventeen."

"Will I ever grow old again?" Miles inquired, hopeful that his youth might be forever preserved.

"Yes. If you want to, you can return to the same date that you tethered away. Once you pass that moment, you'll resume the normal aging process until you chronoshift again. In fact, quite a few of our Order have done that. There are advantages in certain eras to being older. The good thing with that way of aging is that you have control over how much older you get."

"That way?" Miles always hated wrinkles in rules. "Sounds like there's a worse option."

"The inevitable option," Matthias frowned. "Eventually, the present catches up to us all. If you survive long enough for the present to catch up to the moment you left with me, you will start to age again, and nothing you do can stop it."

"Survive long enough," Miles muttered solemnly. "So I can die?"

"Yes," Matthias answered. "We're still flesh and bone. If you're wounded bad enough to bleed out or stop your heart, you'll die."

"That sucks."

"Fear of death is what makes us mortal and our lives, as unusually long as they are, worth living. It makes every moment, every breath, every experience that much more meaningful."

"My teachers always talked about how the ancient gods in mythology envied mortals. Is that the reason why?"

"If you believe the myths. But in my experience, the only god I've ever met doesn't envy us. It wants to wipe us out."

"You mean Gaius."

Matthias nodded. "Remember, though. Outside of our ability to chronoshift, our longevity is our sole advantage over Gaius. We're able to live long enough to become expert tacticians, historians, and warriors. That is what keeps us one step ahead of the demon, and it's the main reason we deliver our children at a time ahead of ours."

"You mean besides making us stronger?" Miles said while making a sarcastic flex of his arms.

"Yes," he answered irritably. "If your mother delivered you in 1647, you'd constantly age and we'd stay young. Without sending you away to live in another time, your life span would be too short. We'd have to watch you grow old and die. No parent wants to outlive their children, not even immortals. And even though you mock the process, being an orphan and living through tough times has prepared you for the kind of life we lead far better than living with us and then being shipped off to live alone in another time to stop the aging process."

Just as Miles prepared his rebuttal to the sorest of subjects, an odd harmonic frequency penetrated the whole of the underground bunker. Miles had felt something similar before, except this time it was massively amplified. It resembled the sound of an old television left on a dead channel; that odd, subtle humming of the air one felt more than heard. And then he remembered, in this time, there were no televisions or electrical equipment that could emit such a frequency. He looked to his father who smiled and rose from his chair.

"We have a visitor," Matthias announced. "Time to meet your brother."

CHAPTER TEN

"My brother?" Miles squeaked. He couldn't hide his excitement and confusion at the idea. "How do you know?"

"That noise you heard, it's made when we tether. It's what a chronovortex sounds like when you're not on top of it."

Miles dug a finger into his right ear, which still rung with discomfort. "Couldn't it be something else?"

"Not likely," Matthias answered without concern. "He's expected home today." He extracted a watch from inside his breeches' pocket and glanced at the face. "And he's late too; was supposed to be home about twenty minutes ago."

With all the time we have on our hands, Miles thought, *he sure is nitpicky about a few minutes.* Miles rose from his chair. His knees wobbled a bit beneath him. He hated feeling nervous.

"C'mon," Matthias urged Miles, moving toward the chamber door, "I'm sure you're dying to meet him."

Miles couldn't deny that. He had no idea the reunion would be so soon though. How would he react? What would he say? This day was shaping up to be more than he could handle.

Following his father through the door, the entire chamber fell into darkness. He reached out and grabbed his father's shoulder. "What was that?"

"Don't worry," he laughed and continued walking, leaving Miles behind. "The whole place shuts down when we move beyond the range of the beacon."

"Oh," Miles sighed and took several quick steps to catch up to his father. "So, what does it work off of, our pulse?"

"If it was that simple it wouldn't be much of a safeguard."

They reached the end of the tunnel and the ladder that led back up to the basement. Matthias stood aside to let his son ascend. Taking hold of a chest-high rung, Miles stopped and gave his father a pleading glance.

"Then how does it work?"

"A conversation for another time," Matthias answered curtly.

Miles grunted his displeasure and climbed out of the secret passage. His father followed shortly thereafter and closed the metal grate in the floor. He led Miles back up the cellar stairs, through the kitchen, and into what he would have referred to as a living room. A great stonework hearth stood at the far edge of the room, bookended by two large windows. The sheer draperies that covered them softened the glow of the late morning sun. More white wainscoting flowed into this part of the house from the foyer. Above it, the plaster walls were painted tawny, reminding him of the sand dunes along the coast. Facing off at the center of the room sat two maroon, empire sofas with cherry woodwork and, between them, a handcrafted coffee table of a similar style. An elegant Persian rug lay beneath them, incorporating both the colors present in the room but also complimentary tones. Ornate book shelves highlighted the four corners of the great room. A collection of several hundred gold-lettered volumes populated them. Nestled between the two windows to his right, Miles noted the circular, cherry pedestal table and two matching Queen Anne chairs.

All of those features made the room comforting, inviting, but what interested Miles the most was the young man who sat turned away at that table, sipping from a steaming mug, and dipping a nib pen into an inkwell before scribbling into a journal.

Miles glanced with hopeful eyes at his father who nodded back with a high cheeked grin.

Matthias grunted and called out, "Alistair!"

When the young man turned about, the resemblance to Matthias was uncanny. Unlike Miles, who got most of his facial appearance from his mother, Alistair looked maybe a year or two younger than their father, but with a neatly coifed head of blazing red hair like their mother. They both shared different aspects of their parents' traits, affirming for Miles that, though separated by more than a century, they all were indeed a family.

"Miles!" Alistair cried out in surprise. He rose from his chair like a jack-in-the-box and hurried around the couch with a hand extended.

Miles stepped forward and held out his hand which met his brother's firm grasp. He thought his neck might snap when Alistair pulled him close and wrapped his arms around him.

"It's so good to see you," Alistair growled as he squeezed his brother in a stranglehold.

"You too," Miles gasped.

Alistair let go of Miles, allowing him to catch his breath. "Sorry." He patted his younger brother on the back. "Got carried away."

"That's okay," Miles grunted in pain. His whole torso ached. "You're strong."

Behind him, Miles heard a muffled cry. He peered back over his shoulder to find his mother, who entered quietly behind Matthias and himself, weeping into his father's chest. At first he worried he had done something wrong, but then he observed a slight smile amidst her sobs. They were tears of joy.

"We're all together," she whimpered and held out her arms towards her sons. "After all this time, we're finally together."

The whole moment felt awkward. For seventeen years he lived without an emotional connection to a family, or for that matter, anyone. Now being thrust into a family, most of whom had been together for what could have been centuries for all Miles knew, was foreign to him. A lifetime of anger for being abandoned now threatened to be unseated in his mind by what could be the equivalent of lifetimes of love and compassion.

Miles watched Alistair move with vigor past him to his mother and father, embracing them. They all contemplated him, unmoving and no doubt seeming quite uncomfortable by the gesture. Even though his parents did their best to explain the reasons they left him to rot in the year 2000, he still harbored ill will toward them for their actions. However, Miles found this moment difficult to deny. Struggling to process all that had happened to him in the last forty-eight hours, his mind sought balance and safety instead of conflict. In the end, the primal need for love and acceptance won out. Walking on heavy feet, Miles joined their embrace and let the moment be everything.

When the tangle of arms and bodies unwound and the tears stopped flowing, the four of them retired to the sofas—Miles and Alistair sat side-by-side on one with their parents together on the opposite one. They rested in each other's company, sipping tea and nibbling on small cakes that Elizabeth brought from the kitchen. The conversation centered on the newest addition.

"Last time I saw you," Alistair said, leaning back against the arm of the sofa, "you were about twelve years old and about yay high." He gestured with his hand just above the top of his head. "You grew."

Miles thought that only his parents had been voyeurs of his pain. The idea floored him. "When did you see me?"

"Plenty of times. We all took turns watching over you for a while. We even met once."

"Bullshit," Miles barked and then winced, peering at his father for the expected glare of displeasure. None was forthcoming. Desperate to know, he asked his brother, "When?"

"It wasn't anything special. You were at the...what do they call it?" He rolled his hand through the air a few times and then snapped his fingers. "The mall. You went holiday shopping with the family you were with before the Lyles."

"The Shepherds?"

"Yup. I passed by you just inside the vestibule. You slipped on the wet tile pretty hard. I was the stranger who picked you up and asked if you were okay."

Miles struggled to recall the memory. It definitely wasn't anything special as Alistair suggested, otherwise his memory of it wouldn't have been so foggy. "I wish I could remember it. You were that close, and I never knew."

"Which is exactly why he was relieved of that duty," Matthias added, sounding a bit pissed about it still. "He risked too much in making contact with you at such a young age."

"When exactly did you plan on coming to get me?" Miles questioned his father.

"They didn't come get me until I was nineteen," Alistair answered before his father could speak up. "My friends and I made a pact after the Japs attacked Pearl Harbor." He shook his fist. "We're all gonna volunteer. Get even with them bastards. It felt like the right thing to do. But on my way to the recruiter, Dad pulled me aside, told me I was throwing my life away for nothing. I was ready to punch him in the face. I mean, I didn't know him from a hole in the ground." He leaned forward, bent elbows resting on his knees, and clasped his hands together. "Then he told me about who we are, you know, about the real war that needed fighting. I took quite a bit of convincing, as I'm sure you did. When he showed me the chronoperpetua and what it could do, how could I say no?" Alistair narrowed his eyes at Miles. "They were waiting for you to be ready, Miles. It's different for everyone. I was ready to go to war at nineteen. And imagine how stupid it would have been to fight and die in a war that wasn't even real."

"The important thing is that you're here," Elizabeth added, "with us now."

"I guess," Miles said, cracking a small smile.

Matthias disagreed, shaking his head. "No. There's no reason to guess. We're stronger together. We're better with you, Miles. You're the part our lives that's been missing for far too long."

Chills raced through Miles. He spent the better part of his life hoping that one of the families who looked after him would care enough to finally adopt him, but it never happened. And not only did his real family finally find him, but to hear that his absence left a hole in their lives was more than he could ask for. His only wish now was that this miracle felt a bit less unlikely and crazy. When was the bottom going to fall out?

From the other side of the house, a muted knocking sound could be heard.

"What's that?" Miles asked.

"Damn," Matthias snarled, "I forgot about Davis."

"Who's Davis?"

Matthias got up from the sofa and passed through the far archway.

Before disappearing into the dining room beyond, he came about, speaking quick and direct. "Liz, warn Miles. I'll keep him busy for a few minutes."

"Warn me about what?" Miles pleaded as his father passed from view, weary at the prospect of more surprises and secrets. He stood up, physically animated as he redirected his question at his mother and brother. "What's he talking about?"

"Calm down," Alistair tried to soothe him. "It's not that big of a deal."

"Really?"

"Davis is a friend of ours," Elizabeth tried to clarify. "You don't need to worry about him. We invited him over so that he could tailor some clothes for you that were a better fit."

"That's what you needed to warn me about?"

"Not exactly," Alistair quipped, moving from the sofa and back to his journaling at the pedestal table.

Elizabeth got to her feet and pointed at her eldest, quite displeased. "You're not helping." The sounds of Matthias and Davis talking in the foyer caused her to look over her shoulder and back with concern. She refocused her attention on Miles. "It's just that he's a lot like the people you're going to meet here; he has no idea *what* we really are. Do you understand?"

"He's not an idiot, Mother," his brother interjected.

Hands on her hips, Elizabeth pivoted and huffed at Alistair, "Enough! I can handle this. Now keep quiet or you'll be cleaning out the stables for the rest of the day."

Alistair lifted his eyebrows in an expression of abhorrence and finished it off with a gesture of buttoning his lips.

Elizabeth took hold of Miles by the shoulders and held him with gentleness, a solemn look on her face. "Miles," she spoke softly, "I need you to listen to me. When we're around people of this time, things are going to be said, things that may bother you. But you have to understand that we love you and you're a member of this family, no matter what you hear."

"I don't understand. What kinds of things?"

"Townsfolk that know us would be suspicious if we suddenly produced a seventeen-year-old son that they never met before. Any of them that remember my last pregnancy were told the child was stillborn."

"You mean me?"

"Yes." She frowned.

"I get it; you had to tell everyone that because you left me in the future." Miles struggled to contain his frustration. He returned her frown. "So what am I, a stable boy?"

"Sort of. Your father told him that you were sent here by my brother to," she used her hands to make air quotes, "cool your blood. A little back-breaking stable work and getting away from the big city'll straighten you out." Elizabeth humorously mocked the southern drawl.

Miles, however, found no humor in her words. "Great, so I'm still a screw up."

"No, no," his mother pleaded and waved her hands at the idea. She paused, placing her fingertips over her mouth. Her saddened look made him ache inside. "Honey, you're no screw up. Whatever happened back there, none of it matters now. This," she pointed to the ground, "here with us, is a clean slate. Please, don't take any of this business to heart. We all have to act, to play a role when we're around normal people. It's just our cover." Her hands gently caressed the sides of his face. She locked eyes with him. "Let it go, sweetie."

The gentleness of his mother's touch soothed him unlike anything he had ever experienced. And she reflected his hurt back at him like a mirror. He had to close his eyes to arrest the tears that threatened to break free. Miles let his head slump until it made contact with hers. "Okay," he whispered.

"Good." Elizabeth smiled and smoothed his hair with her hand.

Alistair broke his silence from the armchair. "Hey, I'm known as the bastard son of a dead mother. You'll get used to it, Miles. After long enough, you get used to just about anything."

"That I know," Miles grumbled to his brother. Wary of the answer he might receive, Miles asked his mother, "Is my name still Miles?"

"Of course," Elizabeth replied soothingly, buttoning the top button of his shirt and straightening his suspenders. Looking him up and down with a satisfied grin she added, "Except you've got my maiden name."

He rolled his eyes. "What's that?"

"Stephens."

"Miles Stephens." He ruminated over it for a moment. "Sounds okay I guess."

She rose to her tip toes and kissed him on the cheek. "Of course it does. It's my father's name. It's who you were named after."

Miles grinned. Another question he always wondered about answered. They gave him his grandfather's name.

The footfalls of hard soled shoes announced the entrance of his father and their friend Davis through the kitchen archway. Miles had pictured in his mind a tall, scraggy, handlebar moustache-sporting frontiersman type for some reason. This Davis character, however, was the antithesis of his imagination: short, thinning hair, round as an orange, and red faced. He kept wiping away the profuse sweat on his brow with a stained, tattered handkerchief from his pocket. As expected of a tailor, his threads were impeccable—very sharp, very showy.

"Is this your new project?" Davis asked Matthias as he waddled across the room. The way he moved and talked had Miles questioning the man's sexuality. He bowed his head to Elizabeth, laying his bowler hat over his chest. "Ma'am." Then, with an aloof air, he regarded Alistair and droned, "Master Draven." Alistair grunted back and went on with his writing, not paying their guest any more attention.

Standing a foot from him, Miles could barely stand Davis' stench. No amount of body spray could have covered up the intense body odor that wafted off of him. His eyes began to tear from the pungent aroma. *Doesn't he know he smells?* Miles considered whether or not deodorant had been invented yet. *Something to research. This dude needs it.*

Davis reached out to touch Miles' arm, but he reeled away, not really wanting to get pawed by this guy. Over the man's shoulder, though, he noticed his father glaring at him. Giving a snort of irritation, he let his arms fall to his sides and held still for inspection.

"Touchy, aren't we?" Davis asked, dramatically offended by the resistance. Then he smiled in a way that gave Miles the willies. "Don't worry, I don't bite."

Throughout the whole ordeal, Miles held perfectly still, even agreeing to let Elizabeth feed him where he stood when he got hungry. Davis did his job with expert precision, measuring and marking the pattern cuts of rough cloth from which to build an array of handmade suits. It was a tedious and prolonged process but curious all the same. Miles had seen it done on television and in movies before, but it was a whole different process in real life.

By the time Davis had packed up his tools and walked out the door, the sun had nearly set and Miles collapsed on the sofa, exhausted. He promised his mother that he would only take a quick nap before dinner, but he fell into a deep, restful sleep instead.

CHAPTER ELEVEN

"What's this?" Miles asked, sneering. He peered through the side of the glass at the cloudy, viscous fluid that slid around within.

"Drink it," Matthias declared. "It won't hurt you."

"I don't know." Miles leaned his nose over the brim and took a whiff. It didn't smell like much of anything. "Looks like someone blew their nose in it."

"Miles, the simulator can't analyze you without it. Either you drink it, or you can't be taught. It's that simple."

Miles mulled over his options and let out an incensed grumble; he really had no choice. His father's devilish grin told Miles that he knew it too. "Fine." Lifting the glass to his lips, he pinched his nose and tipped it back. It slid down his throat like a lightning fast slug. "Blugggh!" Miles shook off the queer sensation. It felt so nasty. A slight tingling began to spread out from his belly to his extremities. The tingling grew quite strong, almost hurting in some places. "Oww! I thought you said it wouldn't hurt?"

"Well, nothing permanent. What you're feeling now is about as bad as it gets. It should dissipate in a few seconds."

Just like his father said, the tingling didn't last long. When the sensations finally subsided, something inside Miles felt strange. No, strange wasn't the right word for it. He felt...better. It was the only way to describe it. "Wow!"

"Did it stop?" Matthias asked.

"Yeah. What was in that glass?"

"Feels good, huh?"

"Amazing!"

"You can thank the nanites for that."

"What?" Miles coughed. He bolted up from his chair. "Nanites? Are you telling me I just drank a bunch of God damn robots?"

"Jesus Christ, Miles! Calm down. They can't hurt you; their programming won't allow it."

"Programming can be altered," Miles protested.

"Yeah, but we'd have to extract them first, and that isn't easy to do. And the only place to reprogram them is in 2042."

"Really?" Miles asked doubtfully.

"Yes. Do you think we'd all use them if they weren't safe?"

"So you have them inside you now?"

Matthias, exasperated, answered, "I have for most of my life. It's what the beacon down here hones in on."

"Oh." He felt somewhat calmed by his father's assertion. "Mom and Alistair?"

"Of course." Matthias sounded irritated. "Here, let me show you something." He rolled up his sleeve and pulled out his boot knife. "The whole reason you feel so good right now is because they've gone through and cleaned you up inside. They can fight off illness and disease at an accelerated rate and even repair minor wounds." His father drew the blade across the middle of his forearm, creating a small, bleeding cut. Wiping the blood off the knife with two quick swipes across his breeches, he sheathed it. "Keep a close eye on this."

Miles and Matthias both watched as the trickle of blood slowed and eventually stopped. Slowly, the small incision closed as though someone drew a tiny zipper across it. Instead of a line of scab marking where the blade made the cut, only a small scar remained.

"Son of a bitch! What about larger wounds?"

"Like I said, only minor wounds. Someone runs you through with a sword or puts a bullet in your head, there's nothing they can do. You'd bleed out before they ever had a chance to repair the damaged cells."

"Still, that's incredible. Will I ever get sick again?"

"Sort of. You're still vulnerable like everyone else, but you'll only feel the effects for a few hours, if that. Once the nanites assess the threat and exterminate it, you'll feel better. What's really great is that things like broken bones heal in a few days instead of weeks. I'm sure you understand that with the life we lead, we can't afford to get bogged down for days by the common cold."

Miles nodded his agreement. He loved the idea of never really getting sick again.

A whirr and three chirping tones came from the simulator at the far end of the mat. Miles and Matthias both turned to regard the device. The hexagonal pad levitated a few inches off the fabric and hung there.

"Nanite collation and analysis complete," a disembodied female voice announced. A flash of radiance rose from the simulator and receded to a tolerable level. Then, amidst the luminous spire, a holographic figure took shape; a short male of uncertain Asian heritage stood before Miles, arms crossed, staring at him through narrowed eyes. His head was bald, but he sported a well-trimmed salt and pepper goatee that made him look particularly bad ass. Over his muscled frame he wore a traditional black kung-fu uniform with white edging and frog buttons. He had the look of an ancient master. It seemed so realistic that it gave Miles the chills.

"Step forward," the thickly accented voice commanded.

Miles flinched. He hopped up onto the mat and walked toward the simulator. When the hologram held out its hand in a halting gesture, he stopped cold.

"I am Combat Instructor Proxy RX-7," the image said calmly. "But you will call me Master. State your name."

"Ma—Miles Draven," he answered weakly.

"Speak up!" the hologram roared.

"Miles Draven!" he repeated with greater power.

"Better." He sounded pleased. "Hmm...another Draven." The figure began pacing back and forth across the mat. It was so realistic that Miles forgot that the simulator floated below it, projecting the image. Its dark eyes flashed white-hot for a moment and returned to normal.

"You're an interesting human, Miles. So much like your father: similar strengths, similar weaknesses." The simulation paused mid-pace, stroked its goatee, and visually examined Miles from head to toe. "Better raw materials though."

Miles smiled.

"We will need to improve your muscle tone throughout, especially your upper body. Enhance flexibility too. Lack of physical activity has kept you from reaching your potential, Miles. I will correct that. Based on your overall body diagnostic, no singular martial art style will fit you best. You would be best served by learning a collection of techniques from a variety of combat styles. I have compiled for you an individualized system that will draw from Tae Kwon Do, Nihon Goshin Aikido, Brazilian Jiu Jitsu, and Krav Maga. Do you accept this training regimen?"

"Yes, Master," Miles barked back, very enthused by what he was about to learn. He was familiar with most of those styles, but Krav Maga was a mystery to him. Either way, it sounded like an amazing mix of skills.

"Matthias," the hologram called aloud and regarded the elder Draven with a bow of respect.

Miles twisted his torso around so that he could watch his father.

"Yes, Master." Matthias took a step toward the simulator and returned the bow.

Its eyes burned white again. "I'm transferring a conditioning regiment for Miles to your digital capsule. He is to begin tomorrow and continue until sufficient improvement has been achieved."

"Yes, Master," he accepted the command and bowed one last time. A cycle of musical tones came from his breeches. They sounded like echoing water drops. Matthias reached inside his pocket and withdrew a small device that appeared to be a handheld rectangle of glass or plexi. Touching his finger to it, the tones ceased. He placed it back in his pocket.

Curious as to what this conditioning regimen might include, Miles whispered, "What is it?" to his father.

"Miles!" the simulator bellowed.

He snapped back around, standing at attention.

"Time for your first lesson," the simulated teacher announced as it closed in on Miles. It flashed a devious grin. "Do you know how to take a hit?"

"What?" Miles asked, confused. In a flash of movement, Master pulled his arms back and unleashed a double palm strike at Miles' chest. He flinched away from the attack by sheer reflex but did little else to stop it because he thought the simulated instructor was made up of nothing more than light. The strike, however, produced an impact of unbelievable power. Miles flew backward, landing sprawled out across the mat. His chest ached. "What the Hell was that?" He rolled onto his side, wincing, and rubbed at the hurt with his hands.

The simulator hovered beside him. Master extended a hand toward Miles, offering to help him up. Despite the power just displayed by the hologram, he still didn't think it capable of any kind of tangible contact.

"Take my hand," the simulation ordered him, shaking its hand with emphasis.

"Yes, Master," Miles grunted and offered his hand in return. The strength of master's grip surprised him nearly as much as the strike. Pulled back to his feet, he asked, "How did you do that?"

"The nanites inside of you serve me just as they do you. As you already know, they provide me with information about your biological design. But when I'm training you, they act within your body to simulate the pressure of my touch. They interact with your brain and nervous system to create the sensation of skin pressure, pain, and injury. When I helped you up, nanites exited your body through the pores of your hand and collaborated with those beneath your skin to pull you upward."

"But I thought they couldn't hurt me," Miles cried and turned to his father for reassurance, but he just sat, observing the lesson without interfering.

Master continued, reassuring Miles that, "No physical injury or pain you'll feel during these exercises is real. But while we are working together, it will feel very real. It's important that you're able to take a hit, fall safely, and sense oppositional force during grappling and blocking. Without being able to physically interact with me through the assistance of the nanites, my training would be as useless to you as trying to learn by watching others train. Do you understand?"

Miles nodded. Though he didn't understand all of what Master told him, the concept mostly made sense. He knew that most boxers and mixed martial artists sparred with other fighters to prepare for upcoming bouts. Master, he concluded, would serve both the purpose of instructor and sparring partner as he learned to fight.

"Excellent," Master smiled. A new hologram joined Master; a magnificent rapier with an ivory handle, emerald pommel, and golden guards and quillion materialized in his grasp. "I will also be working with you on your sword technique. Unfortunately, due to technological limitations I am unable to engage you in tactile combat simulations. All live melee training will be completed by your family members who are all expert swordsmen." The rapier disintegrated from Master's hand. He then unbuttoned his jacket and let it fall off his shoulders, revealing a perfectly etched body. Nary an ounce of fat could be found anywhere on his computerized frame. Craning his neck to both sides with audible cracks, he rolled his shoulders and asked, "Are you ready to begin?"

"Yes, Master!" Miles answered back with eagerness.

"Right side back, fighting stance!" the hologram ordered. Master slid his right leg back, settled his weight on slightly bent knees, and brought his arms up into an open handed guard with a brutal, "Ki-ai!"

Miles flinched at the war cry. He fumbled about, quickly trying to contort his body into the right position.

Master relaxed from his stance to move around Miles slowly, shaking his head and making a clicking sound with his tongue while he assessed his student. He paused and stomped on Miles' right foot. "Wrong leg back."

"Oww!" Miles yelped and switched feet.

Then he moved behind Miles and pushed at the back of his locked knees. "Bend!" Next, Master came back around to face him, grabbed his fists, and pulled them away from his body. "Too close." Finally, he pried open Miles' hands so they were open and relaxed. "Like this."

Moving back a few paces, Master smoothed his goatee carefully, examining Miles. "So much to learn," he mused aloud with a sigh.

CHAPTER TWELVE

The rustle of curtains preceded a flood of sunlight spilling across Miles' face. He clenched his eyelids, scrunched his nose, and rolled away from the rude interruption of his sleep. The quick movement reminded him of just how hard he had trained with the simulator the day before; every muscle felt stiff and achy.

"Let's go, Miles." Elizabeth bopped him on the hip with a small pillow. "Your father's waiting."

Miles groaned, pulling the blanket over his head. "C'mon." He glanced at his digital watch. "It's only six. It's not like I've got a bus to catch."

Elizabeth grabbed a handful of blanket and whipped it down off his face like a magician performing the tablecloth trick. Miles looked to her at the foot of the bed. The sunlight drowned out her shape. He shielded his eyes away from the glare with his hand. She loomed over him. She wore a brown, woolen dress and a damp apron around her waist. A tattered cloth hung over her shoulder. The look on her face was one of complete impatience, as if to say, *Get your ass out of bed,* without being so unladylike.

"You can't keep wearing that thing around," she said as she rounded the foot of the bed in the direction of the door. "If someone sees you wearing that thing they'll start asking questions you won't be able to answer." She stood beside the bed, hand extended and open, waiting for him to surrender the futuristic timepiece.

Miles sighed, unhooked the clasp, and handed it over.

She slipped it into a small pocket on her apron and patted it. "You really should try using the pocket watch we gave you. Aren't they still stylish in your time?"

Miles shrugged his shoulders and answered, "Sort of." He dragged himself up into a sitting position on the side of the bed and ran his fingers through his hair. "What's he teaching me today?" he yawned.

"Strength training." From the back of the doorway, Elizabeth took down an off-white, cotton coulter shirt and a pair of brown canvas trousers with black suspenders and an adjustable back. She tossed them down on the bed beside her son. Miles picked up the trousers to find the material quite course and rugged, more so than the ones he'd been wearing for days.

"Put those and your riding boots on and don't dawdle. A nice, hot breakfast is waiting for you in the kitchen."

Miles narrowed his eyes at the unfamiliar garments, curious as to the methods of training that awaited him. When he thought of endurance he pictured long distance running and lifting weights for strength training. These clothes, for certain, provided a limited range of motion and, after sweating in the afternoon sun, would lead to significant chafing. He was dreading it already.

A few minutes later, he met his mother in the kitchen for a hearty breakfast of eggs and toast. He gave up on the bacon and steak after his first few days in 1863. For someone who never used to eat breakfast because it gave him a stomachache, he had adjusted quite well to the less greasy fare. The cuts of fatty meat, however, did him in quickly. He also found he felt much more awake and energetic through his morning workouts, instead of drifting off or thinking about food as he normally did every morning. Miles wondered how he would have done at school had he tried to eat a healthy breakfast instead of just wolfing down Pop Tarts, cold pizza, or a sausage-egg-and-cheese from Mickey D's. *Oh well*, he thought, *it's all in the past...or in the future. Uggg!* His head suddenly hurt.

Matthias strolled through the kitchen door, dressed in similar clothes to Miles. A faint sheen of perspiration covered his brow. There were streaks of dried dirt all over his shirt and trousers. He walked over to his son and clapped a hand down upon his shoulder. Miles, wiping off his face with a cloth napkin, looked up at his father.

"Ready?"

"I guess so," Miles replied as he stood and tossed the napkin down on his plate. When he walked away, he heard his mother clear her throat purposefully. He turned to her.

"Aren't you forgetting something?" Her wide eyes glared at his plate still sitting on the table and his chair left sticking out.

Annoyed, Miles pushed the chair in and brought the plate over to the sink.

"What kind of manners did those foster parents teach you?" Elizabeth inquired, shaking her head. He handed her the plate. "Thank you, dear."

Matthias led Miles across several acres to the northern border of their property where the very hint of a rock wall had been started next to a stretch of woodland. A foot high layer of stones of varying size and shape stretched several hundred feet along the tree line. Piled up nearby the wall was a heap of stone.

"Here." Matthias handed Miles a pair of tanned-leather work gloves. His son starred back at him unhappily and then glanced at the pile of stone. "What's wrong?" Matthias inquired.

"Is this the training Master wanted me to do?" Miles wasn't pleased. "Moving rocks?"

"Part of it. Lifting and moving them into place will build muscle." Matthias walked over to the pile of stone, rolling up his sleeves. "We don't have free weights and machines for training. Doing this will toughen you up. Besides, there's a certain satisfaction to a good, hard day's work and a job well done." Matthias pulled on his gloves and took hold of a hefty looking stone from the pile. The sinewy muscles in his forearms bulged beneath the skin. He carried the stone to the rock wall and carefully laid it down, contorting its position until it sat secure and even. Making his way back to the pile, he told Miles, "Your turn!"

"Sure," Miles answered unenthusiastically.

So father and son moved stone after stone from the greater pile to the fledgling wall. Matthias taught Miles how to place the stones so that they didn't topple over or collapse under the weight of the others. He also showed his son how to lift the heavier ones with his knees so that he didn't hurt himself. Miles likened the whole experience to a very tiring game of *Jenga* or *Tetris*—one that made his arms and back sore.

By the time the sun had squatted directly overhead, Miles and Matthias had moved the last of the stone. The wall, that in the morning was a mere suggestion of its intended size, had grown nicely and required only one more day of toil and another load of stone to complete.

Miles stood back, nodding and admiring their work. "Nice," he said, elongating the pronunciation. He suddenly looked down at his gloved hands and grimaced while he flexed his fingers.

"You okay?"

Miles carefully removed both gloves to find his hands badly calloused and blistered. Miles sucked in a tense breath through clenched teeth as pain seared through his hands. "Damn, this hurts."

Matthias appeared unmoved by his son's injuries. Cold and emotionless he told Miles, "Hurry inside and have your mother take a look at that."

"Is it bad?" Miles questioned aloud, his lips taut with discomfort.

"I've seen worse," Matthias shrugged. "It's actually quite necessary though. You can work on your studies for a few days until they heal up. The rest of your physical training will wait."

"Wait!" Miles exclaimed. "I thought the nanites could heal stuff like this. Why do I have to wait?"

"They're programmed to let certain injuries heal on their own. If they heal that, the skin on your hands won't be any tougher than it is now. You're better off this way. Trust me."

"This sucks," Miles growled and threw his gloves to the ground. He stalked off toward the house.

Over the next eight days, a consistent rain fell across the countryside. The soggy earth made the outdoor work Matthias had set aside for Miles impossible. Unfortunately, it would be waiting for him when the weather subsided. In the meantime, Miles toiled away reading history texts and studying tethering theory while his mother treated his sore hands; she soaked them in a solution of warm water and Epsom salt, followed by an application of oatmeal paste and sterile gauze wraps to prevent infection.

The blisters on Miles' hands had healed enough after a few days for him to resume his physical training. Desperate to get away from his studies, he joined Alistair in the bunker to work on his marksmanship. Unlike swordplay, firearms were the one area of combat training where Miles caught on quickly. With very little instruction, he squeezed off one round after another, center mass on the paper targets. Even Master's holographic distractions of gunfire and tinges of battle could not break his concentration in simulated combat. From those brief moments of success, Miles let go of his previous failings with swordplay and martial arts, and enjoyed the feeling of not being a total failure in his new life.

When the weather finally cleared, Miles awoke quite late one morning to find a letter from his father on his nightstand. It read:

Miles,

Alistair and I had to go into Richmond this morning for the horse auction. I left some firewood for you to chop out at the main stable. It will help you work on developing your strength a bit more and your hand-to-eye coordination. You'll have to make yourself something to eat as your mother tethered out to visit her brother. I expect that all the wood will be split by the time we get back this evening. The axe is stuck in the old oak stump by the stable. If you run into any wood that's too tough, use the sledgehammer and wedge that I left there. And make sure to put everything back in the stable. We're expecting more rain tonight and the heads will rust.

Dad

"Wonderful," Miles whispered to himself sarcastically. Splitting wood sounded like a fantastic way to spend an afternoon for a redneck. He was seriously starting to miss the days of sitting around the house, playing video games, and vegging out. *This crap's for the birds!*

After getting dressed, grabbing a slice of apple pie that his mother explicitly said was for after dinner, and filling a canteen with water, Miles trudged his way along the muddied footpath until he came to the main stable.

"Damn it!" he swore loudly. "All of this?" Towering over him was a monstrous mountain of firewood that stood nearly as high as the stable roof. "I'm supposed to finish all this by tonight?" He shook his head in disbelief. "He's nuts!"

Knowing he was the only one that would be blamed if the woodpile wasn't split, he reluctantly pulled on his work gloves and picked up one of the smaller logs and placed it, on end, on the stump. With all the confidence of a seasoned lumberjack, Miles took the axe in both hands, raised it over his head, and brought it screaming down at the log. His aim, however, lacked any resemblance to that of a woodcutter. The head of the axe sliced along the side of the log, sheering the bark clean off. Small grooves from woodworms were visible.

"Hmmm," Miles groaned and pursed his lips in thought. He brought the axe up in front of him with both hands to examine it. Having never tried to swing an axe before, he never considered the difficulty in hitting a target. It always seemed so easy to do when he would stop for a few moments to watch the outdoorsman competitions on television; nothing but big, burly men swinging axes at logs and taking out huge chunks. Miles never considered there might be any kind of science or skill to it. He tried to remember exactly how the lumberjacks placed their hands: one hand up by the head of the axe and the other down by the end of the handle. Slowly, he practiced the recalled movements. Miles raised the axe up vertically in front of him with its head hovering directly over his own and his hands lined up with the target. The top hand slid down to meet the other as he carefully brought the axe down toward the log. The bladed edge tapped the center of the piece of wood. Two more times he repeated the technique, feeling confident that the next try would prove more effective.

Exhaling a strong breath, Miles took another swing. *Crack!* Far from perfect but better than before, the axe struck a few inches off center and cleaved the log open. The head lay wedged in the log. Thick fibers of wood held it together. With a grunt, he lifted the axe up in the air with the log still attached to it and brought it down again on the stump, splitting it the rest of the way. *Alright,* he thought. *Put a little more oomph into the next swing.* Picking up another small log, he tried again. With each successive attempt, his accuracy and power grew until he felt he had gotten the hang of it.

When Miles finished chopping the last of the small logs, he found that the large ones provided a new challenge. No matter how hard he swung the axe, no matter where it hit, the thin axe head failed to split the logs. Having pulled the head free of the first of the larger logs, he puzzled over it for a second and then remembered the wedge and sledgehammer. The wedge was a thicker version of the axe head but without a handle to hold on to. Picking it up off the ground, he found it weighed as much, if not more, than the whole axe. The back of it was broad and flat, perfect for slamming with a sledgehammer.

Examining the log, Miles found a deep crack and worked the edge of the wedge into it until it stood upright on its own. Then, practicing the same technique he mastered with the axe, he took the sledgehammer in hand and brought its weight to bear on the flat end of the wedge, forcing it deep into the log with a loud crunch. Splinters of wood erupted into the air and the log, though still clinging together by a few resilient strands, laid otherwise cut in half. With one good tug, Miles ripped the two halves of the log apart and let out a loud roar, like a lion that had just slain an antelope and called the pride to dinner.

Completely exhausted and with the sun near to setting, the last log lay split in half. Miles sat on the stump, drenched with sweat, drinking down the last drops of water from his canteen. The *clop clop* of horse hooves growing nearer heralded the return of Alistair and Matthias from the auction. They had two new horses in tow—a sleek brown mare and a spirited black colt that bucked and snorted with displeasure.

Matthias called out, "Whoa!" to the horses, and the carriage came to rest beside Miles and the woodpile. He glanced proudly up at his father and older brother. The look was not returned.

His father tied the reins off on the dash rail, leaned forward, his elbows on his knees, and cocked an eyebrow at the pile of split logs. His father then glanced at his youngest son with a sense of amusement, snickering into his gloved hand. Alistair hopped down from the carriage with a wide grin, apparently entertained by the same gaffe that escaped Miles.

"What?" Miles whined. "I did what you said, didn't I?" He hopped down from the stump and glared at his work.

Alistair, bringing the mare around to the front of the stable, paused by his brother. "The little logs are one thing, but we'll never fit logs that big," he pointed to the split portions of the larger pieces of wood, "into the woodstove or the smoker."

Miles whirled about to appeal to his father. "But you never said I had to do that. You just said split the wood." He pulled the note out of his pocket and handed it to Matthias.

Alistair shrugged and led the mare the rest of the way into the stable.

Matthias' eyes scrutinized the letter. He then folded it up, stepped down from the carriage, and handed it back to Miles. "So it seems. You can finish the job tomorrow then."

Miles watched his father walk away, mouth agape in disbelief. "But I—I" he stammered.

"C'mon, Miles," his father pleaded. "I could use some help with this one. He's full of piss and wind, just like you."

First, his father wasn't clear with Miles about quartering the wood, not just splitting it. Then he doesn't even thank him for breaking his back splitting the whole woodpile, regardless of the oversight in Matthias' directions. *It sure as Hell didn't split itself.* His frustration grew with each day and with each new, archaic responsibility thrust upon his shoulders. Life in 2016 might have been a pain in the ass, but at least he didn't feel like an unappreciated migrant worker. Chronoshifter, time traveler, whatever the Hell they called themselves, it was no life of adventure they led. It was ball-busting labor with miniscule moments of downtime. For a lifetime he wished to be part of a family, to feel like he belonged to something important instead of just being a piece of driftwood that others tolerated rather than loved. And in three short weeks with his "real" family, all they've made him feel like was a mix between a slave and some sort of weapon that needed sharpening before being sent into battle. He was beginning to doubt just how much they actually cared about him.

Miles moped with leaden feet toward the back of the carriage where his father awaited him. The sleek, black colt shined in the fading sunlight like some kind of buffed, onyx statue. It snorted breaths of hot air out its gaping nostrils. Its hooves scraped at the ground, kicking up dirt that its swooshing tail slapped out of the air.

Matthias held the reins and patted the beast on its broad shoulder. "His name's Colossus."

Fitting name, Miles thought. *What will I have to do, clean up its colossal piles of horseshit?* He forced forth a halfhearted grin.

"And he's yours," Matthias added.

"What? Why?" Miles choked out the words. He didn't understand the gesture.

"I just wanted to make sure you knew your work was appreciated. The adjustment you've made isn't an easy one, and I know I can be a little short with you at times. But you have to trust me, and trust that I know what's best for you right now. It may be difficult to understand and even harder to accept, but there's a good reason for everything I put you through. Just know that it's out of love, out of wanting to keep you safe that I push you so hard."

"But aren't horses a lot of work?" Miles drew closer to Colossus, reaching tentatively for its mane. His father gestured encouragingly for him to touch the horse.

"Yes," Matthias concurred, "but nothing that you wouldn't already do on a ranch. Besides, they're loyal friends. If you take care of him, he'll take care of you."

Miles nodded. The horse's mane was soft and smooth as satin. He never knew that a living creature could feel like that.

"Let me show you how to bed him down for the night." Matthias made a clicking sound with his mouth and led Colossus by the reins toward the stable. Miles followed closely behind.

CHAPTER THIRTEEN

Just after breakfast, Matthias packed a rucksack and led Miles on a hike into the forest that surrounded the ranch. Having passed through the dense exterior foliage, the interior woodland realm was an eerie yet tranquil landscape. Next to nothing thrived at ground level, likely kept from sustained sunlight by the blotting foliage at the tops of the tallest trees. As far as Miles could see, a thick layer of twigs, decaying leaves, and old pine needles blanketed the forest floor. Only the warble of songbirds and the rustle of leaves on the breath of the wind could be heard.

After twenty minutes or so of non-stop walking on uneven ground, Miles grew tired and wanted to rest. He paused, bent down, hands on knees, and whimpered, "How much farther?"

"Just up ahead," Matthias stopped beside him and replied with a grin. A light sheen of sweat covered his brow. He breathed heavily.

"Where are we going?"

"You'll see." Matthias motioned with his hand for Miles to follow, and he resumed his trek.

This better be worth it.

Almost ready to call it quits and head back, Miles saw the forest ahead open up into a small clearing. He trudged forward to find a ring of pencil straight, towering red cedars. Unlike the rest of the forest they travelled through, undergrowth grew here. A thicket of lush fern covered the ground within the ring of trees.

Miles stopped just outside the clearing. He didn't like the look of it. It gave him the impression that it was meant to look picturesque and beautiful, but it was really concealing evil, sparkling vampires or something. His father stood in the center of the clearing, hands on hips, staring up at the tree tops. A cool breeze passed through the woods and Matthias closed his eyes, breathing deeply.

Miles cleared his throat loudly to rouse his father from his sensory trance.

His father called back, unfazed, "Beautiful, isn't it?"

"Sure," Miles answered back. He stood with his arms crossed, watching his father. "What is this place?"

Matthias smiled and opened his eyes. His gaze fell right on Miles. With an excited clap of his hands he strode toward his son. "This is a place I like to visit from time to time—a place to think in peace."

"You brought me all this way to meditate?"

"No. Not this time. I brought you here to practice tethering. I figured you were about ready for your first solo chronoshift."

"Sweet!" Miles cheered and pumped his fist. "I've been waiting for this."

"Good. After how rough our tandem tether went, I feared you might shy away." A snapping twig echoed through the trees. Matthias cupped his hands around his eyes and squinted into the darkness of the forest past Miles.

"What's wrong?" Miles inquired with concern and turned about to see what made the sound. About a hundred feet away, two white tail deer made their way through the woods. They stopped to drink from a meandering stream and the larger of the two peered right back at Miles and his father. He dug at the loam with his hoof and snorted. They then galloped off.

"Nothing. Just trying to make sure we're alone." Matthias put an arm around his son and led him toward the center of the clearing. "Obviously, we can't afford to let anyone else see what we're doing."

"But why way out here? Why didn't we just work on it in the bunker?"

He gestured against the idea with his hands. "Way too dangerous. Anything close to the aperture would get sucked in. After all, the vortex is basically a focused singularity. You open it up in the wrong place and you could take the whole ranch with it."

"Oh," Miles grunted. "I can see how that might be a problem."

"After you get some experience at controlling your chronoperpetua, then we can try tethering closer to home."

"Is it that hard to control?"

"Only one way to find out."

Matthias dropped his rucksack, knelt down, and loosened its straps. Reaching inside, he removed an object wrapped in tan muslin and handed it to Miles.

Miles noticed its deceptive weight. It felt far heavier than its bulk. He peeled back the folds of fabric and found what he believed to be a chronoperpetua. It reminded him of the device his father used to bring him home so many nights before.

"That was your Grandfather Hector's chronoperpetua," Matthias affirmed his son's suspicions. "It's yours now."

Miles crumpled up the cloth and crammed it into his trousers' pocket. His grandfather's chronoperpetua! It had all sorts of dents and scratches on its surface—no doubt battle scars from countless lifetimes of adventure and war. Turning it over, Miles expected to find the leather securing straps worn and frayed, but they were supple and new.

"Your mother replaced the straps some time ago. It's been waiting for you since the day you were born."

Miles nodded and continued his inspection of the device. He slipped each of his fingers in and out of the ring shaped holes at one end, kind of like a pair of brass knuckles. The interior of each finger hole had a padding of soft cloth that left a smidge of wiggle room. Turning it over, he found a recessed button just beneath the finger holes.

"Go ahead, push it," his father urged him.

With a click, a latch within the chronoperpetua released and the cover flipped open on an exterior hinge. A single panel, like the one he saw the night his father rescued him, pivoted upward of its own accord from within the device. His studies told him that this was one of two tethering modules that would help him lock onto a specific time. Since this one possessed a singular actuation ring around its perimeter, it had to be the *return* module. If Miles rotated the outer ring clockwise and activated the chronoperpetua, it would send him back to his last destination. It allowed his kind to flawlessly return to the very moment they departed a previous time. For both the chronoshifter and the people of that time tangent, it would seem like they never left. More important, it served as a good emergency escape measure when they didn't have time to fumble over dials and destinations.

As much as he wanted one of his own, Miles felt somewhat disappointed by the device. He remembered his father's chronoperpetua glowing with unimaginable power in the darkness of the park. But there in the clearing the ambient sunlight drowned out its brilliant emanations. Only a meager sparkle emanated from the chronometric particles that swirled within the panel. It was the presence of that otherwise unknown, undiscovered particle that fueled the device. The more he learned about chronoshifting, the more the mystery and magic of time travel gave way to scientific knowledge. He kind of liked it better the other way.

Closing that cover, Miles flipped it over and opened the other side. This time the *tuning* module rose from the interior. In difference to the return module, this one had five independent adjustment dials around the perimeter. Each one controlled the numbers displayed in each of the five circular panes and a different, measurable moment in time: hours, minutes, days, months, and years. Both modules possessed a large circular cut out at the base of the panel for securing an anchor into the core. This one also possessed an activation ring, much like the perimeter of the return module. Should it be engaged, it would bring the chronoshifter to whatever date they tuned into with the dials.

Finally, Miles tilted the chronoperpetua and peered into its core. There he found the heart and soul of the device—a permanently fixed panel that kept track of the passage of time in the present. Every moment ticked by in the round display panes, unlike the modules where it stayed static until manually altered. The core also had no discernible dials or activation rings, just a socket for securing an anchor. If neither module was activated nor an anchor placed in the core, the device would automatically tether to the present.

Remembering the schematics in his father's journal, Miles fitted his fingers into the device and secured the straps tight against the back of his hand. He rested his thumb to the side of the actuator, careful not to press it. Pushing out a nervous breath, he asked Matthias, "Now what?"

"Here. Take this." His father handed him a new anchor. It had the letters *CA* etched into the crystal.

Miles held it by his thumb and index finger. "Who's *CA*?"

Matthias frowned. "Charles Albright. A very dear friend. His wife died a few months ago."

"Was she one of us?" Miles solicited.

Matthias nodded. "Yes. She was such an amazing woman and one Hell of a warrior. Her death left a big hole in that family."

"Did she die in battle?"

"No," Matthias sighed. "Time caught up to her. She grew old and died."

The idea of growing old and dying after a fulfilling life didn't bother Miles in the least. The thought of dying at the hands of another person, however, now that put a scare into his heart. But watching his father squirm at the thought of dying of natural causes made Miles consider what it must be like for one of their kind not so new to this way of existing. *What will it feel like to live for hundreds of years without aging a single day?* Your loved ones, equally ageless, move with you through time. You forget how truly fragile you all are. Then, without warning, the clock starts ticking and you begin feeling every second of your life bleed away. You get older, weaker, eventually unable to do the things you once did. And meanwhile your wife, your children never age. It gave Miles a moment of pause. Perhaps if he survived a few hundred years, the thought of growing old would haunt him equally. Perhaps, death in his prime and at the hands of a mortal enemy would be far more welcomed of an end.

"Sorry, Dad." The words came out and, for the first time, they felt natural, unforced.

Matthias gave a weak smile back. "I just wanted to go visit him, you know. See how he's doing. Besides, it's a great excuse to introduce you."

"Okay. Let's do it." Miles looked inside his chronoperpetua and held the anchor just above the socket. "So do I just push it in?"

"Yeah."

Miles moved his hand with great care. Pushing the anchor through the hole in the tuning actuator, it dropped right into place. An immediate surge of energy sparked through it. The glass sphere spun about an invisible axis at such speeds that he could no longer make out the letters on its surface.

"Now close the module over it and shut the cover," Matthias instructed.

Miles did as ordered. He felt the whole device buzzing in his hand, acting as though it had an eagerness of its own to be used again.

"Now you're ready." Matthias clapped him on the back and started backing away from his son. From his pocket he withdrew his chronoperpetua and prepared to chronoshift. "Make sure you brace yourself," he called out as he hit the actuator. The energy tether rocketed from his device and pierced the fabric of time. He yelled over the roar of the vortex that formed before him, "The terminus wave will snap your neck if you aren't ready for it."

Miles gave his father a weak salute. Then he bent his knees, leaned back, and squinted cautiously as he hit the actuator with his thumb. His whole body rocked backwards from the force of projecting the tether. *Holy shit!* One arm alone couldn't keep it steady enough to open a vortex. He brought his left hand to his wrist and grabbed it aggressively, steadying the tether. A hurricane like wind rushed over him as the fabric of time peeled back and a chronovortex opened before him.

An unexpected but wholly familiar sensation greeted him next, a tickling prickle moving up his forearm. It was a feeling he had felt only once before, in his bedroom, the day his foster parents were murdered. From an opening at the back of the chronoperpetua, tendrils of energy reached out and wrapped around his wrist. He thought he had seen the wispy remnants of something similar that day, but he had dismissed the thought. Now he didn't know what to think. If he didn't imagine it, then what happened to him defied the laws of chronoshifting; no one could tether without a chronoperpetua.

In his periphery, Miles witnessed his father being drawn into the vortex and it closing behind him. *I have to tell Dad about this*, he decided. *Maybe he'll know what it means.*

Preoccupied by this enigma, Miles let his attention fall from the tether he projected across time. He refocused on the vortex and realized the terminus wave, as his father called it, raced toward him faster than he could have anticipated. His father's warnings nor the papers he had studied could have prepared him for it. Miles reeled away from the oncoming force and failed to brace for contact.

Closing his eyes, Miles felt the wave hit his chronoperpetua and wrench his body into the vortex. Every single cell of his body felt momentarily disconnected from every other cell. It didn't quite hurt, but it didn't feel good either. For a short time, all he understood was an odd, ethereal awareness. After a few moments, though, he felt much better. His awareness of self returned, and Miles remembered the chronoperpetua strapped to his wrist, and the azure tether that dragged him headlong through a wormhole. Swirling streaks of blinding radiance rushed by him. It filled him with a sense of sheer exhilaration. Though his mind beckoned him to whoop aloud, the sound could not be formed.

Memories of the first tether with Matthias, only a few weeks before, lingered as only wisps, impossibly distant for their age. Pain, bone deep cold, and confusion—it was all Miles could remember. But this he knew he'd never forget. Perhaps being dragged along like a tin can on a string caused the amnesia. Maybe the vortex itself wiped his memory clean. Either way, he took pride in knowing that he'd made his first chronoshift. When he saw the end of the line draw near, he knew he belonged. What began as a mere pinhole of bright white light at the visible end of the energy beam swelled in an instant and consumed him whole.

Miles felt the draw of the tether terminate and his body tumbled freely from the mouth of the vortex. A world of spinning, muted colors greeted him as gravity took hold. He cried out in terror, not knowing how far he would plummet before the ground either broke his fall or crushed his bones to powder. A painful smack, like being hit by a giant fly swatter, greeted the side of his body. Harsh lashes whipped at his skin, and soft objects scattered beneath him.

Water! Miles felt wetness wrap around him like a heavy blanket and strip away the air. Then he came to a swift and sudden halt against a wall of slick mud. Twisting about, Miles dug his feet into the muck and pushed upward with great force. His flailing arms sprayed water in all directions as he broke the surface and gasped for air. He found himself standing in a cold, waist deep pond. Wreckage of his impact floated about the surface of the murky water: snapped reed stems, long green leaves, plucked geese feathers, and their angry owners who quacked at him. A particularly irritated pair of the long necked foul pursued him with snapping bills. Miles backed away from them on unsteady feet that slipped and slid in the mud. Finally at the shore of the pond, he climbed out and grabbed a nearby stick to ward off the geese.

An unfamiliar male voice barked at Miles in a thick British accent, "That won't be necessary, Master Draven!"

Miles whipped his head around to find his father and a man in his middle years walking toward him from a large stone manor. The man's outfit seemed much older than those of the 1860s. It reminded Miles of the clothing worn by colonials in his school history books: he wore black riding boots; brown breeches; a dark blue waistcoat that draped over his thighs with wide buttons and red edging; a white, long sleeve shirt with a frilly collar that covered his neck; and a larger tan coat over it all. Atop his head sat a thin field of short gray hair. In his hand he carried a walking cane that he pointed at the geese.

The man dug into his pocket and tossed a handful of bread crumbs into the pond, luring the attention of the geese back toward the water. "Those are my prized geese, boy! Can't have you beating the tar out of them. Each one is worth more than a score of you."

Matthias laughed aloud at the jibe, but any humor was lost on Miles who seethed inside at the cheap appraisal of his worth. *Just an old man with a big mouth*, he told himself. *Probably the gardener or something.*

His father's gait was brisk, confident. The old man, however, seemed to be hobbled by leg problems; he had a noticeable limp with each step.

Miles realized the chronoperpetua was still strapped to his wrist. He crossed his arms in an unnatural hurry, trying to hide the device from sight.

"Ah," the man announced, his gaze following Miles' hand. "I see you have Hector's chronoperpetua."

Miles pulled his hand free, shot his father a bewildered glance, and asked, "He knows?"

"Of course he does, Miles. This is the man I told you about."

"Charles Albright at your service." He nodded respectfully to Miles.

"You're Charles?" Miles inquired, quite confused by the man's physical appearance. "But you're—old."

"I see this one's a real charmer, Matthias."

"I-I'm sorry," Miles stuttered ashamedly, not meaning to insult him. His father said that Charles' wife died of old age, not that time had begun ticking for him too. He felt mislead. "I didn't—"

"No, it's alright, Master Draven." He waved off Miles' apologies. "I'm growing old. After too many lifetimes to count, I'm finally growing old and dying."

Miles didn't know what to say or how to respond to such an affirmation of doom. The whole situation felt quite awkward.

Matthias squinted up to the sky. "Looks like rain."

"It always does," Charles groaned as he reached down to rub at his right knee. "Damned knee's aching. Let's go inside, Matthias. I need to warm my aching bones." He began hobbling his way back to the manor.

"Come on, Miles," his father urged. "Let's get you inside and out of those wet clothes."

Miles stood alone in the library of the Albright manor while his father fetched hot tea from the kitchen, and Charles fetched dry clothes from his son's room. The whole place felt like it came right out of Hogwarts or something. Books lined every square inch of shelf space in the massive room. Most of the titles printed upon the spines didn't ring familiar with Miles. Most sounded like they were written in Latin or some other foreign tongue when he tried to pronounce them. The remainder of the library contained two comfortable armchairs that resided in the natural light that flooded in from the two windows. A small side table stood beside each seat. Miles dared not sit his wet ass down on any of the upholstered furniture. The fabric looked far too lavish to risk damaging.

He entered the adjoining study where a modest fire crackled within a marble hearth at the far end. A large, framed painting hung over the mantle; it appeared to be a family portrait of some kind. Miles figured it might be a painting of the Albrights when they all appeared young, but having never seen anyone other than an aged Charles, it was too hard to tell. In the center of the room stood a circular table with a cherry finish and four matching chairs that Miles had to circumvent on his way to the warmth of the fireplace. He took notice of several other paintings and a tapestry depicting the Albright family crest populating the walls. Unlike the library, the study had only one window—a bay style with a cushioned seat beneath it that ran the whole length. And on the other side of the room, a comfortable enough looking sofa took up much of the lower wall. It felt like a relatively calm space to sit and think.

Having reached the fireplace, Miles put his back to the flames and crouched down. The heat lapped at his wet skin and clothes, chasing away the deep-set cold.

His father returned first. In his hands he carried a wooden tray with three mugs, a teapot, a bowl of sugar, and a ceramic creamer. He laid it down upon the table and poured three drinks.

"Sugar and cream?" he asked his son.

"Sure," Miles answered with interest. "Lots of sugar." He rose to his feet and stepped away from the fire to join his father at the table. The loss of heat brought back a swell of chills from his damp clothes. With both hands he clutched at the mug and drew it to his lips to blow away the steam.

"You've got to be freezing," his father surmised.

"I've been worse." Miles' teeth chattered. Taking a sip, the warmth soothed his shaking. "So how old is Charles?"

"I'm 397-years-old," Charles grumbled from the archway. He limped into the library without his cane. A pair of dark blue breeches and a tan shirt hung over his forearm. A strip of cloth wound around his knee several times, holding water bags to the injured joint.

"You mean 398-years-old, Charles," Matthias adjusted his friend's assessment before taking a seat at the table.

"Bah," he groaned and wove a dismissing hand at Matthias. "Don't tell me how old I am. I was born in 1578." Charles hobbled over to Miles and offered him the dry clothes. "Here, boy. They're my son's. He's a bit taller than you, but they should suffice."

"Thanks!" Miles snatched them away and laid them on the table. With great effort he peeled the damp shirt off.

"Yes," Matthias clarified, leaning back in the chair with a knowing grin, "but it was 1215 when you were born. Now it's 1613. Your math's always been a bit dodgy."

Charles crossed to the couch and collapsed against the soft cushions. He moaned aloud, wincing as he grabbed at his knee. "I see you still haven't learned to respect your elders," Charles declared with a chuckle. He pulled a flask of liquor from his waistcoat pocket and took a luxuriating sip of its contents. Whatever he drank, it brought swift comfort, easing his pained expression.

Still standing in damp trousers, Miles scanned the room for a private area to change out of them. He'd have to strip right down to the skin, and the idea of doing that in front of any other men, family or not, was a situation that made him incredibly uneasy. Just seeing the shower stalls in the gym locker room back at school made him shrink back in terror; three main pipes ran from the floor to the ceiling with three shower heads anchored to each. No stalls. No walls. The thought of showering face-to-face with three other guys with their dicks hanging in the breeze made him sick to his stomach. Thank God he never had to do that. Not that he thought that he was *undersized* or anything, he just hated the idea of being so exposed. Chilled to the bone and soaking wet, however, he was certain there was significant shrinkage going on. Talk about self-conscious.

"Go change out in the hallway, Miles," Charles offered the face-saving advice. "I don't need the painful reminder of what it was like to have a young body."

"Yes, sir," Miles mumbled and shuffled himself out of the study, through the library, and into the outer corridor. He stripped away the last of his wet garments, wadded them up into a dripping ball, and pulled on the dry trousers. Just as Charles thought, the clothes hung a bit too long on his arms and legs, but they got the job done. Miles cuffed the sleeves and ankles for a better fit and returned to the study. He placed his wet clothes on the stone hearth to dry. Then he took a seat across the table from his father, sipping from the much cooler tea.

"So, Matthias," Charles inquired, "will you be attending the gathering?"

Matthias' relaxed posture changed abruptly. He leaned forward and narrowed his eyes at Charles. Something about him, something Miles couldn't put his finger on, had been disturbed greatly by the question. "What gathering?"

"You mean you weren't invited?" Charles countered with confusion.

"No!" Matthias snapped. "Who called this gathering?"

"The Magister Consilio."

"But I'm part of the council," Matthias countered, visibly appalled. "So are you. Were you a part of this decision?"

Miles had no idea what they were talking about. *Magister Consilio?* Judging by the vehemence of their words, he decided to stay out of it and try to figure it out on his own.

"No, Matthias! I resigned from the Consilio. In my condition, I have little want or time to engage in such political maneuverings. I'm trying to *live* my last few years."

"Doesn't it strike you as peculiar though that I wasn't consulted?"

"Well, up until this very moment I had no idea you weren't. But in their defense, they told me that they hadn't been able to reach all the Magisters, which is why they approached me."

"That's because everyone's in hiding," Matthias cried out in anger. "When someone's chopping up little kids and sending their heads to their parents in pine boxes, that's what's going to happen. That's what we're supposed to do when the Order's been compromised—close ranks and isolate." He slammed a fist down on the table. His mug wobbled and toppled, spilling tea all over. Miles reeled back in his chair, holding his drink at a safe distance.

"Our homes are robbed, our children murdered, and they want a meeting?" Matthias shot up from his chair and clenched his hands into fists. The sides of his jaw pulsated as he compressed his teeth rhythmically. "The whole damn thing smells like a trap!"

"That may well be, but it's not only the little ones who are gone,

Matthias," Charles spoke with sadness.

"What are you saying?" Matthias inquired softly, crossing the floor to his friend.

Charles strained with great effort to lift himself up off the sofa. He stood face to face with Matthias. "Annelise and Trevor are gone." Limping, he approached the fireplace and stared longingly at the family portrait. "They disappeared a few weeks ago. At first Trevor was late checking in. I was laid up sick in bed, so I sent Annelise out after him. Hours became days. Days became weeks. When she didn't come back, that's when I started to worry. Something went terribly wrong and I was in no shape to go chasing after them."

"Why didn't you tell me?" Matthias pleaded from across the room. "We could have tethered after them."

"It's not that simple. When I finally got up the strength to chronoshift, I couldn't find any of my anchors. They'd been stolen."

"They're all gone?"

"Yes. It happened at the same time as the other robberies."

"Do you have any idea what happened to the kids?"

"No. I can only guess that Trevor uncovered the conspiracy and—" his voice got caught in his throat. Tears pooled along his eyelids, glistening in the firelight. "I should never have sent Annelise after him. Now they're both gone." He shuddered with silent sobs. "My sweet Abigail. Losing her was hard enough." Charles reached up and touched her image. His hand slid down to the frame. "Now my children. Everything that has mattered to me has been taken. I'd be better off dead."

"Don't say that." Matthias moved to Charles' side, laying a comforting hand on his shoulder. "Don't give up hope just yet."

"Hope?" Charles laughed. "I'm no fool, Matthias. Hope's a young man's poison. I used to drink it like Scotch. I hoped I'd see the day where we'd send Gaius back to Hell. I hoped I'd die valiantly by my beloved's side, long before our children. I was an idiot. Hope's nothing but a blindfold that hides the truth from the eyes of fools. And the truth is that everything we've fought for is falling down around our ears."

"Oh, come on!" Matthias sounded appalled. "It isn't over yet. We haven't lost."

"Five children massacred, an artifact lost, and you think we're winning?"

"I didn't say that," Matthias shot back angrily. "Don't put words in my mouth."

"Look," Charles barked, "I know you think the gathering's a trap. Maybe it is. I don't know. But by walking into it with my eyes open, maybe I can find out who's responsible for this mutiny. And maybe I can find out what happened to my children. I've got to try."

Matthias frowned at his friend. The tension seemed to melt away. "What if things go sideways? What are you going to do?"

"I'm still a Centurion at heart." Charles grinned. "I'll fight to the death. Maybe take a few of those bastards with me."

"Where's the meeting?"

"Edo."

"The Takashima clan," Matthias deduced. His brow furrowed in contemplation.

"Yes. Hideki was the envoy who visited me."

Matthias leaned against the mantle. "That whole clan is bound by the Bushido. If they lied about the meeting, they'd dishonor themselves. No samurai can live with that kind of shame."

"So then maybe they're telling the truth," Charles postulated.

Matthias grinned uncertainly. "Or they're being misled. Then they wouldn't be aware of it. Perhaps the treachery runs far deeper."

"Well, I'm going," Charles declared, "either way."

"I don't like it, but I understand."

Charles gestured toward Miles. "With Miles being the only survivor, you realize that your absence at the meeting will only lead to suspicion."

"I don't care. I have just as good a reason as any for going into exile. If my son was the only survivor, then I have reason to fear he might be targeted again."

Miles didn't like the sound of that. He never even considered that another attempt might be made on his life.

"I'll do my best to explain your absence to the other Magisters. Tell them I've come in your stead."

"You don't have to. Just get in there, find out what you can, and get out in one piece."

"I will." Charles and Matthias shook hands and clapped each other on the back in a brusque hug.

Miles, who had taken in the whole conversation, now had a better understanding of the situation; things were far more precarious then he surmised. The Order itself lay fractured like a smashed mirror. No one knew who to trust or fear. The one thing Miles knew for certain was that his family had nothing to do with the treachery. He only hoped that they could do something to help Charles.

Hope...he too hung every chance of success on that word. Miles wondered if that made him blind and a fool like Charles suggested. He believed that he had witnessed enough in his short time as a member of the Order to not turn a blind eye to the truth. Yet, hope lingered.

"Master Draven," Charles said as he approached Miles, "now that we're warm from our bones to our breeches, would you care for a tour of the manor? There are some impressive trophy heads and suits of armor in the colonnade."

"Sure!" Miles exclaimed as he left the comfort of the chair. It sounded far more stimulating than an old library.

"Excellent!" Charles clapped his hands together. He directed them both toward the entryway of the library. "This way."

CHAPTER FOURTEEN

Miles watched as the simulator pulled back from its projected emulation of Master to demonstrate a wider combat scenario. He appeared to be standing fifty or so feet away, though the projector hadn't moved an inch. The virtual persona stood in a defensive posture, swaying and bouncing nimbly; it told Miles that it was vital to stay supple and ready to react quickly in combat. As a holographic sparring partner came at it with a downward sword strike, Master stepped into the attack. With a fluid, deft movement, the instructor parried the attack with an angled, upward block and followed it up with a disemboweling slash across the assailant's belly. The lesson, meant to teach Miles defensive techniques against strike number six, had eluded him. His frustration and fatigue began to show in his poor posture and slumping form. The latest demo failed to show him anything he hadn't seen all morning.

The deceased, simulated attacker dissolved away. Master refocused its attention on Miles. "Do you understand now?" the instructor proxy asked, its tone exhibiting frustration at its student.

"I guess so," Miles sighed and shrugged.

Master prepared to attack like a cat ready to pounce on its prey. With an angry cry, the hologram sprung at Miles, its sword slashing down at its student's head. Miles reacted by throwing his rapier arm up hard and fast, the blade parallel to the ground with its center directly over his head.

"No, no, no," Alistair barked from his seat beside the training mat. He shook his head emphatically.

"What now?" Miles groaned. He stepped back from Master and

glowered at his brother, impatient with his repeated corrections and interruptions. His sword arm fell limp at his side.

"Pause simulation." Alistair popped up from his chair and stepped onto the mat, stalking toward his brother.

Master bowed its head to Alistair, settled its feet into a comfortable stance, and clasped its hands together. "Simulation paused," the computer projection acknowledged.

"You're gonna get your head split in two if you do that in combat."

"Hey, give me a break," Miles whined. "I'm trying."

Alistair narrowed his eyes and got right in Miles' face. "Are you gonna tell that to Gaius? 'Go easy on me. I'm trying,'" he sniveled condescendingly right back at his brother. "Get your head out of your ass!"

Miles flinched back at his brother's harsh tone. For a guy who always seemed pretty laid back and aloof, he didn't expect Alistair to have such a hot temper. Miles averted his gaze, uneasy with making eye contact at that moment. "Sorry," he mumbled.

Alistair grabbed Miles' rapier hand by the wrist and lifted it up so that the quillion rested about six inches over the right side of his head and the blade tilted down at a 45 degree angle over his left shoulder. His fingers strangled his brother's wrist and shook it for emphasis. "You don't want to outmuscle an opponent. You want to redirect their strike; let it slide off. If the angle's wrong, you'll have a canoe for a scalp."

Stepping back quickly, Alistair unsheathed his rapier and brought it down overhead toward Miles' blade. Miles flinched as the two swords met, but he didn't falter. Alistair's blade slid along the rapier and clear of his body.

"See?" Alistair smacked Miles on the upper arm, his demeanor less angry. "Your blade's got to be angled to parry the strike safely."

Miles nodded.

Alistair smirked at him and withdrew into a fighting stance.

Miles mirrored Alistair's form. He stepped into a back stance, knees bent and steady beneath him, and held his rapier poised in his right hand with his left hand supporting the base of the pommel. He had come to know quite well that devious grin his brother shined at him; it meant pain was coming. *But would he really cut me?* Miles nervously pondered.

"Ready?" Alistair quipped.

Miles swallowed hard. Sweat gathered on his palms, making the pommel slick.

With an angry growl, Alistair came at Miles hard and fast. His rapier cut an exaggerated path through the air toward Miles' left side, but he shuffled back on the balls of his feet and struck out at the blade, knocking it clear. Alistair didn't relent. He advanced, making a quick, short cut at his other side. Miles continued his retreat, swiping his rapier back across his center to barely block the skillful strike. Then Alistair slashed with his blade in a shallow arc over his head and brought it straight down at Miles. This time he stepped into his brother's attack and brought his rapier up. The two swords clanged and the grating sound of metal scraping against metal filled the chamber. The downward pressure of Alistair's sword on Miles' fell away, and he brought his around in a reflexive counterattack. He stopped his parabolic strike just in time. The biting edge of his rapier hovered mere inches from Alistair's neck. His brother stared at the blade and then back to Miles with wide, worried eyes. Both of them stood still, breathing heavy. In his periphery, Miles noticed that Alistair's rapier was drawn back to strike, but he would have been headless long before the arm had a chance to swing forward. Miles had won the encounter.

Master, who had been silent during their exchange broke the silence by clapping.

A sudden smile pursed Alistair's lips. He stepped back from the threatening blade, slapped it away with his own, and shouted, "That's it!"

"Really?" Miles asked with uncertainty.

"Yes," he bubbled with pride. "Did you feel how effortless the parry was?"

Miles nodded. "It also seemed to set me up for the counter strike."

"Exactly! Just remember, it isn't about strength, it's about speed and technique. We're not fighting with claymores and broadswords."

"Yeah, but what do we do when someone comes at us with a

claymore or a broadsword?"

Master chimed in, "Let them exert themselves. Use your speed to avoid their attacks. When they tire and can't lift their weapon, you take their life."

Miles knew exactly what Master meant. "You mean like when Rocky fought Mr. T?"

"Exactly, Miles," Master confirmed.

"Wait! What?" Alistair asked, quite bemused. He looked from Master's projection to his brother.

"*Rocky III*," Miles responded with an air of irritation. He thought everyone knew about those movies. Then he remembered that his brother grew up in the 1930s. "Sorry. It's a boxing movie. You'd like it."

"I'll take your word on that."

The door to the training chamber creaked open and Matthias entered. Both Miles and Alistair turned to greet him.

"Lunch is almost ready, you two," Matthias announced. "It's about time to wrap things up."

"We're almost done," Alistair said.

"How's Miles doing, Master?" the elder Draven inquired.

"Satisfactorily. Footwork is shaky at times, but his basic defensive mechanics are coming along."

"Excellent. You can power down, Master." Matthias bowed at the simulated instructor. Miles and Alistair paid their respects too, and the hologram returned the gesture.

"Powering down," Master said before hologram pixilated and disappeared. The simulator's light emitters went dark and the floating platform settled back upon the mat.

Miles sheathed his rapier and stepped down to the floor. He unbuckled his sword belt as he walked, wrapping the leather straps around the scabbard before he pulled out a chair and collapsed upon it. The sword fell upon the table with a clunk as Miles dropped it and picked up a towel. He wiped at his head and arms, soaking up the sweat that covered him.

"Alistair," Matthias called out as he approached his eldest, "I've got a job for you."

"What is it?"

"After you get something to eat, I want you to go visit Charles. Find out what happened at the gathering."

"Sure. Should I take Miles?"

"No," he answered, glancing over at his youngest, "he needs to rest."

"Thanks," Miles sighed and slouched down in his chair.

Matthias laughed. "What have you been doing to him?"

Alistair shrugged. "I didn't do anything."

"Ha!" Miles guffawed, pulling the towel down over his head.

A low, subsonic tone began digging into Miles' ears like the bit of a drill. He sprang up and pulled the towel down off of his face. Matthias and Alistair too seemed effected by the sound. They squinted in obvious discomfort. It took only a second of exposure before his father and brother came to the same alarmed conclusion. They both dove to the floor and covered their heads with their hands and arms.

"Get down," his father screamed.

Miles rolled sideways and fell from the chair to the floor. A swirling wind filled the training hall. He scrambled toward the wall on his hands and knees, keeping his head down as lighter materials nearby took flight. Pressing his back into the wall, he yelled, "What the fuck's happening?"

"Tether vortex!"

Miles covered his head as one of his brother's books blew off the table and headed in his direction. The binding slammed into the wall just inches above him. When it landed on him, he peered through the gaps between his arms for more projectiles. The whole room threatened to come apart at the seams. Chairs and tables scraped across the floor, bookshelves teetered violently, dumping their contents, and the corners of the training mat peeled up from the wooden frame, kept in place only by the weight of the simulator pad.

Having never been on this end of a chronoshift before, Miles had no idea what to expect. The torrent of wind and the uncomfortable pulsations he remembered, but they never felt so intense before. Just then, the fabric of reality above the training mat transformed as though he was seeing it as a reflection in a funhouse mirror. It puckered in on itself, flexing and warping until the bent portions disappeared from sight and were replaced by an explosion of azure from within the emerging vortex. A flash of brilliance filled the training hall, drowning out the nanite light sources and all attempts to see. Miles spun around to bury his face in the corner where the wall and floor met. He held his eyes squeezed tight until the tempest subsided and a hush fell over the chamber. The next sounds he heard were those of rasping, wheezing breaths that he barely noticed over his own thunderous heartbeat.

Pushing himself up into a kneeling position, Miles surveyed the chamber for the unwelcomed visitor. In his periphery, he saw Matthias and Alistair rise from the floor with haste. Both men immediately went for their weapons; his father pulled a spare rapier from the weapon rack and his brother unsheathed his sword, tossing the scabbard aside. The idea that the intruder could be an enemy struck Miles as a possibility only after watching them scramble for weapons. He lunged on his knees for the table. With his fingertips he clamped onto the tip of the scabbard and pulled it off the table. Miles then drew his sword and hopped up onto his feet.

Matthias signaled in silence for Miles and Alistair to fan out across the near side of the room to search for the intruder. They did as they were told, moving with hesitant, calculated steps. Their heads and eyes shifted about with the predatory precision of a barn owl hunting for rodents at night. Miles, however, didn't see anyone. He halted and glanced back to his father and brother. The three of them exchanged confused shrugs.

Matthias shook his head, took a deep breath, and stepped around the end of the mat toward the bookshelves on the other side. Alistair appeared to follow his lead, tiptoeing up onto the edge of the raised mat, leaving Miles to venture around the other end. He paused just before losing sight of his father and brother. The aisle looked so narrow. If someone jumped out at him, Miles wasn't sure how well he'd handle fighting in such a confined space without his dagger. And it would take time for his father or brother to reach him if he got into trouble.

He gulped hard as he watched Matthias step out of view down the first aisle. Alistair, on the other hand, had reached the far side of the mat and leered with intent at two rows of shelves that had partially fallen in on one another. He seemed too consumed by his analysis of the fallen tomes to notice Miles' uneasy stares. Hoping that he wouldn't be the one to find whoever tethered there, he took careful steps down his aisle. The floor though was littered with toppled books and strewn papers. He tried not to step on any of them for fear that he might not only damage them but cause so loud a rustle as to alert any lurking nasties to his location. The task felt impossible. Then he took notice of a cluster of glowing nanites moving with alacrity at the very end of the row; they returned books to their original shelves faster than a teenage librarian on cocaine. Miles slowed in his pace, hoping the little buggers might move fast enough to clear the way before him.

"Guys!" Alistair cried out to Miles' rear. "Get over here!"

Miles spun about on the balls of his feet and sped back along the aisle. Seconds later he rounded the corner at the end of the row. He drew his rapier back over his left shoulder, poised to strike down the nearest threat. The scene, however, disarmed him; Alistair had laid aside his sword and was kneeling before a mound of toppled texts and dislodged shelving, throwing them aside haphazardly. Miles didn't understand the cause for such alarm at first blush. Then he noticed the limp human hand protruding from the pile. Someone lay buried beneath the rubble.

Alistair laid eyes on Miles and pleaded, "Help me!"

Miles flew to his side and slid along the floor to his knees. He immediately got to work helping to clear the pile away from whoever was trapped beneath. Though he didn't ask aloud, he wondered who it could have been. Before he could consider the possibilities, Miles slid a shelf off to the side and saw the lapel of a blue waistcoat with red edging. He knew it well. "It's Charles!" he burst out.

"I know," Alistair grunted with effort as he tried to push the shelving unit back up onto its feet from his knees. The ponderous load appeared to inexplicably lighten for him as it left his hands and settled upright once again.

With it clear of the fallen chronoshifter, Matthias stood on the other side of the bookshelves, having been the unseen force that helped lift it away. He moved toward them and hovered over Charles' feet. "Help me move him over to the mat," he told his sons.

While Alistair and Miles worked together to lift his upper body off the floor, Matthias took hold of his legs. With shuffling steps, they carried him over to the edge of the platform and laid him down with the utmost care. His clothes were torn and bloodied; numerous gashes and cuts marked his arms, legs, and torso. Most of them had stopped bleeding and began to scab over.

"Is he dead?" Miles asked, stepping back and looking over him. He didn't like standing so close to someone who might be dead.

Matthias checked his wrist for a pulse and then leaned down to listen to his chest. He shook his head and answered, "No, but his pulse and breathing are weak. Go get your mother. Tell her what happened."

Miles took off at a sprint. He raced through the underground tunnel, climbed back up into the basement, and ascended the stairs to find his mother sitting at the kitchen table eating her lunch. "Come quick!" He gasped to her as he tried to catch his breath.

"What's wrong?" Elizabeth asked with fearful urgency. She shot up from her chair.

"It's Charles," Miles answered, turning back to return to the basement. "He's hurt. Come on!"

Without saying another word, she followed Miles back through the bowels of the ranch and into the training hall where Alistair and Matthias had the med kit open and had begun dressing his wounds. She knelt down beside Charles.

"What happened?" she asked.

Matthias replied, "I don't know. He tethered here out of nowhere. We pulled this out of him." He handed his wife a small sliver of metal shaped like a nail file. A purple stain marked the part of the object that wasn't bathed in blood.

"What's that?" Miles asked.

Elizabeth looked at it up close under the light. "A shuriken of some kind." Sniffing the purple coating, she added, "Atropa Belladonna, I'd bet."

"Will he make it?" Matthias inquired with concern.

Elizabeth pulled close the med kit and removed a small, black penlight. "It hasn't killed him yet," she answered while peeling back one upper eyelid. She turned on the light and shined it into one eye and then the other. "It may take a day or so for the effects to wear off, but he should pull through. It must have been a paralytic dose—potent enough to immobilize him but watered down enough to avoid cardiac arrest."

"So whoever did this was trying to capture him, not kill him," Alistair concluded.

"That's my guess," his mother acceded.

"Wait!" Miles broke in, looking down on them. Something was on the tip of his tongue, an idea that he couldn't quite piece together, but he remembered the word that planted the seed. "You said it was a shuriken?"

Elizabeth glanced up at him and nodded.

"So you're talking about ninjas," he clarified.

"Most likely," she agreed.

Matthias squinted at his youngest. "What are you thinking, Miles?"

Miles hated being put on the spot. It made him hesitate for a moment, making sure his idea made sense before he embarrassed himself. Weakly he answered, "The gathering. Charles said it was going to be in Japan. Maybe you were right. Maybe he walked right into a trap."

"Maybe," Matthias concurred. "Alistair and I had discussed that while you were gone. The only thing is if the gathering was a trap, it wasn't what I expected."

"You mean the poison-tipped dart," Alistair concluded, drawing an invisible cord connecting the ideas.

"Precisely. I thought the traitors would try to wipe out the leadership and weaken the whole brotherhood, but they didn't. They wanted prisoners to interrogate. And there's only one reason to capture all the clan heads."

"Oh, my Lord!" Elizabeth gasped. "They're the only ones who know where the artifacts are hidden and how to break the ciphers."

"Well then shouldn't we do something?" Miles asked as he crouched down beside his mother.

"Like what?" Alistair snapped.

"I don't know," Miles admitted in frustration. "Check in with the other clans. Find out what happened."

Matthias shook his head. "It's too risky. The only one I trust outside this family is Charles, and he's of no use to us right now."

"So we have to wait until he wakes up before we can do anything?" Miles asked.

"Unfortunately," his father replied. "So until we find out what happened, no one comes and no one goes. We'll take shifts at watch through the night."

"And I'll stay down here and tend to Charles," Elizabeth volunteered. "We'll need to set up a cot for him to rest on and get some fluids into him."

"I'll take care of that," Alistair said as he jumped to action.

"What about me?" Miles asked. "What should I do?"

Matthias looked around the training hall. "Help your mother get settled down here and then clean up this mess. There's only so much the nanites can do."

While Elizabeth stood constant vigil over Charles, rarely taking a moment for herself, an odd, silent calm fell upon the rest of the Draven household. Alistair anesthetized himself against the boredom with his books. Matthias tended to the horses and checked in on his incapacitated friend. And Miles, alone with his thoughts, wandered the halls and grounds like a specter. Music could provide only a meager distraction from the dullness of waiting, so he eventually abandoned his mp3 player. The simulator was out of the question with the training hall being used as a hospital and studying chronoshifting theory would only bore him more. Everyone else had a place to go, something to do, or a way to make a difference in the interim. What Miles would have given for the feel of an old Genesis controller in his hands or some trashy reality television shows. The only time he felt useful was when it was his turn to take watch—a nerve-wracking, four-hour exploitation of his lack of experience and skill. What the Hell would he do if something went awry while the rest of the family slept? Luckily for him, his two shifts passed without incident.

Roughly forty-eight hours after Charles dropped half-dead into their midst, the chaotic ringing of a small, electronic buzzer sounded in the kitchen. Alistair sprang from the sofa and threw a window open. The clatter woke Miles from a restful nap in the wingback. He snapped awake with a fearful start and fell to the floor.

Alistair's voice bellowed out the window, "Dad! Get in here!"

Disoriented, Miles scrambled to his feet by clawing at the chair. He barked, "What's wrong?" Then the buzzing struck his eardrums. "What's that noise?"

"Come on!" Alistair answered, running past his brother and into the kitchen. "Mom needs us!"

Miles wobbled after his brother, still half-asleep. "Did Charles die?" he called out.

"I don't know!"

"Did he wake up?"

"Jesus, Miles, I don't know."

Miles passed into the kitchen and started shaking out the cobwebs when the kitchen door burst open. His father ran through the doorway. He took heaving breaths. Matthias had to have been in the stables again because his riding boots had an unpleasant sheen of horse manure on them. Smears of brown foulness painted the floorboards with each step. *I'm not cleaning up that shit*, Miles swore to himself.

Letting Matthias go ahead of him, Miles followed his father and Alistair down through the basement. It was a choice he immediately regretted when he descended into the secret passageway; he had to put his hands on the very same rungs where his father's boots stepped. It took all his concentration to not grab a handful of slurry on his way down.

After traversing the muddy tunnel, Miles entered the training hall. His attention focused on his family members. There were no tears, no melancholy faces. Everyone huddled around the makeshift hospital bed where Charles sat up, awake and sipping eagerly from a glass of water. The wall of the training hall acted as a headboard with several pillows supporting his back for comfort.

Charles pulled the glass from his lips and sighed. "How long was I out?" he asked Elizabeth who sat beside him. His voice sounded hoarse, parched.

"Two days," she answered.

He started coughing. "Two days? What the Hell did they do to me?"

"Poisoned you with nightshade," she answered. "It took a while for your metabolism to process the poison."

"Why didn't it kill me?"

"We're pretty sure they wanted to take you alive," Matthias added.

Charles flinched at the sound of his voice as though he had yet to notice him standing at his bedside.

Matthias reached out his hand to Charles who took hold of it weakly. "Just glad you got away."

"I barely got away. You were right, Matthias. The whole damn thing was a trap."

Miles lingered a few feet away from the foot of the cot, not wanting to get too close. The bloodied bandages made him cringe. Alistair, however, stood beside their mother.

Charles handed Elizabeth the glass. "Thank you."

"What happened?" Matthias asked as he settled himself into a chair beside the cot.

"I'm not sure." Charles groaned in pain with the effort of adjusting his injured body. "Only five Magisters attended the gathering, including me."

"Who?" Elizabeth inquired as she started to redress some of his wounds.

Charles hissed when the bloody gauze exposed a deep gash on his forearm. "Hiro Takashima, Mohaymen Ashfar, Gregor Platanov, and Dube Owusu. We all wanted answers. Hiro said that the absentees felt as you did—they thought the whole thing was folly. By God, it all happened so damn fast too. One minute we're discussing the treachery, the next we're overrun by hooded mercenaries."

"Ninja," Miles called out. He stepped closer to the foot of the bed.

Charles squinted at Miles. "Yes, Master Draven, if that's what they're called. They walked right out of the God damn shadows without making a sound."

"Was it Takashima?" Alistair asked.

"No." He shook his head emphatically. "Hiro was the first to fall. The rest of us did our best to fend them off while our tethers locked on."

"You tethered directly here?" Matthias asked, surprised.

"No. I'm old, not stupid," Charles complained. "I tethered home first and waited to see if anyone followed me. When I started getting the shakes bad and light headed, that's when I decided to come here. The poison explains why I couldn't think clearly though. Damn! I knew my wounds weren't bad enough to bleed out. I could hardly keep my wits long enough to activate that second tether."

"If they didn't come after you," Alistair surmised, "they must have gotten what they wanted from someone else."

"That's likely," Matthias said. "Now that I think about it, maybe the other Magisters didn't attend because they couldn't be reached or didn't want to. Maybe they were left out on purpose."

"But why us? What were they after?" Charles wondered aloud.

Miles answered, "Mom thought it might be the artifacts. Since they didn't have the diaries, maybe they'd torture the locations out of you."

"That's a pleasant thought," Charles concluded.

"Wait!" Matthias threw his head into his hands. "Oh, my God, I'm so stupid."

"What?" Elizabeth prodded, reaching across Charles to touch his hand.

Head still buried in his hands, he answered, "They're all on the clock."

The collective whole grunted, "Huh?"

"Mohaymen, Gregor, Dube," he paused and looked to Charles, "and you. You're growing old. You're the only ones that time has caught up to."

Charles droned with understanding, "Easy targets." He let his head fall back against the pillow and stared at the ceiling.

For a few moments, no one spoke. A dark cloud hung over them all. Miles had no idea what to say. Thankfully, his mother broke the silence.

"Should we do something? Try to help the other Magisters."

Matthias fell back against his chair, defeated. "Where would we even start to look?"

"You'd have to start in the present. That's where the gathering was held."

"Wait," Matthias sat forward abruptly and asked, "it wasn't in their time?"

Charles shrugged his shoulders dismissively. "No. Hiro didn't want to chance bringing any traitors into his home. He thought it was the safest place possible."

Matthias rolled his eyes. "Of course. It also happens to be where Gaius has power and influence." Matthias rocked back and forth in his chair, shaking his head. "I think we have to assume the Takashima clan's involved."

Elizabeth tilted her head and regarded her husband with doubtful eyes. "But what about Hiro? Why kill the head of their own clan?"

Matthias threw his arms up in surrender. "I don't know. Maybe he stood in the way. Maybe it was all just an elaborate hoax."

Charles cocked his eyebrows and snickered through his nostrils. "That's one convincing hoax. They cut him to pieces."

"Either way, their whole clan is suspect now."

"So what are we waiting for?" Alistair suggested with zeal.

"What are you suggesting?" his father inquired further.

Alistair answered with crispness, "Go to Edo. Take them out." He slammed one fist into his other palm for emphasis.

"How? There's no safe way to chronoshift there. And travel by land would take weeks."

"But we've done it before," Alistair objected. "Tether to the future, hop on a plane—"

"Just get the damn idea out of your head!" Matthias ordered sternly.

"Matthias!" Elizabeth protested.

"No. It'd be a death sentence to anyone who stepped foot on Japanese soil without the protection of a daimyo. I'd bet my life that's why they held the gathering there. The whole country's an isolationist state. A bunch of uninvited gai-jin sneaking around the capital city?" He snorted derisively. "They'd be executed on sight by samurai. We're going to have to find another way."

"You mean wait," Alistair said with a huff and stormed away from the bedside to the other side of the hall. He growled and slapped a glass of water off of the far table, sending it crashing into the wall in a spray of shards. Collapsing in a chair, he stared at the floor.

"We've no idea who's behind this, Alistair, and the Takashimas are public enemy number one!" Matthias rose from his chair. He sighed an angry breath at his son's attitude. "The only place we're safe is here. If you want a fight, sooner or later they'll bring it to us, and when they do we have to be ready. If we scatter, looking for trouble, we'll have to do it on their terms and then we won't stand a chance."

Alistair sat still as a statue, acting as though he didn't even hear his father.

Even though his brother wanted to jump into action, Miles found himself siding with his father. He did so mainly out of fear, but he did see his father's point. They had home field advantage if trouble came knocking. They knew the lay of the land and could set traps for any intruders. Venturing into territory that could be harboring an enemy or another clan set on defending their territory like the Dravens would likely prove to be disastrous.

Miles approached his brother with calculated steps, stopping a few feet away. "He's right."

"I know," Alistair responded under his breath so that only Miles could hear. "Fine," he barked back louder to his father and stood again. "Then let's get to work. I'm tired of sitting here waiting." Turning his back to them, Alistair disappeared into the passageway.

"Well I'm going to get out of your hair as soon as I can then," Charles offered. "I don't want to get in the way."

Elizabeth dismissed the notion with a wave of her hand. "Don't be silly, Charles. You won't get in the way. Besides, we could use your help."

"And we're the closest thing you have to a family. You should stay with us," Matthias suggested. "There's no reason for you to be on your own right now."

"Such kindness." Charles fell silent, appearing quite consumed by thought. He then flashed a sad grin. "But, I must decline. I have to go back, in case the children come home. I haven't given up on them yet."

"Nor should you." Matthias looked at Miles and shined him a proud smile. "I would do the same."

"At least promise you'll stay a few more days, until your wounds heal. You're in no condition to be chronoshifting." Elizabeth finished redressing the last of his wounds.

Charles examined the array of bandages that covered his wounds like a raggedy mummy. "Agreed."

CHAPTER FIFTEEN

The cargo area of the farm wagon provided a bumpy, painful ride for Miles. He felt every pebble and rut of the road in his ass. His father and brother, however, sat on the far more comfortable, spring-supported box seat at the front of the wagon. They barely even winced as the wagon jostled up and down and side to side.

Despite the discomfort of the ride, getting away from the ranch for a day made it tolerable. After being cooped up on the property for so many days—first waiting for Charles to awaken and then days of preparing defensive measures—they all needed to get some fresh air and a change of scenery. His mother had already gotten her vacay when she tethered back with Charles to make sure he could safely and comfortably finish his recovery. Now that she had returned, the men had their chance to escape.

They left just before dawn for the 17th Street Farmer's Market in Richmond. A dense fog mastered the countryside, enhancing the morning chill with a dampness that burrowed deep into Miles. He had to keep blowing hot breaths into his hands to keep his fingers from freezing solid. They hoped to sell the two horses they kept in tow to the Confederate States Army at the First Market House and then buy supplies with their earnings.

Miles remembered taking several trips to the Market in his first seventeen years of life, but none of them ever took this long. Those visitations all occurred in what Miles now knew as one distant, possible future where the trip would only take thirty minutes to an hour by car. But in 1863, it took four hours under the power of two oat-fed horses just to get a sniff of the outskirts of Richmond.

As the wagon's wheels took hold of the cobblestone streets, the painful bumps of the road became a constant, body-numbing vibration. Yet a new sense of wonder supplanted any physical discomfort the ride produced. He suddenly found himself immersed in a surreal vista that contradicted everything he ever knew of this historical city—aged brick buildings now stood newly mortared; women in ankle length, patterned skirts carried parasols; men in waistcoats, bowler hats, and trousers perused the avenues; horse drawn carriages of every kind rolled up and down the streets; and Confederate soldiers took a break from battle to enjoy the finer things in life.

Alone in the countryside with his family it was easier to overlook the odd clothing and lack of electricity in the lived-in portions of their home, especially with all the technology they had hidden away in the bunker. It was like playing pretend. But being in this thriving, colonial metropolis stripped away any pretense that the world he once knew simply waited for him behind a veil that he could throw aside whenever he pleased. Furthermore, it dashed the illusion created by tourist attractions like Colonial Williamsburg that he visited often as a kid. Sure, they had the right look, the right costumes, and actors who could pull off the ruse, but at the end of the day you still climbed into your car and drove home to the comforts of *modern* day. None of it was real.

Drawing near the marketplace, it wasn't what Miles remembered or what he had expected. His father told him that with the war raging through the countryside, only a few farmers participated in the open market, too fearful that passing soldiers might raid their precious crops. Yet the place still seemed to possess a healthy vigor. Plenty of merchants filled the marketplace to the point where patrons had to move with care and patience to navigate it successfully. In the *future*, the place never felt so busy. If this is what his father meant by *only a few farmers*, he'd hate to see it during a time of peace and prosperity.

The wagon rolled to a stop at the outskirts of the marketplace. Miles unlatched the rear gate and hopped down from the back of the wagon, landing flatfooted on the cobblestone. A jarring ache radiated up through his legs. He reached out and held onto the railing around the wagon for strength as he waited for the sensation to fade. Its recession left him keenly aware of how knotted up his body was from the ride.

Everything tingled in that pins and needles kind of way. *Ugh.* A primal urge to stretch spread outward from his core. He straightened his extremities to their limit and arched his back, reveling in the warmth of circulation breathing life back into strangled muscles and wiping away the nagging tingles. His spine popped like stepping on bubble wrap.

His father and brother stepped down from the box seat. Matthias walked past Miles to the two mares they brought for sale. Alistair came around the other side of the wagon and pulled two feed bags from the cargo area. He handed them to Miles and asked him to feed the horses. Miles took the bags of oats and proceeded to the front of the wagon without complaint. Having affixed them to each horse's muzzle, he affectionately rubbed Hiccup's crest while watching his father unhook the two other mares from the rear of the wagon. The horse grumbled with delight at his touch.

"Miles," his father called him over.

He adjusted his slouch hat by pulling up and then back down on the front brim, hooked his thumbs inside his trouser pockets, and then coolly sauntered to his father. He felt like Doc Holliday in *Tombstone*. Out of the corner of his eye he noticed Alistair staring at him and snickering under his breath. He did his best to ignore him. But when his father caught sight of him and cocked a perplexed eyebrow at Miles, all he wanted to do was crawl under a rock and hide.

"What was that supposed to be?" Matthias solicited in faux seriousness, unable to contain the rumble of laughter in his throat.

"My cowboy impression," Miles answered, feeling quite defeated.

Matthias and Alistair couldn't keep their mirth under wraps any longer. Alistair leaned against the wagon to keep from collapsing in all out laughter. His father laughed so hard he had tears in his eyes. He doubled over and put his hands on knees while he tried to catch his breath. Miles looked around the marketplace to see if people were watching. A few pair of curious onlookers paid mind to their outbursts. He added public embarrassment to his list of chief complaints against his family.

Nearly hyperventilating, Matthias walked over to Miles. It was a perfect imitation of his cowboy amble, which looked completely ridiculous from his point of view. He shot his father a pissy, sarcastic smirk.

"Cute," Miles declared flatly.

"Looks like you got a load in your drawers, boy!" Matthias retorted in the worst mockup of a southern accent he ever heard.

Alistair let out a hair-raising cackle and fell to the ground.

Miles shook his head, dead set on being angry and stern, but he couldn't resist. It was undeniably humorous. He laughed and said, "You guys suck."

The moment passed shortly thereafter. His father, in all seriousness this time, said, "I want you to stick to the market. Take a look around, but don't stray too far. I'll want to head back to the ranch as soon as our business is finished here."

Matthias handed Miles what looked like a ten dollar bill, but he had never seen one quite like it before. On one side it had a portrait of some bearded historical figure he didn't recognize, along with some of the classic calligraphy common on most currency. The backside, however, made his jaw drop. If there was any misunderstanding about what the confederacy stood for, the depiction of a colored man and two colored women picking cotton on the bill said it all. Upon closer inspection of the image, Miles noted how they all wore smiles on their faces. The immortalization of slavery on their currency as a symbol of their way of life was bad enough, but to make the slaves look happy was downright appalling.

"That's messed up."

"Don't worry," Matthias consoled him, "those things will be worthless in a matter of months. Once the North starts to win the war, they fall out of circulation. It'll take another hundred years before anyone cares about those. Kind of a collector's item."

"Still." Miles had difficulty letting it go, regardless of the events the coming months would bring.

"I know."

Miles found some comfort in his father's words. Though he never saw slaves on the ranch or felt comfortable enough to ask his family their position on the matter, it eased his mind. He felt reassured that his family, though operating in this time and place, did not agree with the same barbaric values their countrymen held so dear.

Matthias continued. "Anyway, get yourself a bite to eat or whatever that'll buy you. It changes every day. And try to remember everything I told you. Stay out of trouble."

"I know," Miles reassured him, nodding emphatically.

"Alistair!" his father shouted.

His brother jogged over. "Yes, Sir!"

"Go to Kline's Mercantile right away and get these supplies for your mother." Matthias handed Alistair a slip of paper with about twenty items listed on it and a bill fold. "Don't dawdle either. I don't want to leave your brother by himself for too long."

"I'll be fine," Miles countered, not pleased by the suggestion.

Before Miles knew it, Alistair and Matthias had taken off in different directions and he stood awash in history. He didn't know what to look at first. Taking the first tentative steps away from the wagon, he tried to keep a mental leash on it so that he didn't stray too far. The act left him feeling naked and exposed like a newborn. He didn't understand it completely or like it, but it kept him always looking around and on his toes.

Weaving around patrons, passersby, and vendors, Miles recalled the few times his foster parents dragged him there in the summer months. It was the last place he wanted to be. It all seemed so boring and simple. After all, why would a teenage boy care about fresh fruit and vegetables, handmade crafts, and secondhand items. Yet, something about living in this era made him take half an interest in it. Maybe it was because to him it was the past, history, but to these people it hadn't yet happened. Then to twist it all up and spit it out, none of it had happened yet. It was all so real, so amazingly tangible, yet it was all just a shadow of possibility. Miles breathed it in and enjoyed the thrill of it all.

It took a good half hour for Miles to make his way through most of the market. He saw some really interesting items, but nothing he wanted to waste his money on. From the far end of the market, he could still see the wagon. Neither Matthias nor Alistair had returned from their business. A sudden gurgling of his stomach keyed Miles into a pang of hunger he had been ignoring amidst his perusals, so he decided to spend some of his cash on the fare the food vendors had for sale.

Threading back through the market, he noticed that the stands that sold fresh food seemed thinly stocked. Likewise, the produce appeared to be of a poor quality. All the fruit and vegetables he remembered from his visitations were colorful and crisp. *Probably from all the chemicals and pesticides they used*, Miles concluded. Eventually, he doubled back a bit to visit a farmer whose wagon rested at the edge of the ring of market shops. He must have been in his mid-to-late forties judging by the strands of gray peeking through his dark hair and beard. And by the look of his threadbare clothes, he was a bit down on his luck. The provisions he sold lacked in variety and quantity: a few bushels of strawberries, cherries, green onions, radishes, and mushrooms. Those sparse items, however, excelled in quality; every piece seemed hand polished or carefully tended. Miles gladly turned over the asked price for a handful of juicy, perfectly ripe strawberries.

Heading back toward the wagon to wait for his father and brother to return, Miles popped one of the delicious berries into his mouth. Biting into it, a stream of juice ran down his chin onto his waistcoat.

"Son of a bitch," Miles muttered in frustration. He swiped at the drippings with the palm of his hand, creating a vertical smear. Newly tailored clothes and he had already stained them.

With a huff, Miles tugged down on the bottom of his vest and then threw a hasty hand through his hair which felt oddly wet. Examining the sleeve of his navy great coat he noticed some dark spots forming. He squinted up through the fog at an overcast sky. Cold raindrops pelted his face, which sent a chill through him. The misty air already had a nip of crispness to it, so the rain didn't help him keep warm. Miles pulled the coat closed over his clothes and buttoned it up to his neck.

Miles stared into the flow of bodies along the city sidewalks. He wondered what was keeping his brother. His father told Alistair to hurry back to the marketplace, but he had yet to return after nearly an hour. Miles tried to remember where his father sent him. *Oh, yeah! Kline's Mercantile.* Alistair had headed along Main toward 16th Street. It couldn't be that hard to find or that far away if he made his way by foot.

Though he remembered his father's warning about sticking to the marketplace, he didn't think it would be a problem if he wandered a block or two to look for his brother.

Miles pulled the wires of his earbuds from under his coat and nestled them into his ears. With a pop of his collar, the whole of the device lay discretely hidden from view. He reached into his trousers pocket and pressed play.

Having reached the corner of 16th and Main, Miles had yet to find Kline's. He felt a bit nervous about going any further and wondered if he should turn back. Turning about, the marketplace had yet to fall out of sight. So with trepidation, Miles continued on toward 15th Street.

After only a few steps, he decided that he didn't feel comfortable going any further. When Miles turned around to go back, a strange young woman crossed his path. It wasn't that she acted particularly strange that aroused his suspicion. She was simply different from the common citizens milling about the cobblestone streets. From head to toe, she dressed in a cut and style of clothes that didn't fit with the common look of the period, or any time period for that matter. From her black leather boots to her knee-length whimsical coat, this girl looked about as out of time as Miles felt. He stood watching her, mesmerized. Like a little kid drawn to the eerie chimes of an ice cream truck, he followed her without thought. *Who is she?*

Block after block he walked, trying to keep pace with her. The cautious voice of his father went silent in his mind, smothered by the allure of the chase. He grew agitated, though. While he could keep her in view, getting close enough for an encounter had escaped him. Following her around a bend, she suddenly disappeared.

Where'd she go? Miles wondered, having totally lost track of the mystery girl. The spell broken by losing sight of her, the silenced voice of warning returned with gusto.

"Where the Hell am I?" Miles grumbled. Swept up in the ebb and flow of Richmonders, he found himself lost in an uncomfortably foreign part of the city. "I'm in deep shit now."

A seedier atmosphere gripped this part of the city. The whole nature of the buildings and people reminded Miles of an old Jack the Ripper movie. Where the marketplace felt well maintained and clean, the stonework here appeared slick and grimy to the touch. Wooden shutters looked weathered and longed for care. Filthy windows guarded the likely lawless activities taking place within. Shadowy men lurked about the entrances of equally shadowy establishments, stealing wary glances at their surroundings. Women wore lascivious garments made of bright colored, silky fabrics and contrasting lace accents. The very air around them reeked of syphilis or worse. Miles tried not to lock eyes with a trio of such ladies whom he passed by. They lingered about a lamppost pining for tricks. He shied away from their suggestive gestures and advances, walking by with determination. They cackled at him like hyenas, but he soon left them far behind.

Miles came to a stop along the sidewalk and hopped up on a rickety wooden crate for a better vantage point. Up on his tiptoes, he surveyed his surroundings, but it was no use. Miles felt defeated. He stepped down from the wooden crate and kicked it aside. "Damn!"

A sudden awareness of time struck him. Miles pulled back on his sleeve to check his watch only to find a bare wrist. Following his mother's advice, he had left it on the bedside table and took the pocket watch that day. Irritated with himself, he pulled out the old world timepiece and opened it to learn just how long his excursion had taken. His father told him he'd be back by 9am and it was well after that. *Damn it!* Miles stuffed the watch back into his waistcoat pocket and turned on his heels to head back to the marketplace. With one foot on the cobblestone and the other airborne and mid step, a pair of strong hands strangled the lapel of his coat and yanked him into a dark alleyway. Disoriented and off balance, he had no defense as one of those hands brusquely smashed him against a wall of brick and pinned him where he stood. The addition of a cold blade across his throat had him paralyzed with fear.

The lone sliver of light that fell through the alley landed right in his eyes. The assailant stood an arm's length away, obscured from view. Though Miles couldn't see them, he feared that one of the sketchy characters he spotted on the street had designs on slitting his throat and raping his cold body. He wished he had spent more time in the simulator so there was some chance of fighting his way out of this disaster.

"Who are you?" a harsh yet distinctively female voice barked at Miles.

The sound was so unexpected, so disarming, that he relaxed a bit from his panicky state, despite the threat against him. Bewildered, he answered without first considering if he should. "Miles Draven. Who are you?"

The hand pinning him to the wall relaxed, and the blade against his throat pulled away enough for him to breathe without the sting of pain. His name must have made her question her tactics if only for a moment. She spoke again. "Don't worry about who I am. Just stop following me or next time you won't be so lucky!"

Stop following me? This was the young woman he had been following through Richmond! Judging by her actions, Miles suspected he might be right about her. "Are you a chronoshifter?" he asked with excitement.

In response, she slammed him back against the wall. Her face passed through the shaft of light. An aggressive scowl attempted, without success, to mask her beauty. He had no idea when he watched her at a distance that she could be so exquisite. Framed by a swirl of sable curls was an undeniable collection of facial features so soft and inviting that Miles felt a flame of ardor spark inside his chest. But that excitement extinguished like a match in a hurricane as she jerked him forward and drove a bony knee into his groin. He crumpled to the damp ground in utter anguish.

Curled up in a fetal position, Miles clutched at his throbbing testicles. A nauseating ache permeated his lower abdomen. Despite his agony, he attempted to keep his wavering eyesight locked on her should she decide to lay another blow on him. She did not, however, give him a second thought. Stepping over Miles and moving further into the dark alleyway, the young woman secured a chronoperpetua to her hand. Without adjusting the dials, she activated the tether and the vortex swallowed her up in a blue flash.

Eventually, the discomfort inside Miles calmed to a dull ache. Inch by inch he adjusted his body until he sat upright and leaned against the wall. Once the dizziness dissipated, he performed a careful self-examination of the tenderized flesh. He never forgot the story that Jimmy Allen loved to tell at lunch about how he ruptured his nuts cliff jumping into Abel Lake. It always gave him the chills. But this wasn't as simple as keeping his legs together when he jumped into a lake from really high up. Finally, Miles let out a full body sigh of relief.

"Thank God!" he groaned. She hadn't reduced his boys to paste.

The sound of clacking footfalls raced along the cobblestone sidewalk beyond the alley and then grated to a stop. They hurried back and splashed water on Miles from a nearby puddle.

He flinched away from the cold water. Disinterested in the pain that any quick movements might render, he turned his head slightly until the silhouette of a tall figure came into view. Its chest heaved from apparent exertion.

"Miles," Alistair's shaken voice called to him. "Are you okay?" He cautiously stepped toward him.

"Do I look okay?" Miles groaned.

"Not exactly. What the Hell happened?" Alistair held out both hands to help him up.

"I met a new friend." Miles let out a pained chuckle as his brother pulled him to his feet.

"What?"

"Another chronoshifter. The bitch tethered away after she kneed me in the balls. She's pretty hot though."

Alistair clamped his hands on Miles' shoulders and locked eyes with him. "What did she look like?" his brother inquired with deep concern.

"It's okay, I'll make it," Miles replied, carefully adjusting the crotch of his breeches. "You don't have to go kill her over this."

"It's not you that I'm worried about," Alistair retorted. "Describe her."

Miles shrugged his shoulders. "Dark, curly hair, about five-foot-four, and wearing all black. Why does it matter so much?"

A sudden, concerned look overcame his brother.

"You know her?" Miles asked.

"We need to find Dad, now!" Alistair barked. He grabbed Miles by the sleeve of his overcoat and dragged him out of the alley.

"Wha, why?" Miles stuttered while struggling to get his balance in difference to his brother's strength. Getting roughed up by everyone had gotten on his nerves. He swore that the next person who pushed him around was going to get their ass kicked.

"C'mon!" Alistair demanded. He took off at a jog and never looked back.

Miles followed along as best he could, despite the terrible ache that lingered in his groin. After several city blocks, his brother led him out of the seedy part of town and back to the marketplace where Matthias had returned from his business with the confederates. He had busied himself while he waited for his sons to return by packing up the wagon with newly purchased supplies. When Alistair and Miles arrived at his side, he expressed his displeasure.

"Where were you two?" Matthias howled in anger.

Miles glanced over at his brother, hoping he'd speak up first. To his surprise, Alistair appeared reluctant to talk. In their few days together, his brother struck him as being tough, ready to speak up and defend himself at any moment. But he seemed cowed by their father's anger. Since Miles never bit back his words when facing adversity before, he decided to answer back. When he did, though, his father cut him off.

"You," he pointed at Miles with a stern finger, "weren't supposed to leave the marketplace. And you," he redirected his ire at Alistair, "had a simple job to do. Get the supplies for your mother and get back here to babysit your brother."

"Hey," Miles interjected, feeling affronted, "I don't need a freakin babysitter."

"Really?" his father snapped at him and wrenched the headphones out of his ears.

"Oww!"

Matthias stuffed them down the collar of his son's overcoat and leaned close, whispering in a menacing tone. "Do you know what would happen if someone found you with those?"

Miles didn't answer. He pushed out his jaw and stared back at his father, very uncomfortable with his close proximity.

"Do you?" Matthias yelled.

Miles glared back and rasped, "No."

Matthias lowered his voice again, yet maintained his anger. "They'd lynch you for witchcraft and then come after the rest of us. That's what I meant about staying out of history's way. Don't you ever do anything so stupid again! Do you hear me?"

Miles recognized that his father held the higher ground; taking the mp3 player with him that morning was a dumb ass thing to do. He wondered why he still made such stupid decisions sometimes. He let his hateful stare fall away and replaced it with a shameful grimace. Staring at the ground, he answered resignedly, "Yes, sir."

"Now, where were you?" Matthias probed him further, but he did so with a measure of gentleness.

Miles returned his gaze to his father and noticed that Matthias was no longer in his face. Likewise, his father's change of tone was accompanied by a softer stare and posture. He felt safe to answer the question honestly. He said weakly, "I saw a girl." The moment the words left his lips, Miles knew it sounded childish and idiotic.

His father's boisterous, appalled laugh confirmed the ridiculousness of his answer. "You saw a girl? Are you kidding?"

"It wasn't like that," Miles pleaded, "I swear. There was something about her that seemed out of place. I only meant to follow her for a block or two, but before I knew it, I ended up lost in a really sketchy part of town. Then she beat the," he paused, trying to be mindful of his father's critique of his language in public places, "crap out of me and tethered away."

"A chronoshifter?" Matthias asked, his voice marked with concern. "Here?"

Alistair broke his silence. "That's what I asked Miles when I finally caught up with him."

"I don't get it," Miles interjected. "Why are you so concerned about another one of our kind being here?"

"Because this is *our* tangent, Miles," Matthias spoke with haste, "our responsibility. Everyone in the Order knows it. If another chronoshifter's here but avoiding us, they're either spying on us or worse." Matthias moved with haste to tie down the supplies he purchased at the market. "Get in the wagon. We need to get out of here."

Miles stood motionless, watching his brother silently assist their father in securing the goods. Without warning, the insinuation of his father's words sunk in and he cried out. "Wait a minute!"

Alistair shook his head and continued to work. Matthias, however, paused, looked to the sky as if to appeal to God for help, and rounded on Miles slowly. He held his arms out to the side in a gesture of vexation. "What, Miles? We really don't have time for this."

This time Miles drew closer to his father. "Do you really think she's the traitor?" Miles inquired in disbelief.

"Probably one of them," his father answered without hesitation.

Alistair added, "It makes sense, Miles."

"No, it doesn't! Look, she had me dead to rights. All she had to do was draw that knife across my throat and I'd be dead. But she didn't. When I told her my name, her whole demeanor changed. It was like she didn't expect to find me here. And right before she tethered she told me to stop following her and stay out of her way."

"I don't know," Matthias sounded doubtful.

"Don't you see?" Miles pleaded. "If she was one of the traitors, she wouldn't have given me a warning. She would've made damn sure that I didn't get away this time. I'm a loose end."

Matthias drew closer. He didn't seem angry. His voice sounded even more worried. "Are you absolutely sure that's what happened?"

Miles glanced at his brother and then back to his father. "Yes!"

Alistair came around to their side of the wagon. "It's Annelise," he revealed. "She must be tracking someone. Maybe a conspirator."

"Annelise Albright?" Matthias asked, astonished. "How do you know?"

"Miles described her perfectly."

Miles recalled the likeness of Annelise in the Albright family painting and did his best to compare it to the few glimpses he caught of the girl in the alleyway. They matched. "I thought she looked familiar.

So she's still alive?"

"Apparently," Alistair retorted.

"Dear, God!" Matthias gasped. A look of sheer terror gripped him. He moved with sudden haste, grabbing a long canvas bag and a knapsack he kept stowed on the wagon. He offered the backpack to Alistair who took it without question and strapped it to his back. Matthias threw his bag over his shoulder and pulled the strap tight against his body. Its contents clinked metallically. Putting his hand upon Miles' back, he attempted to usher him from the market. Alistair followed behind, keenly scanning the crowds as they walked.

"Where are we going?" Miles asked, confused.

His father answered, "We have to get home!"

"But the wagon is back there."

"It will take too long. We have to tether home, now!"

"Tether?" Miles stopped and turned to Matthias. "Why?"

"Miles, if you're right about Annelise and she's still loyal, then her only reason for being here, in this tangent, is because she's chasing someone. But my guess is she lost track of them. Whoever it is, they must've tethered here first. When they realized they were in Richmond, they tethered to the only other person who could lead them where they intended to go. Annelise must have made the same calculation when you said your name and tethered after them again."

Alistair, looking quite distraught, chimed in, "Home?" His eyes suddenly opened wide with terror. "Mom!"

"These traitors are working for Gaius," Matthias reminded them. "If they get their hands on the artifact diaries, it's just a matter of time before the bastard collects them all. I just hope we're not too late."

Matthias stopped along the sidewalk as the three of them passed in front of a narrow, empty alley. "We'll go one at a time. Try to make sure no one sees you. And tether directly to your mother. Be ready for anything when you come out of the vortex. We could land in the middle of a trap."

Both Miles and Alistair nodded. Matthias jogged down the corridor and moments later vanished into the vortex. Alistair motioned to Miles to go next.

"You go ahead of me. I'll make sure you're clear," he said as he patted Miles on the shoulder.

Miles puffed out a nervous breath.

"You can do this," Alistair pumped him up. "Believe in yourself."

He nodded back, trying to fill himself with that very belief his brother spoke of. Miles ducked into the alley and dug through his pocket for the chronoperpetua and his mother's anchor. Every nerve jittered. Fumbling about the mechanism with trembling fingers, he finally got the anchor snapped into place and the straps of the device secured around his hand and wrist. Having solo tethered only once before, the experience still scared him. His fear grew to new levels as this crossing might bring him face-to-face with life threatening danger yet again.

Regardless of his fear, Miles didn't want to let his family down. It was the first moment they were depending on him to step up and accept his birthright. Arm quaking, he brought it to bear before him and aimed the chronoperpetua into open space as his father taught him. He steadied his right arm with his left hand, averted his face, and hit the actuator. The beam exploded into the void, anchoring to its target. Before he could brace himself, the terminus wave arrived, and the vortex violently swallowed him up.

CHAPTER SIXTEEN

A static chronoshift, as they termed it, flashed by in a breathless moment. He likened it to a boulder being shot by a powerful catapult in a shallow parabola over the earth. When it hit it didn't dig into the dirt and stop. Its inertia propelled it forward until something got in its way. Miles was that boulder. Before he could brace for the draw of the tether, he had hit his destination, skidding and tumbling violently across the lush lawn of the ranch and sideways into a fencepost. His insides hurt beyond belief, but nothing felt broken.

The intense odor of burning wood and crackling timber sparked his numbed senses back to life. Black swirls of smoke billowed overhead, casting odd shadows across the ground. He scrambled across the dirt on rubbery arms and legs, trying to gain traction and right himself. His eyes wobbled in his head. When the image stabilized, a dreaded sight ripped his heart from his chest. The warm, comfortable home that represented every meaningful dream of his life lay under siege by the rending power of flame. Fire flares exploded through window panes, charring the surrounding wood. Smoke poured from every egress.

"Mom!" Miles screamed at the blaze, uncertain if she had gotten to safety. He stumbled toward the house. A few feet from the front porch stairs, the intensity of the heat made him retreat.

"Miles!" he heard his father calling for him. Shielding his face from the heat with his arm, Miles searched for Matthias. He found him kneeling beside something in the lawn. With sturdier steps, he jogged over to his father. His mother lay there unconscious. A small, bleeding cut on her forehead and a nasty bruise seemed to be her only injuries.

"Is she alright?" Miles implored over the roar of the fire.

"I think so," his father answered back.

The sudden thrum of an emerging chronovortex blared at Miles and Matthias. Both of them sought its source but couldn't find it. Quite a distance to their left, a fissure in the fabric of reality peeled open and coughed Alistair out. He too landed in an awkward heap that skidded more than rolled. Springing to his feet with great speed, he caught sight of Miles and Matthias and sprinted to them.

"What the Hell happened?" Alistair demanded.

Matthias replied, "I don't know. She was lying here when I emerged. Someone got her out."

The splintering snap of lumber thundered from the porch right before it collapsed upon itself. As a result of the structural failure, the second floor buckled and cindered hunks of studs and siding sprayed out across the grass. Matthias shielded Elizabeth with his body while Miles and Alistair averted their eyes from the expressed debris. Amidst the chaos, an odd, tortured sound mixed with the moaning desolation of their home.

"Do you hear that?" Miles cried out.

Matthias and Alistair both stared back at Miles with dumbfounded expressions. Then Alistair's face lit up with alarm.

"The horses!" he yelled.

"Go, go!" Matthias commanded them both.

Alistair took a strangle hold on Miles' coat lapel and dragged him into motion.

"What's wrong?" Miles yelled at his brother mid run.

"The stable's on fire," Alistair answered.

Miles followed hot on Alistair's tail. They passed dangerously close to the house as they ran around the left side. With the barn in sight, the brothers picked up the pace. Fire had engulfed the entire structure. The pained whinnies of the horses grew more distinct. Alistair stopped without warning and held out his arm to bar Miles from running past him. Miles slowed up and gasped at what he saw. A large swath of earth had sunken down several feet. The garden that had once flourished there had been reduced to overturned topsoil and hacked up bits of plants. It looked like a dirt salad.

"They detonated the training hall," Alistair concluded.

"Who?" Miles barked.

"Annelise. Whoever she's chasing. I don't know."

Alistair launched into an all-out sprint around the cave-in and toward the stable doors. He reeled back from the intense heat. Stripping off his overcoat, he dunked it in a rain-filled barrel beside the door. He slipped his arms part way into the sleeves and grabbed the searing hot iron handles. Steam billowed from contact. With brute force he pulled at the doors and they swung open. A flash of heat and flame blew through the doorway. Alistair dropped his coat and dove to the ground, rolling away. Flame took hold of the back of his trousers. He smacked at them with his hands. Miles ran past him, picked up the wet coat, and smothered his brother's legs, extinguishing the flames.

Following Alistair's lead, Miles dunked his coat into the barrel and pensively approached the entryway. Flame rolled out across the top of the door frame. Fiery tongues of red and yellow lapped across the entire interior of the stable. Through the iron bar windows of each stall, Miles saw the desperate inhabitants rearing up on their hind legs, kicking at the doors with their hooves, and calling out for help. He had to get in there and set them free.

Alistair moved up beside Miles, ready to enter. "Hold it over your head, like this," he yelled through the commotion, his coat covering his head as if to ward off rain. Ducking down to safely clear the flames, Alistair slid inside and headed toward the nearest stall. Using the damp coat as insulation against the intolerable heat, he slid open the door of the first stall. A horse charged out wildly, almost running the wrong way before it turned and galloped into the open air and safety.

"Come on, Miles!" Alistair howled at him.

Charging in, Miles headed for an occupied stall. It was Colossus. His massive hooves kicked at the door, knocking slats loose and splintering others. Miles opened the stall and got knocked back by the horse's charge. Its hindquarters were aflame. Colossus charged for the outside, but each clop of his hooves made the flames swell in size, covering more and more of his body. Miles got to his feet in a hurry but didn't know whether to help out his burning steed or free the others.

"Shit!" he snarled, and wrenched open the next stall door. The white mare within kept rearing up at Miles, refusing to leave. He screamed at it to get out but it just snorted back at him. Grabbing a nearby pitchfork, Miles slid it through the window and jabbed it into the horse's thigh, drawing blood. This time it got the message and ran for safety.

A loud cracking from overhead attracted his attention. The long beam that held the roof in place was nothing but a red hot cinder. Bits of it rained down on top of Miles and Alistair. The strain on it was too great. Alistair ran into Miles and pushed him toward the door.

"It's gonna collapse! Run!" Alistair screamed.

Miles pumped his arms and his legs, thundering toward the doorway. The roof gave way and a swell of heat swept down across him. He escaped the stable just before the entire structure collapsed. For a few moments they heard terrible cries of the horses they couldn't save, but they quickly faded out to silence. Miles fell to his hands and knees. Alistair stood hunched over.

"How many did we save?" Miles rasped, trying to catch his breath.

Alistair scanned the yard. Streaks of soot and ash covered his face. "Four."

"That's not even half."

"We're lucky we saved that many."

Alistair straightened up. "Miles," he said sadly. He took slow, lumbering steps past his brother toward a steaming form collapsed just over a small hill.

Miles sat back on his heels, watching his brother. "What?" He pushed himself up from the dirt and grass. The world spun around him. Alistair didn't answer. Taking a few deep breaths, he fought off the lightheadedness and made his way up the hill. There he laid eyes on his horse, Colossus, burnt and blistered on the ground. The poor creature just laid there taking short, wheezing breaths.

"What do we do?" Miles solemnly asked.

Alistair reached for his holstered LeMat revolver. "End his suffering." He took aim at Colossus' head and drew back the hammer with his thumb.

"Wait," Miles said, laying his hand on Alistair's arm. "He's mine. I should be the one to do it."

"Are you sure?"

Miles frowned and nodded. "Yeah, I'm sure."

Alistair took hold of the barrel and extended the revolver to his brother. Miles grabbed the wooden handle and slid his index finger into the trigger guard. With a trembling hand, he took aim at the back of Colossus' head. The horse strained to turn its head and look up at Miles. He saw the pain in those deep, dark eyes that stared at him. The horse snorted, laid its head back down, and closed its eyelids. Just as he was taught, Miles gave the trigger a steady squeeze. He looked away just as the hammer struck the firing pin, sending Colossus to his eternal rest. The lonely report of the fired round echoed through the countryside.

Miles handed the LeMat back to his brother and walked away.

Every part of the ranch lay decimated—an ashen shadow of its former self. The fires had died off to glowing cinders and smoke. Though they lost their home, the Draven family outwardly expressed their thanks that, aside from the deceased horses, their losses weren't graver.

Elizabeth, who awoke shortly after the collapse of the stables, sat on a splintered bench pulled from the wreckage of the garden. She held a wet, bloodied cloth to her wounded forehead. Matthias stood close by, monitoring her for concussion symptoms or other possible problems. He held another damp rag for her.

Alistair knelt before them, laying out a tarp across the dirt. Upon it he laid a few supplies that he scavenged from the property along with the contents of the two bags his father stowed upon the wagon.

Miles stood awash with grief and anger. He picked stones out of the loose dirt and slung them at the smoldering remains of the home he had grown to love in the past few weeks. The ranch represented a fresh start for him and the realization of his life's search for meaning and identity. Though he still attained those dreams, the loss of the material representation of those hopes stung nonetheless. Yet a deeper and far more painful kind of loss disturbed him in a more profound manner; it was the death of Colossus. Not that he didn't mourn the loss of his foster mother, father, and brother, but the raw emotions that he felt at having to put Colossus down could not be measured. The poor thing had no idea what had happened to it, nor did it deserve to die that way. Miles had only worked with him a handful of times, but a bond had formed. And to put a bullet in Colossus' head to end its suffering filled him with grief.

"Were we able to salvage anything?" Matthias asked his eldest son.

Alistair squinted up at his father. "Aside from our main weapons?"

"Yes."

Alistair shook his head in clear frustration. "Not much. They burned everything down. They even dropped hand grenades into our concealed storage lockers. All I could scrounge up were a few empty clips." He picked one up from off the tarp and slung it across the ground like a dealt playing card. It bounced along the dirt. "Even those are banged up. Whoever did this knew exactly how to hurt us."

Matthias knelt down beside his wife and asked, "Lizzie, what happened?"

Elizabeth pulled the cloth from her head. Only a small splotch of blood was visible. The bleeding had nearly stopped; no doubt the work of the nanites. Offering the makeshift bandage to her husband, he took it from her and handed over the clean one. She pressed it to her head, shrugged, and answered, "I don't know. I'd just come downstairs with an armful of bedding to wash. When I reached the foyer, I noticed that the front door had been left open. I thought you might've come home early, so I called out for you, but no one answered. Then I shut the door and went about my business. When I entered the kitchen, a dark shape passed in front of me. Before I could react, something hard hit my head. That's all I remember."

"Was it Annelise?" Miles inquired. He chucked a stone at the collapsed, smoldering structure that was their house. It collided with the last intact window pane. The glass shattered and fell from the compromised frame. "We know she came here."

"I don't know," Alistair confessed. "If her goal was to come do this," he glanced at the decimated house, "then I don't think she would've hung out in Richmond long enough for you to find her. She would have left the moment she realized she wasn't at the ranch. You yourself said she seemed surprised by who you were and then tethered right after. It's possible she had no idea why she was there until that moment."

"Well if you're right," Miles pondered, "then who was she chasing?"

"And why did they come here?" Matthias countered, rising from his crouching position. "Was it to disrupt our activities or something more?"

Elizabeth gasped. "The diary! Maybe they were after the artifact diary!" She stood up quickly. Her knees wobbled and she collapsed back down on the bench, holding her head as she swooned.

Matthias rushed to her and stabilized her with his strong hands. "I moved it after the robbery, remember? They missed it when they came for Miles' anchor. I wasn't about to leave it lying around."

Elizabeth nodded with her eyes shut. "I'm okay." She waved off his hands. "I just got up too fast."

"How are you going to tether in your condition?" Alistair asked and began packing the gathered supplies back into the two bags. "You're in no shape to chronoshift."

Miles broke his gaze from the ruins to look upon his family.

"Just give me a few minutes," Elizabeth snapped back, seeming quite irritated. "I'll be fine." Opening her eyes, she slowly stood up from the bench. With her legs sturdy beneath her, she concluded, "See, I'm fine." She stumbled ever so slightly. When Matthias flinched she shot him a dismissive glare. He backed off immediately.

"Where are we going?" Miles asked.

"Back to Charles'," Matthias answered, reaching down to take one of the two repacked bags from Alistair. "He's got plenty of space and could use our help."

"Come on," Alistair urged Miles, "this place has had it. Time to move on."

Miles couldn't believe what he was hearing. By all accounts, this had been their home for a long time. *How could they just walk away so easily? No hope or want to rebuild?* He had grown so attached to the new home he didn't want to let it go, and he hadn't lived there that long. Miles always hoped that finding his family would mean stability, security. At the very least a house that he could call his own, one he didn't have to fear losing when the family got tired of him. Fires happen, he knew that, but this was no accident. His parents' words echoed to him; they didn't interfere in his troubles for the last seventeen years in order to make him stronger, to prepare him for what life would be like as a chronoshifter. If always being on the move and never having a stable home was part of the deal, he wanted no part of it. He had his fill of that back in 2016. His frustration boiled over. "Isn't this bothering anyone beside me?" he yelled.

Everyone looked taken aback by his outburst.

"So this is how it is? We just watch everything burn to the ground and then walk away?"

"Miles," Elizabeth said with concern and stepped toward him, "we can never rebuild what we had here. It was a beautiful home, but we have to go."

"But it was my home," he cried, "the first real home I've had. I've spent my whole life saying goodbye. I don't want to do it again."

Alistair, being quite matter-of-fact, interjected, "It's just a house. There'll be others."

"I don't want there to be any others. It may be easy for you to see horses die and your home burn to the ground, but it isn't for me. This was supposed to be a new beginning for me, but it feels like the same old bullshit."

"Son, we didn't have a lot of time left here anyway," Matthias explained. "Think about it. We've been here a while. Too long, in fact. Sooner or later people were going to realize that we don't age. Then we'd have no choice but to move on. What happened here today, as bad as it may seem, is a lot easier than walking away by choice. You're right, though. None of this is easy. But we still have each other, and as long as we're together we can find another home in another time where we can be a family. Please try to understand, Miles. It really is for the best."

"Whatever," he snapped back. Miles couldn't even look his father in the eye. All the logic and reasoning in the world at that moment wouldn't have made any sense to him. This was a matter of the heart, of emotion, and the cold resignation needed to walk away escaped him. He strapped his chronoperpetua to his hand with sharp, angry movements. Slapping Charles' anchor into place, he stared indirectly at his parents and brother and barked, "Let's go."

CHAPTER SEVENTEEN

The aggressive rapping of knuckles against the main entryway reverberated through the foyer. Each distinct crack hit Charles' eardrums like an electric shock, rousing him from his siesta on the settee. His eyes peeled open like creaky doors on rusted hinges. A great smudge across his field of view distorted the great room. With a groan of intense effort, he pushed himself up off the settee and heard the knocking again. After rubbing the fatigue from his eyes, he drowsily reached for his walking cane and pulled the handhold free of the main shaft to reveal the narrow blade within.

"Assassins don't usually knock," Charles mumbled to himself. "But just in case." He shoved the concealed pig sticker back into its sheath and attempted to straighten his wrinkled garments. No amount of pulling or pressing could flatten the creases. "Bah!" he growled.

Though he could walk fine without the assistance of his cane, the deception of being infirm gave him a distinct advantage against anyone who dared try to exploit his faux frailty. His joints constantly ached and he lacked the strength and vigor of youth, but should the need be called upon, he could will forth the centurion for one last battle. It was a battle he anticipated coming soon. He only wished the traitorous rogues would have the common decency to confront him on a full belly and a good night's sleep, neither of which he had in recent days. Too many questions kept him awake at night, not to mention the lingering pain of his battle scars. What had become of his children? Would he see them again before he took his last breath?

Charles took hold of the massive doorknob and twisted it. When the latch clicked, a silent, betraying hope manifested in his mind—*please be Annelise or Trevor*. Pulling the door ajar, he peered through the gap to find a sight more unexpected than if fate had fulfilled his greatest hope. Before him in the vestibule, covered in soot and dirt, stood the whole of the Draven clan. Matthias stared at the ground and then locked eyes with Charles. A duffel lay strapped across his back, with another smaller bag clutched in his fist. Elizabeth leaned against him, looking woozy with her head resting on his shoulder. The remnants of a painful gash marked her forehead. Behind them, Miles brooded against the inner wall of the archway. Alistair, conversely, had his back to them all, sword drawn and alert, scanning the landscape. He too carried a heavy duffel. The whole situation stunk of trouble.

Charles gawked, speechless at them while trying to make sense of their presence. Then he found his voice. "What in God's name?"

"We need to talk," Matthias said. "Something's happened."

"Evidently!" Charles stepped aside and gestured to them to come inside with brisk waves of his hand. "Well, come in, come in."

"Thank you," Elizabeth said faintly as she crossed the threshold with her husband's help.

"Are you all right, my dear?" Charles solicited with gentleness, taking her other arm in his for extra support.

"I'll be fine. I just need to rest," she answered with forced confidence.

Miles entered just ahead of Alistair who shut the door and keyed the lock behind him. He sheathed his rapier and let his bag fall to the floor with a clatter.

"Was there a fire?" Charles looked from face to face for an answer.

"A fire," Miles snorted sarcastically. Alistair backhanded him across the chest.

Matthias settled Elizabeth into a claw-footed chair in the foyer with great care. He explained, "We lost the whole ranch. They razed it to the ground."

"Wait. What do you mean 'they'? It wasn't an accident?"

"No."

"Then they came for you," Charles surmised. A sobering reality sank in; capturing the Magisters had either fulfilled its purpose or failed completely, leaving them no other choice but to go on the offensive.

The conspirators had taken the next step. The dark clouds that lingered in the distance had gathered around them, smothering the light.

"That's what we need to talk about," Matthias said. He knelt beside Elizabeth and offered her a drink from his canteen. When she leaned forward to sip from it, she swooned forward in her chair. Matthias grunted and wrapped his arms around her, holding her up. Both brothers moved in to help.

Though Charles had his suspicions that this "talk" might shed some light on the fate of his children, it had to wait. "Let's get her into bed to rest and find a place for everyone else. Then we can have our little talk over some brandy."

The crackling fire within the stone hearth filled the great room with warmth. To his rear, Charles heard the last of the Dravens join them. He glanced over his shoulder to see Miles, who had finally unpacked his few belongings in one of the guest rooms, settle down on the settee beside his father.

Charles tapped the top of the crystal brandy decanter against the rim of an empty sniffer with a clink. The soothing, warm elixir filled the glass to half. With the stopper back in place, he picked up two drinks, pivoted on his heels, and gimped over to where they were all seated.

"Miles?" Charles slid in beside Alistair and extended the youngster a glass of brandy.

"But I'm only seventeen." Miles looked to his father for approval. Matthias just shrugged back. He took the glass from Charles' hand and held it awkwardly.

"And you're in seventeenth century England," Charles countered and struck the bowl of his sniffer against Miles'. "Drink up!"

Miles took a whiff of the brandy and grimaced. Placing the glass to pensive lips, he sipped at the amber spirit, swallowed hard, and coughed. "Jesus!" he gagged.

Charles let out a muted laugh, unable to stir true merriment within himself knowing that his friends just lost everything they owned. He looked at each of them. Alistair leaned forward, elbows on knees, hypnotized by the brandy he swirled in his glass. Matthias sat back against the cushions, legs crossed, and sipped at his drink. He too held a blank stare, just looking off into nothingness while his mind likely delved into dark possibilities. Miles might vomit, he couldn't tell. The liquor probably was a bad idea.

Charles moved his head to engage Matthias' gaze. His friend's face flickered to life. "So talk."

"She's alive, Charles." Matthias didn't smile or react much as the words left his lips. With a great gulp he knocked back the rest of his glass.

A torrent of emotion swelled inside Charles like a storm surge. He leaned forward, clasped his shaking hands together over his mouth and nose, and closed his eyes. Tears spilled down his cheeks. "Thank the Lord," he whispered. He opened his eyes and wiped away the wetness with the heels of his palms. An uncontrollable smile pulled at the corners of his mouth. The muscles in his face hurt from lack of use for so long. "Is she all right?"

Matthias leaned against the arm of the settee and stroked at his chin with his hand. His eyes shifted with uncertainty. Shrugging and shaking his head, he answered with sadness, "I don't know."

Charles took umbrage with his answer. "What do you mean you don't know? You saw her. Someone did." His head flicked nervously from one guest to another. "I want answers."

"Just take it easy," Matthias cautioned his friend. "It isn't so simple. There's more to it than rainbows and butterflies."

"I don't give a damn what it is," Charles countered in anger. "My daughter's alive. That's all that matters to me right now." He glowered at his friend. "Where is she?"

Alistair interjected, "We don't know." He laid his glass down on the end table. "Miles was the only one to actually see her."

"Then how do you know it was my Annelise?"

Alistair explained, "His description of her was spot on. Right down to her spirited nature." He cracked a sarcastic smile.

Charles shifted his penetrating stare to Miles. "You saw her?" he asked.

Miles nodded. "Yes, sir."

"What happened?" Charles pleaded.

Miles took another swig of the brandy, more confident and determined this time. He didn't even cough. He then recounted his run-in with Annelise to Charles, who listened intently. Everything Miles said, from her seeming disoriented to her quick exit after meeting him, told Charles that she was hunting someone. She had a side to her personality that would not let her drop something that she felt mattered, regardless of what anyone else felt. It kept her at odds with Abigail and himself for years after they rescued her from the Gestapo but failed to save her shadow family. After many years she finally let go of it, having fully understood the nature of time and that there was nothing they could have done to save them. So, whatever she had been searching for now, whomever she had been hunting, the task had taken hold of her and possessed her soul. She would not resurface until she found what she sought.

"She's after someone," Charles declared. "There's no other reason for her to be in *your* time and in such close proximity."

"It's possible," Matthias conjectured. "We can't think of any other reason she would have wandered around Richmond for so long if her intended target was the ranch. She would have immediately tethered to another family member if that was the case. It's more likely that she's chasing the conspirators rather than one of them."

"So then she's still on our side," Charles affirmed. "The only question then is who's she chasing?"

"I hate to suggest it, Charles, but you said Trevor disappeared first and then she went out looking for him. Maybe," Matthias paused. He then offered sadly, "She's trying to avenge him."

The very insinuation caused a flood of desperation that threatened to rob Charles of his composure. "I'm not willing to entertain that option yet. She's the only one who knows for sure what happened to Trevor. Until I hear it from her lips, my son's still alive."

"Fine. So we've got to go find her," Matthias concluded.

"How?" Charles cried. "They stole all of my anchors."

"What about her belongings, her room?"

Charles shot up from the settee. He answered with vehemence, "I've tried. It's been scoured clean, just like I taught her. Just like we were all taught. She didn't leave anything behind to put in an anchor." He snorted his frustration then turned away, staring into the fire. "Our only hope is that she comes to us."

"Yeah, before they do," Alistair suggested and finished his brandy.

His words gave Charles pause. He turned around and stared at him with an uncomfortable glance. Miles and Matthias gave him similar expressions. They hardly had the manpower to fight back: two able-bodied fighters, two injured badly enough to make them a liability, and one incredibly green sapling. Before they showed up at his door, Charles only had to worry about himself and in many ways welcomed death at the hands of another man or woman with keen mettle. He had made all the calculations, thought about all the scenarios by which he might lose his life and had resigned himself to the inevitable. His equations, however, never took into account the lives of others he held dear. Things suddenly became far more complicated than he wanted.

Matthias stood up and faced his friend. "Then we wait for her. And if they come for us, we make our stand together." He held out his hand to Charles who took it without thought.

"There's no one I'd rather go into battle with, my friend." He pulled Matthias into him with a brutish tug on his hand and gave him a manly slap hug.

Pulling back from the embrace Matthias looked to his sons. "We've got work to do."

CHAPTER EIGHTEEN

Miles snapped awake and immediately freaked. He didn't recognize where he was. It was the same kind of panic he felt whenever he moved in with a new foster family. He'd forget where he went to sleep and would wake up all disoriented. Then it slowly dribbled back to him— *Charles' house*. After a hearty dinner and one too many brandies, he crashed on the settee in the great room. Sitting up, he scratched at the backs of his arms. The course fabric left imprints on his skin that itched.

As he sat there, Miles noticed an irritating harmonic pulse drilling into his eardrums. The sensation was one he was newly acquainted with—the sound of a chronovortex. *Who the Hell's tethering?* As far as he knew, everyone was accounted for and asleep.

Miles reached for the hurricane lamp on the end table beside him and turned the dial on the oil burner until a sallow, weak glow illuminated the great room. He scanned his surroundings, pivoting his languid torso left and right because his stiff neck protested too vehemently. Nothing seemed amiss. The bizarre humming then dropped off as suddenly as it began.

You're imagining things. He grunted dismissively, adjusted his hips, and laid back down to try sleeping again. Just as his shoulders met the cushion, a loud clatter came from down the hallway. He rolled off the couch, landing with a thud, and scrambled to his feet. Miles instinctively grabbed for the nearest weapon to defend himself. He stood glaring at the entryway to the great room. His chest heaved, amped up on an overabundance of adrenaline, while he stood in a defensive posture in anticipation of something dangerous coming after him. Miles then glimpsed the odd and futile weapon he clutched tightly in his right hand. Unless a myriad of pajama clad, teenage girls came to fight him, a frilly throw pillow would be of little use.

Floor boards creaked and voices whispered out in the hall. They drew closer as each second passed. A terrible mixture of excitement and anxiety consumed his mind. Miles found himself lost in fearful memories: the horrible image of his foster father lying dead in a pool of blood, sprinting down a wet sidewalk under the glow of streetlights, and the explosive report of gunfire in his ears jolting his nervous system. With a forceful yank, he drew himself out of his catatonic state and shook it off.

"Coward," he whispered to himself angrily. That wasn't the kind of productive fear his father told him about. Miles grunted and slung the throw pillow at the couch. He tried to remember where he laid his rapier and dagger, but the jitteriness of his body made it difficult to focus. Scanning the room, he caught a subtle glint of silver and emeralds from under the front edge of the settee—the knuckle guard and pommel of his sword. With haste, Miles dropped to one knee and reached for it with his right hand. Keeping his gaze warily set upon the archway, he groped along the guard, past the quillion and loop until his fingertips found the leather of the two scabbards and belts wrapped around them. He drew them out into the open and unsheathed both weapons.

Miles rose to his feet and took several deep breaths to try to calm his nerves. It did little to allay his condition. The thundering of his pulse and the tremors moving through his body brought further frustration. He remembered being told that fear could be his ally if he learned to master it. But the master at that moment was the fear. From that failure to take control, a fierce maelstrom of wrath gathered inside him. Surrendering to the beast inside had always been an easy and dangerously intoxicating solution when things didn't go his way. But too many times before, it blinded him to the damage that he caused until it was too late. It was how he always imagined how Dr. Banner felt when he became the Hulk. A field of waste and destruction left in his wake when the green skinned monster took over.

A powerful sense of self-awareness came to Miles in that moment. The possibility of coming face-to-face with a life or death situation was too important to subjugate his will to blind rage. Calling his own bluff, Miles chose to master the one part of himself that he refused to control in the past. With every ounce of will he could rally to his cause, he slammed shut the cage door that threatened to let the beast escape. That decision brought a sudden surge of power racing through his body. An invigorating tingle rose from deep within that helped calm the nerves that his fear had teased into a frenzy. He could still think, and he could still control himself. *Maybe that's what Dad meant*, he pondered. *I'm still pissed, but I'm focused. I need to learn to do that with my fear.*

Savoring his small personal victory, Miles forgot about his fear for the moment and readied himself for battle. He craned his neck left and right, popping several vertebrae, and settled into a comfortable fighting stance. The rapier he held angled out and away from his midsection, just as his father taught him—set to parry an oncoming attack. Its companion dagger he gripped tightly in his right hand, drawn back and ready to deliver a deadly thrust. Breathing deeply, Miles took a tentative first step toward the doorway with his left foot, followed by a crossing step with his right. More whispers and queer sounds filled the hallway. He snapped back with silent epithets against the craven thoughts that threatened to stop him. Footfall after footfall, he closed in on the archway until he could stab into the darkness beyond with his rapier.

Miles pressed himself close to the wall and tried to gather his courage. A nearby floorboard beyond his line of sight let out an eerie creek, counteracting his efforts at self-control. His pulse thundered in his ears like a hundred galloping horses, and the levels of adrenaline swirling in his bloodstream made his tremors more pronounced. The grips of his dagger and rapier were damp and slick from sweat; he flexed and wriggled his fingers to get a better grip.

Four figures sprang from the darkness into the great room, all brandishing swords. Miles felt his heart stutter in shock. He stumbled back a step or two but held his weapons strong. The fight or flight instinct kicked in. He stepped forward to parry the outstretched rapier of the nearest assailant and take their life with his dagger. But as blade met blade, a leather-clad hand reached for his thrusting dagger's cutting edge and redirected it with a firm grip. Miles pulled back, trying to free his weapon, but it remained immobilized.

"Miles!" the figure rasped at him.

The voice was familiar. Miles squinted. It took a moment or two to process the man's face through the haze of his anxiety-addled eyes and the dim lighting. Then the tumblers of his mind clicked into place.

"Jesus Christ, Dad!" Miles cursed hoarsely at his father and pushed back against his arresting grip. "Are you trying to give me a heart attack?" He noticed that his father had carelessly thrown on his clothes from the previous day. His shirt hung partially unbuttoned with half of its tail hanging from the waist of his trousers. His suspenders lay twisted over his shoulders. He had been awakened into a state of alarm too.

As the other armed intruders moved around the room, their identities became clear: Elizabeth, Alistair, and Charles. His mother and brother had the same disheveled state of dress as Matthias. She moved with delicate speed to the rightmost window and peeled back the edge of the curtain to look out onto the courtyard and gardens below. There seemed to be no lingering effects of her head injury. Alistair lingered close by their father, listening intently while keeping his eyes trained on the hallway. Charles, on the other hand, stood sentry by the door, poised to strike anything or anyone that approached. He awkwardly wore his sword belt and side arm holster secured over his nightgown.

"Was that you?" Matthias whispered.

"Was what me?" Miles countered.

"The tether wake?"

"No," he responded with subdued outrage. "Why would I be tethering at this hour? I thought *I* was imagining it. That wasn't you banging around in the library?"

"The library?" Charles shuffled close.

"Yeah, just down the hall. At least it sounded like it."

"The diary," Charles declared. "It's kept in the adjoining study."

Matthias made a hissing sound with the back of his throat which attracted everyone's attention. Elizabeth crossed the room and stood nearby.

"Charles, you and I'll take point. Liz, you stay with Miles to our rear. Alistair, you cover our backs. Remember, whoever you see in there isn't a friend, not anymore. They're our enemies. Show them no quarter and protect the diary at all costs."

Normally, Miles might have been put off by the suggestion that he needed protection. In this case, however, he knew better than to argue. He could barely handle one-on-one combat against the simulator let alone a skilled warrior who wanted to skewer him like a kabob. Putting him on the front line of defense served no one's best interests that night. He could think of no greater comfort in his situation than being surrounded by four seasoned warriors who had his back should his own skills fail him.

Everyone nodded and fell into place. Matthias pulled a small penlight from his trousers' pocket, clicked it on, and wedged it into the quillion of his rapier. Then he followed Charles into the darkened hallway, the tip of the blade pointed at the ground before them. Miles tried to follow right after them, but his mother put the back of her hand against his chest. She too produced a similar flashlight. After a few seconds, she lifted her hand and the two of them passed into the darkness. Miles could see a faint silhouette of his father and Charles about ten feet ahead of him, moving with great care. The sound of Alistair's bare feet padding against the hallway carpet behind them completed their defensive formation.

A hollow, metallic clang brought everyone to a sudden, heart pounding halt. His father and Charles stood only feet from the archway of the library. The definitive sounds of rustling papers and whispering voices filtered into the corridor. His mother and father extinguished their lights, casting them all into darkness. From the archway, a soft glow ebbed and flowed from within. There were indeed invaders in Charles' home. They all waited in silence for Matthias' signal to rush forward.

Miles couldn't control the shaking of his hands as he waited. The fear, the nervousness threatened to boil over into a form of paralysis. For the moment, the darkness kept his weakness hidden from view. He hoped that the order to charge would not expose him as a coward.

With a suddenness Miles never expected, his father and Charles rushed forward into the library, weapons brought to bear. Elizabeth took off after them, all the while maintaining a firm grip on Miles to keep him safely by her side. Weakness settled into his knees. Both legs wobbled beneath him like sticks of Jell-O. Passing through the archway, he bore witness to a field of literary carnage; half the shelves of the library were stripped bare. Their collective texts lay scattered and strewn across the floor. Two wall-mounted candelabras provided weak, flickering light that threw strange shadows across the chamber.

Amidst the ruptured spines, severed covers, and torn pages stood a pair of cloaked intruders who brandished their gleaming blades in defensive, threatening postures. The frightening reality of a life or death struggle punched Miles in the gut. It stripped away all of his courage and left him a quivering mass. His trembling hands could not be steadied. No amount of wiping could swab away the sweat amassing in his palms. His mouth ran dry. Though his father, mother, and Charles stood between him and the rending blades of their enemies, Miles felt naked and alone against a tide of evil. He wanted to crawl up into a ball and cry, but he saw nowhere safe to cower. The lone hope for salvation was that his family surrounded him. They stood as a makeshift defensive wall that Miles stood behind. *They won't let me get hurt*, he told himself.

"What are you doing in my home?" Charles growled at the two intruders.

No answer was forthcoming. They held their ground as though waiting for a signal. From the adjoining study, a third figure moved out from the shadows. Their identities lay concealed beneath their draping cowls.

"You know damn well what we're here for, Charles." The voice sounded male, quite young. From beneath the folds of his cloak, the intruder pulled out a small, leather bound journal. "And now that we have it, we'll be on our way."

"Like Hell you will," Matthias barked. "Hand over the artifact diary. You're outnumbered and overmatched."

"And if I don't?" he rasped back, tucking the journal back into his cloak.

"We'll send what's left of you back to your master," Charles explained.

A cold cackle came from the intruder. "I don't think so. Who's going to stop us? A hobbled old man? The three of you with the whelp in tow? Too many hindrances to put up a good fight." He paused to adjust the chronoperpetua strapped to his hand. "No, we're going to walk right out of here, and you're going to let us."

Matthias laughed. "Why would we do that?"

To his rear, Miles heard a swift and subtle rustling of curtains and the friction of a sword being pulled from its scabbard. Before he could turn around to defend himself, the tip of a cold steel blade bit the back of his neck.

"Oh shit!" Miles cried out. It took all of his self-control to not piss himself at that moment. *I'm not ready to die!* Miles begged silently. Fear had arrested all power to turn and brush aside the threatening blade with a spinning parry or any other counter attack. Keeping his head attached to his neck overrode all other instinctive neural pathways that had been forged in the last few weeks. His rapier and dagger fell from his grasp with a muted clang.

Everyone in the room shifted position like a contagious reflex action: feet shuffled, weapon angles altered, and fields of view widened. Miles had become the unwanted center of attention. The balance of power shifted in favor of the intruders.

"Let him go!" Elizabeth shouted.

She took an aggressive step toward Miles, but the intruder that held him at sword point pressed their weapon into his neck. The pain caused Miles to hiss and hold his hands out toward her to stop. Elizabeth did as Miles requested. She sneered with deadly intent at her son's captor.

Miles shifted his fearful gaze to each family member, trying to convince them to do whatever it took to save his life. They all looked back with the same despondent grimace. There was nothing they could do.

"Just as I predicted," the hooded man with the journal reiterated as he moved with nonchalance toward the outer corridor. "We'll be leaving now."

Charles stepped into his path, thrusting the tip of his gladius at the man's chest. It tore through the outer layer of clothing and stopped. "You're not going anywhere with my diary."

The shadowed face tilted down at the sword as though to assess the weapon's quality. His concealed face turned toward Elizabeth and called out, "Your youngest or the diary, Elizabeth. You choose."

Miles watched his mother close her eyes tight, shake her head, and whisper something to herself.

"Elizabeth!" Charles pleaded. "They won't kill him. They know they won't make it out of here alive if they do."

His mother's eyes snapped open and fell on Miles. Tears trickled down her cheeks as she glowered.

Miles' heart sank in his chest. *She's going to let me die?*

Elizabeth then rasped, "Let him go, Charles! It's a risk I can't take."

A swell of relief buoyed Miles up from the depths of despair. He smiled weakly at her.

"Liz?" Charles shouted, more insistent this time.

"Charles," Matthias interrupted despairingly, "it's over. They've won. Let them go!"

Charles snarled at the shrouded man and whipped his blade away from him. The blade hummed as it cut through the air. He stepped aside to let him pass along with his two silent confederates who backed up toward the hallway, protecting their retreat.

The one who held Miles hostage pulled him backward and brought the blade of the sword around to a frontal choke, the keen edge pressed against his trachea. They dragged him backwards toward the archway. Off balance, he struggled to keep his feet beneath him. One wrong move and he'd bleed out. Miles saw the looks of desperation on his mother and father's faces, his brother's pent up desire to go ape shit on his captors, and Charles' frustration at losing the diary. They all followed close by, not letting him get too far away. It was his fault. He had become the weak link. How was he going to get out of this?

The backward momentum stopped and Miles could rest for a second. He didn't understand why they stopped moving, but by the awkward postures and expressions everyone held, something had happened. His captor swung him around and he understood the delay.

The man who did the speaking for the intruders stood rigid with discomfort, his hands held up in front of him as though he were under arrest. His partners threatened to jump at some unseen force in the corridor.

A familiar female voice that Miles couldn't place called out from the darkness, "Stand down or I'll run him through!"

When they didn't relent, the leader lurched forward as though pushed and cried out, "Do as she says!"

The dejected enemy combatants sheathed their weapons. The one holding Miles hostage pulled its sword away from his neck and struck him in the back of the head with the pommel, sending him sprawling across the floor. Elizabeth dropped to her knees and put herself between her son and the intruder. She trained her trembling rapier on them, a clear warning to keep their distance. Alistair shifted his position and stood beside her as an extra measure of protection. Clear of immediate danger, she helped Miles to his feet. He groaned, holding the back of his throbbing head. The whole room wobbled around him.

"Move," the female voice called out again.

Their leader took a few measured steps into the library and stopped. From the darkness of the corridor, Annelise Albright emerged. She held the tip of her gladius pressed square between his shoulder blades, providing an incentive to obey her commands.

Charles stumbled forward, his hand over his gaping mouth. His whole body shuddered with weakness. "Annelise, you're alive! I thought—"

"I've been on the run," she snarled, "chasing down this scumbag for the last few weeks."

"Where's your brother?" he sounded hopeful. "Is he still alive?

"Not for long." Reaching out, she grabbed the back of the intruder's hood and pulled it down, exposing his face to everyone. Alistair and Matthias both gasped aloud in shock. "Say hello to your father, scumbag."

"God, no!" Charles begged, moving closer to his son. "It can't be. Please, tell me this is some kind of joke."

Miles saw the face of the young man, still and speechless, in the flickering candlelight. He glanced at the painting that hung over the fireplace at the far end of the study. Trevor Albright, Charles' own son, had not only betrayed the Order but stolen his father's artifact diary!

Annelise twisted her face into a vicious scowl, digging the blade into her brother's back a little deeper. "Tell him!" she bellowed.

"It's true," he whimpered. "I'm with Gaius now."

"But why?" Charles pleaded.

"I'm tired of wasting away my years for nothing," Trevor snapped at his father. "We all are. For our service, Gaius has promised us true immortality. None of us want to grow old and die like Mom, like you will soon, father. We can all be saved."

The throbbing in Miles' head began to subside and he noticed that amidst the heated conversation, his father and brother inched closer to their adversaries, weapons at the ready. The other traitors took tighter grips of their sword handles. One wrong move and this whole situation would explode like a powder keg.

"Have you lost your mind?" Charles howled at his son. "Did I teach you nothing?"

"No, you taught me well," he rasped. "Too well."

Taking a handful of his cloak, Trevor spun around to his rear. He unsheathed his gladius with his other hand and brought it down in a sweeping arc on his sister's blade, knocking it out of her hands.

Dropping his blade, Charles lunged headlong at Trevor, arms wide. Before he could tackle his son, the rightmost traitor crossed his path and thrust their long sword into his abdomen. He came to a sudden stop, doubled over, and grabbed at his stomach with both hands. When the intruder withdrew its bloodied blade, Charles collapsed to the floor.

Miles felt his insides knot up. His head swam with cowardly thoughts and the grisly images of his murdered foster family returned. With plodding steps, he backed away from the bloody melee that unfolded before him, unable to engage. The heel of his foot bumped into the quillion of his rapier, yet he made no effort to lift it. He watched Annelise scream for her father, clasp her emptied hands together, and ram them into her brother's face, knocking him back. She sprawled across the floor and wrapped her arms around her father's lifeless form. Tears streamed down her face.

The corner of the room stopped Miles from withdrawing any further. He slid down the wall into a cowering crouch. Fear had paralyzed him, disconnecting the lines of communication that controlled his limbs. His eyes, however, still worked. They would not allow him to look away, to shield himself from the chaos and death that unfolded before him. All he could do was bear witness to the outcome of the engagement.

Trevor, recovering from his sister's counter attack, looked down upon his sister and fallen father. He reached out for them, but his co-conspirators retreated into him, pushing him back and into the darkness of the corridor. Swords clashed and clanged, and boots scuffed against the floor as the melee raged on. Matthias and Alistair pushed their adversaries back and away from Annelise and Charles so that Elizabeth could rush to their aid. They landed glancing strikes that drew blood.

The intruders kept losing ground and couldn't fend off the mania of the Dravens any longer. They shouted at Trevor to go, to run, but he fought their overwhelming strength for a few moments more, struggling to get to his father. They finally broke his will and shoved him into the darkness. Loud footfalls resounded through the corridor.

Alistair made a dash for them, but Matthias grabbed him, ordering him to let them go. They slowly turned back to their fallen friend. Charles lay lifeless in his daughter's lap. Annelise howled in agony, unable to contain her anguish. She looked with pleading eyes to Alistair, Matthias, and Elizabeth in turn, but no one could save him. Her gaze drifted to Miles. The features of her face twisted into a cold, angry stare at the sight of him. Did she blame him for her father's death? Had his inability to act let her brother slip away with the diary? Miles hated himself for falling prey to fear, but he didn't think he deserved her derisive stare. At that moment he had the distinct impression that she wanted to end his life.

CHAPTER NINETEEN

Under a heavy, gray sky, a swirling mist enveloped the English countryside. Annelise stood motionless beneath the pall, her heart and soul heavy with the loss of everything in life that mattered. Beside her lay a soggy mound of fresh earth, and six feet below her, her murdered father laid in a pine casket. Though she felt alone, she was not.

Matthias stood beside the headstone and said a few words of comfort and loss to all in attendance before reading the prayer of Eternal Rest from the Albright family Bible. "Réquiem ætérnam dona eis, Dómine, et lux perpétua lúceat eis. Requiéscant in pace. Amen."

The rest of the Draven clan—Miles, Alistair, and Elizabeth—huddled close together around the grave, squinting through the chill rain at Annelise and Matthias. They all wore on their sleeves more emotion than they cared to express. The elder Dravens in particular seemed utterly distraught, having lost a long-time friend and ally in the war against Gaius Lloth. They had showered her with care and concern since Charles' passing, knowing the unenviable burden that lay upon her shoulders. None of them, though, went so far as to ask what drove her brother to such treachery. They danced delicately around the subject, consoling her instead. As much as they claimed to understand what she had been through and that they were there for her, none of them could ever truly fathom her suffering. They were whole, they were a family. She was alone, and it made her resolute to face her problems on her own. Her sole reason to live now hinged on avenging her father, and that meant taking the life of her brother. She tried to convince herself that she was ready for that burden.

Matthias closed the Bible and tucked it inside his coat to protect it from the elements. From the fresh mound of sodden earth he picked out a rock and laid it gently upon the headstone. "You'll be missed, brother," he whispered as he let his hand fall from the smoothed marble. He then pulled the shovel from the pile and cast a wad of dirt down upon the casket. It hit with a thump, dispersing across the wooden lid.

Elizabeth followed closely behind, placing another stone upon the grave marker and shoveling an offering of dirt down upon Charles. Then Alistair paid his respects, leaving only Miles and Annelise to say their goodbyes.

Miles approached the shovel and cast a heaping load of earth into the grave. "You seemed like a good man," he surmised. "Too good to die that way. We'll make sure it wasn't in vain."

Annelise narrowed her eyes at Miles, displeased by his assertion. *It's not your war, boy. I'll be the one getting even.* She had her fair share of issues with the fledgling chronoshifter. He was too green at a time when the Order needed seasoned warriors, not whimpering, spoon fed half-wits. Beyond that, Miles basked in the glow of being newly reunited with his family after a lifelong absence. In her seventy or so years with her family, those were the few memories that the distance of time hadn't sullied or dulled. She had nothing left, but Annelise remembered those early years and envied, no, hated Miles for finding them when her only companion was pain and despair.

Miles held the shovel in both hands and looked to Annelise.

She knelt by the headstone and scrawled her hand across his name, memorizing length, cut, and depth of every letter etched into the stone. Then below it, only the year of his death—*1656*. To inscribe his birth year of *1215* would only arouse suspicion in later generations. Leaning close, Annelise placed a loving kiss upon the cold marble. Then she rose to her full height, brushed the damp dirt from her knees, and placed the final stone upon the grave marker.

After slogging through the mud to Miles' side, she wrenched the shovel from his grasp and leered at him. "Thanks." He subtly shook his head at her with a distressed grimace. Annelise ignored his displeasure and, with a great heave, threw a heavy chunk of soil down upon the casket. Turning about, she jammed the spade into the ground at Miles' feet, and plodded past him back toward the mansion.

After drying off and getting into fresh garments, everyone gathered around the fireplace in the great room to chase away the bone-deep chill brought on by the rain. The logs crackled as the rending tongues of a rolling fire burned away at them. Miles sat on the floor beside the fire, cross-legged beneath a heavy blanket, sipping a hot cup of Earl Grey. Alistair sat in one of the two mahogany open armchairs that occupied the far corner of the room. He distracted himself from the moment by reading Euripides' *Iphigenia in Aulis*. Elizabeth sat nearby upon a matching chaise lounge, mending a tear in her riding breeches. The patriarch of the family rested by the fireside sipping whiskey from a flask. He prodded the glowing embers with the iron poker, stirring the flames to burn brighter and hotter.

Annelise kept herself apart from them. She sat at the mahogany reading table at the far end of the room, elbows resting on her knees, head in her hands. She didn't want to talk to anyone, but the damned silence of the room gnawed at her. As much as she wanted to keep from her reluctant companions what happened between Trevor and herself, Annelise knew it was no private war. She had a vendetta against her brother, there was no doubt, but the Dravens were still members of the same Order and her allies. They had a right to know how deep the treachery went.

With a grunt, she rose from her chair and crossed the room. All eyes locked on her as she approached Miles and Matthias.

"It's time you all knew the truth," Annelise grumbled. "I'm sorry I didn't tell you sooner, but it's my family, my responsibility. I wasn't ready."

Matthias held his hands out to stop her. "No reason to apologize. You've been through Hell." Though it was her home, he offered her a seat on the settee. The rest of the family joined them, though none sat beside Annelise. They all kept their distance.

Slowly, she began to recount the moment she discovered her brother's treachery.

Annelise's tether through the space-time continuum dropped her into an inhospitable environment. Winds swirled all about her. The very air burned at her lungs. Above her, crimson clouds streaked across the sky. Towering before her stood a hillside of shale and pebble atop which her brother stood, back to her. Her feet slid in the loose stone with each trudging step upwards. Legs aching and short of breath, Annelise reached the crest. She bent down, hands on knees, and breathed painful breaths.

Trevor did nothing to acknowledge her presence. He had been growing more and more moody as the weeks since their mother's passing wore on. Death was nothing new to their Order, but somehow, watching their mother grow old and die warped him deep inside. Annelise couldn't put a finger on just what was different about her brother, but he had changed.

Having caught her breath, Annelise stepped forward and stood side-by-side with Trevor.

"Hey!" she sighed. "I thought you were out on reconnaissance."

"I was," Trevor answered coldly. He didn't move. He just stared into the distance.

Annelise looked out upon the world to see if something in particular had stolen him away. A sudden feeling of both fear and disgust swelled within her. Before them stretched the nondescript ruins of a bygone civilization. She wondered why he would come to such a toxic, barren wasteland. Buildings crumbled to the Earth, collapsed bridges, and rusted out corpses of automobiles. Annelise felt like she was staring straight into the face of a nightmare. She had never laid eyes upon anything like it in all her travels.

"Where are we?" Annelise asked, confused by their surroundings.

"Manhattan."

"No, it can't..." her voice trailed off as the reality of his answer struck her like a kick to the guts. He was right. Like a transparent overlay, Annelise's memories of the titanic metropolis acted as a mental map for the wreckage that stretched as far as her eyes could see. A strange object jutting out of a roiling sea of waste was no rock; it was the spiked crown of the Statue of Liberty, fractured and rusty. The George Washington Bridge lay twisted and buckled with its support cables strewn about from it like the tentacles of a dead behemoth. They had travelled to the forbidden zone, a time and place beyond reprieve; a sobering reminder of what failure on the part of the Order could mean.

"Trevor," her voice trembled as she leaned into his side for comfort, "we shouldn't be here."

"Why?" he rasped.

"Because it's dangerous. Can't you feel it? This whole place is toxic."

"I don't feel much of anything anymore."

Pulling her attention away from the disturbing landscape, Annelise asked her brother, "What are you doing here?" The burning of her lungs brought forth a painful convulsion. She threw her arm over her mouth and nose to stifle an uncontrollable coughing fit. Having subsided, she drew a portion of her coat over her mouth to breathe through the fabric. It seemed to be an improvement.

"Thinking," he whispered.

"About what?" she demanded, growing short on patience.

Trevor finally broke his gaze from the apocalypse and looked down upon her. His features seemed worn, haggard, his frame slumped. She knew that look. Whatever thoughts brought him there, it was eating him alive. Annelise had her suspicions, but she waited for Trevor to admit it.

"No matter what we do, no matter how many times we push back, nothing changes. Every time I tether forward, this is the future I find."

"Things will change, we just have to keep fighting. You know what dad says, 'Every moment is a chance to build a better future.' You can't just give up because things look too bleak."

"I don't intend to give up."

"Then what are you saying, Trevor?"

He paused to stare back out over the devastation. "Do you still think about mom?"

Annelise's voice rose to a shrieking pitch. "What does that have to do with anything?"

"Just answer the question," Trevor snapped back.

"Every damn day. How could I not?"

"She's all I ever think about. You watched her die. Growing older and weaker every day. In the end she could barely hold her eyes open, and all the while having to look at us, young and ageless. She spent her life fighting a losing battle instead of living a simple, happy life."

"She was happy, Trevor. You know that. She lived a far better life than she ever would have had she stayed in her own time, the daughter of a penniless clerk with no dowry. Mom would have ended up a servant. She told us," she stammered, "she told you not to feel sorry for her for those very reasons. Mom saw that look in your eyes, the same look you've got now. She married Dad knowing full well what it meant to become one of our kind."

"Well I don't want any part of this life anymore. No one asked me if I wanted to be part of this war. It was forced upon me, just like it was forced upon you."

"But I thought you said you weren't giving up. It sure sounds to me like you are."

"I'm not going to kill myself if that's what you're hinting at. Quite the opposite, Annie. I've made a deal."

Annelise felt her features crinkle into a grimace of sheer disbelief. "A deal? With whom?"

"One that will ensure my immortality and that of my loved ones. I'll never have to grow old and die. Neither will you, Annie, if you come with me."

"What are you talking about? Come with you? Where?"

"I'm fighting for the side that'll win this war. No more wasted lives. I've traded my allegiance for what matters most to me."

"Oh, my God! Trevor, tell me you didn't! Please, tell me you're joking!"

"It's the only way, Annie. The cause doesn't matter to me anymore. All that I care about is protecting what I have. Protecting you and Dad. All the rest of them are going to die anyway."

"You don't know that! There's still time to change the future. But giving that demon unfettered access to chronoshifters will sway the tide of this war greatly in its favor. How do you know all of this," she thrust an accusative arm at the putrid landscape surrounding them, "isn't happening because of you?" Annelise reached out and grabbed hold of his coat lapels, strangling the fabric. Trevor remained stoic, unaffected.

"You don't have to do this, Trevor. Walk away before it's too late."

"I can't, sis." Trevor peeled her hands off of his coat and stepped back from her. "I've done things. Things I can't come back from."

"No. That's not true."

"I have no choice!" he yelled back, finally showing emotion.

"Bullshit!" Annelise barked, stalked toward him and punched him square in the cheek. She then doubled over in pain, coughing into her hands. "You have a choice. Please, don't do this," she begged through gasps of air. "If you join Gaius, if you betray the Order, you'll be hunted and killed."

"But I won't be able to protect you or father otherwise."

"Well that's a risk you're going to have to take," she rasped, drawing her pistol and training it on his chest. "Isn't it, traitor?"

"So you're not coming with me then?" Trevor asked, anger flashing in his eyes. He glared down the cobalt barrel at her.

"No!" Annelise screamed and fell to her knees, unable to get a full breath. The pistol dropped from her grasp. "Did you really expect me to join you?" she wheezed out each syllable. The veins in her neck and face bulged and her skin flushed red from the strain.

"I had hoped..." Trevor reached out a helping hand toward her, then balled it up into a fist and pulled it away. He clenched his jaw, grinding his teeth together behind a grimace of utter disgust. He jammed his fist into his trouser pocket, pulled out his chronoperpetua, and strapped it to his hand.

Annelise felt the nauseating sensation of the world spinning uncontrollably around her. She fought to stand, to not let Trevor escape, but the lack of oxygen left her barely able to lift her head and see him dialing in a new set of time coordinates into his chronoperpetua. Though the pain of losing her mother ripped her apart, Trevor's betrayal now threatened to burn to ash those pieces of her that remained. Everything that meant something to her in this crazy world was being ripped away. She gathered up enough air for one final, hopeful plea. "If you do this, you betray everything mom stood for." Tears of pain and sorrow broke through. Annelise gathered her handgun and struggled to raise it. "If you loved her you wouldn't do this."

"I disagree." A sapphire bolt of energy erupted from his chronoperpetua and hooked onto its target. "Stay out of my way, Annie." With a flash, Trevor vanished.

"Noooooo!" Annelise raged. With trembling hands, she holstered her pistol and fumbled about in for her chronoperpetua. Activating it, she escaped the forbidden zone.

The room was still. Annelise wiped away her gathering tears with the palms of her hands. She looked at her companions and decided she had never seen more mournful faces in all her years. Friends had come and gone, allies had fallen, but this was something more for them all. Eons of struggle now hinged on their ability to fight back the treachery that had wormed its way inside their Order. That treachery now had a name and a face. That knowledge, however, was of little consolation to Annelise.

"I hate to ask this of you, Annelise," Elizabeth probed, "but was Trevor the one who murdered the other children?"

Annelise closed her eyes tight, wincing in pained concentration. The answer came at a price. The images were too stark, too gruesome to believe. Trevor's words resounded in her mind. *I've done things. Things I can't come back from.* She shook her head, telling the memories to leave her mind, but they wouldn't. She wished that she had never found out what his words meant. But Annelise saw his handiwork with her own two eyes, which slowly opened to find four eager faces waiting on her answer.

Annelise swallowed hard to push down the lump in her throat. "It was a few weeks ago. I'd been following him relentlessly since that encounter; trying to get an idea of what he was up to, you know, without getting too close. But he just kept tethering from one time to another. I didn't know what he was up to but I kept at it." She paused as she came to the moment that haunted her thoughts. "Eventually I found myself in Nice, France. I think it was December of 1952. I knew that none of our kind had made camp that far into the future, and since the artifacts only exist in the present, I didn't understand why he was there.

"So I strolled through the streets, looking around, marveling at how little things had changed since 1942. Even though it wasn't Germany and it was a decade later, it all felt so comfortable, so familiar. At least for a moment it did. I think my body knew what was happening before my brain did because I had a sudden case of tremors. And then a frightening realization hit me. The only reason he could be so far into the future was for the children.

"Without thinking, I took off in a panic. I only hoped I could stop him before it was too late. I finally caught up to him, but all I saw was him disappear into a vortex with a child in tandem. I did my best to track him after that. He eventually led me to Highgate Cemetery. What I found," she shook her head in disbelief, "made me collapse: a freshly dug grave, an unmarked stone, and a spade jammed into the soil. Bloodstains lingered on the grass. I had to know. I started digging until I hit something soft. It was the body of a mutilated little girl. He didn't even have the decency to put her in a casket." She snickered angrily, "'Things that I can't come back from,' the bastard! He murdered a child and cut off her head, for God sake."

"It must've been Antoinette Michaud," Elizabeth added.

"Pierre's little girl?" Annelise asked.

"Yes," Matthias answered solemnly.

"She was only twelve-years-old!" Annelise raged. "She didn't pose a threat to anyone. Why kill her?" More tears rushed to her eyes and ran down her cheeks.

"So then it was Trevor all along," Alistair concluded.

"I'm not so sure," Matthias interjected. "He may have killed Antoinette, but the assassins who came after Miles, they weren't chronoshifters. They were way too careless and sloppy—using firearms out in the open and killing an entire family to get to one person."

"Could they have been hired hitmen?" Alistair posed.

Matthias scratched at the back of his head and winced thoughtfully. "It's possible."

"He's obviously working with others of our Order," Annelise added. She glanced from Matthias to Miles. "Maybe they went after you. Hired the hitmen at least. All I know is that Trevor never once led me to your time."

"We've had our suspicions that there were several traitors in our midst," Matthias said. "Do you have any names? Any leads to go on?"

Annelise shook her head. "I'm sorry. I wish I knew, but I never heard any names or got a clear glimpse at anyone's face."

"We thought perhaps the Takashima clan had a part in this," Matthias alluded, "but we have no proof. Your father was ambushed at a gathering in Edo."

"Well, Charles did proclaim Hiro's innocence, Matthias," Elizabeth interjected. She turned to Annelise. "Your father swore that ninja assassinated him before he escaped."

"But that doesn't recuse the rest of the clan," Alistair amended. "They could still have had a hand in it." He shot up from his chair in frustration. "Just too many damn questions left unanswered."

Matthias stood up too. "Just calm down. What do we know for sure? We know Trevor and others are working for Gaius, and that they went after the children, probably meant as some sort of offering of loyalty."

"Or Gaius' pathetic way of making sure the 'prophecy' didn't see the light of day," Alistair mocked the idea.

"What prophecy?" Miles questioned.

Elizabeth answered, "It's one of Nostradamus' lost quatrains. It speaks of a deliverer, a set of twins. But no one in the order has ever given birth to multiples. It's pure nonsense."

"Whether you think it's nonsense or not," Annelise countered, "if a demon from the Netherworld takes stock in it, that should be good enough for all of us."

"Either way," Matthias barked over them, "we also know that Gaius is after the artifacts. That was the whole reason Trevor and the others broke in last night and stole the diary."

"But what about yesterday?" Miles questioned everyone aloud. Then he pointedly asked Annelise, "Why were you in Richmond? What the Hell happened there?"

She flashed Miles an angry stare. Her defenses already up, his inquiry felt like an accusation. Then she remembered the day before and her chance encounter with him. It wasn't exactly cordial. Taking a deep breath to calm her nerves, Annelise softened and replied, "I was hunting

Trevor. I think he spotted me in the crowd, though, and led me on a wild goose chase. I wandered around for a while looking for him. Unfortunately, I couldn't hear him tether away with all the noise. It wasn't until after I ran into you," she looked pointedly at Miles, "that I knew why he was here. Well, maybe not exactly why, but it had to do with your family. He was after your Artifact diary."

"Thank God you moved it, Matthias," Elizabeth sighed and laid a hand upon his shoulder.

"I know," he agreed, placing his hand on hers.

"That's probably why he detonated the charges and set fire to the ranch; if he couldn't find where you hid it, he'd make sure no one did. I had to let him go so that I could pull you out of the house, Elizabeth. He left you there to die." Her gaze fell to the window and the freshly dug grave outside.

"So what do we do now?" Elizabeth wondered aloud. "They've got Charles' diary. We can't let Gaius get his hands on Excalibur."

Matthias looked to Annelise. "Do you know its last resting place?"

Annelise swallowed her sadness with a grunt. With her forearm she dried all her tears and shut off the valve. She breathed deep and replied, "Maybe. Dad didn't tell us when he was moving it, but I spent a lot of late nights trying to crack his cipher."

Her companions aimed a collection of doubtful glances in her direction. She waved off their visible concern. She hadn't let slip a secret that would implicate her in some crime. "No, he asked me to do it, to test it. Dad was always trying to fortify it, make it harder to crack."

"Did you crack it?" Alistair asked. He leaned forward in his seat, seeming eager for her response.

She nodded. "I was able to figure out a few of them, but that was fifteen years ago. He may have moved it since."

"Well," Matthias redirected everyone's attention, "then that's where we'll start. We'll split up, tether to different times for safety, and investigate those locations. If we're lucky, we'll find it before they do."

CHAPTER TWENTY

Annelise hated using Trevor's anchor to tether after him. Anchors left too much room for error, for the unexpected. She never knew when or where the chronoperpetua would dump her, but with her brother constantly on the move, it remained her only option to track him. This blind foray into the time-space continuum did not disappoint. When the gaping throat of the blue vortex peeled back and coughed her out, the sensation of free-fall took hold of her. Spinning and flipping, turning and falling, she couldn't get her bearings. The g-force felt like the crushing hands of a giant trying to roll her body into a ball as if she were clay. Inexplicable streaks of light and dark whipped across her field of vision, consuming her mind in an all-out assault on the senses.

With a painful crash of her body against a hard but oddly forgiving force, the torture of her plummet gave way to another kind of suffering—the acrid burning of saltwater filling her lungs. A frantic scramble to reach the surface ensued, but she had no idea which way was up. The primal part of her mind fought to smother her ability to reason, begging her to take another breath. A glimmer of muted light and rising bubbles helped her push back against the irrational impulse. She kicked desperately and reached out for the glowing orb above. Cresting the surface, Annelise expelled the painful fluid in a heaving cough and gasped a refreshing, invigorating breath of fresh air. Lapping waves slapped her in the face. She spit back the putrid water that invaded her mouth and vigorously kicked her legs to keep her head above the waves. Bobbing like a cork, Annelise searched for the light that guided her from the depths. It was the moon, half-full and glowing. It cast a dull blue glow upon the rippling surface of the water. Below it danced tiny, eerie sparks of light that appeared to speckle the horizon.

Then it hit her—the angle of the lights, the taste of the water. She refocused her eyes to take in the whole landscape, moon and all. Staring into the darkness, the subtle silhouette of London Bridge slowly appeared. A few flickering flames lit the windows of the apartments perched above the roadway. Those eerie sparks were nothing more than some well-to-do merchants or middle class Londoners wasting expensive candlelight on evening revelries. Annelise knew she had landed in the Thames. That realization brought a swift and sudden panic to her heart knowing she landed so close to the bridge. If she got sucked into the timber starlings that surrounded the stone footings, she'd be crushed. That fear, however, quickly passed as she realized that she landed east of the bridge and out of danger. But she likewise knew she had to get to the shore before its temperamental current swept her too far downstream and away from her brother's dealings. Quickly scanning the banks of the Thames, Annelise decided she treaded much closer to the south bank. So she came about and began swimming in that direction.

Thrashing her limbs, Annelise fought the will of the water in the hopes she might find soft footing in the muddy shore at low tide. She kept snatching peeks of the shadowy south bank between feverish strokes. When fatigue overwhelmed her, she stretched her legs down toward the riverbed, but her boot tips just flailed at the open water. Bankside stood only feet away, and it grew closer with every jostling wave. *Damn*, she thought angrily to herself. *High tide.* She knew she'd find no shore to stand upon, and she bobbed too far below the walkway above to gain purchase.

A sudden wave lifted and slammed her into the stone retaining wall. Her head hit with a crack. Disoriented, Annelise started to drift and spin uncontrollably downstream. She groped at the slick stone, desperate to find a handhold to stop her slide. Then, as luck would have it, she collided with a flight of watermen's stairs. The jagged edges of the steps dug into her side, but she did not cry out in pain. She just laid there for a moment, saying a silent Hebrew prayer of thanks for the fortunate landing. A haggard grunt escaped her as she pulled herself out of the water and sat on a cold stone step. Waves nipped at her boots as she gathered herself. After a few deep breaths, she stood up and ascended the stairs.

At the top step, Annelise paused again. The side of her head throbbed dully. She pressed her palm against the painful egg on her temple. Pulling her hand away, she examined it under the weak lighting cast down from above. *No blood*, she concluded. *Probably just a concussion*. Not the best condition for her to be in at that time, but as long as she avoided combat she knew she'd be fine.

Trevor had tethered near the river several times in the last few days, always evading her in the narrows of London. She had yet to discover the nature of his dealings, but she knew it had a great deal to do with her father's artifact diary. Annelise flipped open her chronoperpetua to see her current time frame. She didn't expect what she found. *June 28, 1613*. Taken aback, she opened the back panel and found that her current time and the present time were in sync. While the previous tethers after her brother brought her to a variety of different tangents in both Tudor and Jacobean London, none of them had led her to the present. Only a handful of reasons could lead a chronoshifter to tether to the present: resetting for a tether to the future, doing recon on Gaius, or relocating an artifact. She wagered that Trevor journeyed to the present day for one of the latter two, though the circumstances likely pointed toward a more nefarious combination of them both.

Annelise surveyed her surroundings. A long, dirt road ran the length of Thames in both directions. During the day, Bankside had the reputation for being a festering sore of licentiousness beyond the jurisdiction of London. But under the cover of dark, few dared roam the highways and byways of Southwark. As far as she could see, the river walk lay dark and abandoned. The normally busy tenements and merchant shops that lined the road stood lifeless. Only a few candle lit windows provided any proof that life went on after dark. Everything was still and relatively silent. If it wasn't for the constant slosh of lapping waves against the barrier wall and docked boats, the silence would drive her mad.

Trevor's other tethers to London never brought her to this side of the river. Annelise hoped she didn't swim herself out of position. The lack of action along the Bank didn't fill her with confidence that she made the right choice. However, she knew it would take too long to make her way across London Bridge and to the north bank. So she put her faith in blind luck, jogged across the road to the stone sidewalk that ran alongside it, and made her way westward in search of an inlet through the buildings. Rose Alley was the first major roadway that crossed her path. It led away from the river toward the old Bear Trapping grounds where the popular theaters of the time had popped up in the latter half century. It seemed an unlikely place for her father to hide the artifact, but it was the only card she had to play.

Turning down Rose Alley, Annelise put distance between herself and the Thames quickly. The rush of water faded away and the only sounds she heard were her boots against the damp stone and her heart beating in her ears. At each intersection along the way, she paused to peer into each street, sidewalk, and alleyway to ensure she didn't overlook even the slightest oddity. There was no sign of her brother.

Annelise cleared the tenements that occupied several hundred feet of riverfront without incident and entered an area where the land took on a wholly different shape. The stone sidewalks and roads fell off to open marshland. The cover that the tightly spaced buildings provided gave way. Annelise now stood out in the open, exposed and vulnerable; it felt like being naked. A crisp breeze blew across her body and joined forces with her damp clothes to bring about a fierce wave of chills.

Knowing a marksman could target her from any number of vantage points, Annelise crouched down and moved with desperate speed toward a nearby, semi-circular structure that stood amid the soggy earth. It was a theatre of some kind, but in the darkness she couldn't tell if it was the Rose, the Globe, or another playhouse of the day. Its white, vertical panels rose some thirty feet into the air and stretched about fifteen feet wide. Each section joined with the next at a slight angle, forming the outer structure. Along the joints and at measured intervals, dark accent boards gave the theatre a distinct appearance. And atop it all, a peaked roof of thatch hung over the edge.

Within a few feet of the building, something painful scratched at her arms and face. She swore under her breath and reeled away. A line of tall, evergreen hedges surrounded the theatre, and Annelise walked right into them. Holding still, she scanned the surrounding countryside for any movement her disturbance might have aroused. An eerie stillness prevailed.

Though she saw nothing to arouse suspicion, the sounds of muted groans and whispering voices drew her attention to the theatre itself. Rather than circumvent the hedges and remain out in the open, Annelise ducked down and crawled beneath the lowest branches to get closer to the wall. Having cleared the pine boughs, she stood up into a narrow gap between the structure and the hedges. It was just big enough for her to move without brushing against the wall or disturbing the branches. She could move in safety, completely obscured from view. With careful steps, she shuffled along the exterior and examined the seams between each panel for a gap wide enough to spy through. Finally, Annelise came upon a narrow separation from which to eavesdrop. Very little of the theatre interior could be seen through the narrow gap, though; only vague forms flashed back and forth, in and out of view.

The garbled voices became clearer, more distinct. It sounded like many people embroiled in a struggle. One of the voices shouted out above the others, pleading for help. It was the voice of a man scared beyond all reason.

"Shut up!" another lower, harsh voice yelled at the panic-stricken man. When he didn't comply, the sharp sound of scuffing boots preceded a thud and a pained grunt.

Frustrated by her limited view, Annelise continued skirting around the theatre until she reached the end of the hedges and the main gate. The door sat slightly ajar with no guard. She knelt down in the muck and pressed her face to the gap. Looking within, she concluded it was in fact the Globe: the unmistakable design of the thrust stage, the ornately painted columns and tiring house, and the Heavens. It definitely served as the kind of location her father might have hid Excalibur; a major historical landmark that would show up in history texts.

Several figures filled the interior of the theatre. In the pit, a whimpering man stood bent over in apparent agony as two larger, stronger looking men restrained him. To the side, another person held a burning torch overhead, casting light on the whole scene. Three additional figures stood upon the stage, watching the action taking place in the pit below. Hooded cloaks shrouded their faces from view but not the distinctive bulk of their male physiques.

One figure gave off an eerie air that felt quite different from the rest. Covered in an ornamental, hooded robe, this one slithered out from the shadows in a manner that gave Annelise the chills. Though she had no proof, her gut told her that it was Gaius Lloth. She had lucked out after all! Now she knew why all her attempts to scour London proper for Trevor never amounted to anything.

Annelise held her position and kept a watchful eye over the events unfolding before her.

"John Lowin," the hooded figure observed, standing at a distance. "We've been looking for you."

"Who, who are you?" the man named John stuttered with fear. "I have no money! Please, don't hurt me!" His plump face and neck quivered with each abrupt turn of his head from one captor to the other. The gray, thinning hair upon his head clung to his sweaty face.

The shadowy figure removed its hood. A middle aged man with red hair and a matching beard came into view. He reached beneath the lapel of his cloak and produced a long blade that reflected the torchlight.

"Oh, my God!" John blubbered. "I have a wife and children. Take anything you want, just don't kill me!" Twisting and pulling against the strength of the two men who held him, John struggled in futility to get free.

The ginger halted a few feet from John. An evil grimace corrupted his features. "Fear not, Mr. Lowin. I don't intend to kill you." With an aggressive thrust, the man sunk the tip of the blade into his own chest. Collapsing to his knees and gasping for breath, he cackled in pained ecstasy. Then he fell limp at John's feet and there was total silence. A small, pulsating orb of green light materialized next to the corpse.

It must be the Talaria, Annelise concluded. She had never before witnessed any of the artifacts take on their ethereal form.

John gasped and stared slack-jawed at the dead man lying before him. He turned his gaze of confusion back to his captors. "I, I don't understand," his voice still trembled. "Why did he do that?"

Driving a foot into the back of his knees, the brutes that held John forced him to the ground. They pushed him down so that his face lingered mere inches from the corpse.

Seemingly put off by the action below, the middlemost figure on the stage turned away. For a brief moment, the torchlight framed his face and Annelise gasped. *Trevor!* He headed for the center door of the tiring house. His companions lingered for a second or two more and then followed suit.

From the very air around them, a deeply disturbing, ethereal voice answered John, "So that I could become you." A hideous spectral form leapt from the corpse and enveloped John. He cried out in utter agony. The strongmen that held him close let go abruptly and withdrew.

Nothing could have prepared her for what she saw. Annelise averted her gaze and leaned back against the door frame. The demon's true form proved far too ghastly to look upon. While she fought to shake the image from her mind, she took comfort in the reliability of her intuition. She had not only found Gaius, she found Trevor too. It instigated a sudden, consuming urge to throw the door wide and rush into battle against her enemies. That frenzy to spill blood, she knew, would not serve anyone's vested interests that night. Seven opponents were far more than she could handle on her own, even if they were all poorly trained henchmen. But she knew at least one of them was her brother, a trained warrior. And more than likely, the men who stood with him at a distance from the demon once fought for the Order too. Anyone with more than a lifetime's worth of combat and training could not be merely handled by any one person. Furthermore, any confrontation would put her at too great a risk of being possessed by Gaius. And if there was one universal absolute for dealing with the demon, it was never let it get close enough to touch you when you make the killing strike. If it ever took over a chronoshifter, there's no telling how much damage the bastard could do across the ages.

Annelise resumed her surveillance, hoping the transformation had been completed. To her relief, it was. John Lowin, who had screamed in terror only moments before, crouched low by the fallen vessel. Reaching down, he unclasped the ornamental cloak and lifted it up and around to his own shoulders with one fluid move. Then John reached out for the artifact. It whisked across the ground toward his open hand and joined with him. A perverse smile pursed his lips. With unnatural speed, he rose to his feet. Standing erect, he stretched out his limbs so that every bone inside popped. A ripple of movement, of something lurking beneath the flesh, cascaded along his body. He was no longer John Lowin. He had become an it, a demon reborn in the skin of another. *But to what end?* Annelise considered.

The three men who stood nearby it, bowed their heads low and murmured, "Master."

The demon faced the stage. "Where did they go?"

"Up there," the man with the torch spoke in a thick Irish accent. He pointed toward the hidden area above the stage. "Making sure everything's in order for the morrow."

"This all feels too easy," Gaius growled.

One of the brutes who held the real John Lowin rubbed his hands and blew into them. "Easy? That's not how I'd describe it. I've never been one to play with fire."

The other strongman grunted his agreement.

"Not that," the demon answered. "This could be an elaborate trap. I can't get a true sense of their intentions yet. My power is still too limited."

"Aye," the Irishman responded, "but they took all those heads. That's got to be worth something, Master."

Gaius ignored the man's comments and sniffed at the air like a hunting dog. "The artifact is here. They're not lying about that."

"So let's take it now!" the Irishman demanded. He raised his fist at Gaius and clenched it in an aggressive manner.

In an instant, the demon disintegrated into a dark mist which swirled behind its insistent servant and rematerialized just as fast. Gaius stood behind him, growling. It pulled the man backward and off balance with its knife pressed hard against his throat. The demon hissed, "You serve me, Jacob. You'd be wise to remember that."

The other men stepped back, putting distance between themselves and the demon's rage.

Jacob winced and shook his head sharply. "Yes, Master," he cried.

Just as abruptly as it fell upon the Irishman, Gaius teleported back to its previous position in the pit. Jacob grabbed his throat and rubbed at it. He examined his hand, likely looking for blood, and then stared at the ground.

Annelise speculated, from her observations, that the power and influence of the demon drew followers to its cause. Like courtiers of kings and queens, these men knew that being in the service of such power meant that great treasures and power may too be imbued upon them. But that very same power could turn against them at the slightest transgression. Those in court often forgot their station in life and, in turn, paid the price with their head. The fear of punishment not only kept these lackeys in their place, but in some ways proved to be just as intoxicating a motivation as the rewards such service provided.

Loud footsteps from the back of the theatre attracted the attention of Gaius and its men. Trevor and his companions exited the tiring house and walked to the front of the stage. All of their faces were now bathed in the torchlight. The other men had distinctively Asian features. *Takashima.*

Though their betrayal surprised and worried Annelise, at least she now knew what she and the Dravens were up against. The Takashima clan had seven members, each one more cunning and bloodthirsty than the next. But their moral code, the Bushido, should have kept them from such dark treachery. *They'll be a handful.*

Trevor announced, "Everything appears to be in order." He removed his chronoperpetua from under his cloak. His companions did the same, verifying Annelise's suspicions. The three of them adjusted the dials on their devices, preparing to tether away to another tangent.

Gaius rubbed its hands together, "Excellent. Then we're all set for tomorrow?"

"Yes," Trevor responded, tightening the straps around his wrist and hand. He gave the demon a final, unpleasant glance. "Just play your part and everything will go as planned. And dump that body in the river. It will be washed out to sea by daybreak."

Trevor and the Takashimas activated their chronoperpetuas, firing the energy tethers in different directions. Annelise took the opportunity to slip away unnoticed. She had to act quickly if she wanted to use the sound of their vortexes to mask her own. Backing away from the door, she withdrew her device, strapped it into place, and slapped her father's anchor into the core. He and, hopefully, the rest of the Draven clan would be awaiting her return. In a flash of brilliant azure, the energy tether extracted Annelise from the present.

CHAPTER TWENTY-ONE

The main entryway door to the Albright Manor opened and shut with a slam. The ruckus alerted Miles and his mother, who had been resting after their return trip from the recent past, that they had company. They hoped Matthias and Alistair, or perhaps even Annelise, had finally made their way back home with good news after being apart for two days. Not ready to take chances, however, Miles drew his Beretta, his mother her rapier, and they rushed to the vestibule. He kept his sights aimed ahead of her every movement to gun down anything that might get to her before she could raise her weapon.

To their collective relief, Matthias and Alistair awaited them when they arrived. They stood wet and muddied from head to toe. Their expressions spoke of an exhaustive adventure, one that did not go well. Neither man moved with any sense of spirit—quite the opposite, in fact. Alistair collapsed into the nearest chair, let the back of his head thud against the wall, and stared at the ceiling. With a massive sigh, he leaned forward, elbows on knees, and then began to untie his boots. Matthias, on the other hand, staggered toward his wife, peeling off his drenched coat. His silver P226 bounced under his armpit.

"What happened to you?" Elizabeth asked with concern. She sheathed her rapier and rushed to Matthias.

He shook his head and answered, "It wasn't there." Their bodies collided in a strong embrace. They held each other close for a moment before letting go. Laying his forehead against hers he added, "The damn tide rolled up on us too fast. We must have looked like fools mudlarking while everyone else fled to the upper bank. Probably think we drowned." He smiled at her, brushing his fingertips across her cheek.

"And you?" Matthias looked from her to Miles with hopeful eyes. "Did you find it?"

Miles holstered his Beretta, then drew near his parents. "Sorry. We didn't find it either."

The small glimmer in his father's eyes faded away to resignation. Matthias frowned and wrapped his arms around his son, hugging him tight. "It's okay, Miles. I'm just glad you're both safe."

"We're fine," Elizabeth added. "It wasn't a complete loss, though."

"How so?" Matthias asked.

Alistair glanced toward them with interest. He rose to his feet and crossed the floor.

"We found this," she answered, motioning to Miles.

He knew exactly what she wanted. From his pocket he produced a piece of folded up butcher paper. Once unfolded, it revealed a charcoal rubbing from Mên-on-Tol. He held it out for them all to see. Amidst the undulations and crevices that the impression captured, the letters "WS" were clearly visible.

"Where was it inscribed?" Matthias asked.

Miles replied, "Along the top of the holed stone. We found it as soon as we got down from our horses."

"WS?" Alistair leaned over his father's shoulder to view the parchment. He looked to Miles, his face contorted in confusion. "What does it mean?"

Elizabeth shrugged. "I don't know. Hopefully Annelise can shed some light on it when she gets back."

Matthias furrowed his brown. "She isn't back yet?"

"Not yet," Miles answered. "She's been gone longer than any of us."

"Are you worried?" Elizabeth asked.

He shook his head. "No, she can take care of herself. I just wish she'd tell me what she's up to. If she gets—"

A sudden, powerful tremor shook the house. The entire foundation vibrated beneath them. Everyone grabbed for the nearest heavy object to cling to and ducked down for safety. From all around, a deafening cacophony filled the air: pots and pans clanking together in the kitchen, the shattering of picture frames as they slipped from the walls, and fine china bouncing along shelves before smashing against the hard floor.

"Earthquake?" Miles yelled over the clamor.

"No!" Alistair countered. "Chronovortex!"

Miles shook his head and shrugged. He strained his sense of hearing to pick up the signature harmonic, but the din drowned out his senses.

Matthias drew his sidearm and said, "Alistair's right! Someone's tethering into the manor!"

Miles yelled back, "I can't hear it!" He felt his mother's hand fall on his arm. She nodded to him that she heard it too. He felt dejected that he couldn't make it out.

Everything fell calm in an instant; the vibrations ceased and the noise dropped off to silence. All they could hear were their collective breaths and the light squeak of an overhead chandelier set into slow motion like a pendulum. Weapons drawn, they rose to their feet and slithered into the main hall. Matthias and Miles swept back and forth across each archway they approached, covering all the interior angles in search of the latest intruder. Alistair and Elizabeth kept a keen eye on their rear as they progressed. Then they heard it—a rustling coming from the library, just like the other night. *Had someone else come looking for the diary too?* Miles felt big time déjà vu.

Stopping at the edge of the doorway, Matthias looked back at his family members. Miles knew he awaited a "good-to-go" nod from each of them. Miles gave the nonverbal reply without much thought, which surprised him. He didn't feel so scared this time. His grip on his Beretta was firm, confident. Perhaps brandishing a deadly firearm that didn't require as much skill as a rapier to take down an enemy gave him more confidence. Point and shoot and they go down. Simple. He knew he could handle that.

Matthias then threw his hand up with three extended fingers—a countdown. One by one they closed back on his hand until a balled fist crunched into shape.

Matthias rounded the corner of the archway and Miles shuffled across the face of it, training his sights on anything that moved within. Alistair and his mother filed into the library as he cleared away. They halted, their weapons trained on a familiar form that moved about erratically, scrutinizing the book shelves.

Annelise, startled, rounded on them. "What the Hell?"

A giant knot of tension within Miles relaxed. He let his gun fall to his side with a sigh of relief. "You sure know how to make an entrance." Miles thrust his Beretta back into his holster.

"Yeah," she barked back at him, "because I have control over where the damn vortex opens."

Matthias advanced across the floor. "Where've you been?"

Annelise huffed and turned her attention back toward the books. "Finding my brother." Her stare followed the movement of her finger from the spine of one tome to another. Then she halted and jabbed a finger against one book in particular. "And Excalibur. Yes! There you are!" She squeezed her fingertips between the covers of a few tightly packed texts and pried free a thick, dusty textbook. Then she carried it over to the table in the study, slamming it down.

Miles looked to his brother and parents who all wore the same uncertain expression. Then he moved into the study to see what she was up to. The others followed. Taking hold of a satiny red bookmark, Annelise swung the tome open. Its dry binding cracked from the strain. She jabbed her right index finger against the page. There sat a hand-drawn image of William Shakespeare's Globe Theater.

"That's it! This is where my father hid the artifact."

Everyone else leaned in closer. Matthias pulled another candle closer to the text. "How do you know?"

"I went after Trevor. I found him and two members of the Takashima clan casing the grounds. Gaius was with them."

"How do you know it was Gaius?" Alistair probed. "It's always disguised."

Annelise made a painful grimace. "I watched it take over a man."

Elizabeth covered her mouth and gasped. "You saw it?"

Annelise nodded back. "Only part. I couldn't watch."

The room fell silent. The collection of candlelit faces examined each other in quiet contemplation. Though Miles knew little about the demon's true form, he gathered from their reaction that it must be horrific, like Pazuzu from *The Exorcist*. If he ever saw anything like that he knew he'd shit his pants.

"It makes sense, Matthias," Elizabeth interrupted the silence. "The *WS* we found could mean William Shakespeare."

"But wait," Miles interrupted. "Wouldn't people notice if Excalibur was sitting out in the open?"

Alistair shook his head at Miles. "Not necessarily. It might be encased in another object or even buried beneath the theater."

"So then what's it waiting for?" Miles retorted. "Why doesn't Gaius just go and take it?"

"With chronoshifters on his side, he's likely waiting for some event in history to mask his movements so we don't detect it."

"Oh, my God!" Miles shouted, shoved his brother's arms out of the way, and violently pulled the history text across the table to himself. He began to frantically search the pages.

"What?" Annelise demanded with an annoyed tone.

Miles ignored her and hastily asked, "What's the date?"

Matthias withdrew his chronoperpetua. "April 15th. Why?"

"No," Miles shook his head vehemently, "the present!"

"Oh, sorry." Matthias flipped over the device and popped open the back. "June 28th."

"1613, right?"

"Yes," Matthias answered his son.

Annelise gasped. "You don't mean?"

"I remembered my teacher saying something about it in English class. June something. In 1613. The Globe's going to burn to the ground during a performance of," Miles paused, scanning the page. "Here it is! *Henry VIII!* The theater's destroyed on June 29th, 1613 in a massive fire!" He looked up to see the rest of their stunned faces staring back at him, framed by the flickering candlelight. "Hey, don't be so surprised I actually learned something in school. Well?"

Alistair nodded. "He's right. With people frantically trying to escape that tinderbox, it's the perfect chance to slip inside and recover the sword. No one would be the wiser when they sifted through the rubble."

Elizabeth grabbed Miles by the sides of his face and planted a big, wet kiss on his forehead. "That's my boy."

Alistair mussed Miles' hair with his hand. "Not bad, Miles. Not bad."

Miles felt a surge of excitement in his body akin to a volcano before it erupts. He couldn't wait to finally be part of a battle, unlike the skirmish in the study. The thought of a life or death battle did cause fear to stream through him, but Miles knew his destiny was to be part of this Order and fight. And he remembered what his father told him. *True bravery, true courage is facing your fear and mastering it in the moment.* He now knew what his father meant by mastering his fear; like his anger, he needed to stay in control and do what was necessary despite it. On the night that they lost Charles, he locked up, could barely react when his life was in danger because of fear. Miles had done nothing to prove he was ready, but he knew it was time to test it.

"So what's our plan?" Elizabeth asked.

Everyone looked to Matthias for an answer. Everyone, that is, but Annelise. She took hold of the text book and turned to the next page where a sketch of the theatre's interior lay. The three tiers of seating that surrounded the stage were dissected and drawn as independent rings to show the detail of each. She pushed the tome back to the middle of the table and pointed to a portion of one of the levels.

"I'll position myself here in the lower level seats," Annelise added with confidence. "From what I saw, it's the best spot to monitor the whole theatre during the performance. Elizabeth," she directed, "you take up position on this side of the theatre. Matthias, you're by far our best swordsman. If you linger with the groundlings on the right you can be the first line of defense when the fighting breaks out. And Alistair, guard the gate. Anyone tries to escape once the fighting starts, you cut 'em down."

"Wait! What about me?" Miles contended, pissed that she left him out. "I'm ready."

Annelise snorted a dismissive breath. "You?" she asked snidely, looking him up and down with a disgusted smirk. "You're not ready."

"Bullshit!" Miles barked. He closed on Annelise, his face inches from hers.

"What are you gonna do about it? Huh?" she snapped back, leering closer.

Matthias yelled, "Enough!" and pushed his way between them. Miles tried to shove his way past his father but he stonewalled him. "I said enough!" Mathias growled at his son, "Sit down."

Miles swallowed his pride and did as his father said. He never wanted to punch a girl in the mouth so much in his life.

Matthias, quite flustered, straightened his posture and heaved a sigh. Turning from his son, he regarded Annelise with concern. With a careful, measured tone, he said, "Look, I know I've got no right to try to stop you or even ask you to bow out tomorrow, but I think we might be better off if you stay back."

"What?" she shrieked. "You don't have enough warm bodies to win this fight and you're asking me to sit this one out? You know what? You're right," she snapped at him like a crazed dog, unhinged by his suggestion. "You don't have the right."

"Fine," Matthias answered her with contrasting gentleness. Her aggressiveness didn't seem to dissuade him from his strategy. "I just want to make sure we're straight with each other before the curtain goes up. The way I see it, Trevor's still your brother. Despite your constant denials, I'm worried it's going to compromise your ability to do the right thing, should it come to that."

"How dare you? I'm not a rookie halfwit like your son," she snapped back and leered at Miles. "You want to worry about someone screwing up out there, worry about him."

Matthias' whole body knotted up in anger, and his face became flushed. Her attack on Miles must have crossed some invisible line in the sand. His father leveled a trembling finger at her and growled, "Leave Miles out of this. He's not your concern. I'm talking about you. I need to be sure you're not going to be a liability out there."

It filled Miles with a vengeful satisfaction to see her getting reamed out by his father instead of being on the receiving end himself.

"Who do you think you are? My father?" Annelise yelled as her hand fell to the pommel of her gladius. "You're nothing to me, none of you! I'm in this for me, that's all. I'm going and that's the end of it. And if you don't like it, you can see yourself out. Remember, Matthias, you're guests in *my* house now, not my father's."

He scrunched his lips together in a tight, angry stare. The sides of his jaw flexed as he clenched down. Breaking his short silence, he grumbled, "Fine, we'll do it your way."

"Fine!" Annelise stalked past Matthias, bumping shoulders with him.

He scowled at her over his shoulder. When she passed through the archway and out of sight, he rolled his eyes and sighed. "I guess that's settled."

Alistair approached Matthias. "Not a bad plan, minus the psychotic part."

Matthias snorted a laugh at his son's wry humor.

"Yeah, that's a great plan," Miles whined sarcastically, "except for the part where I'm left behind." Ogling the diagram of the Globe and eager for his assignment, he asked, "So where do you want me?"

Alistair and Elizabeth stood by idly. Neither of them seemed to want to make eye contact with Miles. Instead, they shot Matthias half-hearted glances. Miles could tell something was wrong. They all looked uncomfortable in their own skins. No one seemed to want to talk, and that told Miles everything he needed to know.

"No," Miles pleaded, shaking his head. "Please tell me I'm not being left back."

"I'm sorry, son." Matthias frowned.

"Damn it! Why?" Miles whined.

Matthias shook his head apologetically. He laid his firm hands on Miles' shoulders and looked him in the eye. "Miles, this isn't to punish you. You've done nothing wrong. You're just not ready yet, and that's my fault. If I hadn't waited so long we might have had more time to prepare you. But none of us can do the job we need to do if we're worried about your safety."

"You've got to be kidding me!" Miles slapped his father's hands away. "You dragged me here, ripped me away from my shitty life to be a part of this family, this war. And now you want me to stand by while you all walk into a God damn buzz saw?"

"Miles," Matthias pleaded, his eyes ringed with red. "I'm not going to have your blood on my hands."

"But I can do this," Miles contended, looking to Elizabeth and Alistair for help. "I can help you."

Neither of them said a word. They seemed content to let Matthias speak for the family.

Miles collapsed in a chair and held his head in his hands, distraught. In an instant, a wave of grief crashed over him and tears spilled down his cheeks. He muffled his sobs as best as he could, but he knew they could hear him and see his shuddering.

Matthias pulled up a chair beside his son. "I know this isn't what you hoped for. But you've got a much bigger responsibility now; if we don't make it back, you've got to pick up the pieces and keep on fighting. Hook up with another clan and keep hunting Gaius."

Lifting his head from his hands, Miles cried, "But this isn't fair. I don't want to be left alone again, not after all of this. Please!"

"None of us want to leave you. Do you think this is what we want?"

"No," Miles droned. He felt the warmth of his mother reach down over his back and wrap around him. She squeezed him tight, her head on his shoulder. He could feel the wet of her tears penetrating his shirt. It only made the pain run deeper.

"You're our future now, Miles," his father sniffled, himself overcome by emotion. "And you're smart, smarter than anyone has ever given you credit for. If we fall, I know you'll find a way to defeat that bastard."

Miles quietly took control of his emotions, letting the outside still express his grief. Inside, however, he contemplated the situation. He knew nothing he said could convince his father to change his mind. If he stood up and walked away in seeming defeat, perhaps his father would leave him with his anchors. Then he could just tether to them after they leave.

Rising from his seat, Miles put on a good show. He wiped his tears away with his sleeve and sucked in a shuddering breath. "Fine. I'll stay behind. But if you don't come back, I'll never forgive you." He cast everyone a final, pained glance to put the nail in the coffin and then stalked away from the table. At the entryway of the room, Miles heard Matthias clear his throat.

Shit! Miles winced and came about.

Matthias rose from his seat and crossed the room to Miles. He held out his hand. "I need your anchors, son. I know you too well to let you keep them."

"No trust," Miles snapped at his father. He jammed his fist into his pocket, pulling out the glass orbs and handing them over forcefully.

His father handed him back one of the anchors. It was Charles'. "Keep this."

"Why?"

"You'll need it to get back here the next time you tether."

Miles shrugged. "But, he's dead. How will it bring me back to him?"

"Dead or not, this is where he's buried. The anchor will always bring you back to where he rests."

"Thanks."

Without his anchors, a major blow had been dealt to his clandestine plan. He would have to secretly petition his mother and brother for help, though he doubted they'd be complicit in disobeying Matthias. The last thing Miles wanted, though, was to appeal to Annelise. That contingency nauseated him. He went off in search of an alternate solution to his dilemma.

CHAPTER TWENTY-TWO

Miles approached his mother in confidence, hoping she might see things his way. However, she protested vehemently. Just as his father had said before, she reiterated how Miles represented their last hope should their mission fail. Besides, he was her baby and she didn't want to send him into danger. Foolishly, he compared himself to Alistair without thinking it through. His mother quickly reminded Miles that while his brother appeared to be a year or two older, he had lived as long as the average mortal in the twenty-first century. Her counter argument shut him down cold. Though he knew better than to try, he approached Alistair next. His brother's response didn't surprise him. He had their father's back, almost repeating Mathias' ultimatum word-for-word. Should something unthinkable befall the family patriarch, Alistair was every bit ready to assume the mantle of leadership without missing a beat. Their father had groomed him well.

Miles stood in the estate gardens, brooding over the quagmire that his life had become. Neither the beauty of the neatly manicured tiers of shrubberies, nor the colorful bloom of spring, nor the shafts of sunlight bathing his face in warmth could lift his spirits. The hardened freeze of a desolate winter wind clutched at his heart. Not a single argument gave him leverage over his family members. When his mother, father, and brother tethered into danger that night, he would find himself alone again and quite possibly forever. He wanted to believe that they were all wrong, that the little bit of training he had over the past few weeks made him a worthy combatant, and that he was truly ready to plunge into battle. But in a moment of brutal honesty with himself, Miles admitted that if their roles were reversed, he knew he'd be just as vigilant against his participation that night.

He reached down for the nearest stone, picked it up, reared back, and let it fly as hard and as far as he could. It spun through the air until it collided with a large spruce tree and fell on top of Charles' headstone, knocking off all of the stones placed there on the day of his burial. Miles sighed audibly and crossed the yard. Picking them up one at a time, he placed them back atop the grave. The last one he placed he recognized as Annelise's. He shook his head thinking about her. *Pain in the ass!* Miles looked to the house and wondered where she'd be sulking. He hated himself for what he knew he had to do.

Annelise was different; she was a wildcard that no one could count on. She came and went as she pleased and didn't take to Matthias' leadership. And while Miles' relationship with her was anything but cordial, she at least provided him with one last, unfortunate option. He cringed inside at the thought of approaching her. She bristled every time he spoke to her as though the sound of his voice made her physically uncomfortable. It had become clear to Miles that she had no respect for him or his abilities. Annelise had a singular mindset, focused solely on revenge, and anything standing in her way would confront the darkness that lurked within her. He had been privy to her dark side far too often for his liking, but he knew that he had no choice. He now had to beg her for help.

"Damn it!" he grunted to himself. With bounding steps, he climbed the tiers of the garden and entered the manor through the cook's entrance. Like most of the house since Charles died, the kitchen stood cold and dark. He weaved his way past the butcher block and ascended the servant's back stairwell that led to the formal dining room above. Matthias, Alistair, and Elizabeth sat at the baronial table reviewing the small details of their battle plan. Miles stole a glance or two at their battle plans before they noticed him. They intended on blending into the crowd as groundlings so that they stood as close to the stage as possible when the theater burst into flames. That would keep them from being swept out of the theater by the swell of panicking patrons. They had no idea who Gaius would be masquerading as, but they felt confident that it had to have assumed the form of one of the actors or stagehands in order to allay suspicion and gain insight into the theater's workings.

"Miles," his mother gasped as she turned about abruptly and clasped one hand over her chest and another on her son's arm. "My dear, you scared the life out of me."

He frowned sheepishly. "Sorry, Mom." His father and brother looked upon him with forced smiles. Neither of them seemed to exude confidence. He felt like they were all looking upon one another for the last time. The ache inside him grew with each passing moment. "Has anyone seen Annelise?"

Alistair furrowed his brow in thought and replied, "I think I saw her in the library a little while ago, getting ready to tether."

"Why?" his father pried suspiciously. "What's wrong, Miles?"

Miles shook his head and frowned. "Nothing. I just wanted to say good-bye to her. Never know if I'll get the chance again."

"The way you two have gone at it over the past few days I didn't think you'd even care." Elizabeth rose from her chair and hugged her son. Miles closed his eyes, focusing on the gentle touch of his mother. It was another memory he wanted to store away in his little cigar box, but he couldn't preserve the moment, only remember it. As Elizabeth pulled away she continued, "You're a very kind young man. I hope she can look past her problems for a moment and appreciate the gesture."

Moments later, Miles stood in the entryway of the library. The whole place sat quiet and lonely. Taking a few steps inside, Miles could see through the inner archway to the study, which too seemed empty. Well, not entirely empty. On the center table sat Annelise's coat, balled up into a heap, and her travel bag open with its contents sprawled about. He passed through the library to investigate the rest of the study.

Miles heard the creak of floorboards behind him and a displeased sigh. Craning his head around to his rear, he laid eyes on Annelise who looked quite irritated. She huffed with indignation and attempted to cross the room to collect her belongings. Miles stepped in front of her to block her path to the sitting room.

"What do you want?" she inquired nastily.

"Please, Annelise," Miles begged. "I need your help."

"Why should I help you?" Annelise snarled. She looked him up and down with a snide grimace. It was as if he were a bug she'd no sooner crush under her boot than avoid stepping on. Annelise exhaled a sharp breath through her nose and narrowed her eyes at him. "You'll probably just get in the way, get somebody killed." She stalked past him into the sitting room and under her breath muttered, "Moron." Then she sat down upon the window seat, one leg folded up beneath her, and glanced over her shoulder out the window.

The sunlight that filled the room played off the auburn highlights in her dark hair. She possessed an aggressive, predatory nature that he found both intimidating and beautiful all at once. The paradox infuriated him.

"I'm not moron! And by the looks of things, sweetheart, you're about five minutes older than me, so don't give me any of that 'kid' crap either."

"Looks can be deceiving," she responded coolly, without giving Miles even a cursory glance. "You're what, sixteen?"

He took a moment to answer, wondering where this question was headed. "No, seventeen. So what! How old are you?"

"Well, by all accounts, around seventy-five." Her tone changed from factual to snide. "I've lost track over time."

"Fine! Whatever!" Miles shot back angrily. He wasn't interested in the finer details of her sordid history. He knew she was notably older, he just never knew how much older. Keeping track of his time on Earth let alone his fellow time travelers was going to be a tough task now that age was no longer a visible, tangible thing. Just another annoying part of life he needed to acculturate himself to. He was pissed that she sucked him into her trap. "But I'm no idiot. I know what we're up against out there."

Annelise leaned back against the window frame. She pulled her right foot up onto the window seat so that her knee was tucked against her chest. She glared at Miles. Her eyebrows furrowed in protest. "Oh, I'm sure. You've had what, four of five weeks of study and maybe some simulated combat?" She leaned forward. "Ever face death?" With a swift and violent yank Annelise drew her pistol from its holster and held it with intent against her temple. She started getting loud. "Ever have a gun pointed at your head or a blade pressed so tight to your throat that you can feel your skin splitting?" She jerked the pistol away from her head and let her arm hang over her knee.

Miles placed his hand across his throat, remembering their first encounter back in the alleyway. "Yeah, I've got some experience with that. No thanks to you."

She scowled at him from across the room. "That was nothing."

"You know what?" Miles crossed the room, pointing at her menacingly. "Before I got ripped away from my shitty life I didn't have to deal with those things." He stopped just feet from her. It was his turn to yell. "But since then I've had to outrun assassins after they murdered my foster-family and deal with your bullshit! And now that I've finally found my real family, the last thing I want is to be orphaned again, only this time because I didn't do anything to try to stop it."

"Boo hoo," she said snidely, wiping away imaginary tears of pity. "Do you think you're something special?" Annelise hopped down from the seat and took an aggressive step toward him so their faces were mere inches apart. "We've all suffered loss. None of us had it easy. I had to listen to the screams and cries of my adoptive family the night the Gestapo broke down the door and took them away. And what did I do? I hid like a coward in a broom closet until my real parents came and found me. So don't give me your sob stories about not being able to do anything to stop it. At least your foster family was put out of their misery quickly. God only knows what Hell mine faced before the Nazis finally executed them."

"That's right," Miles derided her, "you've got it bad. You've lost everything that matters to you. But you know what? I don't intend on losing all that I have left. So you can take your experience and shove it! I'm not going to stand by and do nothing this time." He leaned in and scowled menacingly at Annelise, pointing at her. "I refuse to end up like you."

"Go to Hell," Annelise fired back, staring him down. She clenched her trembling jaw. Redness circled the whites of her eyes where a line of tears pooled along the lids.

Not in the mood to listen to her cries, Miles turned away to leave. But when he reached the archway his feet stopped. There were no whimpers, no cries of sadness to hear. Instead, he felt a great ache of grief welling up inside of him. It was not the kind of grief that came from being helpless. Miles knew that pain all too well. This was a different kind of grief, the kind he wished someone at some time felt for him. It was grief that came from knowing he hurt someone with his words. Back in his time, words, cruel phrases, and evil taunts were the tools of his tormentors. They used them to break him down, to dehumanize him for their entertainment. And even though he did not intend his words to serve the same ends, he had hurt her nevertheless. Yes, she may have been somewhat deserving for the lack of kindness and respect she showed him, but it still didn't make it right. Nor could Miles ignore the pain that he knew she had to be feeling.

Miles turned back to her. He saw Annelise sitting upon the window seat, diligently cleaning the inner workings of her opal-handled pistol with an oiled rag. She wore a steely cold look of hatred upon her face. That look reminded him of the mask he wore when he felt the most pain inside. *Anger beguiles those that seek weakness and chases away those that may desire intimacy.* It was a quote his social worker read to him once from some dusty old psych textbook. It took until that moment, looking at Annelise, to understand it and how it applied to him. When you've lost the things that you hold most dear to you, especially loved ones, you don't want anyone getting close to you for fear the same terrible loss may come again.

Miles moved toward the fireplace. He stared at the Albright family portrait that hung above the green marble mantle. It was a painting depicting a truly happier time when mother, father, son, and daughter were still at peace: before Abigail's painful death, Trevor's betrayal of the Order, and Charles' subsequent murder at his son's hands. Annelise was alone, and that feeling was something he had lived with his entire life. Even if she wouldn't admit it, they shared a great many things in common.

"I don't envy you one bit," Miles admitted, his voice sad and consoling. He turned in her direction and frowned apologetically.

Annelise cast him a confused, squinty glare. "What do you mean?" A hint of displeasure accented her voice.

"What you have to do tonight." Miles paused, searching for the right words. He couldn't find any that seemed appropriate, so he stared at the wood floor, kicked at a rough knot in the hardwood, and painfully uttered the only thing that came to mind. "Hunting down your brother, I mean."

"He's not my brother," she replied, not breaking stride with her weapon maintenance.

With cautious steps, Miles approached Annelise and sat beside her on the window seat. She made no move to make him believe his presence was unwelcome.

"It wasn't enough for him to betray the Order, but to let that happen to our father." She shook her head, slapped a freshly loaded clip into the pistol, and jerked it hard into its holster. "My brother's dead. Tonight's about revenge." When she closed her eyes, the surface tension that held back the wall of welled-up tears broke and lines of wetness spilled down across her cheeks. She rose from her seat and made her way to the fireplace. Annelise stood glaring at the painting.

Miles leaned forward where he sat, laying his forearms across his knees, his fingers intertwined. He tried not to look at her. "I know what it's like to be alone."

"I'm sure you do, Miles." She paused for a moment. "Look, I can't help being jealous. You still have your family. You're not alone anymore. My mother and father are gone, and now I have to kill Trevor. You're right. You don't want to end up like me. All I have left is hate. That isn't much to live for, or fight for."

Miles lifted his head and let his gaze fall on her. She no longer glared at the painting. She now stood, shoulders hunched, looking down at the fireplace and subtly shaking her head. The impregnable stone fortress she erected around her emotions lay in ruins. Miles hopped down from the window seat and approached her. He pensively laid a hand on her right shoulder, expecting her to round on him and take a swing. Instead, she reached up with her left hand and laid it upon his. She trembled.

Miles felt nervous; his voice cracked as he spoke. "Hey, we might not be your family, but as long as we're alive, you're not alone."

Annelise turned her head just enough to see him out of the corners of her eyes. Her young face seemed suddenly worn and aged. "I'm sorry I called you stupid, Miles. You're not. In fact, you're pretty damn sharp. Sharp enough, I'll bet, to figure out a way to follow us." She straightened her posture and wiped away the tears with her sleeve.

"But how? My father took all my anchors."

"You still have your chronoperpetua, right?"

Miles threw up his hands in defeat. "Yeah. But I'll never make it there in time without an anchor. That's what I was hoping you could help me with."

"I'm sorry, Miles." Annelise shrugged. "I can't. I don't have any to give." Leaning close, she whispered, "But that doesn't mean you can't make a new one." She pulled back and gleamed a wry smile at Miles.

Make a new anchor? Is that what she means? Miles wondered if it could be that simple.

Clapping him on the upper arm, Annelise walked past him and withdrew her chronoperpetua from her pocket. With a few deft adjustments of the dials, she set her course, and turned back one last time to Miles. "Your father's right, though. If we fail, someone's got to carry on after we're gone...someone strong."

Miles puffed himself up a bit and stood tall to fit the bill. "We won't fail."

"I hope you're right." Annelise slid her fingers into the grips of the chronoperpetua and secured the strap around her wrist. Pointing it at the center of the room, she activated the device. A ribbon of azure energy shot from it, ripping a hole in the space-time continuum. The tether raced through the rift in search of its anchor point. Rippling tendrils, like squid tentacles, weaved a braid along her forearm and took hold. As the terminus wave swept back along the energy pulse toward Annelise, she called out to Miles through the deafening din. "Take care, Miles."

"You too!" he yelled back. "Good luck!"

When the wave met the chronoperpetua, the vacuum of the continuum engulfed her in a wrenching tug, and she was gone. In her place, a lingering emptiness remained. Yet it was not a tangible vacancy.

It was one Miles, to his amazement, felt inside. One he felt at seeing Annelise leave. A few days earlier, he wouldn't have believed he'd feel any emotion for her besides anger and resentment. But the wisps of a bond that formed between them in those short moments before her departure had his heart and mind whispering to him for more. He hoped beyond hope that this wasn't the last time they'd see each other.

With her gone, Miles immediately recalled all the materials that could be used to fill an anchor: fingernail clippings, flakes of skin, blood samples, or hair trimmings. *How am I going to get any of those without somebody getting suspicious?* And where would he find an empty anchor to put the genetic residue in once he obtained it. A sudden, instant jolt of excitement ran through him as an idea sparked to life. He'd have to wait until everyone left, but he had an idea that just might work. Trying to control his excitement, Miles did his best to fake his disappointment in staying behind. Then he went off to help his family prepare for battle.

CHAPTER TWENTY-THREE

A gloomy sky lingered over London and the countryside of Southwark, just beyond the Thames. The loss of sunlight kept the temperatures cool but not so low as to keep patrons of the arts from attending William Shakespeare's latest play. People from all walks of life slowly filtered into the circular confines of the Globe, handing over their meager earnings to escape from the drudgeries of life. Many of those handing over a mere penny for a groundling admission squinted at the bleak veil overhead and grumbled of their hopes that the skies would not open up on them during the performance. Others appeared to disregard the imperfect weather completely, having spent the better part of their lives working in the muck and filth.

Those with the means to do so, surrendered upwards of three pence for covered seating beneath the thatch that conveniently provided shelter from the elements and distance from the stench of the groundlings. A clear dichotomy existed between the haves and have-nots of British society; from the quality of their clothes to cleanliness of their bodies, everyone knew their place and kept with their own. And only Shakespeare's carefully scripted homage to Queen Elizabeth's father in the form of *Henry VIII* could bring them all together.

Annelise entered at the head of all the patrons and sat herself down dead center in the backmost row of the lower level—the perfect vantage point by which to monitor the events within. The constant flow of people into the theatre brought the house to maximum capacity in very little time at all. Yet, through the mass of humanity, she had no trouble picking out her allies for the impending encounter. Matthias, dressed in the garb of a field hand, stood in the shadow of the down-left pillar of the thrust stage, mingling with the rest of the impoverished. To Annelise's ten o'clock, Elizabeth sat rail side in the dress of a house servant. Her eldest son stood vigil at the main gate, ensuring that their prey did not escape. Miles, however, she didn't see. She felt certain he would succeed in fashioning an anchor, but if he delayed any longer, he might be too late to help.

Within moments of closing the gate, the sound of horns and strings from the Heavens called the audience to attention. When the music faded, a young man entered the stage from the left balcony door, dressed in the costume of a servant. He laid his hands upon the rail and began to sing.

"I come no more to make you laugh: things now, that bear a weighty and a serious brow, sad, high, and working, full of state and woe, such noble scenes as draw the eye to flow, we now present—"

His voice trailed on through the chorus of the play while Annelise's mind perseverated on those first lines. They carried an irony that did not escape her. There would be no laughter once the real life drama soon to play out supplanted that of Shakespeare's company. Blood and tears would flow from those soon to perish upon these hallowed grounds. And though none of them shared a common noble ancestry, their cause, their struggle was perhaps the most noble of all. The actor sang about history, about paying homage to those who had passed from this Earth by these staged imitations. If the Order failed in their mission, the histories yet to be written and the songs yet to be sung might express a wholly different tenor and feeling than the natural course of time might otherwise inspire.

Her thoughts drifted from the greater cause to the one that stirred her blood—vengeance. Annelise understood all too well that the battle ahead would breed few possible outcomes and believed herself prepared to face them all. But as she waited for the boom of the cannon to rouse her to action, a stark realization breached her psychological defenses and attempted to rob her of the hatred that gave her power. Could she really spill the blood of the man she'd known as her beloved brother for the last few decades? It brought her to the brink of an emotional upheaval she felt powerless to stop. The once impervious fortress that protected her innermost feelings continued to crack and crumble. It took marshaling every wisp of self-control within to keep her composure. Annelise pushed back at the weakness, reminding herself that Trevor left her no choice. It was his decisions that brought them all to this moment. Those thoughts reunited her with the anger that once before gave her strength. Brick by brick, a new fortress rose from the rubble and ruin to protect her heart. Her resolve strengthened, Annelise took pause and banished any lingering doubt or fear. She was ready.

When Annelise finally broke from her contemplations, she found the play in full swing and drawing close to the very moment that she and the Dravens awaited. She reached into her coat and pulled from the inside pocket a crinkled, folded-up page torn from her father's copy of the first folio. Listening to the words of the actors, Annelise scanned the page to find a match.

"Your grace is noble," the voice of an unknown character echoed in the theatre. "Let me have such a bowl may hold my thanks, and save me so much talking."

Annelise glanced up at the action on stage and tried to identify who had just spoken. An older gentleman, dressed in the frock of a Catholic Cardinal, moved around a table occupied by two younger looking gentlemen and a boy made up to be a woman. They all wore the fancy linens of courtiers.

The older man, who Annelise identified as Cardinal Wolsey, said, "My Lord Sands, I am beholding to you: cheer your neighbours. Ladies, you are not merry: gentlemen, whose fault is this?"

Sands and Wolsey talking in the same scene, Annelise noted. The action had progressed to act I, scene iv, when the history on stage would soon turn to tragedy beyond. She searched feverishly to find her place on the page.

"The red wine first must rise in their fair cheeks, my lord," the actor portraying Lord Sands, answered back. "Then we shall have 'em talk us to silence."

The voice of Anne Boleyn replied with false modesty, "You are a merry gamester, my Lord Sands."

Annelise found her place in the play. In her periphery, she could see the key lines of the script circled in ink. The moment when the entire theatre would erupt in hysterics drew at a pace. Letting the scrap of paper fall from her hands, Annelise tried to calm the swirling butterflies in her stomach by focusing on the action of the play.

"Yes," Lord Sands answered Anne, "if I make my play. Here's to your ladyship," he raised an empty goblet up high. "And pledge it, madam, for 'tis to such a thing,—"

The effeminate young man who portrayed Anne Boleyn played the part well. Annelise had to remind herself of his gender as she watched. "You cannot show me."

"I told your grace they would talk anon," Lord Sands concluded joyfully.

From above, a sizzling boom echoed through the theatre. The whole audience jumped at the abnormally loud blast from the cannon. Frightened faces locked on the ball of flame that shot from the front window of the Heavens as it traced a hissing arc toward the thatch roof.

Cardinal Wolsey recoiled and ducked down behind the table where the other actors cowered. Still trying to stay in character but clearly overcome by worry, he shouted "What's that?"

The moment the fireball hit the roof, the crackle of tinder and the smell of pitch overwhelmed the theatre. Men and women alike screamed with terror at the sight of a massive inferno encircling the top of the theatre with unimaginable speed. The theatregoers rushed for the exits, trampling over one another to escape to the safety of the open streets. Annelise, the Dravens, and a large number of unidentified others held their positions, unfazed by the hysterics of the crowd.

The leftmost door of the tiring house blew off its hinges and sprayed chunks of wood across the stage floor. From a swirling cloud of smoke, a man stepped out onto the stage dressed as Henry VIII.

Annelise rose from her seat at the sight of him. It was John Lowin, the man who Gaius took possession of the night before. "That's him!" Annelise shouted over the fading din of the dispersing crowd and leapt over the railing. Elizabeth and Alistair sprang to her side. Matthias backed away from the demon, drawing his weapons.

Gaius growled at them all. "Keep them busy," he growled. With a wave of his hand, the right front corner of the stage tore away. Boards and splinters of wood exploded outward. The nameless confederates who lingered in the theatre sprang with drawn swords at the small group of chronoshifters. The fight for the future had begun.

CHAPTER TWENTY-FOUR

Alone again. The unbearable stillness of the Albright mansion closed in on Miles. It stood as a haunting reminder of what his life might be if his family failed in their mission. Though he had only been a part of this family for a few weeks, he knew that he didn't want to go on without them if they perished that night. He had no plans to forge on. Miles had resigned himself to whatever their fate may be—living or dying by the sword.

With reckless determination, Miles scrambled off toward the north wing of the mansion and the bedrooms. Somehow he had to construct an anchor and use that to tether into battle. He had his chronoperpetua, but simply travelling to the present wouldn't solve his dilemma. Miles would never be able to reach the theatre in time. Only a direct tether would land him in the Globe, by their side. His father thankfully left Miles with the means to achieve the first part of his plan. Charles' anchor could be repurposed to tether to another target. After all, it was filled with his genetic material and would always bring Miles back to where his decomposing body lay. So if he emptied the contents and replaced them with someone else's leavings, it should, in theory, take him to that person.

Miles entered his parents' bedroom first in the hopes that he might find what he needed. First, however, he needed to empty the old anchor. At his parents' bedside sat a half-empty pot of cold water used for washing. Removing Charles' anchor from his pocket, Miles gripped each side of the crystal orb and twisted the two halves in opposite directions. The two pieces came apart with some effort. He quickly dumped out the contents on the floor before submerging the anchor in the water. Using his fingers, Miles rubbed at the smooth interior to dislodge any clinging particles. Then he removed it from the water and wiped the inside dry with an unused hand towel that sat beside the pot. After inspecting the two halves closely, Miles felt confident that the anchor was clean.

He immediately crossed the room to inspect the vanity in search of genetic material. Miles glanced over the collected belongings that rested there: a music box filled with hairpins, broaches, jewelry, cosmetics, and an opal handled hairbrush. The hairpins and brush held the best chance for success. Miles grabbed the music box and dumped its contents on the vanity. Kneeling down to eyelevel, he scrutinized each bent metal wire for a single filament of his mother's hair. Just one would be sufficient for the chronoperpetua to hone in on. Nothing. Not a damn thing. Then he took hold of the hairbrush and brushed his hand against the bristles, looking for any hairs that might pop up from within. The brush couldn't have been cleaner were it new. Not even a flake of dandruff fell from it. He knew, especially in those uncertain times of betrayal, that his mother, father, and brother would have carefully disposed of any and all physical residue they might leave behind, and they preached it to him constantly. You didn't want anyone following you unless you wanted them to.

Frustrated, Miles rose from his kneeling position, spun on his heels, and flung the brush across the room with a grunt. It clattered into the headboard of the bed and fell on the pillow beneath. *The pillow!* Hairbrushes and hairpins stood out and were obvious places to search. Perhaps they never considered scouring their pillows.

Miles crossed to the room in three massive strides, fueled by the possibility of success. He picked up one pillow and then the other, analyzing every inch of the stark white cotton for any red or brown hairs that lingered. Again, his efforts resulted in defeat. He knew he was running out of time and options.

With no other viable sources of genetic material to sift through, Miles stalked from his parent's room and down the hall to his brother's room. He threw open the door and stepped inside. Alistair's belongings, he thought, were the least likely to produce any leavings. His brother was more clean-cut than Jack, his old nemesis, and even more exacting than his parents. Miles always pictured him scrubbing down his skin and hair at night like an "In-valid" from *Gattaca* using a "borrowed ladder." And his bedroom, even this one that he'd only been using for a few short days, spoke to his anal nature. Miles knew just looking at the place that he wouldn't find anything to aid his cause. A cursory examination confirmed his suspicions. Nothing.

Miles stepped back out into the hallway, leaned against the wall, and puzzled over what he would do next. The only three people he could tether to were gone, along with their genetic residue. How was he ever going to find any material to fill a sphere? Miles closed his eyes and let the back of his skull drum against the plaster wall. He let his head hit with enough force that he felt a sting of pain, which immediately sparked to the forefront a distant memory—the very first moment he met Annelise. She jumped out from the shadow of an alleyway, kneed him in the balls, and slammed the back of his head against a brick wall. That was the Annelise he had known for the past few weeks: a snotty, stuck-up, self-centered bitch. It was hardly a tender memory, other than the bruising of his testicles.

Then Miles clenched his jaw and moved past that thought to a more recent, singular moment of vulnerability where her defenses lay strewn across the floor in tatters before him. It was the moment he came to realize that a fearful, hurt little girl still lingered beneath her protective exterior. She wanted everyone to believe that she viewed her mission that night as a business transaction. Kill Trevor and avenge her father's death—simple, cold calculation. But deep down, Annelise didn't relish her mission. Trevor, regardless of what she would admit, was still her brother, and she had to kill him to set things right. It quietly tore her apart inside. Miles truly never believed her capable of such emotion. In that brief moment that she let her guard down, however, he found a kindred spirit who he understood and empathized with. And the tears that wet her soft, ruddy cheeks only a short time before had set aflutter the wings of a hundred hummingbirds in his chest. Perhaps he finally found someone just like himself, someone who he understood and who understood him in return. Perhaps he hated her because he saw so much of himself in her. Perhaps...perhaps he might fall for her if they had yet to spend their last moment together.

His eyes snapped open with a jolt. "Of course!" Miles shouted, "Annelise!" Maybe she left something behind for him to use. She was a bit of a nomad, always coming and going from the house, and she didn't seem to take the time or care to erase any evidence of her existence in her travels. In fact, Annelise didn't give a damn if anyone followed her, especially Trevor. She wanted him to. Her desperation to end her brother's life and possibly her own made her reckless. It was that reckless spirit that Miles affixed his last hopes to.

Miles sprinted down the hallway to Annelise's bedchamber. With a wrenching twist, he turned the knob and ran into the door with his shoulder. The dense oak didn't budge. *Locked!* Of course, of all the rooms in the house, hers had to be locked. She may not have been a teenager anymore, but she sure acted like it at times.

Sprinting back to his room, Miles grabbed for his overcoat. He reached for the inside pocket, pulled out his lock pick set, and let the garment fall to the floor. In a blink he was back at her door, working his warded pick into the old-style lock. Being relatively new to the art of lock picking, Miles struggled to manipulate the pick. He knew he had to be patient and feel his way through it. His fingertips trembled and sweat dripped down his brow. Just when Miles was about to rip the pick out and throw it down the hallway, he felt it slide freely past the internal wards of the lock and heard the locking mechanism pop open.

A great sigh escaped Miles. He rose to his feet, returned the ward pick to its case, and wiped his forehead with his sleeve. Giving the doorknob a second try, it gave no resistance and turned with a click. Miles stepped forward, pushing the door open. The room stood in near total darkness. He couldn't see a damn thing. Gingerly, Miles crossed the room and reached for a pair of drapes. With a firm yank, he pulled them apart.

A stinging wash of sunlight cast Annelise's pigsty of a room into clear focus. From the cloud of dust that erupted from the fabric, Miles suspected the drapes hadn't been opened in years. The air was alive with sparkling particles that drifted about aimlessly in the light. His suspicions were confirmed by the hundreds of burnt out candle nubs that littered the room. As he took in the scene, a bit of shock overcame Miles. He had no idea what kind of a person Annelise was before her father's untimely death, but it was clear that she had been simmering in a pit of darkness. Red markings covered the chalk white walls, spelling out her brother's name in erratic, eerie writing. He wondered briefly if Annelise used blood to write his name, but then he caught sight of a small can of red paint on her vanity. If this was what she spent her quiet hours musing over, she was treading a very fine line between sanity and bat-shit crazy.

An oddity then struck Miles. It was obvious at first blush that Annelise was not the clean-freak her father claimed. He found it hard to believe from the condition of her room that she diligently disposed of any genetic residue she left behind. The mess wasn't just the result of a few weeks of melancholy. This pigsty hadn't been cleaned in years. *But why lie about it? What was Charles trying to hide?* The only reason Miles could think of was that he didn't want to find Annelise or Trevor. It was a mystery for which Miles didn't have time.

He turned his attention to the vanity, examining the objects that rested there. "Yes!" Miles hissed, swinging a clenched fist in celebration. Annelise's belongings didn't disappoint. A large clump of her auburn hair lay tangled in the bristles of her hairbrush. He pulled it free and used his fingertips to roll it up into a misshapen ball. Then he pulled the emptied anchor from his pocket. Miles pressed the wad of hair into one side of the sphere and then attached the other side, twisting them until the threads meshed together. Finished closing the sphere, Miles held it up to eye level and examined the newly formed anchor; the pieces of Annelise's hair sat safely nestled within the smoky crystalline orb.

Miles jammed the orb into his trousers and raced off to his room to collect his belongings. He stripped down to his bare chest and boxers, pulled a light body armor vest over his head, and secured the Velcro panels. Over it he wore a loose fitting white shirt and a black lace-up doublet. He pulled on matching black gusseted breeches and riding boots, all pieces that wouldn't make him stand out in Elizabethan England should he be stranded there.

Around his shoulders and his waist he strapped his double holster and added a full cache of clips. Miles understood that his Berretta didn't fit the time period he was preparing to tether to and that firearms were a last resort weapon, but he refused to go into such a life or death encounter without it. If it came down to it, if pulling the trigger saved his loved ones, he wouldn't think twice. Having affixed a suppressor to the end of the barrel, Miles jerked the slide back to chamber a round before securing it under his arm. Just below the belt portion of his holster he secured a second belt from which his Italian three ring rapier and dagger hung. And over it all he threw a black cloak and secured the top clasp to keep it on his shoulders.

Miles exhaled a nervous breath. There was no turning back once he tethered. He'd never truly been in a battle outside of the night Charles was murdered and the day he beat Jack to a pulp outside the gym. But this was for real. There stood a very real chance that he would not live to see another sunrise. Maybe Annelise was right, maybe he wasn't ready. Miles felt himself shaking inside. He wanted to throw up.

Miles shook his head and swore at himself under his breath, cursing his cowardice. He swallowed hard, trying to muster all his courage, and strapped the chronoperpetua to his hand. Each strap was pulled taut until it choked off the flow of blood to his fingers. Flipping open the core of the device, Miles laid the new anchor in place, closed it, and turned the locking ring. He grabbed hold of his right wrist with his left hand, raised both arms before him, and targeted an open space in the room. With a few quick breaths to steel himself, Miles closed his fingers down on the chronoperpetua. A snaking tether of blue energy erupted from the device and tore open a hole in the fabric of time. His body jolted back from the force of the beam. Tendrils of chronometric particles crawled up his forearm and latched hold just as the terminus wave struck. Miles closed his eyes and held his breath as the vortex consumed him with wrenching power. The cold of chronospace welcomed the traveler back.

CHAPTER TWENTY-FIVE

Miles emerged from the vortex like a rock skipping across a pond. He hit hard and fast, his momentum sending him into a painful tumble that left him skidding on his back through a swath of mud and slop. His nerve endings screamed out in pain. The discomfort caused him to suck in a convulsive gasp that reeked of pitch and burning pine. No sooner had his lungs filled with the distasteful air than they expelled the irritant with violent force.

His fight or flight instincts kicked in. Miles rolled over onto his side, grabbed a handful of his cloak, and drew it over his nose and mouth, desperate for clean oxygen. After a few filtered breaths, his coughing subsided enough to think beyond the pain. A deafening hissing and crackling from above begged of his attention. Craning his neck, he looked up into the nighttime sky. Though pelting raindrops made his eyelids flutter, they couldn't blind him to the angry flames that besieged the encircling thatch roof of the Globe Theater nor could they snuff out its power. The rending flames tore at the straw and sprayed cinders all about, which swirled and pirouetted through the air like fireflies. Many extinguished with a hiss when they collided with rain drops mid-air, falling to the earth as ashen rain. The others, however, survived the fall only to fizzle out in the mud. And what Miles assumed, at first glance, to be a sunless sky turned out to be a wall of thick, black smoke that billowed upwards from the blaze, blotting out the sun as if night had fallen. Dark, swirling vapors wafted down into the theater grounds from above—a vaporous octopus reaching out for passing prey. It was a nightmarish sight that his best efforts to prepare himself for had failed miserably. His pupils dilated with fear at the sight of it, and his heart kicked into an adrenaline-fueled overdrive. A nervous queasiness filled his belly.

The sudden clatter and clang of swordplay then struck at Miles, drawing his attention away from the ring of Hellfire above. His head pivoted left and right as he tried desperately to key in on any immediate danger. The groundling section teemed with warriors, both friend and foe, engaged in frenzied swordplay, but no one had taken notice of Miles yet. Turning over onto his stomach, he attempted to push himself up onto his hands and knees to stand, but he found that his arrival had robbed him of his strength. His weakened limbs wobbled beneath him. Unable to push himself up, Miles sat back with his legs bent beneath him and waited for his muscles to recover.

As he watched the fray unfolding before him, Miles felt his mouth go dry without warning. It was a sensation that had haunted him since it took control of him back in the manor the night they lost Charles. It caused him to withdraw, to lose all courage when it was needed the most. This time, however, it didn't blind him by a fog of gut wrenching memories. This time he told those memories and the doubt to go fuck themselves. Miles willed himself to focus his every thought on his inadequacy, on his craven actions that may have cost them the life of a dear friend. A swell of anger rose in him which took control of the fear and fused with it. The synergy of his greatest strength and his greatest weakness provided Miles with clarity he had never experienced in all of his painful years—a far cry from the day he nearly beat Jack to death.

Miles unfolded his right leg and planted that foot firmly into the mud. Gritting his teeth, he took a deep breath, pushed off on his knee with both hands, and rose from the muck with a grunt of determination. At full height, however, a surge of lightheadedness swept over him. The whole world spun and swayed. He teetered a bit, but did not topple over. Closing his eyes for a moment, he steadied himself and shook off the dizziness like a wet dog. When they opened again, a calmer, more confident view of the world greeted him. Taking a relaxed, supple grip of both his dagger and his rapier, he drew them from their scabbards and launched himself forward at a sprint. The whole theater bounced in his scanning frame of vision as he dashed into battle. His legs drove him straight toward his mother the moment he recognized her shape and her desperate defensive movements.

Two men wielding massive broadswords unleashed a furious barrage of strikes at her. Her sword and dagger cut through the air in zigzagging patterns that intercepted the paths of their humming blades. Each cut came within a hair's breadth of landing a fatal blow. The pace had started to overwhelm her physically. She gave ground as she parried each strike, pushed backward by the sheer force of their weapons. Strained grunts escaped her with each frantic clang of metal.

The larger of the two burly swordsmen swung his blade down overhead, which she caught with a crossing guard. The moment Elizabeth committed both of her keen blades to defending his strike, he brought a meaty foot up into her stomach. The blow threw her into the mud. Both weapons jumped from her grasp on impact and skittered across the ground. Then her opponents took the advantage, closing in on her with blood-thirsty grins. She wriggled away from their advances by digging her elbows and heels into the mud, but they overcame her feeble attempt with only a few steps. They raised their broadswords up over their heads, ready to hack her to pieces.

Instead of harnessing all his power to drop the fatal blow on Elizabeth, the largest of the two men flinched back with a look of fearful surprise. Without warning, Miles flashed before him, thrusting his dagger between the man's arms, and straight through his trachea. The blade severed his spine, and he fell into a limp, asphyxiating heap. When he fell away, Miles stomped on his back and leapt at the other warrior, thrusting his rapier at his midsection. Caught completely off guard, his blade failed to sweep Miles' weapon clear, and the tip of the sword dug into his hip. The assailant wailed in pain, gnashed his teeth, and swung his sword laterally at Miles. His sword and his hand, however, came away from the rest of his arm as Elizabeth jumped to her feet and swung her rapier at him, severing the limb. The man grabbed his gushing wrist, screaming in utter anguish. With a thrust of his dagger to the chest, Miles silenced him.

"Miles," his mother screamed and then threw her arms around him. "What are you doing here?"

Her arms squeezed the air right out of him. "Saving you apparently," he gasped while scanning the rest of the theater.

Elizabeth let go of him. She shook her head in clear disapproval of his presence. "You shouldn't be here!"

"I couldn't stay away."

"I know," she said, reaching up on her tiptoes to kiss him. Then her eyes suddenly flashed wide when she glanced over his shoulder. Her face contorted into a grimace of desperation. "Miles!" she screamed, pushing him aside. Both her blades swept back across her body, parrying a thrust by another would-be attacker.

Miles acted out of instinct and manipulated the momentum his mother provided so that he slid into a strong defensive posture. Stable despite the soggy earth and ready to reengage, he watched as the attacker stumbled toward Elizabeth. The man wasn't a member of the Order, Miles felt certain by his actions; he had sacrificed sure footing, laying a heavy wager for a killing strike. That gamble turned out to be a losing hand when his mother's sword came back across the man's chest and cleaved a cavernous wound that felled him. Even Miles, in his few weeks of training, had learned that lesson in oftentimes painful ways at both his brother and Master's hands. This man hadn't fought like a well-trained warrior at all; he fought like a brute swinging a sword. For that matter, neither had the two other men he and his mother had just dispatched. That's all they were...hired thugs.

A certain confidence rose up in Miles—if he could avoid the other chronoshifters and focus on those mercenaries, he might be able to hold his own in combat. That very assumption, however, immediately robbed him of his newly found confidence. He thought he had taken out two of their Order and now witnessed a third fall. He believed that his skills were up to par with his fellow chronoshifters. He'd been fooled. These men simply acted as human shields to cover Gaius and the other chronoshifters from danger while they pillaged the grounds, searching for Excalibur. The deadliest of combatants still awaited him.

Miles resumed his feverish search, squinting through the rain to find where they needed to take the battle. He located his brother and father nearby, engaged in fierce combat against multiple combatants, none of which appeared to be members of the Order either. Annelise had broken off from the rest of the pack and fought with a trio of her own at the other corner of the stage.

Takishima, Miles remembered. He fought off the glare of flickering firelight for anyone who appeared to be of Japanese heritage. Beyond the teeming swarm of warm bodies that monopolized his brother and father's attention stood a hooded figure that overlooked a team of men digging with great vigor. Several other men kept vigil over the excavation. All but one of them carried slender, curved swords at the ready to cut down anyone who got too close. *Katana blades*, Miles realized. A samurai's weapon of choice. The other man carried a weapon Miles recognized from his time with the Albrights—a gladius. "Trevor!" he gasped.

Miles raced to his mother as she whipped her rapier aside in an emphatic display of *chiburui*. His feet slipped a bit in the mud, but she caught his arm to stabilize him.

"Come on! We have to get over there!" he shouted through the din of combat. He pointed to the ravaged front corner of the thrust stage where the diggers labored beyond the protective guard.

"I know!" she yelled back, "but we can't get close enough without being swarmed."

He turned away from his mother and galloped through the mud toward his brother and father. Elizabeth called out to Miles from behind, but he didn't look back. Digging his heels into the ground, he brought himself to a halt between them.

His father caught sight of him and yelled, "Miles! What the Hell are you doing here?"

"Miles?" Alistair called out in surprise.

"Yeah," Miles admitted, "I don't listen very well."

Beads of sweat and rain dripped from Annelise as she battled against the dauntless mercenaries who came at her. What they lacked in skill, they made up for with strength and determination. They kept her on her toes but, thankfully, they couldn't coordinate their efforts worth a damn. She continued dodging and parrying their barrage of blades, patiently waiting for a chance to strike the fatal blow. Her battle had separated her from the rest of the Draven clan.

Annelise stole glances across the battleground to keep a wary eye on her brother. If Trevor made a break for it, tried to escape before she could exact her revenge, she planned on cutting him off. But from what she could see, he had no intentions of fleeing. For that matter, he didn't seem to have any intention of entering into combat either. While he held his gladius and pugio, they laid limp at his side. He stood beside Gaius, shifting his nervous gaze from the excavation to the battle unfolding before him.

Trevor showed no resemblance to the warrior she once knew and loved; instead of a bloodthirsty lion waiting to pounce on its prey and tear it to ribbons, Annelise saw a caged, skittish animal that would no sooner cower away from a threat than fight back. She expected more from such a callous, cold-blooded murderer. Plunging her gladius into the chest of such an adversary would usually bring her a depraved sort of joy. Watching the life ebb out of an enemy who had no right to live while better people died carried with it the best satisfaction imaginable for a warrior. Yet, killing this poor bastard would provide no such delight. She'd no sooner slay a child for bad language than waste her mettle on such a pathetic figure. *Perhaps that was Trevor's plan all along*, she postulated. Maybe he hoped it would defeat her resolve, weaken her spirit so that he could then exploit that weakness. She convinced herself that was the case and resolved that she wouldn't succumb to his manipulations.

A war cry from a nearby opponent called her full attention back to the melee. He came at her in a full-on bull rush, his sword drawn back to his right with both hands. She knew that if she stood her ground, he would overpower her before she could react. In an instant, she brought her gladius across her left side and fell to the ground beneath his sweeping blade. Annelise's left shin collided with his ankles while her right leg hooked around the back of his knees like a pair of scissors. He cried out in surprise. The lever action of her legs broke his balance, and he slammed face first into the mud, which muffled his objections. Before he could wrench his face free, Annelise whipped her gladius back around to her right, imbedding the blade halfway through the back of his skull. His body twitched and then fell still.

For a fleeting moment, she laid upon the cold, wet earth, staring up at the relentless, flaming beast. It razed the structure with a casual benevolence, seemingly content to devour it at a slow pace while savoring every morsel. Its lapping tongues penetrated through the topmost tier of seating while its wiry tentacles stretched down along the framework. With a sudden, echoing snap, the uppermost support beams gave way, crushed beneath the weight of the beast. The flaming thatch collapsed, spraying a swirl of angry cinders down across the grounds. They glided toward the embattled warriors like a billion blazing samaras. While her opponents covered up and cowered beneath the maelstrom, she lavished in its mesmerizing beauty. Annelise felt a passing calm sweep through her, and she beamed a tantalizing smile as the cinders drew so close that she could almost kiss them.

In no hurry to feel the sting of countless fiery barbs, Annelise rolled over onto her hands and knees in the instant before contact and drew her hood back up over her head. The sparks rained down across her back, burning out when they impacted against the damp cloth. Each cinder left behind tickling warmth that penetrated to her clothing but didn't burn.

Annelise looked down at her feet for the man's head, kicked at it, and pulled her gladius in the opposite direction to free her sword. Still clutching her pugio, she planted her left fist into the mud and rose with a slashing spin. She settled into a sturdy back stance, her gladius and pugio poised to attack. The pair of men that awaited her held bewitched looks upon their faces. They gazed at the lifeless man who lay at her feet.

The man to her left snapped out of his trance to blink at her through the rain. He surveyed the whole theater and then back at her. His features softened. The broadsword fell from his grasp. With the back of his hand, he smacked the chest of the other man who jolted to attention. "Fuck this, mate! Nothin's worth dyin like that."

"Right!" his partner barked back, throwing his sword to the ground. The two men took off running for the main gate. They stumbled and slipped through the mud like an awkward comedy act. Annelise watched them the whole way, not the least bit sorry for letting them get away. These people weren't mere shadows that she could dispatch without remorse; they had lives to live that might matter to the passage of time. And though they took up arms against her for a short time, they realized they had played the fool and escaped with their lives. Perhaps they'd yet make something of themselves.

Annelise turned her attention back to the Dravens, who had greatly thinned the remaining mercenaries. Once vanquished, the true battle would begin against their former brethren, and she would exact her revenge. Worry gripped her mind, though, as she recognized the fatigue in her limbs. From what she could see, her companions' movements lacked briskness too. They were going to be greatly disadvantaged against equally skilled yet rested opponents. Their only chance was to stand together when things came to a head. She couldn't stand with them though. Trevor was her responsibility, not theirs.

A massive brute headed toward Miles with deadly intent. He tossed a heavy sabre from hand to hand as though it weighed nothing. His long, greasy hair and the sinewy muscles that flexed in his forearms reminded Miles of his foster father.

"Bring it, shit head!" Miles taunted him and began bouncing like an MMA fighter ready to go to work. Both his dagger and rapier sat at the ready. Then the brute came hard at him, spinning the sabre across his chest in a crisscrossing flourish. The sword hummed through the air. Miles hadn't been trained to deal with this kind of attack yet, and he feared for his safety. The blade came within inches of his face. With careful steps, Miles retreated, shifting his weight from side to side. He hoped that if he kept his distance, an opening might be exposed.

Alistair, already engaged with two opponents of his own, stole a glance at Miles over his shoulder. He spun his dagger into a forearm guard to check a thrust to his chest. With fluidity and grace, his right hand came up under the man's arm, severing it at the elbow, and then sweeping back across his throat. Coming about to face his brother, he growled, "Oh, no you don't!" and whipped his dagger through the air at the brute. The narrow blade flew tip over pommel at its target. It hit hard and deep, but imbedded itself in the man's shoulder blade instead of his heart.

"Damn!" Alistair screamed and refocused on his remaining combatant.

For a brief moment, the man reeled back in pain. Then he reached back and plucked the dagger out. It looked like a toothpick in his giant hands. He angrily hurled it, tip first, deep into the mud. During the mercenary's throes of pain, Miles had found his opening. With a quick pivot of his left foot, he unleashed a swift, right round kick to the side of the man's knee. Though the joint bent inward at an awkward angle, it didn't break. The man dropped his sabre and the dagger, howling in pain. He took an angry step forward, but his shredded knee couldn't handle the weight and he stumbled. Miles knew he had to finish him off quickly. He drew his rapier across his body and slashed back with all his power, hoping to end him with one fell blow. Midway through the air, however, a strangling grasp arrested his hand. The crushing power forced his hand open, and the rapier toppled to the ground.

The thug yanked Miles close. "Bullocks!" he barked and punctuated his words with a right cross to his nose.

Miles flinched back, his eyes closed. On impact, a bright spark flashed before him. The crack of bone rattled his skull. He couldn't open his eyes. The force of the blow spun him around and face down into the mud. Both eyes and his nose throbbed with an unimaginable ache. He pitched his hips backward up over his heels, dropped his dagger, and grabbed at his face with both hands, coddling the injury. A mix of blood and rain flowed from his face like a faucet. The cartilage that once gave his nose form now felt like jagged crumbles of shale shifting beneath the surface. Though Miles wanted to cry from the intense, shooting pain that raged through his face, he fought back the tears. He knew the nanites would repair the damage in a few hours, but only if he got up and made it through this nightmare.

Miles whipped his head around in a panic, looking for Karl's doppelganger. He quickly spotted the bear-sized man slopping through the mud behind him, having reclaimed his hefty sword. *Where's my rapier?* Miles thought fretfully. He needed something more substantial than his dagger to defend himself. Then he caught sight of the flickering yellows and reds of the firelight above reflecting in the steel of his blade. It lay in the mud a few paces behind his adversary. Having shrugged off some of the pain, he pretended to still be agonizing over his broken nose. He moaned and lurched on his knees. When the man drew within arm's reach and drew back his weapon for the kill, Miles once again kicked at the mercenary's knee. His heel struck just below the patella. This time, it cracked on contact. The man collapsed forward, straight at Miles with the tip of his sabre driving down at him. Miles snatched his dagger from the mud, rolled out of the way, and scrambled to his feet. With desperate, slipping strides he crossed the grounds toward his rapier. He lost his footing, slid face first across the ground, and came to rest beside his sword. Taking a firm grasp of the handle, Miles rose to his feet and rounded on the brute.

The muscled warrior used his sword as leverage against the soft earth to push himself back up onto his feet. Erect but wobbly, he regarded Miles with an angry sneer and brandished his sabre at him. Miles returned the glare, sheathed his dagger, and grasped the rapier with both hands. With powerful, confident steps he stalked through the mud toward his opponent. Within striking distance, the brute swung wildly at him, but his desperate attack whiffed. Miles ducked beneath the whistling edge of the blade, remembering what Master told him. He knew his blade wasn't strong enough to directly clash blow for blow with the sabre, so he didn't try. Another counter cut came at Miles, but he slid his feet back and leaned away. He watched the tip of the blade cut the air within inches of his nose. *Stay back, stay out of the way. Let him wear himself out.*

Swing after swing, the brute came at him. Miles used every way of evading an attack that he had learned, and they were paying dividends. He had even managed to land a few feint cuts as he ducked and dodged each violent attack. Bleeding lacerations, like tiger stripes, marked the man's arms, legs, and torso. The brute's breathing had grown vapid, and he seemed to take more and more time to recover after each attack. The sinewy muscles of his arms struggled to keep the sword aloft. Its tip rested against the ground.

Miles' evasive maneuvers had taken a personal toll too. Though he hadn't been hurt, his legs grew rubbery and he didn't know how many more strikes he could avoid safely. He tried not to let his fatigue show.

The brute flinched forward with a growl but didn't raise his sabre. Miles too flinched in response and the man grumbled a low laugh.

"Come on!" Miles howled, spreading his arms in an inviting manner. "Kill me!"

The brute smiled painfully, brought his sword up over his head, and lunged at Miles with a screaming, downward strike. All of his lessons, all of his training came together at that moment; Miles stepped instinctively into the attack, thrusting his rapier up over his head in an angled block to his left. The sabre struck hard against his sword, but it slid clear away as he side-stepped to the right. When the downward pressure ceased, his rapier came around and slashed down across the brute's chest, cleaving a gaping wound that exposed severed ribs and organs beneath. A spasmodic cough of blood shot from his mouth and he fell at Miles' feet.

Miles stood over his kill, fighting to catch his breath. His heart thudded like a paint mixer and his body trembled from the adrenaline flooding his bloodstream. Then a sudden whoosh of sound hit his ears as though they just popped. He hadn't even noticed but his senses had blocked out the tinges of battle around him: the clink of swords clashing, the grunts and groans of exertion, and the cries of warriors being injured in the melee. The regained sense of awareness sent his thoughts right to his family. Miles turned about in a complete circle, hoping to find them all still standing, still fighting. To his relief and surprise, he found himself amidst them, their enemies thinned dramatically but not completely dispatched. Their clothes had small tears where they had taken minor wounds, but the nanites had already sewn them closed. No one had landed a fatal blow on them like the wounds that marked the twenty or so lifeless forms that littered the grounds of the theater. Miles couldn't take his eyes off them—not because it was the same primal fear of death he felt back when the assassins came for him. No. This was a distinct sadness for the mothers, fathers, wives, sons, and daughters who would never see these men again. He knew what it was like to live without, and he now understood that pain would be shared with many others in the coming days. Whatever that damned demon had promised them and whatever they'd done, their lives shouldn't have ended that way.

Splintering cracks echoed down from the rafters and support beams above. It shook Miles out of his melancholic musings and caused everyone around him to recoil, drawing their eyes to the flames. The ring of unforgiving fire had chewed its way further and further down the structure. It had completely engulfed the top two tiers of seating and the roof that sat overtop of the stage. Despite the coolness of the rain that continued to fall, the heat pressed down on them all. The battle had to be brought to an end soon.

Miles whirled around, rapier drawn back over his shoulder, at the sound of closing footfalls splashing through the mud from behind. Jaw clenched, he anticipated hacking away at an advancing adversary. To his surprise and relief, Annelise raced across the grounds of the theater toward him with her weapons sheathed.

She came to a halt just a few feet from him and smiled through the rain and hail of cinder. "You made it!"

He relaxed his weapon and wiped at the blood streaming from his nose with a soaked sleeve. "Wouldn't miss it," he replied with a wealth of sarcasm. A small crack emanated from his nose as some of the splinters of bone set back into place. He winced and opened his mouth to stretch his face.

More hectic boot splashes filled the air amidst the crackle of burning timber. Miles followed the sounds and realized that the remaining mercenaries had disengaged from combat and fled toward the exits. Moments later, Miles, Annelise, and his family members stood temporarily unopposed. They took hard breaths, trying to recover from what had felt like an endless struggle. He exchanged woeful glances with his mother and father from across the grounds. It wasn't enough that Gaius' distraction had worn them down or delayed their efforts to stop the demon. They now had to face their traitorous brethren in order to accomplish their mission. Through the intensifying heat and treacherous plumes of burning ash erupting from razed timber, the Draven clan closed ranks and stood together for strength.

Annelise, however, stood alone. She drew forth her gladius and pugio and screamed into the rain. "Trevor!" The veins in her neck bulged to the surface.

Miles regarded her with confusion. "What are you doing?" he begged. "Stand with us."

Annelise frowned and shook her head. "I can't. I have to take care of my brother. You stay by their side and protect each other." She turned away from Miles and shouted again at her brother.

The demon stood above its frenzied crew, watching them excavate the ground beneath the shattered stage. They couldn't dig fast enough to satisfy Gaius. Imperceptible waves of energy pulsed outward from the ground with growing strength as the diggers cast aside shovel full after shovel full of loose earth. The pulsations fed the demon's thirst for the power that the artifact promised. No longer did it care to obscure its primal nature. John Lowin's body strained to contain the true form that lurked within. Spittle seeped from its mortal lips, and queer disfigurations rippled beneath the façade of flesh.

A sudden, shrill sound like the wail of a thousand cats in heat soured the entire experience for the demon. Gaius hissed, threw back the hood from atop its mortal head, and turned its attention toward the theater grounds. Most of the mortal minions the demon had cast into battle against the chronoshifters lay dead amidst the muck and mud. The rest of the men had fled the theater, no doubt in fear of losing their lives. It mattered not. The pawns had served their purpose and held the chronoshifters at bay long enough. And there stood the source of irritation; Annelise Albright, Trevor's sister, beckoning him to fight. The demon had had enough of their intrusions.

"Put an end to this now!" Gaius growled at his turncoats.

The traitorous chronoshifters, who formed a defensive wall to protect the dig, cast disdainful glances at the demon. They drew their weapons, turned to face their former brethren, and stalked through the rain. Trevor, however, remained as a last line of defense. Gaius decided that it was an unnecessary measure.

"No, Daisuke," the demon called out the samurai who had been moving straight toward Annelise. He stopped and turned back to face his master. "Trevor will do the honors."

Trevor rounded on the demon, distraught. "What? I...I thought I was to be your personal guard?"

Gaius laughed. "I have no need of your protection now, traveler. The artifact is within my grasp, and your kin aren't foolish enough to harm my mortal form."

Trevor glanced out over the grounds to his sister who held him in a menacing glare.

"Is there a problem?" the demon inquired with amusement. Though the chronoshifter's innermost thoughts were not yet privy to Gaius, it lavished in the palpable anguish the reluctant servant suffered at the thought of facing his sibling in mortal combat. The screws needed tightening. "It's time to prove your devotion."

"Devotion?" Trevor barked, aghast. He closed to within inches of the demon's face. "Is slaughtering children not enough for you?"

With a slow, menacing grin, Gaius answered, "No. I don't trust you and never have. Any of you. Take her life and I will consider not taking yours."

"This was never part of the bargain," he howled.

Gaius took an aloof air and whispered, "And I told you that bargains do not suit me. I take what I want. And if you can't see her from this world, know that I will in ways so deliciously agonizing that no mortal could ever conceive." The demon licked its lips.

Trevor scowled at his master and turned away from its demented gesticulations. He glanced down at his weapons and then to his sister. With firm steps, he began a slow trek through the slopping mud toward Annelise.

Daisuke reached out to stop Trevor as he passed by. His wet, jet-black top knot glistened in the firelight. "Can you carry out your duties, Albright San?"

Trevor stared into the mud, shaking his head. "She's my sister," he reminded Daisuke with sadness. "I don't have a choice. All I can do is make it quick and painless." He glared back through the rain to Gaius and then back to the youngest of the Takashima clan. "I can't let that bastard have its way with her."

With a grunt, the samurai nodded and let his hand fall aside. Before Trevor could take a step, Daisuke added, "If you fall, I will end her for you."

Trevor nodded. "Domo."

Annelise screamed his name. Turning to face her, Trevor breathed a heavy sigh, and took the final few steps toward his destiny.

The veil that shrouded the depth of the betrayal within the Order peeled back to reveal the known conspirators. The Draven family stood in a protective cluster, each facing out at the circling threat. As suspected, the Takashima clan was rotten to the core; Hiro, the patriarch, had successfully faked his own death. He stood beside his two eldest sons, Daisuke and Hideki. They had abandoned every principle of Bushido and honor in order to betray their sworn oath to stop Gaius. They walked a slow perimeter around Miles and his family, waiting to pounce. Their partner, however, presented a shocking insight into the events of the last few days. While it was believed that the other Magisters who attended the ill-fated gathering with Charles were subsequently tortured and put to death, the reality turned out to be far more nefarious than previously thought. Miles glanced back over his shoulder to where Gregor Plantanov, the Russian patriarch, stepped out from the shadows to be counted amongst the conspirators. The Cossack's salt and pepper hair lay matted down from the weight of the rain. Wetness dripped from his ashen beard. Deep creases marked his aged face in the sallow firelight. In his hands he loosely clutched his kindjal dagger, which looked more like Annelise's gladius but with a thinner blade. His curved shashka sword borrowed greatly in design from the katana, though it lacked any form of guard and had a grip half as long.

Matthias begged of the traitors, "Why are you doing this?"

"Time has caught me, brother," Gregor asserted, pointing his kindjal dagger at Matthias, "as it will you one day." He tilted his head back to scan the flames that crackled above them. The top two tiers burned with a radiant rage. The Cossack squinted, blinking against the hail of raindrops falling upon his face. Flashes of red, yellow, and orange glistened across the surface of his eyes. He exhaled and held his weapons out at his sides. "The fire of time burns us all, Matthias. It lurks as embers in the darkness, watching, waiting in silence to expose our mortality. We're lulled into a sense of comfort for centuries, forgetting that we're not eternal. And that's when it strikes us down. It engulfs us like dried kindling that burns in the blink of an eye." He lowered his weapons. His gaze returned to Matthias. "I don't want to die an old man, lying in bed, wishing I had more time." Gregor shook his head, droning, "I'm tired of this war, Matthias. We all are."

"But that doesn't give you the right to murder children!" Matthias howled. He looked to each of the traitors in turn. "We either die fighting, or survive long enough to see our time expire. That's how it is! Your children all had the chance to grow up, to follow in your footsteps," he snarled and glared at the Takashimas. "How dare you rob our children of that very same chance?"

The traitors erupted in a collective cackle. Hideki grumbled, "Kodomo to iu mono wa tsukaisute de gozaru."

Gregor provided his own translation. "Children are expendable. When we live forever, we can make as many as we want. Their sacrifice was the price of our allegiance—a price I was more than willing to pay."

Elizabeth broke her silence. "What in God's name broke inside you, Gregor? In all of you?" she screamed. "You're speaking of our children, not random shadows."

"You clearly don't understand. You're still young. You've yet to feel the inescapable stranglehold of time. What Gaius offered me, what it offered all of us, was a chance to wind the gears back and extinguish those rending flames forever. If you were in my shoes you wouldn't question what I've done. Not like the others."

"The others?" Matthias asked. "You mean Dube and Mohaymen."

"Fools 'til the bitter end! Gaius offered them true immortality and they spat in its face. By standing side-by-side with the demon, we can end this war. Why waste our lives fighting against an inexorable tide?"

"I think I've heard about enough," Matthias growled. "Let's finish this."

"As you wish," Gregor conceded, spinning both of his blades around into reverse grips. Bending his knees and twisting his torso, he dropped into a ready stance. He brought his dagger up in front of his face, just below eye level and parallel with the ground, while his sword arm recoiled toward his backside, the tip pointing skyward. Then the samurai followed suit, each preparing for the inevitability of combat. They contorted their frames into warlike postures and grasped their sword handles with deadly intent.

Miles felt his father's firm hand grasp his wrist, turn him around, and pull him into the middle of his family. His heart sank in his chest the moment he saw his father's face. The confidence, the strength he had grown to know in his father over the past few weeks seemed to have been supplanted by uncertainty. His eyes flitted about nervously at their opponents before locking on Miles. *Is he worried we'll lose?* Miles wondered.

"Stay between us," his father commanded. "Only fight if you have to. We can handle them. Do you understand?"

Miles felt all of his confidence leaving him like a deflated balloon. Now he felt his own worries seep back in.

Matthias shook him and yelled, "Do you understand?"

Miles flinched at the outburst, nodding. He stammered, "I understand."

His father yanked him close and wrapped one arm around him to hug him tight. "I love you, Miles."

Those words completely disarmed him. He was certain now that his father believed this to be their last stand. Why else would he say that to him? As best as he could, Miles tried to answer back but all he could produce was a muted "Dad." Matthias let go of him, stepping away toward the encircling threat. Both his mother and brother distanced themselves from the center, leaving Miles alone at the hub of the wheel. Around Miles the deadly dance began.

The tinges of battle raged nearby, yet Annelise paid them no matter.

She knew that the Dravens could take care of one another while she settled this personal score. Standing stoic amidst the rain and hail of cinder, she leered at her traitorous brother who stopped a few feet away from her. The mere proximity of her sworn enemy marshaled forth every trace of anger within her. Her fingers flexed upon the pommels of both blades.

"This isn't how I wanted it to end, Annie," Trevor explained. He held his gladius and pugio limp at his sides. "None of this was supposed to happen."

"What you wanted, brother, is irrelevant," she spat back at him. She couldn't believe his arrogance. *Not even prepared to defend himself.* Did he think her skills so lacking? Did he believe his words would quell her mania? She wanted blood. "But you'll pay for everything you've done."

"You don't understand," he begged.

"Oh," Annelise snarled, "I understand perfectly." Without warning, she grunted and launched herself at her brother with all her might. Her gladius cut through the air at Trevor's throat, but he ducked beneath the arc of the humming blade.

"Wait!" he yelled and countered with a flick of his wrist that spun his sword upward along the side of his head and into her gladius with enough force to send her off-balance. With a shuffle of his feet, he stepped past her, pivoted to his right, and punched her in the shoulder. The added weight of his pugio intensified the power of the strike, making her stumble.

A deep ache radiated down her whole arm. Pissed off, Annelise rounded on Trevor by whipping both blades through the air in an effort to ward off any attack from behind. She didn't figure he would do something so stupid against her, but it was one of his favorite counters to a lunge; decades spent as sparring partners eliminated any possibility for surprise when they fought for keeps. They had to get creative most of the time just to keep each other on their toes. So while she expected him to hang back to avoid her subsequent counter attack, finding him flatfooted and shying away from battle sent her over the precipice. A blind rage supplanted the anger within, muting the discomfort in her shoulder and erasing her previous hesitancy to vanquish an unwilling opponent. All that mattered was his complete and total annihilation.

Annelise attacked with unrelenting ferocity. She grunted with each savage swing of her sword and dagger. The speed and power of her strikes kept Trevor from taking advantage of the openings her all-or-nothing assault exposed; he just deflected each attack in turn, constantly retreating until the railing of the lower seating sections left splinters in his back. What began as cindering wisps of thatch falling down upon them like fiery snow turned to a raining torrent this close to the outer edge of the theater grounds.

Unleashing a hair-raising war cry, Annelise brought the blade of her gladius down like a sledgehammer at Trevor's head. He sidestepped just in time to slip out of the way and slide around to a rear position, but he didn't get away completely unscathed. The chipped edge of her sword ripped a chunk of flesh from his right shoulder. The wound bled down his limp arm in pulsating waves. Trevor clumsily sheathed his pugio and clamped that hand over the wound, wincing on contact. Biting his lower lip, he tried to raise his sword arm to no avail. He couldn't lift it. The handle began to slip from his fingertips. Collapsing to one knee, he stared back at Annelise as she tried to free her blade from the railing. Her desperate, shifting gaze switched back and forth from her wedged gladius to her brother. *What's he waiting for?*

Miles held his dagger and rapier with trembling hands. He could barely keep up with the pace of battle. Though he kept moving to avoid getting caught up in the melee, as his father ordered, the action surrounding him kept shifting too fast. What started as a circle he could easily hunker down in, flexed and bowed until it possessed no discernible form.

The three Takashimas came at his mother and brother with all their might, coordinating their attacks. Their swordsmanship appeared to be without equal, on the verge of overwhelming Alistair and Elizabeth. Every cut, every parry seemed part of a calculated effort to separate his mother and brother to create exploitable vulnerabilities. If it wasn't for the samurai's commitment to fighting solely with their katana, the strategy would have resulted in their speedy demise. His family's dual bladed style of swordsmanship, however, gave them a fighting chance.

Stealing a glance over his shoulder, Miles found his father engrossed in one-on-one combat with Gregor. Each violent attack brought them one step closer to the excavation and Gaius. At first he thought that the natural ebb and flow of their movements sent them in that direction, but then he recognized his father's strategy; when Gregor tried to move to his right, his father outstepped him and cut against the grain with his rapier. Then he drove him back further with furious slashes at his sides and jabs with his dagger. Matthias was trying to get closer to the demon! As much as he trusted his father, his actions went against everything he had been taught. He briefly considered rushing to his father's side to stop him from making a mistake, but someone flashed toward him in his periphery.

Daisuke, the youngest of the three Takashimas, forced his way past his mother and brother to take a shot at Miles. Before he could react, the samurai was right on top of him. His speed and power were overwhelming. With clumsy steps and uncertain swipes of his rapier, Miles defended the first few attacks—a thrust, two lateral cuts at his waist, and a downward slash at his neck. Miles could feel his heart racing in his chest. He fought to catch his breath. The next attack, he feared, might be his last. The samurai smiled wryly at him and cackled, readying his katana for the killing strike. Daisuke unleashed a hair raising kiap and rushed at Miles, his weapon cutting a whistling arc through the air. But before that strike could land, Elizabeth slide tackled the samurai. He lost his footing and fell directly on top of her.

Miles backed away from the danger. Watching his mother wrestle against Daisuke in the mud and his brother try to fend off two samurai at once made him feel so lost, so vulnerable. He promised to stay out of the battle and now he really understood why. Against one of their own, he didn't stand much of a chance. They were too fast, too skilled against his meager training. But he had come so far, learned so much to stand by and watch when it mattered. Though it meant breaking his promise to his father, he had to do something.

His blood boiled at the sight of his mother pinned down by Daisuke. With one hand the samurai tried to wrestle the dagger out of her hand,

and with the other he deflected her weak attempts to punch him. If he wrestled the dagger from her grasp, he would kill her. But if Miles could free her, the battle would be balanced yet again.

Having sheathed his rapier and dagger, Miles launched himself at Daisuke's back without a care for his safety. He took two fistfuls of his overcoat and wrenched him off of Elizabeth. He kept dragging him through the mud, pulling the samurai clear of his mother. He thought he had gotten the best of Daisuke. In an instant, the samurai dropped his katana, brought his knees to his chest, and kicked out with both feet at Miles' chest. Both boot heels struck square. The power of his legs threw Miles back through the air. He crashed flat on his back against the ground; the impact knocked the wind out of him. Gasping for air, he rolled onto his side. All he could do in his incapacitated state was fight for breath while he watched Daisuke and his mother rise from the muck and reengage.

Their life and death struggle eclipsed anything he had ever witnessed on film or read in a book. They didn't swing at each other's swords to make it look good or move around in some wildly choreographed ballet for the eyes. Both warriors exchanged vicious blows. Every slash, every stab was delivered with the intent to rend flesh in order to take a life. Despite the rain, the smoke that swirled around them, and the hot fireflies of ash that pelted them, neither combatant could seize the advantage.

A thrust to Elizabeth's midsection by Daisuke found an immediate counter as she slid back along a diagonal and brought her rapier down across the katana until her quillion block locked up against his tsuba, pushing the blade clear of her body. She tried to come right back at him with a jab to his neck, but he ducked beneath her arm and snapped out a side kick into her ribs. The strike sent her stumbling back, covering the injured area with her elbow. They both stood back for a few seconds, catching their breath. Miles too had found the rhythm of his lungs and diaphragm again. Turning over onto his stomach, he sat up on his knees with both arms wrapped around his chest.

The two warriors rushed forward into battle once more. Their blades clashed in a dizzying blur. Elizabeth cut at the samurai with a zigzagging motion of her two blades. A misstep, though, sent her off balance, and Daisuke took advantage by slashing at her stomach. Her quick reflexes saved her from disembowelment; she kicked her hips back and made a wild swing at the sweeping katana with her dagger. The impact of the smaller blade set the samurai's on a lower trajectory where it gouged out a gill-like cut in her upper thigh. She winced and cried out in pain. Clenching her jaw, Elizabeth brought her dagger back around to her left. Then she cut back across her body with both blades while driving her body forward. Daisuke dropped into a shoulder roll to evade her. He popped up into a back stance to her rear. She rounded on him. With a nod, he acknowledged her keen mettle in battle. His eyes then shifted, narrowing on something behind Elizabeth. She followed his gaze all the way to the far end of the theater where Annelise hacked away at her brother, pushing him straight into the lower railing. Her fury landed a deep gash along his upper arm. Trevor stood completely helpless as she tried to wrench her gladius from the railing. Once she freed the blade, her revenge would be complete.

Two hurried, splashing footsteps brought Elizabeth's attention back to Daisuke, but she was too late. He rammed into the middle of her side with his shoulder, knocking her to the ground, and headed straight toward Annelise. Scrambling to her feet, she gave one look to Alistair, who was losing ground against both Hideki and Hiro, and then back to Annelise.

"Shit!" she barked and rushed to her son's aid.

Running footsteps caught Annelise's attention. Daisuke sprinted at her with his katana drawn back over his right shoulder, ready to strike the fatal blow where her brother couldn't. He didn't appear to be concerned with anything else but the kill.

Annelise's gladius broke free from the stubborn railing just as the samurai moved within striking range. With both hands she raised her sword into an upward guard in anticipation of his blade coming down at her neck. But with a suddenness that took her by surprise, Daisuke's head came clean off, spinning up and backwards while his body collapsed, tumbling across the muddy earth. A fine mist of blood spiraled through the air. She jumped out of the way just before his remains crashed against the wall. Annelise fell back against the rail and fought to catch her breath. She regarded her fallen foe and then searched the grounds for her savior. Expecting to see Miles or one of the other Dravens having come to her aid, the truth threw her mind into a spiral.

At the point where the samurai's head took leave of his body, Trevor stood with his back to her, his bloodied gladius clasped firmly in his left hand. He glanced from side to side, constantly scanning the field of battle. Then he turned about to stalk toward her on unsteady feet. His chest heaved with each step. A few feet from her, he stopped. Trevor threw both his gladius and pugio aside and held his hands out at his sides, leaving him unarmed and vulnerable.

Neither Trevor's apparent surrender nor his slaying of Daisuke minimized the weight of his crimes in her mind or that she should grant him quarter. *It's a trick*, she warned herself. *Kill him!* Annelise resumed her onslaught, swinging at Trevor with both blades. He managed to duck and dodge most of her strikes without his weapons, but he couldn't stop them all. A cut to the upper thigh, a shallow stab to the stomach, and a slash across his chest took their toll. Trevor began to fade, stumbling with each step. His bloodied, rain-soaked garments glistened in the raging firelight from above. Near the front of the thrust stage, the mortally engaged siblings circled. Annelise looked for an opening to take his life and exact her revenge while Trevor looked back woefully.

"I'm going to end this!" Annelise spat at him. "Everything you've done, I'm going to make right again." She hunkered down into a battle-ready pose, twisting her feet for better traction in the mud.

Trevor held himself like a noble warrior, refusing to back down in the face of death. The blood line of Roman Centurions still surged within, like his sister. To die in battle meant everything to them. Barely able to hold himself up, he set his feet in the soggy earth and held his arms at the ready to engage Annelise. "It's not what you think, Annie!"

"Shut up!" She slashed at the air. "You're a God damn traitor. You hunted down all those children. And father!" Annelise let all her rage explode in a rush. She leapt forward, swinging her blade down hard in an effort to cleave his head in two.

Trevor's eyes flashed and he moved into her. "Stop!" Trevor shouted, brought his left hand up on an intercepting course with her wrist, and halted the downward strike of her gladius. "The kids are alive!"

"What? No! You killed them!" she growled, trying to wrench her hand free. He released his grasp as she swung her pugio at his neck.

Trevor recoiled away from the edge of the dagger and slapped at her hand as it passed by, setting her off balance. Sliding into her with his shoulder, he knocked her back into the stage. When her arm came back across for a counter slash, he clamped his left hand down on her wrist and muscled her arm back across her own throat. Grunting, she tried to slash at his midsection with her gladius, but he managed enough power in his injured arm to bring the knife edge of his hand down hard on the bundle of nerves in the middle of her forearm. The sword fell into the mud.

"No!" he screamed. "They're safe. I didn't kill them. I hid them."

Annelise fought to overpower him, but she wasn't strong enough. "I don't believe you," she cried. "This is a trick!" Though her arms were immobilized, her legs were not. With a swift, upward swing of her knee to his groin, Annelise dropped her brother. She stood over him, trying to make sense of her thoughts. *Could he be telling the truth?* As much as she dared to believe him, the evidence weighed too heavily against Trevor. She berated him in disgust, "You didn't hide them, you sent their heads to their parents in boxes, you fucking animal! Did you think I didn't know?" she screamed.

Trevor knelt in the mud and groaned. He lifted his head and gazed at her with pain-filled eyes. "I took them somewhere safe, Annie. Those were the heads of their shadows."

His words struck a chord. She hadn't considered the possibility that the murdered children weren't the real ones. That fact alone wasn't enough to disarm her rage.

"What about our father?" Annelise howled. "It's because of you he died!" She grabbed his collar with both hands and punched him in the side of the face.

Trevor grabbed at his jaw. "It's what he wanted."

Her voice rose to an ear shattering pitch. "Liar!" She jerked him closer, hitting him again.

He spit out blood and groaned, "It's true, Annie, you know him. He didn't want to die like Mom. He wanted to die in battle, a warrior. When I told him about my plan, he decided it was how he wanted to go out. I refused to go along with it. But when he told me how much he missed her, how much he wanted to be with her again, I couldn't say no." He slumped forward.

Annelise shook her head, awash with grief. The truth hurt too much. "But why?" she cried. "Why didn't you tell me? Why leave me in the dark? I could've helped."

"You did help," Trevor reassured her. He looked up at Annelise, squinting through the rain. "It was your determination to pursue me, to get revenge that convinced Gaius. It was the only way to put on a convincing show."

"But I—"

"No," he countered, "you couldn't. Your greatest asset is your sheer determination, not your acting." Trevor smiled weakly at her. He laughed between groans of pain. "If you knew it was a ruse, it wouldn't have been the same."

An explosive crack emanated from the stage. Annelise turned away from her brother to glimpse the source of the threatening sound; the conflagration above had chewed its way down through the heavens and sank its teeth into the remaining support pillar. The column had fractured along its length and ruptured in the middle like a shredded reed. With an eerie groan, the pillar bent, tipping the entirety of the Heavens to the verge of collapse.

Miles got back to his feet and drew both his dagger and rapier, waiting to see where he was needed most. His mother and brother were wearing down the Takashimas while Matthias drove relentlessly at Gregor, pushing him closer to Gaius with every step. Gregor's breath grew labored as he fought off the onslaught. His aged body couldn't keep up with Matthias' ferocity. The look in his eyes, one of desperation and fear, made Miles wonder if the Cossack regretted his betrayal; he yearned for youth, for immortality, but his ambitions bore poisonous fruit and Matthias was the reaper.

Gregor shuffled away from another well-aimed strike, his heels biting at the edge of the pit. The sudden loss of footing made him lose his balance. Dirt spilled back down on top of the diggers who protested aloud in anger. Instead of fighting against his unsteadiness, the Cossack turned into his fall, heaving his body across the pit. He tumbled across the ground and scrabbled to his feet. A pained grimace came over him when he came about to face Matthias. The pit may have protected him against a cutting rapier, but it did little to defend against a well-thrown dagger. Matthias slung the smaller blade through the air and it struck Gregor in the chest. He fell backward at the feet of the demon, gasping for air amidst a flood of blood filling his throat. His hands clutched at Gaius' robes. Silently he pleaded for mercy from a merciless God. The demon slapped away its servants hands and stepped down on the pommel of the dagger with such power that the cross guard broke through his ribs. Gregor convulsed before stillness overcame him for good.

With no other adversary before him that he could attack safely, Matthias turned his attention on the diggers working in the pit. He thrust his rapier at the unsuspecting men beneath him. Miles couldn't see them from where he stood, but he heard their cries loud and clear. Desperate hands clutched at the softened dirt surrounding the pit only to lose purchase. They couldn't escape and Gaius raged at Matthias for it. The demon shifted left and right, trying desperately to get to him, but Matthias kept the pit squarely between them while he continued eliminating the diggers.

Gaius hunched over in a seething loss of control. Hot spires of breath shot from its nostrils. The foul beast uttered some unintelligible words in its native tongue, then reached back with its hand. The flesh that once comprised the vessel's arm ruptured and fell away, leaving only tatters of skin and bone dangling from the shoulder socket. Blood sprayed from severed arteries and veins. A terrifying glimpse of the demonic form that once lurked beneath the surface of John Lowin's body came into view. An inconceivably massive limb, covered in bony spikes and greyish, glistening scales emerged. Long, jagged nails extended from the tips of its three hulking fingers and a thorn-like protrusion extended backward from the elbow.

A bellowing growl that shook the ground burst forth from within the demon. Gaius lashed out at Matthias with the back of its grotesque hand. Though massive, it moved through the air with blinding speed. Matthias narrowly avoided the powerful swipe by dropping flat to the ground. In its attempt to flatten the chronoshifter, Gaius overshot the target and slammed its hand into shattered remains of the stage. The power of the strike brought about a cascade of failures that compromised what remained of the structure's integrity. God awful groans and splintering cracks echoed within the confines of the theater, beckoning all within earshot to pay homage to its death throes. The combatants all froze in place, awed by the spectacle before them. The front left corner of the Heavens pitched downward at an awkward angle. Flaming chunks of wood erupted from the beams that gave way under the strain. The entire roof lurched sharply to the left and snapped loose from the rest of the theater. It plummeted toward the ground in an instant. Miles looked on in horror as the Heavens crashed to the earth with his father trapped beneath.

"Matthias!" Elizabeth screamed.

Her utterances snapped everyone out of their hypnosis and the battle resumed.

Standing mere feet from one another, Alistair told his mother, "I've got this. Go help him!"

"Are you sure?" she asked, sidestepping one of Hiro's lunging slashes.

"Go!" Alistair cross-blocked Hideki's katana, and brought his elbow down on the nerve bundle in his forearm, disarming him. Wheeling back his shoulders, he drove the crown of his head into the samurai's nose with a loud crunch. Hideki stumbled backward, his hands coddling his face. Blood seeped from between his fingers.

Elizabeth slipped behind Alistair and raced toward the flaming bulk of the collapsed stage. Hiro shifted his weight to make a run for her, but

Alistair cut him off with a grin.

"You're mine," Alistair sneered at the master samurai. He whipped his blades around in a defensive flourish and settled with both weapons brought to bear in a relaxed back stance.

Miles took a step in Alistair's direction. He could take out the unarmed samurai, that he felt certain. His brother, however, did not feel so confident.

Leering back at him in his periphery, Alistair ordered him, "Stay back!"

"But I can help!" Miles answered.

"No!"

Hiro glanced at his eldest and then slowly back to Alistair. Bending his knees, he lowered himself into an identical stance. He drew back his katana slowly and then up over his right shoulder. Both men shouted as they launched forward, swords clashing. Every cut of the samurai's katana met a blending parry and counterstrike from Alistair. They were equally matched foes.

Miles flinched and moved as his brother did, living vicariously through his battle. He wouldn't have lasted five seconds against Hiro whose skill and speed were mindboggling. The level of respect he felt for his brother's skills could not be measured. He only hoped he'd get the chance to tell him when all of this was over.

He was so focused on the swordplay that he didn't notice Hideki gather himself up and move around to Alistair's rear. His brother hadn't noticed him either. Rushing forward a few steps, Miles shouted, "Alistair, behind you!"

Before his brother could turn around, Hideki landed a brutal side kick to Alistair's lower back. Alistair's blades tumbled from his grasp, and he flew straight at Hiro. The master samurai side-stepped him and then rammed the pommel of his katana into the side of Alistair's head. His eyes rolled back in his head, and he toppled to the ground. Hideki slogged through the mud to collect his katana. He shook it in his hand to remove the mud, then he returned to Alistair. Stepping over him, the samurai raised his sword for the killing strike.

"Hideki!" Hiro barked. "Let him burn in the flames." He scanned the interior of the theater. "Where's your brother?" His shifting gaze locked on a decapitated body at the other end of the theater. It was Daisuke. His entire body trembled. A pained cry escaped him. He came about in a whirl, every muscle tensed. Thrusting the point of his katana at Alistair, he roared, "Change of plan. Make this one watch his brother die!" Leaving his son's side, he stalked off into the swirling smoke.

Hideki reached down to grab Alistair by the collar and dragged him through the mud. He stalked at Miles. It was his turn. He had no choice. It was his meager skills against a master swordsman. Miles kept a firm grip on his dagger and rapier, retreating away from the samurai as he closed in. He tried to see where Hiro went, but the smoke and debris made it hard to see past the foundation of the stage. Then he searched for his mother; she moved along the burning structure, calling out to Matthias. *Come on, Dad. Where are you?*

His eyes snapped back to Hideki. The samurai slammed Alistair down into the mud and came hard at Miles. The second he got within striking range, Miles slashed at him with his rapier. The samurai parried the attack with ease and stripped the weapon right out of his hand. The subsequent thrust of his dagger at Hideki's chest left Miles in an exaggerated lurch. Before he could try to put on the brakes, the samurai reversed direction on him, bent his palm back over his wrist, and flipped him through the air.

Miles hit the ground with a thud. He scrambled away from Hideki on all fours, his dagger now out of his possession. The samurai slogged through the mud toward him, holding his blade in a reverse grip, tip down, intent on skewering him. A few feet away, he watched his brother struggle to his feet. There was no time for Alistair to reach him, and without his dagger or rapier, Miles was as good as dead. His hands slipped in the mud and he crashed down on his side. A sharp object dug into his armpit and ribs. As Hideki stepped over him and raised his katana over his head, Miles remembered his pistol. Jerking it from the holster, he squared his shoulders against the ground, aimed the muzzle at the samurai, and unloaded three shots, center mass. The bullets left the chamber with a hiss, slicing through muscle and bone. Hideki's facial features contorted in a tortured grimace. He stumbled off to the side a few steps. Miles kept the pistol trained on him the whole way, waiting to unload more rounds, but it wasn't necessary. The katana fell from his hands and then he collapsed to the ground.

Miles clambered to his feet and circled the fallen samurai, never taking his sights off of him. He'd seen enough movies to know to keep his distance. This bad guy, however, didn't look like he was going to leap up and fight despite his mortal wounds. He was dead. But where was Hiro? He ordered his son to take Miles' life, but where did he go? Miles searched frantically for him. When he found him, a desperate fear gripped his heart.

"Oh, my God!" he uttered to himself. He took off at a sprint across the theater grounds.

"Holy shit!" Annelise yelped. She grabbed Trevor's coat, yanked him to his feet, and pushed him back from the stage. The roof broke loose, collapsing to the ground. "Matthias was under there!"

"Can I help?" Trevor clutched at his oozing wound.

"No," she answered. The damage she had done to her brother sickened her. He was a busted up mess and it was her fault. "Get out of here. There's nothing more you can do."

Before she could leave his side, Trevor arched his back and gasped. His face convulsed in sheer agony as the crackle of bone rumbled through his chest. Instead of calling out in a tortured cry, the gurgle of blood filled his mouth and splattered on his sister in a gasp. His good hand reached out for her arm as the tip of a katana erupted through his chest. Annelise shrieked and flinched back. With a violent jerk, the blade withdrew from his body and Trevor fell to his knees. She dropped with him, catching his weight as he fell forward onto her. Her brother's weight pinned her against the ground. Unable to reach her strewn weapons or get out from under Trevor, she waited for Hiro Takashima, who loomed over them, to take her life and finish off her brother.

Every muscle in his body trembled. The patriarch of the Takashima clan glowered at them both. Slowly, he drew the handle of his katana back over his shoulder and coiled his torso so the sword pointed directly at Annelise. "Sochi wa sesshya no musuko wo koroshita!" the samurai growled.

"Speak English, asshole!" Annelise spat back with fearless vehemence.

"You killed my son," he repeated irately.

"He's a traitor, just like you!"

Hiro screamed and lunged forward. Annelise closed her eyes, squeezing her brother's limp form. She hoped it would be over quickly for them both. A sharp hiss cut through the air followed by the splash of something heavy against the sloppy ground. The cold plunge of hardened steel ripping through her body never came. Peeking through narrowed eyelids, she saw Hiro lying a few feet away with an entry wound in the side of his head. Brain splash and hunks of skull littered the ground beside him. The other side of his head had been completely blown off. Blood flowed hot and steamy into the rain-chilled mud, forming a soupy swirl.

From her right, Miles came sprinting over, the muzzle of his pistol still smoking in his hand. He holstered it and stood over her. "Are you okay?"

She nodded. "Help me!"

Miles took hold of Trevor's shoulder and strained to pry his limp form off of her.

Annelise added her muscle power to his, pushing Trevor onto his back. She knelt over him and put her head to his chest, listening for a heartbeat.

"Leave him!" Miles ordered her. He grabbed a fist full of her coat and tugged. "We have to go!"

"No!" she shrieked, hitting his hand to break his grip on her coat. "I'm not going to leave him here."

He tugged at her harder while deflecting her blows. "He betrayed us all! Let him die! That's what you wanted, remember?"

She shook her head and cried, "No. I was wrong. He fooled us all. He didn't do it!"

"What?" Miles asked, looking completely aghast by the revelation.

A groan pursed Trevor's lips. He tried to speak, but his words were inaudible. She leaned in closer, clutching his clothes.

"Take the diary," he rasped. Trevor lifted a trembling hand to his coat. His fingers tugged at the bloodied lapel only to fall away. A rectangular shape bulged through his soaked outer garments. Annelise peeled the coat away from his chest. Tucked within the inside pocket was a small bound volume which she pulled free and slid inside her own.

A pained wheeze escaped Trevor as he exhaled. He winced at the next intake of breath and cried out. The veins of his neck and face pulsated beneath the surface of his skin.

"Hold on, Trevor," Annelise beseeched him. "God damn it, don't you die on me now!"

Miles knelt down. "We can't save him!" he said to her, but his voice didn't register. "He's bleeding out."

"I'm sorry," Trevor whimpered, craning his neck to look her in the eye. Blood trickled from the corners of his mouth and joined with the rain. "Miles is right. You can't save me. Let me go, Annie. Please, save yourself."

"I can't!" Annelise wailed. She collapsed into his chest sobbing. "I lost you once. I'm not going to lose you again."

Trevor lifted his hand and let it fall on the back of her head. He took a shallow, shuddering breath that ended in a long, hissing exhale. His head fell to the side. A blank stare washed over him and his limp form sagged into the mud.

Annelise howled into the rain. As if brought to the brink by the power of her melancholy, the upper two floors to the right of the stage sloughed off into the inner grounds, setting off a cascade of collapses around the theater that threatened to bury them all in a fiery grave.

"Come on, Annelise!" Miles shouted over the crackling din of the inferno. "Either we go now or we're going to die!"

Annelise heard him this time, but she couldn't pull herself away. She had lost everything that mattered to her and wanted nothing more than to be lost in the fire herself—to be burnt to ash and mixed with her brother's. On the other side of Trevor, Miles knelt down in the mud. Annelise regarded him with sadness. His rain-soaked face looked right back at her. There was a look in his eyes, in those deep blue eyes that struck a chord with her. He took her hands in his and squeezed them.

"He's gone," Miles said with gentleness. "Please, Annelise, I don't want to die here." He shook his head, looking across the grounds. They had dispatched all their enemies. The battle had ended. His mother and Alistair knelt down beside Matthias, whom they pulled out from under the collapsed roof. Miles turned back to her. Those same eyes that touched her deeply now pleaded with her to fight another day. His words told a different story. He bravely said, "But I won't leave you either. I won't let you die alone."

Suddenly, she realized that maybe she hadn't lost everything in the fire. Maybe she did have something to live for. If Trevor wasn't the monster they all thought he was then it was her duty to prove it. And maybe, just maybe, she had another reason to go on. With a touch of her hand, Annelise closed Trevor's eyelids. She then laid his hands over his chest, placed a heartfelt kiss upon his cheek, and rose from the mud.

"We're not going to die today." She gave Miles a confident nod. "Let's get out of here!"

The two of them sprinted away from Trevor's resting place. In a matter of seconds they had reached the others. Matthias was awake and groaning, but with a nasty gash on his forehead. Alistair fought to get him to his feet, but his father's strength wavered. Miles quickly slid beneath his other arm to help hold him up. More and more of the theater crumbled. Hunks of flaming timber flew at them. The wind drove a pelting spray of hot cinders all around.

"What happened to Gaius?" Annelise asked over the roar of the blaze.

Matthias motioned weakly with his head back toward the collapsed stage. "Still in there."

"Alive?" she asked.

"Not for long," Matthias groaned before swooning in his sons' arms.

More of the theater came down around them. The seating above the main gate, their only way out of the ring of flaming death, collapsed downward, partially covering it. If it collapsed any further, they'd be trapped. Acting as though they shared a singular consciousness, the survivors drove for the gate. Annelise and Elizabeth cleared the path ahead of the men. Using their arms to shield their faces, they began kicking at the doorway desperately. Each strike rocked the fire-chewed frame and the collapsed floors that teetered precariously above them threatened to collapse at any moment. Back and forth they battered the gate to the sounds of splintering wood. The door, however, wouldn't budge. It only jostled back and forth within its frame.

"Come on!" Annelise howled as her boot heel struck the gate a split second after Elizabeth. A fire-charred support beam above their heads groaned. It cracked under the strain causing it to shift down suddenly. It came to a stop less than a foot from their heads.

Before Annelise could unleash another kick, Elizabeth stopped her. "Maybe if we do it together."

Annelise nodded. "On three?"

"On three," Elizabeth agreed.

Annelise counted off, "One...two...three!" Together they kicked at the gate, rupturing the wooden frame. It fell away, as did the floors above them. Annelise and Elizabeth grabbed hold of Miles, Alistair, and Matthias and dragged them through the opening as the entire theater collapsed.

CHAPTER TWENTY-SIX

Miles, Annelise, and the rest of the family escaped with not a moment to spare. A spray of spark and ash puffed out from the razed timbers, frightening the crowd that had gathered around the Globe. Those very same curiosity seekers stepped aside to let the fleeing chronoshifters pass. A few kind individuals solicited as to their health while others offered to assist them. Miles and Alistair, however, rebuffed their kindness by shaking their heads and repeating, "No, thank you," as they assisted their lame father through the line. Annelise and Elizabeth followed close behind, ready to draw their weapons should any minions of Gaius be lurking in the crowd to cut them down. Having safely passed through into the open, they stopped to catch their collective breath. Miles turned back to look upon the devastation that they escaped unscathed.

Nearly every thread of history had proclaimed that the Globe would rise again—that much was certain. While the previously penned, future texts of history had declared the fire miraculously non-fatal, all records would now be rewritten to account for all the bodies that would be uncovered in the rubble. And though no names would be attributed to those bodies beside John Lowin, Miles knew better. Their Order, however fractured by treachery, suffered immeasurably in the blaze. Despite being lured away from the path they swore to follow, the loss of the Takashima clan and Gregor Platanov was still palpable. An entire family turned traitors had died for their crimes while another clan had come under scrutiny. And the suspected ringleader, the one who had seemingly torn his own family asunder in an apparent power-grab, turned out to be their greatest ally in the end. His body now smoldered in the ashes with the other fallen.

They kept moving, putting more and more distance between themselves and the crowd of onlookers, along Maiden lane before heading down Rose Alley toward the Thames. Under the cover of an overhang, they stopped to gather themselves. Miles glanced over his shoulder at poor Annelise who stood beside him. He felt a terrible ache well up inside for her. While everything that made her life worth living had been stripped away in a cruel twist of fate, providence had yet again shined upon his family with his father being pulled from the flames. It seemed as though no tragedy could sink its claws into them. Yet it was a pain he understood all too well, even though those memories of hurt felt so far away at that moment. What was once a bitter hatred for Annelise had blossomed into a kinship that at least *he* felt. He hoped when the smoke cleared that she might feel the same. Regardless, he resolved that he would not let her feel alone again in this world. They were her family now.

She held a leather-bound tome at her waist, staring down at it. It was the very same one her brother entrusted to her before he breathed his last breath. Drops of rain pelted the cover. Miles couldn't tell if the wetness on her cheeks came from the clouds overhead or her sullen eyes.

"Is that?" Miles wondered aloud.

"My father's journal." She smiled, tears streaking down her cheeks. "Yes."

Miles frowned back at her. He felt only sorrow now. She had lost everything and that pain must have been infinitely greater to know that Trevor was no traitor.

Annelise unwound the cord that held the journal closed. The worn, dry spine crackled as she grabbed the satin bookmark and lifted it against the weight of the pages. Once opened, a secret compartment was revealed; the backside of the journal had a circular chunk dug out of it, and an anchor lay nestled snugly within. Distinctively masculine handwriting was scrawled upon the lines of the opposing page. Her eyes darted back and forth, top to bottom, tracing each line of text. She closed her eyes. Her facial features slumped into a look of consuming sadness. New tears flowed down her cheeks and onto the pages. The ink ran, obscuring the scribblings. With a sniffle, she looked away from the journal and rubbed at her runny nose.

"What does it say?" Miles solicited with gentleness.

"Miles!" his mother protested.

"No," Annelise corrected her, "it's okay. You all need to hear this." Miles pulled a handkerchief from his pocket and handed it to her. She accepted it with a grin and began to read.

My dear Annelise,

If you are reading this letter, then my flame has likely been extinguished. But do not mourn me for this is the way I wished to depart. Having sat by your mother's side in her final days, I wished I could have passed with her. I have grown weary of this decrepit body and long for the comfort of her smile. Celebrate my life. Light a candle for me on my birthday, as you do your mother, and know that we are always in your heart.

I regret that neither your brother nor I made you privy to the truth about his dealings. To protect his true purpose, it was necessary to mislead you and set you on his trail. Your determination to avenge even the slightest wrong, even by your own kin, kept the ruse alive and him safe from suspicion. Despite what you witnessed, I assure you that your brother is no monster. What he says is true. They're alive. But do not take our word for it. Follow this anchor, especially if we've both fallen to Gaius. Go and set the truth free.

Papa

Annelise pinched the anchor, pulled it from the journal, and tucked the diary back into her overcoat. She then removed her chronoperpetua, securing the glass orb in the core. Though redness and tears marked her eyes, a hopeful smile perched on her lips. "Give me a few minutes and then follow me," she told them all. Everyone nodded their agreement. Annelise scrutinized the narrow lane behind them. A moment later, she made her way between the buildings.

Miles turned away from the alley, standing shoulder to shoulder with the rest of his family to obscure the view of Londoners flocking to the inferno. An azure glow splashed across the building façades behind them, followed by a strong wind that whipped at their backs, throwing each of them off balance. Alistair ducked away into the alley after her vortex closed. Miles glanced over his shoulder at his brother. Upon turning back to his parents, he caught sight of his father and felt a pang of concern. The nanites didn't appear to be repairing his father's injuries with any kind of haste. The cut had yet to fully close and a significant amount of bruising still lingered. His posture appeared weak, unsteady. The look upon his face was unlike any Miles had ever witnessed. It was either one of sheer disgust or discomfort, he couldn't decide. Leaning closer, he grabbed his father's shoulder. "Hey, are you okay?"

The nasty grimace vanished from his face. He turned and locked eyes on Miles. Something was different about his stare, something broken. "I'm just dizzy...lightheaded." He pressed his palm against the gash. His balance faltered for a brief moment before Matthias caught himself.

Miles slid his arm across his father's chest to help him stay on his feet. "Well you took one Hell of a hit to the head. You're lucky you can stand."

The near fall drew Elizabeth's attention. She glanced with concern at Matthias and rushed to him. "What's wrong?" Her eyes fell upon the lingering cut. "Why isn't this healing?"

Matthias shrugged. "I'm fine," he told her, "really." He rose back to his full height and straightened his garments.

"Are you sure?" she asked further. "Maybe you shouldn't tether just yet."

"Yes," Matthias caressed her face with great gentleness. "I'm sure."

Elizabeth shot him a doubtful, sideways glare, and laid her hands on his as they fell away from her face. "If you insist." She shifted her attention to Miles. "You're next, my dear."

Miles nodded to her. As he stepped past her into the alley, she reached out and grabbed hold of his arm.

"Be careful."

"I will," Miles assured her. He took off at a jog down the alley. When he reached a safe distance from his parents, Miles strapped his chronoperpetua to his hand. He paused to think back on just how far he had come since he had been reunited with his family. Miles hadn't quite gotten the handle of tethering, nor was he a great warrior. Yet, he had absorbed enough information over the past few weeks to successfully follow his family into the heart of danger, despite their best efforts, and helped thwart the greatest mutiny in the history of the Order. "Not bad, Miles," he muttered to himself, "not bad."

Aiming into the open space at the back of the alleyway, Miles hit the actuator on the chronoperpetua. The energy tether punctured the fabric of reality, drew it wide like a gaping mouth, and sucked him into the bitter cold of the chronovortex.

The vortex expelled Miles into another unknown destination. In an instant, he found himself awash in a swirl of green, blue, and brown. When the spinning stopped and his body ground to a halt along the ground, Miles picked himself up to dust off.

Shaking loose the cobwebs brought about by impact, he began surveying his immediate area while he put away his chronoperpetua. He had crashed upon a dirt footpath nestled between rows of lush trees and dense vegetation beneath. Scattered throughout the foliage stood tall, hand-sculpted stones that the growth of algae and moss had tinted green. Miles stepped away from the path to examine the nearest of those slabs. He knelt down before it. Upon closer inspection, it was no mere sculpture but a grave marker. The inscription upon its face had been worn away by the eroding hand of time.

"Miles!" a familiar, echoing voice called out to him. He looked left and then right before he spotted his brother and Annelise standing together in the foreground of a sizeable stone archway. Jumping up, Miles jogged over to them. As he drew closer, he took notice of the intricacies of the archway. It felt like it was straight out of a pyramid in Cairo, especially the stone obelisks that flanked two pair of similarly styled pillars. And just inside the main archway a set of iron gates creaked as they swung back and forth in the wind. Surrounding the entire structure on both sides stood a host of mature ash trees, and beneath them, a dense cover of ferns obscured the ground alongside the dirt path. The gateway stood apart from the rest of the property in every way imaginable. Miles wondered what secrets lurked within the darkness. Within a few feet of Alistair and Annelise, he slowed in his gait and walked the rest of the way.

"A graveyard?" Miles asked between heavy breaths. "We're supposed to find survivors here? Ironic."

Annelise shielded her eyes against the sunlight, peering past Miles and down the footpath. "Trevor said the children he murdered were just shadows. That the real ones are still alive."

"Wait a minute!" Miles blurted out, completely flabbergasted. "So he still killed all those kids and sent their heads to their parents, but because they're not the 'real kids'," he motioned with air quotes, "it's okay?"

"It was the only way to prove himself," Alistair added. "Gaius probably never considered the fact that they could have been alternates."

"Still. It's pretty fucked up."

Annelise's eyes snapped back to Miles. She glowered at him, shaking her head.

"So where are they?" Miles probed.

Annelise opened the artifact diary to a hand-drawn map. She scrutinized the image. "Down there." She sighed and raised a hand, pointing down the long tunnel.

Miles gazed down the length of the archway. Several darkened doorways at regular intervals broke the monotony of the stone passage. Sunlight filled the archway on the other side.

"There's an enclosed ring of mausoleums at the other end. We'll find them there." She looked down the footpath behind Miles and slammed the diary closed. "Ugh. Where are they?" she huffed, tucking the diary back inside her coat.

"Relax. They shouldn't be too far behind," Alistair reassured her. "They sent you first, right?"

Miles nodded. He glanced up at the archway. "So where are we?"

"Highgate Cemetery," Annelise answered while continuing to scan the grounds for Matthias and Elizabeth. "Later twentieth, early twenty-first century I'd guess. The stonework's crumbling, signs of vandalism..." her voice trailed off. She popped open her chronoperpetua to refer to the tuning module. "August 18th, 2001." Annelise tucked it back into her pocket. "With the West Cemetery closed to visitors, any of these crypts are the perfect place to safely hide the kids. Tour guides keep people on a tight leash."

In the distance, the hum of a materializing chronovortex caused the air to vibrate. It was joined almost immediately by the sound of a second aperture breaking through the fabric of time. A fierce wind whipped up dust devils and caused the treetops to sway violently. Miles braced himself against the torrent, covering up his face with his arms to deflect the pelting spray of dirt. Behind him the two iron gates clanged hard against the inside of the passageway.

The first vortex puckered into view, belching out Elizabeth into the woods. Her knees bent as she hit the ground and lurched into a controlled shoulder roll, nearly ramming into a headstone. She whipped her head down and back to flip her hair out of her face. Twigs and leaves stuck out like haphazard ornaments.

The second vortex blasted through some fifteen feet in the air and into a tangle of tree limbs. His father's aim was dangerously off target this time. Matthias, prone and out of control, shot from the vortex. A sturdy branch caught him across the chest and deadened his momentum. He fell to the ground while branches lashed across his body, slowing his decent. He hit with a thud. Everyone took off at a sprint to check on him.

Elizabeth reached him mere moments before the children. Matthias growled at her. He extended a stammering hand that kept her from lending assistance.

"Leave me be."

By the time Miles reached his father he had already gotten back to his feet. Matthias looked decidedly pissed but no worse for wear after such a brutal tether. He straightened his garments with a huff.

Alistair leaned close and whispered to Miles, "In all the years I've known him, that's never happened."

"What?"

"Coming out of a tether like that," Alistair answered. "I've seen you be more graceful on re-entry."

Now that was saying something. Miles was taken aback by the revelation. He thought everyone, even experienced chronoshifters, had a bad tether from time to time; if your trajectory's a bit off or you're not prepared for re-entry the end result was usually painful. Miles still felt the ache from his last tether. But according to Alistair, their father had mastered every aspect of tethering. *Just how much damage*, he wondered, *did that hit to the head cause?*

"That's not good," Miles concluded. "We need to get him back home to rest."

"Agreed."

Matthias crossed to Annelise who stood behind Miles and Alistair. The brothers parted to let their father pass. It was like he didn't even see them standing there. He had a determined look in his eyes that bore down on her.

"Where are they?" Matthias asked. His voice sounded deep, serious.

"Over here," Annelise replied and motioned for everyone to follow her. She didn't seem affected by his tone. She led everyone back toward Egyptian Avenue, through the iron gates, and down the corridor of stone tombs. Not a single crypt's door sat ajar. Miles feared that at any moment a vampire or zombie could come bursting through and fall upon them. It was an irrational fear, but the place gave him the creeps.

At the other end of the passage, Miles passed back into the warm sunlight. Once his eyes adjusted, an incredible work of architecture greeted him. He stood within a circular path of grass worn thin by the tramp of feet. Stone tombs, similar to the ones within the passageway, lined both sides of the walkway. The walls they formed stood too high to scale, giving the whole structure a very claustrophobic design. The only egresses, beside the tunnel they had just passed through, were a few stone stairways that led up out of the ring of tombs. But the part of the structure that begged of Miles' attention was an ancient cedar that rose from the roof of the inner circle. Its branches swept out over the edge like an umbrella, reminding all that even from death, life springs eternal. It was a message that he understood.

Miles, still staring at the cedar, had missed that everyone had kept moving. When he noticed, he turned to catch up to them, but he heard voices and the shuffling of feet to his rear. "Hey," he called out to Annelise and his family without trying to be too loud.

Alistair glanced over his shoulder at his brother. He told the others to wait, and the procession stopped. "What?" he asked Miles as he caught up to them.

"Someone's coming!"

"Tour group," Annelise rasped nervously. "Where's the damn tomb?" She moved with haste, quickly eyeballing the placards above the door of each burial chamber for a specific name. The others lent their assistance.

Miles walked backwards, close on their heels, to keep a watchful eye to the rear of their position. The voices and footfalls grew closer with each passing second. The grating echo of iron rubbing against stone and angry hinges screeching in protest against their usage ricocheted along the circle in all directions. He spun around to find the disturbance.

"Quick, in here!" his mother called out to everyone from around the bend with a harsh whisper.

Miles rushed toward her voice. She stood in the doorway to a darkened tomb. The others passed by her into the gloom and he followed. Behind them, she pushed the door shut.

Uncomfortable being surrounded by corpses in the pitch black, Miles pleaded, "Can someone light a—"

"Shhh," his brother cut him off.

Miles did as Alistair asked and immediately understood why. Loud voices, somewhat muted by the thick stone walls and iron door, could be heard moving outside along the walkway. With the noise at its peak, the movement stopped. One voice in particular could be heard speaking full-throat above all others, possibly the tour guide. Subdued exchanges intermixed with the louder voice, and then a booming cacophony of laughter burst forth. Finally, the mass of bodies shuffled off until they could be heard no more.

A brief silence lingered until Miles heard what sounded like pieces of plastic being fumbled about in the darkness, followed by a few crackles. A green glow began to emanate from Alistair's hands. Miles squinted through the gloom at the mysterious source of illumination. *Glow sticks*, he concluded. Alistair shook the handful of glowing tubes vigorously. The light they produced increased two fold, and the whole tomb was soon cast in a bizarre green radiance, like looking through a pair of night-vision goggles.

After he handed each of them a glow stick, they began examining the chamber. It didn't take long to figure out that there wasn't much to see. Set within the outer walls of the tomb were several deep alcoves where rickety caskets and their deceased inhabitants rested. A dense layer of undisturbed dust covered the coffins; no one had touched them in ages. The only other feature that stood out was an ornately sculptured stone sarcophagus that sat square in the middle of the floor upon a hefty base of similar craftsmanship. The lid had been cast aside and laid upturned some distance away. Pensively, Miles lowered his glow stick into the open casket. The light fell upon a haggard, almost completely decomposed corpse that stared back at him through empty eye sockets. He turned away in disgust to see if anyone had found anything noteworthy.

His father stood scowling in front of the closed entryway, his hands on his hips. "Empty," Matthias groaned. "There's no one here."

Miles motioned over his shoulder toward the sarcophagus while Alistair inspected the other side. "No one alive at least."

Annelise, searching the confines of the alcoves, turned about in frustration. She fumed, "Where the Hell are they?"

"Is this the right mausoleum?" Matthias challenged her. Every muscle in his body appeared tensed.

"Yes! I'm certain," she answered back in anger.

"Hold on!" Alistair exclaimed, knelt down, and touched the floor. "Look at this."

Miles made his way around the coffin while Matthias and Annelise drew near.

Elizabeth, who had been inspecting the torch sconces along the walls, squatted down beside Alistair. "Scratches in the stone?" she quietly mused.

"What did you say, Lizzie?" Matthias asked her.

Regarding her son with a hopeful grin, she said, "You don't think..."

Alistair nodded. "Give me a hand with the sarcophagus," he implored the others.

Elizabeth and Alistair stood and moved around to the other side of the coffin. Everyone joined them and laid their hands along the cold stone.

"On three," Alistair told them. "One, two, three!"

Miles lent his muscle to the middle of the sarcophagus as they pushed it across the floor. It surprised him how little effort it took to move the coffin given the combined bulk of it and its base. After a foot or so of movement, Miles caught sight of a large cutout in the floor that the coffin hid, and he pulled back to avoid falling in. A warm light radiated up through the hole, across his body, and filled the chamber. Miles knelt down to peer into the opening. In his periphery, the others ceased in their efforts and circled around him, trying to catch a glimpse.

"What do you see?" Annelise asked with eagerness.

Miles couldn't see too far. Right below him, a makeshift ladder crafted from branches and bound with twine provided a way to climb in and out of the underground passage. It looked rickety, unsafe. The passage itself was well lit and stretched off into the distance. And though Miles couldn't see anyone, he heard whispering voices. He turned to Annelise and answered, "Not much." Miles then leaned back down toward the passage and called out, "Hello!"

The whispering voices fell silent.

"I'm going down," Miles announced. Turning around, he stepped down onto the topmost rung with his right leg. A few gentle kicks at the branch validated its strength. It felt secure enough to support the full burden of his weight. Miles exhaled and began his descent.

After he cleared the first few rungs, Annelise followed, then Alistair, and lastly his parents. At the bottom of the ladder, Miles turned about to examine the confines. At the other end of the chamber he discovered a curly, dark haired girl with a cutely round face sitting upon an unzipped sleeping bag. She seemed to be only a few years younger than

Miles, but he couldn't be sure. Huddled close to her side was a girl with golden, shoulder length hair, wearing a yellow sundress, and an off-white sweater. She couldn't have been much older than seven or eight. Both of the girls were filthy. They must have been down there for weeks and were badly in need of baths. They smelled like it too; the air reeked of foulness, no doubt emanating from a nearby porta-potty that was greatly in need of emptying. He wondered how they could stand breathing it in day after day.

Desperate to get away from the aroma of shit soup, Miles approached the children with cautious steps. His eyes kept scanning the room. Right next to where they sat, he spotted a battery powered lantern that kept the area well lit, along with a few boxes of D cells. Scattered around it on the ground were a collection of water bottles, packets of beef jerky, military-issue food rations, and additional hand-held flashlights. Strewn about the sleeping bag were a few paperback novels, some coloring books, and crayons. Miles realized just how hard Trevor had worked to keep the children not only hidden away but alive while he maintained his ruse; though he didn't understand the difference between murdering shadows and real children, he decided that Annelise's brother must have been a good man nonetheless.

When Miles closed within a few feet of the children, he saw the little girl recoil into the older one. She trembled in fear; tears welled up in her eyes. Miles didn't want to scare either of them, so he immediately halted, gestured with his hands for them to relax, and explained with gentleness, "I'm not going to hurt you."

The older girl pulled the other in even closer to herself. "Who are you?" she snapped at him with a distinct French accent.

"I'm Miles. I'm one of the ones that got away, just like you."

She leaned to her left and her right, trying to peer past him. "Well if that's true, then where's Trevor? If he saved you, then why isn't he with you?"

"He didn't save me. My father did."

"And who are they?" the girl inquired, motioning with her head toward the rest of his family as they climbed down into the passage.

"They're my family." Miles nodded at Annelise as she filed in beside him. "And friends. We're here to help."

"What's your name, sweetie?" Annelise asked the girl. "I'm Annelise. Trevor's sister."

"Antoinette," she replied.

"Antoinette Michaud?"

She nodded. "Oui. That's the name Trevor gave me." A sudden look of confusion came over her. Antoinette shook her head in a fluster and quickly uttered, "Je ne comprends pas! Si vous êtes sa soeur, donc où est il?"

Annelise calmingly requested, "Dans l'anglais, s'il vous plaît. Nous tous ne parlons pas de français." With deliberate steps, she moved closer to Antoinette and the young girl. Just as the tips of her boots touched the foot of the sleeping bag, Antoinette reached down under the edge of the sleeping bag and raised the muzzle of a handgun at her face.

Annelise didn't flinch. She knelt down, held her arms out to her sides, and stared down the barrel. "He's gone, sweetie."

"Gone?" Antoinette's lip trembled. "You mean dead."

"Yes. He died keeping you safe." Annelise wiped tears from her own eyes.

The rest of the Draven clan joined Miles and Annelise. Antoinette lowered the pistol.

Alistair stepped forward. He reached into the anchor pouch he kept attached to his belt. "Are you ready to go home?" He pulled out a few anchors and bounced them up and down in his hand like loose change.

Both of the children nodded.

"Good." Alistair smiled. "Did Trevor tell you about your real families? Did he tell you who you really are?"

"Oui. We're," Antoinette stammered over her words before answering, "chronoshifters. Whatever that means."

"It means you're not orphans anymore," Miles added.

Antoinette got to her feet. The little one clung to her the whole way. She rubbed her head with great affection. "It's alright, Hannah. We're going home to our true parents."

"We are?" Hannah squeaked. She had a thick Scandinavian accent. Her words sounded broken, forced. "But what about our other families?

Will we see them again?" She glanced from Antoinette to the others.

Annelise shook her head. "I'm sorry, Hannah. You probably won't see them for a very long time."

Antoinette knelt down before her, wiping the tears from her face. "We'll be okay. I'm sure our real parents love us very much, and we'll love them too."

Hannah smiled.

Miles turned back to his family. "So what do we do now?"

"We go get their parents," Elizabeth said.

"Mom and I will go," Alistair clarified. "Dad's too beat up, and you don't know the Michauds or the Thorvoldsons."

Miles couldn't argue with that logic. They wouldn't know him from a hole in the ground and his father just didn't look right; he kept looking around like he didn't understand what was happening. He stared at Antoinette and Hannah with a vicious scowl. The only place Matthias was going was home.

Alistair handed his mother one anchor and took the other for himself. They then climbed back out of the chamber and tethered off in search of the girls' parents.

Not long after they left, his mother returned with Eric Thorvoldson, Hannah's father, followed shortly thereafter by Alistair and Antoinette's parents, Pierre and Madeline Michaud. The emotional tide their reunions evoked could not be measured or equaled. Miles couldn't fathom what it would be like for a parent to bury a beloved child only to have them miraculously returned to them alive and well. He guessed that his parents must have undoubtedly experienced something similar at having saved him from the sights of an assassin's gun. But was it anything like the pure elation that the girls' parents experienced? His parents never had to deal with the turmoil of believing him dead, so he guessed that it likely paled in comparison.

The whole scene made him wish that he had embraced his parents when they came back into this life instead of lashing out at them for abandoning him. Maybe he should have let them tell their side of the story first. Neither of the girls screamed at their parents about being thrown to the wolves like he did, and they were orphaned too. However, they didn't exactly bubble over with love at meeting them either; as a matter of fact, they seemed rather uncomfortable being hugged and kissed profusely by people they didn't really know. It was an understandable reaction. Then he noticed that their standoffishness melted away the longer they embraced. Perhaps that first embrace awoke the same undeniable sense of kinship that Miles felt towards his mother at first but stubbornly resisted. Perhaps it didn't matter how many centuries separated a child from its parent—it was a connection that could transcend any barrier or time.

Before taking their leave of one another, Miles' parents, the Michauds, and Eric Thorvoldson vowed that no more children would be cast blindly into the future to be raised by strangers. The horrific tragedies that had cost the Order the lives of three children and nearly torn them asunder had forever changed the landscape of their reality. Though they could live in any place at any time, they couldn't escape the specter of betrayal and the fact that Gaius would rise again one day. And when the demon did return, they had to be ready.

For Miles, being ready meant understanding that everything that truly mattered to him could be ripped away at any moment. He once believed that he had steeled himself against such pain—that being rejected over and over again had made him immune to the pain of loss. The events of the past few weeks had crushed that notion into dust.

Where he once lived off of the anger and pain of his life, he decided to live for every moment he had left with his family. He swore that as long as he lived, he would never take them for granted. Matthias told him that it took many years for him to forgive Miles' grandparents for abandoning him. His father hoped that he would one day forgive them too. As he cast his tether into the void, he realized that he didn't need years to absolve them of any perceived wrong doing. Without knowing it, he had already forgiven them.

ABOUT THE AUTHOR

C.W.J. Henderson resides in New York's Capital Region with his wife and twin sons. By day, he's a 7th grade English teacher at a suburban school district in Rensselaer County. By night, he's an author of sci-fi and fantasy literature. He holds both a bachelor's degree in English and a master's degree in secondary English education from the University at Albany. The greatest influences on his writing are the role-playing games he played in his youth and a lifetime of martial arts experience. His favorite authors include J.K. Rowling, Lois Lowry, Gregory Bear, George R.R. Martin, and Jim Butcher. C.W.J. is currently trying his hand at screenwriting while working on the sequels to *Miles Away* and *Fenicus Flint & the Dragons of Berathor*.

Follow C.W.J. Henderson on Facebook, Goodreads, and Twitter (@Fenicus) for more information. Also, visit www.cwjhenderson.com for more news and information regarding his current and future works.

CPSIA information can be obtained
at www.ICGtesting.com
Printed in the USA
LVOW08s1740230517
535559LV00004B/605/P